THE NEXT BLAST WOULD
RIP HIM TO SHREDS

Bedoya Dam swung crazily, as if it were about to topple, then rocked back, flinging Bolan into the wall with a crash. He grabbed at the metal rail and vaulted over the ledge, landing in the road.

The Executioner scrambled to his feet and shouted into his throat mike, determined to get one final message to the Farm. But there was a sudden shift in the pavement. To survive, he had to get off the road and make it to the mountain, still two hundred feet away.

The road buckled under him, and the great mass of the dam started to collapse.

Time was up, and Mack Bolan's options were down to zero.

DON PENDLETON'S

MACK BOLAN®

STONY MAN®

Thirst for Power

A GOLD EAGLE BOOK FROM

WORLDWIDE.

TORONTO • NEW YORK • LONDON
AMSTERDAM • PARIS • SYDNEY • HAMBURG
STOCKHOLM • ATHENS • TOKYO • MILAN
MADRID • WARSAW • BUDAPEST • AUCKLAND

First edition January 2000

ISBN 0-373-61928-6

Special thanks and acknowledgment to
Tim Somheil for his contribution to this work.

THIRST FOR POWER

Printed in U.S.A.

Thirst for Power

CHAPTER ONE

Peru

The blackness came to life. When the guard turned and saw the living, mutant shadow looming over him, he opened his mouth to scream. But before he made a sound the creature lunged, slashing his throat with a steel claw. The guard's scream hissed out the gaping wound as he sank to his knees, his vision dimming. His terror escalated as he died, for he saw that the thing that loomed over him seemed to be some sort of alien cyborg monstrosity, its skull half dull, anodized metal and half flesh. The guard didn't have time to rationalize the horror he was witnessing before his self-awareness emptied into nothingness.

The "cyborg" grabbed the fallen guard by the collar and dragged him into the shadows at the base of the outcropping, kicking the fallen shotgun after him, then moved down the trail at a hurried, but cautious pace.

"Stony Base, Striker here. I've found what I was looking for."

The figure moved to the rocky ledge and peered into the expansive darkness beneath. The vast emptiness of the three-hundred-foot drop was cut down the middle by a meandering ribbon of black water, but there was no sign of human presence.

Mack Bolan pushed at the mask that covered the top half of his face, sliding it onto his forehead. The bizarre green of the night-vision glasses transformed to natural darkness, and he waited, as still as a hunting cat. While his sight adjusted, he listened to the night. Both senses failed to detect anyone else in the vicinity, but Bolan didn't believe that evidence. They were down there. He could feel their presence in his bones.

He followed the earthen trail down the cliff, watching for any sign of life on the trail ahead of him or below in the canyon.

"Striker?" The voice was that of a woman, coming through the tiny earphone in his headset.

"Go ahead, Stony Base," he murmured.

"A satellite assist is out of the question for another four hours." The woman spoke with quiet authority. "There are no orbitals in position, even if we could get access."

"Then I go in blind."

"You could hold off."

"I'm proceeding." He spoke in a tone that left no room for argument, even from Barbara Price, mission controller for Stony Man Farm.

Bolan had once been a soldier, but his days of taking orders from anyone were long gone. Now he relied solely on his own judgment, in all things. He expected no further discussion on the matter, and he received none.

"Affirmative," Price's voice said in his ear. The headset also contained a microphone, which allowed him to listen and speak without using his hands. The unit was on a radio frequency that carried communications to and from a satellite uplink unit in the rear of a Chevrolet sport utility vehicle parked a half mile away, just off the highway. The satellite relayed messages between Stony Man Farm in the mountains of Virginia and Bolan's present location, somewhere along the Reyes River in south-central Peru.

Bolan heard something else, something out in the real world, but so quiet he couldn't immediately identify it. He quickly moved off the trail into the scant shrubbery that straggled out of the rocky soil of the cliff side and fisted a Ka-bar fighting knife. Within a half minute a pair of armed men emerged from the darkness, each toting an automatic rifle. They reached the spot where Bolan crouched without noticing him.

One of them never saw it coming. A powerful push from Bolan propelled him into the cliff wall with the force of a battering ram. He was out like a light.

The second man pivoted, almost losing his balance, and for a moment he knew the same terror his comrade had felt in his final moments. By the time he realized his attacker was human, he was overcome. Bolan snapped the armed man in the forehead with the palm of his hand, and his precarious balance gave way. As he collapsed into the cliff wall, the gunner swung his weapon wildly, but Bolan snap-kicked it away. The man's skull slammed into the rock and he sat on the dirt trail, dazed, becoming aware of cold, wet steel biting into the flesh under his chin.

Bolan watched the man's eyes focus, his body grow tense. "What organization are you with?"

The man registered surprise at Bolan's spoken English, but he answered without hesitation. *"Ejército Peruano."*

The Executioner exerted a substantial increase in

pressure, slicing thinly into the man's skin and pressing against his jawbone. "Tell the truth, and tell it in English."

"I tell the truth! We're army!"

"You're a mercenary. Who hired you?"

The man misjudged his interrogator and the consequences were severe. With a sweeping movement he slammed his forearm into Bolan's to push the knife away from his throat, but he hadn't counted on his adversary's faster reflexes. The Executioner slashed the knife across the mercenary's arm. Terrified by the line of crimson fluid spilling from the gash, the man panicked and tried to scream. Bolan rammed a fist against his temple and he toppled. Plastic riot cuffs secured the man's hands and feet, and a piece of his shirtsleeve stuffed in his mouth would prevent his crying out.

Following the trail, Bolan heard and saw no further signs of life until he reached level earth at the bottom of the canyon. He jogged easily across the empty ground, scanning the area for signs of life.

They were here. Somewhere.

Reaching the narrow river, its water as black as oil, his feet crunched quietly on the gravel. The smooth-flowing current reflected nothing. The sky was moonless, masked by dense clouds. The lights that would normally have guarded the high nearby cliffs from low-flying aircraft had winked out an hour earlier.

But there was light, and Bolan squinted into the blackness until he could make it out—the slimmest sliver of white light originated a half mile away at river level. He started the trek upstream. Towering above him, inconceivably massive, was the great white concrete face of the Bedoya Dam. The tiny light Bolan had seen was at the base of the structure.

There was a crackling in his ear, and beneath a torrent of static he could make out the voice of Barbara Price, trying to contact him. The words were unintelligible behind the static. "Striker here," he replied. "Do you read?"

The answer was more static. The cliff to his right was blocking the signal to the satellite uplink in his SUV. He turned down the unit's volume. Stony Man didn't have anything to offer him during this probe, and he could do without the distraction.

Coming within a hundred yards of the dam, he saw a glowing square that seemed to embrace the earth. It was a large tent that had been staked in the earth against the base of the sharp incline of the dam. The light inside was seeping through the canvas material and showed as a feeble glow in the blackness of the night. A front flap opened slightly, and Bolan saw the tiny sliver of light again.

He sank to the ground and examined the scene over the slight incline of the riverbank. It took him two minutes to identify the guards he knew would be present. One flanked the right side of the tent, while another man stood in the scraggly, knee-high grass along the base of the dam, maybe a hundred paces from the tent. If there was a third guard on the left, Bolan couldn't find him in the darkness. He'd deal with him if or when he showed himself.

Crouching, the Executioner crossed the darkness, sprinting between clumps of weeds. He could barely make out the guard in the darkness, even though he knew where to look for him. Bolan also knew that at any moment he might be made and find himself dodging automatic rifle fire. He reached the dam and felt the cold wall pressed against his back. He paused there, feeling the unforgiving strength of the concrete, feeling for a moment as if the massive tonnage of the concrete and the millions of tons of water it held back were weighing against his spine.

The soldier peered directly up the side of the enormous wall, and now he could see other figures, clinging like flies to the concrete, as silent as spiders. They were dressed in black and working by the dim green light of chemical glow sticks.

Creeping along the concrete, he spied the guard. The man was facing away from the dam into the darkness of the canyon, oblivious to the danger encroaching from the side.

Catching sight of slight movement, Bolan froze. It was the guard flanking the right side of the tent, now walking to the front of it. He lifted a flap and was dimly visible for a half second before he disappeared inside. The guard closer to Bolan was now alone.

The soldier knew his advantageous situation wouldn't last. At fifty paces he stopped, unwilling to press his luck any longer, and drew the Beretta 93-R. When he took up a shooter's stance the guard sensed him somehow, turning in his direction. A quick triburst punched the sentry to the ground.

Bolan moved quickly to the fallen guard. He didn't know if he'd scored with all three of the rounds, but a glance told him one of the 9 mm bullets hit the man squarely in the face.

He continued along the base of the dam, watching the front corner of the tent. If the shots had been heard, somebody would emerge at any second. He flipped the fire selector switch to single-shot mode and waited, his back to the concrete. Twenty seconds, then thirty passed. Several hundred feet above him, the tiny black figures clinging to the dam wall were still working slowly on their perches. Bolan judged his luck was holding.

Not that he truly believed in luck. He was too much of a pragmatist to put his faith in coincidence and too well-disciplined to depend on happenstance. He was the kind of man who made things happen, anticipated worst-case scenarios and was always prepared to react to them.

Eyes focused on the front of the tent, the soldier approached it from the side, listening to the activity inside. Voices were speaking quietly. Bolan shifted his gaze from the front of the tent to make a quick examination. A solid canvas wall faced him. No windows or entrances. The canvas flaps had been secured to the concrete with nails.

He now recognized that the voices spoke rapid-fire Spanish. Bolan heard several words he knew, "countdown" and "detonation" among them.

The soldier nudged at the canvas flap, saw nothing immediately within, then stepped inside. The air was heavy and stale, and a single, battery lantern was hooked to a ceiling loop. The tent was empty.

The voices he had heard were coming from inside the wall, from within a ragged tunnel that looked as if it had been blasted into Bedoya Dam with small, strategically placed plastique charges.

Not for the first time Bolan found himself wondering what the men were up to.

Whatever their plan, they were carrying it out with expertise and skill far beyond the capabilities of a ragtag South American mercenary group. The soldiers on the cliff above were strictly hired hands, but the brains behind the actual operation, whatever its purpose, were unknown entities.

The faces and descriptions Bolan had communicated to Stony Man Farm hadn't been useful. The digital images had all turned out to be those of small-time mercenaries without known ties to major crime or terrorist organizations. None of them could have been a major player in this operation. The perpetrators' politics, motivations and intentions remained unknown factors.

The only thing Bolan knew for sure was that these men had purchased explosives on the black market on a scale unprecedented in the history of South American terrorism. It was enough to turn a skyscraper to rubble or blow away the side of a mountain.

Or puncture one of the world's largest dams.

Bright lights were flashing inside the tunnel and Bolan headed for them, then pulled back when a figure appeared. As the man ducked to exit the tunnel, the Executioner grabbed him by the throat, lifted him bodily and slammed him against the concrete wall. The iron grip on the guard's throat allowed no air in or out. He struggled weakly, his eyes wildly trying to focus on the big Beretta when it nudged him in the chin.

"Do you speak English?"

The guard nodded.

"Stay silent or you'll die," Bolan growled. The man nodded weakly and Bolan relaxed his grip. The man stood there, gasping for air.

"What organization are you with? Answer quietly."

"No organization. I am just a soldier."

"This operation isn't part of the Tupac Amaru initiative?"

"No," the man whispered, shaking his head.

"So what's the reason for it?"

"I do not know."

"Why are you part of it?"

The man rubbed his fingers together.

Bolan directed his prisoner into the tunnel, which extended a full fifteen feet at a sharp angle into the wall, hanging with stalactites of ragged concrete that threatened to tear at their heads and shoulders. They found three men at the end of the tunnel, gathered around a box of electronics. The closest of the three, who probably was supposed to have been guarding them, glanced up and shouted, raising his AK-47 into firing position. Bolan gave his prisoner a sudden shove with his foot and sent him careering into the gunner, both of them shouting as they went down in a tangle of limbs. One of the other men snatched at the handgun holstered under his left armpit but never even drew the weapon fully from the leather. The 93-R coughed once, and the man collapsed in a heap.

The survivor was calm. An older, olive-skinned figure with balding white hair, he opened his hands at his sides and glared at Bolan with hatred.

Bolan's first question died in his throat when his eyes fell on what lay at the end of the tunnel. Floor to ceiling, it was stacked with boxes of explosives, wired to one another and strapped in by a crisscrossing network of small nylon ropes bolted into the walls.

For the first time since embarking on the trail of the explosives, Bolan knew conclusively their purpose.

To destroy Bedoya Dam.

He snagged the fallen AK with his foot and hoisted it into his hands without ever taking his eyes off the prisoners, then gestured to the box.

"Disconnect it."

"I can't," the older man replied in English.

"Then I will." Bolan leveled the Beretta at the box and fired two rounds.

"No!" the white-haired man shouted in panic. "You will blow us all to pieces, you stupid fool!" He knelt quickly at the box of electronics and used a single finger on each hand to begin spinning the corner wing nuts that held on the cover. "Thank God you missed! You would have annihilated all of us."

Bolan didn't feel the need to tell the man he had missed the box on purpose. As the old man lifted the cover and began to probe inside, Bolan gestured for the two fallen men to get to their feet.

A man called out as he entered the tent, then shouted something at the opening to the tunnel. Bolan didn't understand the Spanish. His prisoners were looking at him expectantly.

"Say nothing," he ordered quietly.

The second call that came from the tent was shorter and more inquisitive. A name. Then footfalls approached, and Bolan directed his handgun toward the newcomer while covering the prisoners with the AK. Idly, he considered that perhaps Barbara Price had been correct when she said he would be outgunned on this probe.

No matter. There was no one on hand to provide assistance, and there was no way he could walk away.

The newcomer came into sight and reacted with a surprised grunt when he spotted the stranger, then stopped. It was one of the prisoners who reacted foolishly—the older man launched himself at Bolan's AK and tried to rip it out of his hands, but the soldier detected the movement and turned in time to trigger four rounds as the man's hands landed on the automatic weapon, drilling him through the gut from a range of eighteen inches. Bolan pivoted to face the newcomer and found him, too, leveling his automatic rifle. A round from the Beretta chopped into his elbow and nearly severed the arm, sending the rifle clattering to the floor. The newcomer stared at the dangling limb, his mouth dropping open in shock. When the pain suddenly hit him he inhaled for a great agonized scream, but Bolan's next round slammed into his rib cage, turning off his breathing completely.

"How about you two? You want to play hero?"

The two remaining prisoners shook their heads, horrified.

Bolan stepped over the body of the white-haired man, his back to the wall of explosives, and made a quick examination of the detonator electronics, including a battery, transformer, CPU and keyboard. The small, illuminated LED screen read Disengaged.

The Executioner would simply have to trust what it said.

CHAPTER TWO

The black-painted Bell 430 helicopter crouched in the darkness in a dip in the uneven terrain at the top of the canyon wall. Hidden behind a rise in the rock, the aircraft wasn't visible from the opposite approach to the dam.

Even in a worst-case scenario—the arrival of an unforeseen army, alerted to his plans—Clint Mahoney would be able to make an escape well before they could reach him.

His thoughts didn't even consider that possibility now. An hour had passed, and the operation was going as planned and ahead of schedule.

"They were worth it after all," Mahoney declared.

Thomas McDonough was at his side, surveying the scene with his own pair of night-vision binoculars.

Mahoney lowered his glasses and addressed the younger man directly. "I told you the mercenaries would meet my expectations."

"They do so far," McDonough admitted.

"They'll continue, too. They're professionals, and they're being paid well."

"Most importantly, they'll take the blame."

"Only if necessary. And I don't think it will be necessary."

Observing the operation from the flat promontory on the edge of the canyon, their vantage point gave them an unobstructed view of the dam. They could make out the initial blast-point camp, which was at the base of the massive concrete structure. From their perch, a full twenty feet higher than the top of the dam itself, they could watch the activity. For an hour since the apprehension of the dam maintenance crew, the mercenaries had been at work.

Thousands of feet of nylon lines were used to lower the preconfigured explosive charges into position on the face of the dam. The workers were lowered along with them, armed with industrial-grade nail guns driving six-inch stainless-steel spikes, which made staccato sounds that reached the observation platform as distant pops. Securing each explosive package was simply a matter of triggering eight nails through the support straps, then cutting the nylon rope.

Each package had been prepared with a radio receiver and detonator. Once the bomb was secure, the worker simply flipped a small switch to power up the receiver. When the staging was completed, the worker could move on to the next package. A quality control operator—the only one of Mahoney's men in the field—followed the crews, checking their work. They had started at the bottom of the dam and worked their way up, so the pace increased the nearer they came to placing the last charge.

It was a very efficient process that theoretically allowed twenty untrained mercenaries to stage fifteen packages of explosives in ninety minutes.

A more-distant chatter erupted from the blackness below.

"What was that?" McDonough demanded.

The tent at the bottom of the canyon was too distant and dark to be visible as more than a blur in their optics, so they stared at each other in silence, straining to hear the noise repeated. It didn't come again.

Mahoney radioed his field supervisor for an explanation.

BOLAN HEARD an electronic hiss and a squawk of Spanish from a walkie-talkie out in the tent. Whoever was calling sounded urgent. The AK fire had been heard above.

Without hesitation Bolan ordered the guards to the ground on either side of the electronic box. "On your stomachs, hands behind your back," he commanded. He quickly secured their wrists with disposable plastic handcuffs, then sliced a length of the nylon rope holding up the explosives. The rope was secured to a steel spike in the wall.

"What are you doing?" one of his prisoners demanded as Bolan tied the rope to each of their wrists. "You can't leave us here!"

"I'm going to stop the others. Then I'll come back and remove you from the tunnel. Or the Peruvian authorities will take you out when they arrive. They should be here in an hour."

"You'll never make it!" the prisoner gasped. "There are twenty men at the top of the dam. You could never hope to take them all out. They'll cut you down, then we'll be trapped here when the dam blows."

"You'd better hope not."

The prisoner was panicking. "You can't leave us here to die!"

Bolan crouched next to the prisoner. "If your plan succeeds and this dam cracks, it will wash away at least four villages. A thousand murders will be on your head. Do you think I should care whether you live or die?''

The second prisoner began praying in Spanish while the first man decided to bargain. ''All right. I will give you whatever you want!''

''Information. What are the men at the top of the dam doing?''

''Planting more explosives,'' the prisoner said quickly. ''They figured out the best way to blow it up. The explosions will start right here, and the other explosions will weaken it all the way up.''

''Why the overkill?'' Bolan demanded. ''One good blast should be enough to damage it.''

''But it must be too broken to fix,'' the prisoner declared.

''Why?''

''I don't know! That is what we were hired to do!''

''Who hired you?''

''No one told me! I am just a soldier!''

Bolan rose and checked the rope. ''You should be able to pull yourselves free in a while if you really work at it.''

''But the dam is going to blow!'' the prisoner protested.

''Not if I can help it. This batch of explosives has been neutralized.''

''They're planting explosives all over the dam face. You'll never stop them all,'' the prisoner cried. ''We'll get smashed or we'll drown in here!''

''Then you'd better get to work.''

Bolan retreated to the tent, grabbing the walkie-talkie and switching it off before he probed outside the tent carefully. There was no sign of more guards on the canyon floor. He tucked the Beretta inside his armpit holster and walked outside in plain view, waving up at the tiny insects clinging to the side of the dam far above.

He approached the dam, unable to see the response from the workers above, grabbing for the rope ladder. He knew the workers wouldn't yell. They had been commanded to silence. But he half expected to hear the ping of bullets from suppressed weapons' fire.

His only hope was to behave like he belonged, so he started up the ladder without hesitation. At ten feet from the ground the rope ladder brought him to the permanent steel rungs bolted into the dam.

At two hundred feet above the floor of the canyon he reached the first of the mercenaries planting explosives and gave a quick wave. Hanging on a series of cables dangling from the top of the dam and several yards away from the ladder, the man gave Bolan a look and a quick wave. He went back to what he was doing, inspecting the explosives carefully with a shielded flashlight. Bolan knew he had to be fulfilling some sort of an inspection role, as he was the only worker Bolan could see with a light source better than the faintly glowing chemical sticks.

Another fifty feet up Bolan passed a second workman, who seemed to be wrapping up his activity. He gave a low grunt, and Bolan waved him off, continuing up.

The workman spoke sharply and when Bolan turned, the guy was working his way across the face of the dam in Bolan's direction, dangling without concern from his nylon safety cable. As he neared the soldier, he reached out a hand, apparently providing his life story in a nonstop stream of Spanish. Bolan said nothing as he gave the man a hand onto the ladder, and somehow, in the darkness, the workman suddenly realized Bolan wasn't what he pretended to be.

The Executioner's preternaturally honed instincts detected the sudden change in the worker's demeanor, and he grabbed the man by the wrist with one hand and yanked him close. With his other hand he grabbed one of the two nylon safety ropes hanging from the distant lip of the dam. He hoisted the workman skyward, looping the rope around his neck in a single swoop and dropping him like a dead-weight. The workman clawed at his throat and kicked his rubber-soled shoes hard against the concrete until his legs and arms grew limp. He dangled, swinging at the end of the rope like a pendulum.

Bolan hurried skyward. If there were as many men at the dam as he assumed there were, then he was outgunned on a large scale.

But the price of failure was uncountable innocent lives.

Bolan simply had no choice but to proceed.

He heard a shout from the top of the dam and stopped long enough to peer up the gently sloping surface, then he dragged the night-vision glasses over his face. A handful of figures appeared out of the blackness fifty feet above him. One of them leaned over and shouted again, meaningless words. The figure bent over the edge and triggered a rifle. A volley of rounds chipped at the concrete face, homing in on Bolan, who leaped off the ladder, dangling by the grip of one hand. The sudden barrage halted when the last couple of rounds pinged off the metal rungs. Bolan jerked himself onto the ladder again and drew the Beretta, aiming skyward and firing at the gunner. There was a cry of pain, then the gunner lost his balance and fell, screaming all the way down, skidding against the concave concrete. He flopped wildly and slammed into the wall again, suddenly silent as he disappeared into the blackness below.

Bolan picked out other figures above and fired four rounds into the night. There was a ping when one of them hit the rim, but there was no indication that the other bullets were wasted. As if a supernova was erupting in the Peruvian night sky, the weird green view suddenly became a massive, blinding brilliance. The soldier snapped his eyes shut and pushed away the night vision mask. The enemy had a spotlight up there and had decided it was time to use it. He targeted the brightness and fired two rounds, and was rewarded with an abrupt return to darkness and a tinkle of glass.

He reached the top of the ladder just as a gunner leaned over the concrete, swinging an Uzi submachine gun in his direction. Bolan made a wild grab for the Israeli-made weapon, snatching it by the muzzle from the gunner's hands so quickly the man made a wide-eyed expression of surprise. He was even more surprised when Bolan tossed the Uzi into the open air with one hand, caught it deftly at the trigger and fired. A short burst slammed into the bewildered man and he slumped to the concrete surface at the top of the dam.

Bolan peered through the rails, forcing his light-blinded eyes to seek the darkness for other gunners. There was a confusion of men milling nearby, each unwilling to be the next to poke his head over the edge of the dam and get it blown off. The Executioner didn't give them the opportunity to find him in the darkness. He extracted one of the two grenades he carried, armed the bomb and lobbed it over the top of the dam, retreating quickly down the ladder a half-dozen steps to ride out the blast with his eyes squeezed shut and his head tucked between his arms. A blinding flash erupted with a shriek of noise.

The soldier vaulted the rail like a fighter pilot ejecting from a doomed jet, triggering the Uzi in the same instant his feet touched the pavement. He swept a wicked figure eight of machine fire into five guards and workmen, who were holding their ears and eyes in pain from the flash grenade detonation. The helpless screams of terror were cut off abruptly.

He heard a scrape of noise and instantly identified its source. He dove to the ground and rolled to the railing at the edge of the dam, then leaped to his feet, grabbing at the man in black who was climbing up the ladder. It was the inspector, the man who had been working with a flashlight. The man croaked. Bolan's arm was locked around his neck, and that was about all he could manage. The Executioner manhandled him to the top of the railing,

"Where are the others?" Bolan demanded.

"They have left."

"Where to?"

"To watch." He gestured in the general direction of one of the high peaks towering over the top of the dam.

"Who hired you to destroy the Bedoya Dam?"

"I don't know."

"We're not playing any more games here," Bolan declared in a quiet voice, inches from the man's ear. "I get a name or I let go of you. Then you're nothing more than a red stain down the side of this dam. Got it?"

Bolan felt the man shudder. "Clint Mahoney."

"Who's he?"

"An Irishman. He is in charge. Thomas McDonough is his engineer. He figured out how to blow the dam."

"What's the reason for it?"

"Make money. He has desalination technology to sell the Peruvians. He made a deal with the guy who developed the technology. Joshua Icahn. It is worth billions. He wants to finance a terrorist war against the English."

Bolan considered that for a full five seconds. It could very well be a lie. Then he dragged the man over the top of the railing and allowed him to flop to the ground.

"Stand up," Bolan ordered. "You and I are going to dismantle these explosives."

The inspector grimaced into the darkness, not quite looking in Bolan's direction. "You are too late for that."

"We'll see. Explain how you've got the charges set up."

The man hesitated, then spoke sharply and succinctly. "Plastique charges packed in hollowed-out, six-inch-thick steel plates, all set up along the weakest structural rib in the design of the dam. The initial shock at the base of the dam will weaken the rib. When the other charges go off, they will force the metal through the dam like knife blades, creating fifteen perforations, bottom to top. The dam's integrity will be critically compromised."

"The base charge won't be going off," Bolan declared simply.

The inspector gaped at him, then smiled. "It will not matter. Bedoya Dam will be opened navel to neck."

"You and I are going to make sure this crime does not occur," Bolan said. "Stand up."

"I'm not going to help you. There's no reason I should. I'm as good as dead."

"Consider it a step toward redemption."

"I don't ask for redemption!" the inspector spit

through clenched teeth, then made a grab for the fallen body of a nearby guard. He knew he was a dead man, and he didn't want to delay the inevitable. Bolan didn't ask him to. When the inspector snatched at a fallen AK and swung it in the soldier's direction, the Uzi issued a short burst that cut him down. He flopped on top of his comrade.

The night was strangely silent, and Bolan didn't like it one bit. There was nothing but the hush of a very slight breeze and the gentle lapping of the man-made lake on the other side of the dam—a mass of black water so newly formed by the construction of Bedoya Dam it didn't even have a name yet.

Bolan had followed truckloads of men up the narrow, freshly paved Andes mountain road. Thirty men, minimum. He'd taken down one-third of that number.

Then he heard their footsteps in the darkness.

They were invisible in the blackness of the cloud-shadowed night, but he could hear them walking along the road that topped the dam. Then more steps sounded behind him, approaching from the other direction. Bolan could barely make the figures out, approaching without a word, three abreast, rifles aimed in his direction like riot police.

There were some situations the most highly skilled warrior could never expect to survive. This was one of them. Bolan stepped to the edge of the dam and jumped onto the rail lightly, making a grab for one of the dangling nylon cords the demolition team had used. When the autofire started, the Executioner jumped into the open air some thirty stories above the hard, stony ground. Despite the utter blackness of the night, the world swung wildly in his vision, then he slammed into the concrete eight feet below the rail with a crunch that creaked through his rib cage. Like blazing phosphorous, the rope burned into his flesh and he dropped the Uzi to grab it with both hands.

Pausing no more than a half second to get a breath, he stood against the dam and hoisted the rope around his waist, holding on to his position with his good hand and reaching for his other handgun, a Desert Eagle. The big handgun was loaded with .44 Magnum rounds, and he fired at the first head to appear. The head vanished and there was suddenly an exclamation of voices from the quiet troops. Another figure reached over with an AK and triggered a quick burst, but Bolan returned it. The Magnum round slammed into the concrete inches from the shooter's chin, then careered through his jaw-bone and skull.

"STOP! HOLD YOUR FIRE!"

The mercenary leader grabbed the walkie-talkie from his belt and shouted a quick order above the shooting, bringing the gunfire to an instant halt.

"How many down?" a voice asked in English.

"Two of my men down," the mercenary leader said in broken English. "All original detail down."

"Jesus! How many do you estimate in the team?"

"We have one gunman. He is trapped on dam face. Should we take him out?"

CLINT MAHONEY RAISED his night-vision binoculars to his face again and peered through them, touching the electronic focus switch. The vision blurred slightly, then readjusted to the sharpest possible detail.

There he was, the little cockroach, clinging to one of the ropes. He wasn't going anywhere.

"Any word from the ground floor?" he demanded of his radio man.

"Nothing."

"Damn!" Mahoney moved the binoculars down the wall. At the base of the dam the tent was silent and dark. One of the guards was clearly out of commission, slumped on the cold rock a dozen yards from the tent and cooling rapidly. There should be a whole team down there, finishing their work and heading up the ladder.

"We'll have to assume they're dead," Thomas McDonough declared.

"Who is it?" demanded Javier Arbulu, field supervisor of the three hired mercenary teams.

"It can't be only one man. There must be others below trying to figure out how to dismantle the detonator without blowing themselves to smithereens." Mahoney's head snapped up. "Which means we need to start the detonation immediately before they succeed."

Arbulu grabbed the microphone out of the hands of Mahoney's radio operator. *"Encalada! Cacares!"* he shouted in Spanish. "Fall back! Get off the dam!"

"Initiate countdown," Mahoney ordered McDonough, who was serving as triggerman.

"Ten," McDonough said in a loud, clear voice.

Arbulu's voice took on a sort of panicked high pitch. "You've got just a few seconds!"

"Nine."

"Get off the dam now!"

"Eight."

THE SHOOTING HAD STOPPED, and Bolan allowed the rope to slide through his fingers, ignoring the fire in his flesh. He came to a stop next to the first of the devices affixed to the dam wall. The concave steel plate had to have weighed a couple hundred pounds, and it was shrink-wrapped in blue translucent plastic with a mound of whitish putty bricks. Bolan had rarely seen so much plastique in one place at one time. When that much plastique exploded, it would transform the steel almost instantly into a semimolten state. The shape of the charge would blast it through the concrete of the dam in a millisecond. Fifteen such holes would compromise the integrity of the dam. Failure would be critical and irreparable.

Unless Bolan could stop it. The detonator was embedded in the mass of plastique and glowing with a series of red lights. The soldier examined it quickly, probing the wires, trying to read the labels in the scarlet glow. He found the wire he thought he needed and grabbed it. If he was wrong, he would be incinerated in the blast so quickly he wouldn't see the light or feel the heat. He would be gone.

He yanked on the wire, and the detonator lights went dark. Bolan started down to the next explosive when he realized he was hearing the fast retreat of the men on the dam.

Were the mercenaries simply quick to obey an order, or were they running for their lives.

Bolan wondered just how much time he had left.

"FOUR," McDonough said.

"My men aren't clear!" Arbulu protested.

"Three."

"They'd better get clear," Mahoney replied icily.

"Two."

"Mahoney, you son of a bitch!"

"One." McDonough opened the clear plastic cover over a red button on his small radio pack.

"Run!" Arbulu shouted into the radio. "Run, you bastards!"

"Detonation."

The night over the Andes Mountains of Peru was frighteningly still.

"No response from the ground floor," McDonough stated without emotion.

Mahoney took in a great lungful of air and swung the night-vision goggles to his eyes, letting the air seep from between his teeth angrily as he focused on the lone figure on the dam face. "You devil. You did this to me."

Then he realized what the lone figure was attempting to do and said in a louder voice, "Proceed with the others."

"Ten," McDonough stated evenly.

"No countdown—just fire!"

McDonough flipped the plastic cover with his thumb and jabbed at the second red button on the radio pack.

BOLAN WAS MAKING a grab for the detonator on the second of fifteen explosive fixtures when the blast came, cracking through the dam, the mountain, the very air. He grabbed wildly for the rope and slammed into the dam face for the second time in a minute. The pain from his ribs sliced through his torso and his hands were singing with fire, but somehow he managed to get his feet against the concrete again. He craned his head over his shoulder, trying to see what was going on.

Even as he was gazing down into the dim gray expanse of the dam, the night erupted with brilliance and thunder from a second blast, and the image of billowing fire, smoke and shattered concrete burned into his retinas.

The blasting had started. There was no way he was going to stop it.

Bolan reached for the detonator on the second fixture and snatched out the wires. Two down, plus the primary charge at ground level. Maybe that would be enough to thwart the destruction of Bedoya. But already he thought he heard the distant rush of high-pressure water spray. The third blast came when he was expecting it and he rode it out, hanging on hard, then started clawing his way back to the top.

The fourth blast shook the dam like a massive tremor, and Bolan's hearing was getting muddled by the onslaught, so that he felt the blasts more than heard them. He determined they were going off in five-second increments, chasing him up the dam. It was a race he didn't think he could win. At any moment the dam might split down the middle, directly beneath him, or he might be shaken loose like a puppet on frayed strings.

He willed greater energy into his weakening limbs, pushing hard against the tenuous grip his rubber-clad feet had on the concrete face, riding out blast after blast. They came closer, louder, slamming into him. The night was filled with alternating chaos and darkness, without a single moment of clear sight. Bolan had no idea how far away the top of the dam still was.

His fingers were rebelling against the continued abuse and started to release the rope; he clawed at the thin nylon for a better grip but his fingernails screamed in protest, and when the next blast came his left hand slipped. The soldier's feet lost their grip and he swung wildly, hanging for a long two seconds by nothing but his one hand. Then he felt in the rope the rumble of the dam. It was trembling like an old man about to collapse from old age, and Bolan was going to go down with it.

Somehow, the soldier reached into his gut for his last reserve of strength and grim determination, clenching his teeth so that the pain shot through his jaws and down his neck, pulling against gravity with muscles that should have had nothing left to give. He swung his free, bloodied hand into the sky, grabbed the nylon rope and groaned against the exertion. Another blast crashed through the dam, and he held his position as the impact rocked through him, feeling the crashing of tiny debris against his back, then willed himself to hang on. The next blast buffeted underneath him, almost propelling him up and sending a cloud of high-velocity projectiles tearing into his arms, back and legs.

The next blast would rip him to shreds with flying concrete. Bedoya Dam swung crazily as if it were about to topple, then rocked back, flinging Bolan into the wall with a crash, slamming his chest into the ledge at the top of the wall. He was up.

He grabbed for the metal rail, yanked himself to his feet and was about to tumble over the rail when the final blast came only twenty yards behind him. The concussive force tossed him into the road. He pushed hard against the asphalt, ignoring his body's demands for the rest of unconsciousness, and found himself on his feet, twisting and wheeling while the road turned to gelatin.

Out of nowhere it occurred to Bolan he wasn't alone. The radio strapped to his shoulder should still be operating.

"Stony Base!" he shouted into the mike that dangled under his chin. If Stony Man Farm responded, he couldn't hear it. His hearing could very well be permanently destroyed.

Bolan tried to shout again, to deliver a final message to the Farm, but there was a sudden twenty-degree shift in the pavement. He fought on, propelling himself along the road. His only hope for survival was to get off the dam, get to the mountain, still two hundred feet away. But it wasn't to be. The road bucked against him, as if he were trying to walk the spine of an angry, giant serpent. Finally, the great mass started to collapse.

Time was up and his options were narrowed to zero, and Mack Bolan leaped off the road, diving over the twisting metal rail on the other side of the road, falling, falling into blackness. He was enveloped in cool black wetness, and he clawed to the surface as the world tipped. Bedoya Dam burst from top to bottom and poured out the contents of the lake like a spilled glass of milk.

CHAPTER THREE

"Get me Jared," Mahoney said without turning his face away from the view of the green Andes foothills unrolling like a carpet beneath the helicopter.

Thomas McDonough hit the speed dial code on the Iridium phone and listened for the connection.

"On second thought, give me O'Connell first," Mahoney said suddenly.

McDonough nodded and heard the second ring get cut off. It was tough to distinguish voices over the thrum of the rotors. "O'Connell, is that you?"

"Yes, sir," Marty O'Connell said.

McDonough placed the phone in his boss's hand.

"Mahoney here," he announced into the receiver. "Give me a status report."

"Everything is going as planned."

"You should have the placement effort well underway at this stage," Mahoney stated, glancing at his watch.

"We do, sir," O'Connell said. "We had some trouble early on. Some of the hired help got it in their skulls to demand more information than we were prepared to give them. We dealt with that situation."

"Explain."

"We told them that they had agreed to do the job no

questions asked. We explained that if they no longer wished to abide by those terms they were free to leave.''

"Who performed the negotiating?''

"Sir?''

"Was it you or my son?''

There was a pause on the phone. "I did, sir.''

"Why not Jared?''

"He tried sir. Just couldn't seem to get them to listen to him, is all. Then he turned it over to me. I think because he's just a young lad, sir, they don't see him as an authority figure.''

"But they listened to you.''

"You got to admit I don't look like a twenty-one-year-old.''

"That you're not, O'Connell.'' Mahoney sighed. "Give me the boy.''

"Just a minute.''

It took a lot longer than a minute. After sitting there with the phone pressed to his ear for five minutes, Mahoney hung up. Let the boy call him back.

California

WHEN O'CONNELL STEPPED out the door and onto the front steps of the small suite of mobile-home offices, it caused the entire structure to tilt on its supports and creak like old bedsprings. The mobile homes were situated on the rim of the El Rosa Canyon, where they had served as a construction office during the erection of the new dam. Now more construction had started, this time on the new phase that would install turbine generators at the base of the dam. None of those construction crews were on the scene yet. Just a few engineers, performing preliminary work.

The engineers, along with the dam staff and a pair of guards, totaled just nine men. The only arms among them, the guards' revolvers, had never even been raised in defense of the massive structure when the Mahoney team had descended on them. Two of them had been killed, regardless, during the attack, and the other seven were now shackled in chairs in the office, gagged and blindfolded in the mobile-home office.

O'Connell and Clint Mahoney's son, Jared, the official leader of the team, were using the mobile-home offices as their command base. It was ideal in that it allowed an overlook of the efforts going on in the canyon below and on the face of the dam. But none of the hired help would be able to get a make on them from that distance.

The only problem was that Jared was missing. O'Connell strolled to the edge of the canyon and looked up and down the dam. A pair of Mahoney's guards were nearby watching the scene without emotion, their automatic rifles gripped in both hands. Their orders were to shoot to kill anyone outside the immediate team who attempted to get close to the command base.

Clint Mahoney was a fanatic about protecting the identity of himself and his team.

"Where's Jared?" O'Connell called to the guards.

They didn't answer, but one of them pointed to the small concrete bunker-type building that topped the dam.

O'Connell swore silently and marched along the cliff's edge. "One of you come with me," he muttered in aggravation.

The guards followed him, pulling on ski masks. Wearing the masks was considered standard operating procedure any time they moved to within fifty paces of the hired help. O'Connell dragged on his own, his face immediately itchy and dank in the morning Southern California sun. That only served to exacerbate his anger.

He stomped down the concrete steps from the canyon edge to the narrow walkway atop the dam, then pounded on the steel door of the small building. "Jay! What are you up to, lad?"

The door flew open a moment later and Jared stood there, pointing a machine pistol at them, his eyes wide and his ski mask shoved up on his forehead. It took him a moment to recognize O'Connell, then he laughed. The sound had a strangely hysterical edge to it, and he moved drunkenly. "O'Connell!" he shouted. "I could've shot your fool head off!"

"Jay, what are you doing, you fool!" O'Connell answered, suddenly furious. Two young men—a black man and a Hispanic—were standing around a small steel table, grinning just as stupidly as Jared.

"Just checking on the progress, O'Connell." Jared tried to look straight and failed.

"Get back to the trailers!" O'Connell said in a low growl. "And here! Your da' is on the phone for you."

Jared looked momentarily shamed as he took the Iridium phone and began to walk away. Then he turned back. "There's nobody there."

"He probably hung up by this time," O'Connell said.

Jared continued to walk back to the canyon edge and pushed the speed dial.

O'CONNELL GOT THE NAMES and affiliation of the pair in the building, ordering them back to work. He would much rather have shot them dead on the spot. That wouldn't have been beneficial for the smooth operation of the project. They had seen Jared's face, and they would eventually require silencing.

All such minor issues could wait until later. He watched over the efforts proceeding on the face of the dam. Mahoney's team engineers were shouting orders, plainly frustrated at the slow pace and ineptness of their workers.

But these were gang members and street trash, and their ineptitude had been accommodated in the time line. They were a vital factor in the destruction of the dam, and not for their engineering skills.

Mahoney knew this group of hoodlums couldn't possibly keep their mouths shut about their involvement in what would be a widely publicized and dramatic event. They would be nailed with the blame. They would be held accountable, taking the heat off the Mahoney team.

That was the plan anyway. Jared appeared determined to screw it up.

O'Connell strode back to the cliff's edge, where he saw the guards looking oddly at the mobile-home offices. Then he heard it too—the laughter of a maniac was floating out of the offices, and the maniac was clearly Jared Mahoney.

O'Connell jogged to the trailer and peered into the office through one of the windows. Jared Mahoney was inside, snorting a line of white power off the desktop. As soon as the line was gone, he laughed like a barking hyena and jumped across the office, out of sight. There was a huge crack and a muffled moan.

O'Connell ripped open the door and stormed in. The seven surviving prisoners were covered in blood. Shackled wrist to wrist and ankle to ankle in their chairs, they were helpless as Jared lashed out at them with a two-foot length of concrete reinforcement rod.

The three-quarter-inch-thick piece of rusty metal cracked into the skull of one of the helpless engineers, then careened into the face of the security guard sitting next to him. The engineer slumped lifeless, but the security guard tried to scream in agony. Through the gag he could only groan.

"Jay! What in God's name are you doing, boy?"

"Having some fun, O'Connell."

"Put that bloody club down."

"Now, why would I do that?" Jared's next swing slammed into the shoulder of one of the helpless men with such force the steel folding chair underneath him collapsed. The man shouted into his gag with fear and pain as he slumped on the ruined scrap of metal, dragging his bloodied, wounded companions half out of their own chairs. The silent mass of men moved bizarrely like a gory, partially squashed caterpillar.

"Stop what you're doing!"

"Why? What's it matter?" Jared asked, his manic hysteria transforming into utter fury. He faced O'Connell with his weapon gripped like a baseball bat on his shoulder. "They're going to die anyway, O'Connell. Who cares how it happens?"

O'Connell saw the youth's eyes virtually dancing in their sockets. He was incapable of focusing them on O'Connell for more than a half second at a time.

"These blokes aren't scheduled to die, Jay," O'Connell said, trying to sound soothing and reasonable.

"Why the hell not?"

"You know the plan." He felt like he was trying to reason with a toddler in the midst of a tantrum.

Jared looked at him with a screwed-up expression. "Oh, yeah. Is it time for that, yet?"

O'Connell sighed. "Yes. Why don't you go fetch them?" he suggested. As Jared headed eagerly for the door he added, "And put on your bloody mask."

Jared pulled on his ski mask and headed for the dam. O'Connell had to clean up after the boy. He got a new chair for the man whose chair had collapsed, feeling a kind of disgust as he dragged the prisoner into it. The man was moaning from the pain of his shattered shoulder.

Jared returned minutes later with the same pair of gang members who had been dealing him drugs. They would be dead soon as a result of having seen Jared's face. That didn't matter. What mattered was that the prisoners saw who they were and recognized their gang affiliation.

O'Connell began ripping blindfolds off the shackled engineers and guards, except for the man with the caved-in skull. The man was limp, probably dead. When his neighbors realized that, they began to scream into their gags and drag at their shackles, as if they could somehow drag themselves free of the giant, fourteen-legged being they had become.

"Jesus H.," muttered Johnson, one of the gang members, as he stood in the center of the room, hands on hips and staring with astonishment and admiration at the brutal scene. "These guys sure must have pissed you off."

"They tried to fuck with us," O'Connell said. He wasn't above making use of the mayhem Jared had caused. "Doesn't matter, really. They're going down with the dam. You boys here to get paid?"

"That's right," Jiminez, a Hispanic gangbanger said, giving Johnson a disdainful look. "I want my money."

"You'll both get paid. Fifty percent now. Fifty percent when the dam goes down. Plus a bonus."

That piqued their interest. "What bonus?" Jiminez asked.

"A twenty percent bonus over and above everything else we've given you."

"You bullshitting me?" Johnson asked.

"The payout has already been approved by the man in charge of this operation," O'Connell said.

"He must be one rich, crazy man."

"He's got the bucks all right," Jared stated.

"Why would he give us extra money?" Jiminez demanded.

"Because he wants the job to go smoothly and on schedule," O'Connell explained. "Look at the twenty percent as a gratuity. It only gets paid if you both do a good job." He looked pointedly from one man to the other. "I know it's asking a lot to throw the Latin Rangers and the Black Kings together and expect everybody to get along like good friends."

Johnson grinned widely. "For an extra twenty percent I'd call this man my brother for the next two hours."

O'Connell smiled behind his ski mask and put two wads of cash into the hands of the gang captains. Jared accompanied them out of the office and O'Connell quickly began replacing the prisoners' blindfolds.

They had seen enough.

"GIVE ME SOME MORE of that shit, man," Jared demanded. He was already feeling groggy and angry. The euphoria of the speed high was always followed by bitterness as well as lethargy.

"Sure, man, whatever you need," piped up the Black

Kings captain, who handed him a plastic bag full of the stuff. Several hundred dollars' worth, to be sure. Jared smiled broadly and looked at the Latin Rangers' leader expectantly.

"Sorry, man, you cleaned me out."

Jared was instantly agitated. "Screw you, then."

"Hey, man, if I'd known that was a part of the deal, I would've brought more," Jiminez protested.

"A little late for that now," Jared retorted. They had reached the small concrete enclosure at the top of the dam, and he gestured angrily at the stairway. "Get out of here. Get back to work," he ordered Jiminez. The Black Kings captain watched with amusement.

Jiminez didn't budge. "What's that supposed to mean, man? Am I cut out of the cash because we used my stuff first, is that it?"

"Fuck you!" Jared retorted, his arms and hands starting to shake with the anticipation of ingesting more of the speed. Then the air was pierced by a high-pitched beeping sound that cut into Jared's skull.

It was the Iridium phone, which he had forgotten was clipped to his belt. If he had taken even a second to think about it, he would have realized who was calling and he would have ignored it. At least disengaged the ringer. But all he knew was he had to stop the piercing ring before it occurred again. He flipped it open. "What?"

"It's me," his father said. "Where have you been?"

"Hey, man, I'm talking to you," Jiminez said.

"Shut up!" Jared shouted.

"I ain't shuttin' up, man. I want my money."

"Jared, what's going on there?" Clint Mahoney demanded.

Jared was feeling confused and disoriented. He

wanted the meth and he wanted it now, and as far as he cared nothing else mattered. "Get out!" he hissed at Jiminez. He turned to Johnson, a muscular man in his early thirties. "Get him out of here!"

Before the words were even out of his mouth, Jiminez had flipped a switchblade out of his belt. "You touch me and I carve you," he said emotionlessly to the Black Kings captain. "And fuck you, man. I'm walking and I'm taking the Latins with me."

"Talk to me Jared," Mahoney demanded. "What's the problem?"

Jared could almost see the collapse of the world at the edge of his vision. He didn't need this, and he didn't want it. At the same time he knew he couldn't let the Latins leave. The projects needed the manpower. He didn't know what to say to his father. He was literally trembling with indecision. To his shock he realized Jiminez was already gone, and Johnson was grinning at him idiotically.

"Jared!" the phone squeaked.

"Dammit!" He dropped the phone and held the small plastic bag of meth to his chest, bursting through the steel door. He was suddenly outside, shaking and trembling on top of the huge Southern Californian dam, with the large man-made lake stretching out to one side of him and an endless drop into the canyon floor on the other side. The only protection from either eternity was a fence of thin steel cables, and as Jared's shaking feet ran, he could feel his body bouncing against them. It was incredible that the cables didn't break open, allowing him to plummet into one abyss or the other.

Then he reached the steps and staggered up them, weaving from side to side despite his best efforts to stay in the center of them. When he was on the ground again, he veered away from the cliff. Whatever was happening to him might easily force him to run right off the ledge.

With incredible effort he managed to reach the offices, which were swimming in his vision, but when he tried to slow down and walk steadily to the front door of the building, he found his feet inexplicably speeding him at breakneck pace toward the cliff ledge. He couldn't see it properly, and he tried to recall exactly how far the edge was from the front door to the mobile home. Seemed like at least twenty feet. Vaguely he made out the guards, his father's hired guns, watching him curiously with their automatic rifles in their hands. They were taunting him by perching themselves within inches of the cliff drop-off.

Jared slumped heavily against the walls of the trailer and stared at the bare, rocky ground.

O'CONNELL HEARD THE THUMP against the wall of the mobile home and with a swift, smooth movement drew his handgun, a 9 mm Glock. He swept the gun over the interior of the office, seeing nothing out of the ordinary. The prisoners were secure: bound, blindfolded, gagged. He looked out the front door and again saw nothing out of the ordinary.

"Mr. O'Connell?" someone said from the radio on his belt. He grabbed it.

"What's going on?"

"It's the kid," one of the guards said.

O'Connell swore and stepped out of the mobile home. He found Jared Mahoney stretched on the ground like a corpse, his shoulders propped against the aluminium cover on the wheels and his eyes closed as he buried his nose and mouth in a clear plastic bag of white power. He inhaled from the bag deeply, serenely.

"Stupid piece of shit," O'Connell muttered.

Jared's yellowed eyes opened and he rolled them up at O'Connell. "It's all going to hell down there."

"What do you mean?"

"The Latins are leaving. They want their money."

"Why are they leaving?"

"I don't know."

O'Connell knew he was lying. "What did you tell them?"

"Nothing!"

O'Connell felt his bile rising. Nothing nauseated him worse than a drug addict, and Jared Mahoney clearly was one. He hadn't realized before allowing Clint Mahoney to team him up with the idiot kid, and he guessed the old man was having trouble admitting it to himself. Otherwise he would never have put his son officially in command of this operation.

Now the kid's trembling body was becoming visibly more stable as he got his fix of cocaine or whatever was in the bag. With growing energy he started to stand. O'Connell's gun hand descended on his skull, slamming the heavy grip of the Browning down on his head. It was like the corner of a brick falling, from a hundred feet, slamming into his skull. Jared slumped again.

O'CONNELL FOUND the Iridium phone in the concrete enclosure at the top of the dam. As soon as he hung it up it began ringing furiously and he answered it. "O'Connell here."

"O'Connell, where's Jared!" Clint Mahoney demanded.

"Incapacitated, sir."

"What's that supposed to mean?"

O'Connell's patience ran out and he said, "Too high

to function is what I mean, sir. He bought a big bag of white powder from one of the gangs and got totally wasted.''

There was an icy silence on the line. ''What are you trying to pull, O'Connell?''

''I'm not trying to pull anything, sir. All I'm trying to do is salvage this operation.''

''What's the problem?''

''I don't know yet. As of ten minutes ago everything was running smoothly. We went through with the exposure routine as planned, and Jared was escorting the gang captains away from the base office. Then he came running back saying that the Latins are leaving. Then he passed out. I'm on my way to investigate now.''

The line was strangely, ominously quiet. ''Do what you have to do to keep the project running on schedule, O'Connell.''

''You want me to offer the Latins more cash than I've already promised them?''

''Yes. And keep Jared from screwing things up further. Take whatever steps are needed.''

''Such as?''

''Do I have to spell it out for you, O'Connell?''

''Yes, sir, you absolutely do. What, precisely, should I do to keep Jared from hampering this project?''

There was a long moment, then Mahoney said, ''You have my permission to shoot him between the eyes, but only if it's absolutely necessary.''

CHAPTER FOUR

Stony Man Farm, Virginia

Resting under the dispassionate peak of Stony Man Mountain, the U.S. government complex was hidden from the world behind the facade of a working agricultural enterprise. Not that it was a false front; the complex was a working farm. Some years it even pulled a profit.

But few farms had so many visitors on any given morning. They came in before and during a blazing, orange and yellow dawn that on any other morning might have been called spectacular. Nobody noticed it that day.

They gathered at the huge table with blank faces and glazed eyes. Some of them stared at the walls. Some stared at their hands. None looked at one another while the tape was playing.

The sounds of the blasts were explosions of static and thunder, each one louder than the last, and then there was an impact that might have been flesh on metal. They heard a single, final phrase: "Stony Base!" The background reverberation turned into a rumble that drowned any other sounds the microphone might have picked up. Suddenly there was a splash, and for less than a second the rumbles could still be heard through a blanket of water.

After which the silence was eloquent.

Barbara Price had forgotten that she had started the tape. She was staring at the high-gloss surface of the tabletop, not moving, hardly breathing. Jack Grimaldi stood from his seat, leaned over and flipped off the tape player that sat at Price's elbow, then sat again. No one spoke and no one else moved.

Hal Brognola finally exhaled, long and low, and said, "Katz?"

Yakov Katzenelenbogen leaned forward and lifted a piece of paper off the table in front of him. He didn't need it. After reading it seven times he had memorized every word.

"The Bedoya Dam, 155 miles southeast of Lima, Peru, broke at 3:15 a.m. local time following a series of catastrophic explosions along its face. The flooding swept away most of four villages with at least two hundred dead and another three hundred missing. Rescue teams are finding bodies by the minute. Water rationing has already commenced in Lima. Red Cross teams on the scene are anticipating severe water shortages, and U.S. Centers for Disease Control are rushing in teams to assist the Peruvian government with efforts to minimize anticipated outbreaks of infectious diseases."

Rafael Encizo muttered something harsh and lurid under his breath.

"That's the best the U.S. can do?" Hermann Schwarz demanded.

"Lima has been on the brink of a severe water shortage for years," Brognola explained. The big Fed rolled an unlit cigar in the corner of his mouth and leaned back in his chair. "Its water infrastructure is antiquated and operating far beyond capacity, with new pipeline construction lagging well behind population growth. Because of the poor state of the infrastructure, much of the water that makes it into city pipes is wasted in the ground or contaminated. The Bedoya Dam was designed to take some of the demand off other water sources. When it went on-line last year, three other water arteries into the city were shut down. They're totally dismantled. They can't be operational again for eight months, minimum.''

"So the city is helpless," Encizo stated flatly.

"Unless the people of Peru can learn to stomach seawater," Brognola muttered.

"Somebody did this on purpose," David McCarter stated. The Briton was the leader of Phoenix Force, one of the two special operations groups based at Stony Man Farm. "So what's the purpose?"

"Unknown," Katzenelenbogen replied.

"What do we know about the parties responsible?"

"Every newspaper and television station in Peru received a photocopied letter, supposedly from the Tupac Amaru, claiming responsibility."

"You believe that, Katz?" McCarter asked.

"I don't think anybody does."

McCarter leaned over the table and wrinkled his brow. "What intel did Mack procure on these guys?"

"Not much," Price stated. "He didn't have time for digging. It took him a week to track down one of the buyers of the explosives. That was yesterday, and the explosives were transported almost directly to the dam. Once he realized what was going down he threw himself into it. There was no time for backup to arrive, in any form. Even the local police were an hour behind him. By then it was too late."

"We have a line on the buyers, I understand?" Brognola asked.

"Yes. South American mercenaries. Highly skilled but nothing out of the ordinary. Surely not the brains behind the operation," Katzenelenbogen explained.

"This doesn't smell like the Tupac Amaru to me. What other extremist groups are operating in Peru?" Brognola asked.

"The Shining Path," Katzenelenbogen said. "But neither group has demonstrated a propensity for using mercenaries. They wouldn't trust them even if they could afford them. Especially not for a task as important as taking delivery of a very expensive shipment of explosives. And neither of those groups makes a habit of engaging in acts of mass murder."

"So who does have that propensity?" T. J. Hawkins asked. His eyes blazed with quiet intensity, the only evidence of the turmoil going on in his mind—the same mounting frustration they were all feeling. They had lost one of their own. To have so little to act upon was infuriating. "Anybody in Peru?" he asked. "Anybody in South America?"

There were silent exchanges of looks. "This just doesn't fit any patterns we've seen from the Latin American guerrilla groups," Price said.

"Let's look at it from the perspective of motive," Brognola suggested. "What would anybody, anywhere, have to gain by the destruction of the Bedoya Dam?"

Price and Katzenelenbogen met each other's gaze. "We've been through that, too, Hal," Katz said resignedly. "We haven't been able to come up with anything. Certainly the only real good that might come from such an act is to make those responsible more terrible in the eyes of the people."

"They'd alienate their supporters in the Peruvian population." The speaker was Calvin James, a trim black man sporting a pencil-thin mustache.

"That alienation would turn to vilification in a matter of weeks," Katzenelenbogen added grimly. "A month from now, barring a miracle, Lima's going to be turning its gymnasiums into infectious disease wards to handle hospital overflow."

"Dammit, this is getting us nowhere." Brognola's cigar twitched and spun in his mouth.

"Is there anybody else out there with any better ideas?" McCarter asked.

Brognola shook his head and finally withdrew the cigar with a crooked finger. "Nobody. The CIA is clueless. The Peruvians have no leads that they are willing to talk about. I thought for sure we'd be the ones with enough to go on."

"To go on?" Price asked sharply. "Of course we have enough to go on, Hal. We can have both teams in Peru this afternoon. They can retrace Mack's steps, shake down the explosive suppliers, follow up on the names of the mercenaries we IDed."

"We have no authority to go in on this one, Barb."

"No authority?" Her voice was low and accusatory, carrying deadly weight. "Hal, Mack is gone."

"We don't know that for sure."

"Hal—"

"He's come out of some tight scrapes in the past. I'm not counting Striker out." The big Fed made this declaration with such determined confidence even Price couldn't bring herself to argue the point.

"This has become a personal matter," Price said. "You can't tell me it's not."

"That's a bad reason to mobilize two SOG teams," Brognola retorted tersely.

"Not from my perspective," Price snapped.

"We don't have the okay to proceed with any such operation," Brognola concluded. "It's not going to be easy to talk the President into authorizing a mission on foreign soil. Outside the loss of one agent—not even an official agent—what U.S. interests are at stake here? Don't look at me that way, dammit! I'm giving it to you from the bureaucrat's point of view and you know it! This is strictly a domestic Peruvian issue."

"Not anymore, Hal."

All heads turned. The door to the War Room had opened as Brognola delivered his speech. The figure in the doorway was a black man, with the dignified and proud demeanor of a college professor or a research scientist. Dr. Huntington Wethers had, in fact, been a professor of computer science at Berkeley in a former life. Now he served as a cybernetics expert on Aaron Kurtzman's computer team. "Another dam was just destroyed. This time it's in our own backyard."

He grabbed the remote that activated the large wall screen, and an instant later the image of a southwestern canyon, taken from a helicopter-mounted camera, was displayed with the familiar CNN logo in the corner of the screen.

"Less than an hour ago," Wethers said. "The media is just arriving on the scene. This is the new Southern California Water Conservation Authority Dam. It channels seventy percent of San Diego's water."

"Are they sure an explosion downed it?" Brognola asked.

"More like twenty explosions, according to survivors."

The roomful of people watched as the helicopter swung over the jumble of broken concrete collapsed between two tattered walls of reinforced concrete. The walls were yards thick at the base; the blasts required to puncture such a structure had to have been huge.

The anchor announced that CNN now had a camera in the air over the Bedoya catastrophe, and suddenly the scene on the display changed dramatically—at least part of it did. The desert canyons on either side of the broken dam became wooded green mountains. What remained the same from the previous picture was the ruin of a great dam in the middle of the screen. The news anchor was describing the Bedoya Dam, which had collapsed similarly just eight hours prior to the one in Southern California, under equally mysterious circumstances.

The Peruvian news helicopter was moving in closer, bringing the devastation into vivid clarity on the flat television screen. Every person in the room in Virginia was wondering what it had to have been like to be on that dam while it exploded, over and over again, and finally disintegrated.

Every single one of them was wondering if it was possible to survive such a cataclysm.

Few of them could bring themselves to believe that it was.

The Oval Office, Washington, D.C.

THE PRESIDENT LOOKED PALE. He had asked Brognola to bring the audio tape recording, but now he regretted it. The explosions, one after another, deafening and monstrous, and the one, final spoken phrase, weren't nearly as bad as the abrupt silence when it was all over.

"How in the world did you manage to get this?" he asked.

"My mission controller, Barbara Price, had a satellite uplink established with Striker before he went in. The signal went to hell when he descended into the canyon—the uplink unit couldn't receive through the canyon walls. She unexpectedly started getting a clear signal again a little later, assumedly when Bolan had climbed to the top of the dam and could get a radio signal over the walls. We're not positive, sir, but our acoustic analysis suggests he went into the water just as the dam was bursting."

"Good God." The Man was wondering what that had to have been like, and he found himself curiously moved and shaken by the loss of Mack Bolan. More than once Bolan had rescued him from a bad situation. There probably wasn't a soldier alive who had given more for so long to his country and humanity, taking down the scum of the earth on his own terms. After enduring endless years of government protocol, the Man envied that kind of freedom.

Then he caught himself. Despite his one-of-a-kind lone-wolf status, despite his flagrant disregard of legalities in favor of justice, Mack Bolan hadn't been free at all. Something had chained him to the life he led—some powerful trauma had transformed the soldier's lifework from career to compulsion.

What the hell could have done that to a man?

The President looked squarely at Brognola. "I'm sorry about Striker, Hal."

"We're not counting him out of the picture, yet, Mr. President."

The President delivered his best smile, but he couldn't bring himself to say anything. He had counted agents out of commission more than he cared to remember during his long tenure as the leader of the last global superpower. Those agents didn't tend to come back.

The Man got back to business. "Here's the CIA file, such as it is, on Bedoya."

Brognola took the folder. It was awfully thin. "Am I going to find anything new in here?"

"No."

"And the San Diego dam?"

"Not a scrap. The FBI has only been on the scene for an hour, and our special teams won't get there until afternoon." He shook his head. "This is going to be a disaster. We'll have to send water trucks into San Diego by the thousands. It might be months before a new pipeline is in place. A large percentage of the population will flee and the city will almost certainly be bankrupted without federal aid—which we'll have to provide, of course. This one is going to run into the billions." He exhaled, long and low. "And it's a crappy way to end a presidency."

"Mr. President," Brognola asked frankly, "is there any doubt in your mind these occurrences are related?"

"None at all. The odds against it are astronomical."

"Then you have no problem with my teams initiating their investigations?"

The Man pushed across an envelope bearing the seal of the President of the United States of America. "Signed before you got here. You'll have full access to any and all CIA and FBI intelligence."

"Good to hear," Brognola said, putting the paperwork in a steel briefcase. "My teams are standing by. I'll make a phone call and have them in the air five minutes after I leave this office."

"Wish them luck for me," the Man said. "Ask them,

as a personal favor to me, to wrap this one up quick and neat. After all I've done, I'd rather not be remembered for this."

"I'll tell them, sir," Brognola said. "But to be perfectly honest, they have other personal reasons for going into this one."

"Yes, of course," the President said softly, chastised by his own realization that he had already factored Mack Bolan out of the scheme.

One of the best things about leaving office, he thought, not for the first time, would be the freedom to think of people as human beings again, and not as elements in political equations.

Cajamarca, Peru

STILL CHEWING a tough piece of beef from a roast feeding himself and his eight business partners, Javier Arbulu emerged from the tiny eating establishment in the village square of Cajamarca. The villagers were gathering, the children shouting in excitement. They had never seen an aircraft this close.

The Bell helicopter carefully took up a position over the wide, dirt square that was the heart of the little village, descending with just three feet to spare at the front. A slip of the hand would have sent the rotors ripping through one of the town's buildings. The people of Cajamarca wouldn't have minded so much; it was a government building.

Arbulu approached the helicopter as it rested its weight on the landing skids. He was familiar with the black, unmarked Bell 430. It belonged to the man who had said they would never again see or speak to each other.

The mercenary was monitoring the behavior of the occupants carefully as he approached the opening side door. His employer stepped out with a condescending smile on his face for the villagers. The armed escort remained in the helicopter.

"Hello, Javier," the man said over the roar. The rotors were in idle but not stopping. He wasn't staying long.

"You told me to never try to contact you again. I assumed you would do the same for me."

The man took Arbulu by the arm and led him to the front of the chopper. "That stipulation was intended to protect us from being linked to each other in case either of us becomes tied to the Bedoya Dam occurrence. Now a situation has arisen that might put us in danger of just such a link. Together I think we can handle it, however."

"Why don't we go in out of this racket?" Arbulu suggested.

"No time for that, I'm afraid, Javier."

The man was large and powerful, but with a wide, pale face that belonged on the body of one of those morbidly obese people who never left home. He had green eyes and sandy, auburn hair, which was hidden in a red scarf. He looked like an Irishman, and his voice carried the telltale brogue. His politeness was a ruse. Arbulu knew that, and he was trying to see past it without success.

"Why don't you tell me what's going on, then?" the Peruvian mercenary commander asked.

"At Bedoya, you might have noticed, I kept myself and my staff out of sight of the other hired teams, just in case they were later tied to the event and questioned.

None of them knew my name or the names of my staff. None of them saw any of us face-to-face.''

"No one except me. As we planned.''

"You were never even told my name, but I needed to have face-to-face meetings with you, Javier, in order to gain your confidence. Once I had you convinced I knew you would be able to get the other teams of soldiers on board. But there's more to the plan than you know.''

"Such as?''

The man shrugged. His eyes sparkled as if he were about to tell Arbulu a dirty limerick. "Sorry, Javier. The plan is for there to be no one left who knows who I am or what I look like.''

The man's mouth cracked into a grin, as if the punch line had been delivered and he was waiting for the chuckle from his audience. Arbulu frowned, trying to get a handle on the explanation and feeling sure it was somehow a threat. Then he glimpsed the barrel of a machine gun protruding from the darkness inside the Bell helicopter. The shots slammed into him with magnificent force, ripping through his chest, the sound of it so loud it was audible over the thrum of the rotors.

Arbulu didn't hear it. He was already dead.

The man turned to the crowd as they became terrified. Most of them probably hadn't recognized the sound of the shot until they saw Arbulu fall, and the realization was washing over them like a wave. The women began to scream.

The man pulled out a flag, red on both ends. It was white in the middle with a scrawled emblem and the letters *MRTA*. It was the flag of the Tupac Amaru Revolutionary Movement. The man waved it, making sure the villagers got a good look.

That would keep them guessing.

He scrambled for the helicopter and jumped inside as the engine intensity increased and the weight of the great bird lifted off the landing skids. The tavern door burst open. The mercenaries who had until thirty seconds ago been under the command of Javier Arbulu raised their weapons at the chopper.

Thomas McDonough had been waiting for them with the Browning machine gun. Before the mercenaries could react, the Browning opened fire with a murderous storm of .50-caliber violence. It cut them to pieces and chopped through the building's front like an invisible hatchet moving at lightning speed.

Mahoney put on his headset to speak to the pilot. "Swing over the square. Over the crowd."

The pilot did as instructed, following a large group of the residents of the once-peaceful village. Panicking, they were trampling a man and woman who had collapsed on the earthen street. Mahoney tossed out the balled Tupac Amaru flag, watching it unfurl in the downwash from the rotors and drape the unmoving man. Mahoney laughed at that. He couldn't have asked for a more dramatic souvenir. He just wished there was a news crew around to shoot it.

CHAPTER FIVE

Southwestern Turkmenistan

The Turkmen Central Waterway would be what he was remembered for. Boris Rahmonov had contemplated, half seriously, requesting that an etching of its path be placed on his headstone.

He wasn't that old, he told himself. Not as old as he felt. Maybe he would actually accomplish something even more impressive than this prior to his death.

The waterway began in the desert mountains of southwestern Turkmenistan, where one of the few fresh-water springs grew out of the unimpressive, rocky peaks. For just a couple of miles these streams came together into a modest river before branching into multiple rivulets and streams again, finally seeping back into the earth before traveling far into the desert.

It had been a cruel trick played by Mother Nature on the people of Turkmenistan, long before the Turkmen's arrival. For tens of thousands of years these precious streams of water had collected, come together for a brief period of greatness, then teasingly gone their separate paths.

It had taken a man of Rahmonov's vision and engi-neering skill to imagine a plan for correcting this great geological mistake. It had taken a man of Rahmonov's fortitude and ambition to see it to fruition. The fact that this nation of five million people was on the brink of nationwide drought had been a helpful impetus.

With hard manual labor provided out of the cities of Nebit-Dag, Kum-Dag and Kazandzhik, and vast supplies of materials and heavy equipment courtesy of the United Nations, Rahmonov's great work had finally got off the ground in the late 1990s.

Rahmonov, with the help of French UN engineers, managed to train the Turkmen workers in dam construction. The slow work resulted in an unattractive but perfectly serviceable dam that stopped the flow of the Ahal River forever. The ten-thousand-year-old canyon would grow no farther. The water that had once followed the canyon into the desert, where it sank unused into the earth, now backflowed into the Turkmen Central Waterway.

One down, fifteen to go.

They built two more small dams before Rahmonov was confident enough to split his team into many smaller groups. Then, simultaneously, the remainder of the dams rose in the low mountains.

Finally, as the feasibility of the project became tangible, it was time to construct the Turkmen Central Dam, the largest and most complicated of them all. This would be the dam that held back the backflowed waters. Here, finally, would be the Ahal Lake, holding and controlling enough water to sustain the cities of Kazandzhik, Bami and Bakharden, and even to jump-start the meager agricultural industry that was faltering in the southern Turkmen desert.

The Aral Sea was as dead as a nuclear fallout zone. The Karakumskiy Kanal was no longer able to provide sufficient water for the southern cities of Turkmenistan. Even as water shortages were threatening the cities along the Turkmenistan-Iran border with wide-scale disease and crop failure, the great dam was completed. UN teams arrived to assist the Turkmen government in laying the great pipeline to carry the water into the cities. The great, years-long project finally came to a day-by-day countdown.

When Rahmonov stood with the city officials at Bakharden, 250 kilometers from his dam, and watched the water begin to flow into the city reservoirs to the cheering of a gathered crowd, he had never been so proud and happy.

Work continued at the dam. As a bonus, a new hydroelectric facility had just been green-lighted by the Turkmen government, generating enough power to support half a city.

But when Rahmonov heard the distant thrum of helicopters on that hot, harsh morning, he had a strange premonition that it was about to all come crashing down.

Two major dams had been blown to smithereens within eight hours of each other. No one knew why, nor did anyone believe that the regional terrorist group in Peru or a street gang in the U.S. had destroyed the dams in their respective countries.

So who was responsible? What could their motivation possible be? And why were they targeting dams, of all things?

This project was Rahmonov's entire life. He was paranoid, and he knew it.

He watched the ridge above the base of the Turkmen Central Dam as the thrum became a roar and a black helicopter came into view, sweeping over the workers who stood with their heads bent back. Rahmonov felt the color of the aircraft was ominous. As it landed, he saw the huge white letters emblazoned on the body of the chopper: URAT.

"It's the Urat," his foreman exclaimed, bewildered.

"It can't be," Rahmonov replied. "It's impossible."

The chopper doors pulled open, and armed men began jumping out, falling into formation in an ever-widening line. They held a mean-looking selection of automatic weapons, rifles and handguns, and the guns were directed at Rahmonov's workers. Soon their approaching line was spread across the uneven terrain at the bottom of the canyon. Behind the workers was the dam. No escape there.

The dream was about to end abruptly, but Rahmonov couldn't allow that to happen. "Get up to the top," he ordered his foreman in a low voice. "Get to the office and call for help. I will try to distract their attention while you go."

The foreman nodded and started making his way to the rear of the crowd of workmen, who were milling about with fear in their eyes, the name of God on their lips. They were not fighting men.

"What is this?" Rahmonov demanded, striding forward to meet the oncoming soldiers. "Who are you people?"

"We are the Urat. Can't you read?" The man who spoke was tall, gaunt and dark-eyed. His hair was cut short and bristly, and was a dirty-blond color. He hadn't shaved in weeks, and his desert-camouflage clothing carried much of the desert dust with it.

"You're Russian," Rahmonov stated accusingly. "You've got a Russian accent."

The man swung the butt of his AK-74 across Rahmonov's face so quickly he didn't see it coming. Suddenly his neck cracked as his head snapped to the side. The pain exploded in his jaw as he fell to the rocky ground. "You've got a Russian accent as well, my friend, but you speak it far too much."

When Rahmonov tried to speak again the pain intensified, and he could only moan.

"I assume you are Boris Rahmonov."

Rahmonov tried to nod. His vision was blinded with pain, and he was barely able to hear the words.

"You have stolen our water. You've left us with no way to irrigate our crops or water our livestock. We've come to take back what is ours."

When he focused through the white mist of pain, Rahmonov witnessed the Russian raise the AK-74 in both hands and fire the weapon briefly in his direction. More lightning bolts of pain shot through him, and his breath burst from his body. When he looked down at his legs he saw masses of blood at his knees. He felt as if he were in another world, passed through a dimensional door opened by pain and confusion.

The Russian who claimed to be a member of the Urat ethnic group was shouting orders and pointing at the crowds of workmen.

Even smothered in a haze, Rahmonov realized what the Russian was up to.

Rahmonov reached out and grabbed a rock. He managed to drag his body onto his stomach, but when he tried to crawl his limbs failed to cooperate. He pulled himself forward on his hands as best he could, trying to shout but croaking out nothing above a whisper.

"No. Spare them."

He watched with detached horror as the line of gunmen converged on the workmen, carefully keeping their formation, a net that none of the workmen could have slipped through. None of them was brave or foolish enough to attempt an escape.

The soldiers formed a firing squad, their expressions devoid of mercy. Devoid of any humanity.

Rahmonov couldn't speak, and his moans died on his swollen lips. He became aware of a shadow passing over him, and craning his neck from his prone position he could see a second helicopter hovering over the top of the dam. There was a ladder swinging from beneath it, with soldiers descending one after another.

"We've got a lurker," came a strange voice from nowhere. Rahmonov realized it was the Russian's walkie-talkie.

The Russian grabbed the radio from his belt and spoke. "Yes?"

"Just one," the voice from the walkie-talkie said. "He must have seen us coming. He was trying to get to the office, I believe. They've got a phone line set up there."

"We'll make an example of him," the Russian said without hesitation. "Send him down."

Then the Russian was shouting to the workmen and pointing to the top of the dam. "This is what happens to men who steal from the Urat!"

Rahmonov's foreman appeared, leaning from the lip of the dam. His mouth was open and the sound of his shouts were tiny from three hundred feet. Then he was propelled into open space, arms windmilling, legs pedaling an imaginary bicycle at top speed, his scream of terror growing like the approaching whistle of a train. Rahmonov's head refused to turn to follow the descent, but he felt the impact in the earth and the sudden silence.

He felt empty, a complete and all-encompassing hopelessness. He gave into it and sank into blackness.

AYA ENDOVIK WITNESSED the terror in the eyes of the workmen. He had them where he wanted them, which was terrified beyond thought. When men allowed themselves to be enslaved by the terror of an imminent, violent death they went stupid. The workmen were now convinced that they were about to be shot down by the firing squad or maybe sent flying off the top of the dam one after another.

"Put them inside," he ordered.

His handpicked mercenaries began herding the prisoners into the interior of the dam, into the vast enclosure being readied for the hydroelectric equipment. There was nothing there now except for the great water-lock that was opened and closed to control the escape of the precious water into the massive, welded steel piping that stretched away through the canyon and across southern Turkmenistan.

Beneath the steel grate of the floor were huge overflow tanks, which would eventually be dug out to allow the overflow into the canyon, into the now-dry riverbed, before it rose to the height of the turbines. One of the gunmen lifted the single opening in the grate and ordered the prisoners inside with a gesture. Within minutes the prisoners had taken the ladder to the bottom of the trench and stood there, looking up through the grate like animals in a cage.

Endovik appeared and watched them dispassionately for a moment.

"Some of you will live to spread the message. The Urat will not be robbed of their land and their life," he said. "Anyone who tries to escape will be shot. Understand?'' He walked away without waiting for a response.

Endovik left just four gunmen with the prisoners, which was unnecessary. The workmen weren't going anywhere. The only way out of the trench was through the grate. No more than one at a time could take that exit. If they tried to escape, a single man could pick them off without effort.

The job was easy, considering the magnitude of it. He'd been provided what he needed in terms of transportation, explosives and ammunition. He already had the men.

Really, almost anybody could have accomplished the task. But the man who hired him was intent on getting trained, experienced military men.

Every one of Endovik's men met those requirements. They were ex-Soviet soldiers, many of whom had served time with Endovik in Afghanistan, and every one of them had been in multiple combat situations.

For a group like his, this operation was no great challenge.

Afterward was another story, and that was why the job paid so well. The repercussions could be substantial.

Endovik was transported in the big Soviet-era chopper to the top of the first dam on the hit list. The Central dam blocked off a deep, narrow gorge, too crowded to allow the chopper safe entrance. When he marched to the lip of the gorge and strolled out onto the dam, which was just ten feet wide at the top, he found his teams already rappelling down the front and placing charges in the corner where the dam intersected the canyon wall.

There would be fifteen shaped explosive charges set into the dam at each wall. When the explosions occurred, much of the force of each blast would be directed into the stone canyon wall itself. Endovik had been told that such a blast would make the restoration of the dam exceedingly difficult and time-consuming. By increasing the breadth of the opening that the dam would need to fill, the structural dynamics of the dam would be altered. To repair it, the Turkmen builders might just find it easier to move down to another narrow place in the gorge and start from scratch.

Endovik turned to the newly formed man-made lake that the series of dams in the Turkmen Central Waterway created. By sundown it would be erased. The waters would have rushed out into the desert and evaporated into the soil.

The Russian was chauffeured by the chopper pilot from dam to dam, where his teams were making quick work of setting up the hundreds of pounds of prepared explosives they had been provided. The exercise took less than two hours. Then Endovik returned to the prisoners at the base of the main dam, ordering them out of the trench and into the canyon.

"You see the explosives?" he said to the workmen. "This dam required nearly a ton of explosives set just above the turbine enclosure. That is the weakest point on the dam. The blast will put a great big hole in the middle. The other charges will follow after the first at fifteen-second intervals and will help rip the apron of the dam into two parts. Simultaneously, charges will explode along the face of all the other six dams that make up the Turkmen Central Waterway. The water will rush out in all directions simultaneously, and soon the streams that once sustained the Urat people will be restored."

"You're not Urat," ventured one of the prisoners, made bold during his imprisonment. "You're a miserable terrorist and a murderer. The people of this country need this water. They depend on it. Without it there will be drought and sickness for months, maybe years. Who knows how many will die?''

Endovik gave a small, sideways motion of his head, and without discussion one of his soldiers approached the workman and aimed his automatic rifle at the man's legs. The workman recoiled and tried to run, but the rifle stuttered, the bullets chopping into his legs and sending him crashing to the ground.

''Does anyone else have something to say?'' Endovik demanded over the man's screams of pain.

The workmen glared at him silently.

Endovik glanced at his watch. ''You have nineteen minutes. In that time, some of you might make it to a low descent on the right side of the canyon wall a few kilometers down. That will save you from the water.''

Their fear and hostility became uncertainty until Endovik said, ''I suggest you hurry.''

Then the race began.

ASCENDING TO 250 meters, Endovik directed his chopper pilot to plant them in a spot directly to the east of the main dam, from where they could see across the man-made lake and to the other dams. He watched with growing excitement as the minutes ticked away. He found himself wishing he had a video camera to record the event. He was going to look back on this for the rest of his life.

''How are our friends doing?'' Endovik yelled over the roar to one of his soldiers.

The soldier on the other side of the chopper, looking through a porthole, laughed and said in Russian, ''Running like bugs! A few of them might actually make it to safety."

Endovik had to see for himself. He could barely make them out, far down the canyon, running and tripping on the uneven surface. A few of them were limping on sprained ankles. The man with the gun-shot legs was bouncing along between a pair of helpers, but the three of them were well behind the front-runners.

Then the wounded man fell and one of his helpmates gave up on him, bolting away.

Endovik shook his head and glanced at his watch. They were too far away. None of that trio was going to make it.

He moved back to the side of the chopper where the door was pulled open for an unobstructed view of the dam and the lake.

Two minutes.

RAHMONOV EXERTED a great effort to bring himself out of semiconsciousness, aware that there was no more nearby activity. Where had everyone gone? Why was that thought ominous?

Raising his head, he stared across the canyon floor to the dam. No movement. No voices. There was a strange, faraway thrum, which sounded like the helicopter but which was neither retreating nor approaching. Maybe he was imagining the sound.

He pushed against the ground with his hands, ignoring the streaks of fresh pain in his legs, and peered at the face of the great dam, his dam. There was something strange about it. A strange mass had been applied to the face of the dam directly above the enclosure. There was a bright blue plastic cover and a webbing of black straps holding it in place. The straps had to be bolted on, he decided. It had the appearance of some bizarre sort of monster's egg sac. Smaller such packages were placed every fifteen meters or so up the side of the dam.

When it dawned on him what the packages contained, he experienced the greatest sorrow he had ever known.

His great dream was about to end. He was almost glad to be ending with it.

Rahmonov collapsed to the ground, his cheek striking the rock, and when the massive blast occurred he didn't even turn his head to face it.

ENDOVIK WAS SPEECHLESS when the massive crater appeared in the face of the dam, as if it had been hit by a giant, invisible asteroid. As the water began rushing out in a white torrent, another explosion above the opening tore out a second huge section, then another, until the dam was burst entirely into two halves that were nudged open farther by the torrent of water. Great white explosions were bursting from the other dams, and the water in the man-made lake churned and shook like the Atlantic in a raging storm, the level falling so fast that it looked like a cheap model in a bad disaster movie.

In minutes, the floor of the lake began to appear and the walls of water were sweeping down the mountains, into the villages of the Urat people and into the vast, sandy desert of southern Turkmenistan, where it would seep away, wasted.

Endovik smiled at his men and ordered the pilot to signal the second helicopter. It was time to leave. People were going to know about this soon. Endovik and his mercenary army would have to be far removed when the time came.

As the chopper tilted and sped north over the desert,

he found he couldn't tear his eyes off the cataclysm he had created. Endovik hadn't asked and didn't know the reason for the dam's destruction, but he certainly felt a sense of accomplishment.

Over the Eastern United States

THE THINLY PADDED SEAT of the long-range U.S. Air Force troop transport jet was less than comfortable, and the barrel-chested figure scooted around in it for a more comfortable position, scratching an old scar on his left hand and idly watching the earth dwindle beneath him. The heavy-machinery whine of the motors directly under the floor beneath his feet ended with a bump. The wheels were up, the bay doors closed with a quick hum, and the Stony Man pilot gave her the gas. With a roar, the engines increased their whine and the aircraft began ascending with added g-forces. The angle of ascent was such that Gary Manning could no longer see the earth unless he craned his neck to peer back down at the rear end of the aircraft.

"Somebody told Jack we're in a hurry," Hermann "Gadgets" Schwarz commented. Schwarz was a slim figure in the seat across the aisle. His tanned face made him look younger than his comrades in Able Team, which he was. Able Team was one of the two Stony Man Farm action teams—a team that normally had just three members.

Manning was officially a member of the second Stony Man group. Phoenix Force had taken off in a similar military aircraft less than a minute prior to Able Team, headed for Central Asia.

The news had come down the wire about the third burst dam just minutes before the teams were scheduled to be underway. Phoenix had been preparing to head to Peru. A quick change in plans sent them on their way to Turkmenistan. Able Team was now scheduled to head into Peru, once they learned what they could in Southern California.

"Nice to have you along for the ride," Schwarz said, giving him a clap on the shoulder. He added in a mock whisper, "To be honest, these guys can get on my nerves."

"I heard that," growled Carl "Ironman" Lyons, the Able Team leader, seated directly behind Schwarz.

Manning gave them a grin, but their friendly barbs didn't ease his distress. The loss of Striker in South America had rocked his world. Not that he was unfamiliar with death. Far from it. He'd experienced more than his fair share. But somehow the thought of a world without Mack Bolan seemed surreal.

The mystery made it worse. Until Bolan's body was found, there would be a nagging uncertainty. Hal Brognola was able to turn that uncertainty into optimism, but Manning was having difficulty doing so.

He also found it subtly disturbing to be removed from the Phoenix Force fold at a time like this. He was fast friends with the Able Team warriors, but he didn't share the sense of, well, family that he knew in Phoenix Force. Right now the guys would be sharing their own almost ritualistic barbs and private jokes, reassuring one another that, despite what had happened, life went on.

There was a good reason to have him on the San Diego probe. Manning was an expert in the use of military and commercial explosives. In San Diego, the team had been promised the full cooperation of the federal investigating teams. Manning would be able to make a close examination of the ruin of the dam and maybe even make an on-the-spot analysis of the explosives used. That would, perhaps, lead the team to a source for the explosives, which could, possibly, give them a line on the perpetrators.

Those were awfully big maybes, but it might be all they had to go on. In Turkmenistan the local authorities would have no reason to allow an anonymous U.S. team in on the investigation, so it had been decided to lump Manning in with Able Team's California probe.

"I need some java," Manning said as suddenly as the thought occurred to him.

"I don't think we rate a flight attendant," the stocky figure in the seat directly behind Manning said. Rosario Blancanales was grayed almost to white, but nothing outside of his hair gave him the appearance of an old man. He had clear eyes, as black as the waters of a mountain lake on a starless night. His build was powerful. This wasn't the kind of guy you messed with if you ran into him in a bar.

Blancanales was highly adept at understanding the human psyche. His Able Team comrades had witnessed him turn the most virulent Hispanic-hating bigot into his good buddy when the need arose. His ability to handle almost any personality had long ago earned him the nickname "Politician." But Politician didn't roll off the tongue, so he was Pol for short.

He rose from his seat and joined Manning in the tiny galley area at the front of the plane, ostensibly to get a cup of coffee for himself. They watched the black, steaming liquid trickle into the steel pot.

"This is a tough one for me," Blancanales said. He didn't have to explain what he meant.

Manning didn't look away from the coffee, but he

nodded and leaned back against the wall, folding his
arms.

"Yeah, me too," he said finally.

Blancanales grabbed two cups of coffee and entered
the cockpit.

Strangely, that was enough to ease, just a little, the
anxiety resting like a sack of lead weights on Manning's
shoulders.

Jack Grimaldi took the cup Blancanales handed him
with a nod of thanks, sipping it without allowing it to
cool. He didn't notice that his tongue burned.

"We at cruising altitude yet?" Blancanales asked.

"Not quite," Grimaldi replied.

"But we're sure not wasting any time," added the
blacksuit in the copilot's seat. He was one of the young
military men whose duty rotated him through a stint at
the Farm. It was a unique but thankless position, requiring an exemplary military record and a high level
of security clearance. That same need for ultrahigh security insured that the position would be recorded on
the airman's permanent record in only the vaguest of
terms, and he wouldn't be allowed to speak of it as long
as he lived.

"In this baby we won't need to stop for gas," Grimaldi explained. "We're good to go all the way to
Southern California. Have you there in time for a late
lunch."

The pilot's inflection was more tense than he tried to
sound. Blancanales didn't blame him. Jack Grimaldi
had been as good a friend as Mack Bolan had. Grimaldi
credited Bolan with turning his life around. When the
Executioner ran across him, Grimaldi had been a pilot
for the Mob, without a sense of self-respect. With Bolan's encouragement he had left the organized crime

business, got his head screwed on straight and eventually joined the team at Stony Man Farm full time. Officially, he was listed on the roster as pilot, but high-level Farm staff tended to go above and beyond their job descriptions, and more times than he could count he acted in the capacity of a warrior as well. He fought from time to time at Mack Bolan's side, and the Executioner's unmatched skills had saved Grimaldi's life in those situations more than once.

Blancanales handed the second cup of coffee to the copilot and stared out into the empty landscape of clouds. For a man who was virtually without family, for a man who spent weeks and months at a time alone and fighting his own private war, there were going to be a lot of people affected by Mack Bolan's loss.

If he was truly gone. Blancanales had to keep reminding himself that the Sarge wasn't dead until the body was found.

Maybe, he speculated, the body would never be found. And that way Bolan would live forever.

CHAPTER SIX

Santa Fe, New Mexico

Clint Mahoney didn't stand when Jared entered the office. He glared at his son as if he were an employee who had just blown a major business deal through careless ineptitude. That was exactly how Mahoney saw it.

Jared's eyes were half closed and he walked like a zombie, his feet barely lifting off the carpet. He didn't look at his father, didn't greet him. He simply shuffled to the small bar along the wall and tugged at the cabinet doors. The doors didn't open.

"Your liquor is locked."

"For a reason."

"I want some whiskey," Jared stated simply.

"You aren't having any."

The younger Mahoney looked at his father with some surprise, as if he couldn't believe what he was hearing. Then he shrugged and turned away. "Then I ain't staying."

"Sit, Jared."

Jared ignored him. The elder Mahoney grabbed the phone and spoke into it briefly. Within seconds, before Jared reached the office doors, they slammed shut. Jared grabbed the brass knobs and rattled them.

"What is this, Dad?"

"You screwed up, Jared. We're going to discuss it."

"You don't like the way I do my work? Then I won't work for you."

"I don't like the fact that you are a drug addict, like any other piece of trash from the streets of this country."

"So get rid of me," Jared said, moving back to the middle of the room and glaring at his father.

"Do you have no interest in taking responsibility for yourself?"

"Why won't you let me take responsibility for myself? Let me do what is right for me."

"Which is what?"

"Go where I want to go, do what I want to do!"

"You're not going anywhere. Your place is at my side. You're going to get clean, stay clean and learn to act like my son and my father's grandson."

Jared slumped into a chair. "Yeah, yeah, yeah. I've heard it a million times. When will you get it through your head, Dad? I don't care. I don't care about your father and I don't care about some fucking country I've never seen!"

"Ireland is your homeland."

"It's your homeland. I've never been there."

"It's your heritage."

"I don't know anything about it."

"That's because your mother didn't teach you!" Mahoney declared with sudden viciousness. "She didn't teach you about your past, she didn't teach you to be proud of who you were, she didn't teach you anything!"

"You picked her. Not me. Then you went away for eighteen years. I don't owe you anything."

"You continue to live in my house. You use my money to buy yourself women and cars. And now drugs."

"Then I'll leave." Jared jumped to his feet and grabbed the door, shaking it violently.

"Jared, sit down!"

"Give me a bottle of whiskey, or I'll break the door down and you'll never see me again."

Clint Mahoney sighed deeply. If this was any other man who ever worked for him, he would have killed the insolent bastard by now. But he rose, grabbed a key ring from his pocket and stepped around the desk, unlocking the liquor cabinet. Jared yanked it open and grabbed a bottle of Irish whiskey, throwing the cap on the ground and sucking back a long swallow as he slumped in the chair.

"You want to work for me or not?" Mahoney asked evenly.

"Not on your terms."

"You do enjoy my money, however."

"Not on your terms."

"What if I changed the terms."

"How?"

"I'm thinking of giving you a different sort of responsibility."

"Such as?"

"Dr. Icahn needs someone to watch over him."

"You want me to baby-sit that guy?"

"We need to keep an eye on him. I want you to accompany him on his sales calls. Make sure he behaves and acts in the best interests of the Mahoneys. Instead of giving you an allowance from my money, I'll give you a percentage of whatever Icahn gets from each sale. How about ten percent?"

"Twenty."

For the first time, Mahoney smiled. He found the button he was looking for. "Ten percent of the Lima sales. If you do well, you'll get fifteen percent of the Turkmenistan deal and twenty percent of sales to San Diego. And on any subsequent sales."

"You plan on expanding after the Turkmen units are delivered?"

"Wrong. I plan to expand before the Turkmen units are delivered. Soon, there will be many more people in need of emergency water supplies."

San Diego, California

ROSARIO BLANCANALES was behind the wheel of the Ford Explorer, slowing it to a stop at a corner that was dominated by the burned-out hulk of a liquor store and guarded by a sixteen-year-old Hispanic kid in jeans big enough for a morbidly obese man.

"You want to help out, kid? I'm looking for Romeo Guitierez."

The kid returned a withering, scornful frown. "Man, are you on the wrong side of the street. He's with the Latin Rangers. I ain't no Latin."

"Neither are we, and this is not going to be a social call." He pulled open his jacket just far enough to reveal a holstered, automatic handgun.

The sixteen-year-old grinned hatefully. "You gonna mess him up?"

"Maybe."

"You gonna waste his ass?"

"We can't touch him until we can find him."

The kid tried to see through the dark-tinted windows of the sports utility vehicle, but he couldn't make out much of the figures of the other men. The guy in the passenger seat he could see. A white man, but the kind of white man you didn't mess with.

"You guys cops?"

"We're not cops. Now is this your turf or not?"

"So what if it is?"

"I thought you were some sort of a player in this part of town. I guess I was wrong." Blancanales started to roll up the window, and he let his foot off the brake.

"What the fuck? You never heard of me? I'm José Vallarta, man."

"Oh, yeah?"

"Yeah. And I know everything that goes down around here. Even with the Latins."

"Oh, yeah? Where is Romeo Guitierez, then?"

"He's at El Toro Loco. That's where he runs things from, starting this week. Used to work mostly out of his apartment, but then his old lady got busted for being with him. She kicked him out of the house, man! That's the Latins for ya."

"So he takes his business to the bar."

"That's right. Now how about a little something for my trouble?"

"All right, José Vallarta." Blancanales's hand extended suddenly from the open window of the Explorer, latching on to Vallarta's collar and dragging him into the door with a thump. Blancanales pressed the kid's neck against the window frame with one hand while he jammed his hand in the kid's pockets with the other, then released him so suddenly the kid toppled on his backside on the sidewalk.

"Hey, what the fuck, man!"

"Here's a little something for you, kid," Blancanales said, displaying the packages of crack he'd extracted from Vallarta's pocket. "It's good advice so you ought to listen to me: get out of this business. You're not very good at it. You're gonna end up dead or in jail just like everybody you hang with."

"Gimme that back!"

"Sorry, José. If I did I would have to bust you." He flashed his federal badge just fast enough for Vallarta to see it and register his surprise, then Blancanales pulled away.

"I'D STAND OUT like a sore thumb in a place like that," Carl Lyons said as they cruised past the ancient plastic sign for El Toro Loco.

"You think?" Hermann Schwarz quipped. "So how are we going to get into that place without scaring everybody away or starting some gunfire?"

Lyons was considering that.

"I probably should go in solo," Blancanales said.

"No way," Lyons stated flatly. "They wouldn't trust you for a second. Once you started asking questions they'd figure you for a spy for a rival gang."

"I'll tell them I'm a cop."

"Then you won't get anything," Gary Manning argued.

"That's right. We need good, solid information and we need it soon," Lyons said. "We're not going to trick it out of them, that's for sure. And they're not going to cooperate without some coercion. We're going to have to play hardball." He directed Blancanales to take a couple of right turns, bringing them into an alley behind the El Toro Loco. Several huge plastic garbage cans huddled there, the clouds of flies around them kept out of the bar by an old aluminium screen door at the bottom of three cracked concrete steps.

"Stop here," Lyons said.

Blancanales pulled to a stop. Schwarz and Manning jumped out after receiving their instructions. As the Explorer moved away, they crept to the rear steps of the tavern, Schwarz carrying a long, purple gym bag. At the bottom of the steps each man drew a piece of hardware, then Schwarz dropped the bag and they stepped through the screen door into the small, grimy kitchen of the bar.

The youth who was washing the dishes, probably barely into his teens, stood there gaping at them, hands dripping suds onto the floor. Schwarz gestured to the screen door and said quietly, "Out."

The kid took off, pushed through the door so fast he had disappeared before the door slapped shut again. The swing doors to the public areas opened a moment later. An old Mexican man stepped through and would have frozen if Schwarz hadn't pulled him by his shirt farther into the kitchen, allowing the door to close again. He had glimpsed a poorly lit, unhealthy-looking tavern with a sparse population of young male Mexican customers.

Schwarz held a finger to his lips. The old man was afraid enough to obey except for his one overriding concern. "Where's my grandson?"

"We sent him away. Are those all Latin Rangers?"

"Yes. Are you with the Latins?"

"No. Are you sure there is nobody else in the bar?"

"They are all Latins. They won't let anybody else come here now. Are you police?"

"Federal agents."

The old man's fear suddenly transformed into defiance. "You will take all the Latins away? So I can run this place like I used to?"

Schwarz shrugged. "We'll see what we can do. You leave for now."

The old man was out the door and ascending the back steps when Schwarz grabbed the walkie-talkie from his belt and beeped the Explorer.

"Go ahead," Lyons said.

"The proprietor says everybody in the tavern is from the Latin Rangers. We gave him the afternoon off."

"Good. We're going to put on a light and sound extravaganza for these blokes. In thirty."

"Understood and out," Schwarz said, twisting his arm to see his watch. He and Manning put their backs to the wall on either side of the door with their lead weapons held ready. Schwarz stared at his watch closely.

"Twenty," Schwarz said.

"Jorge!" One of the patrons of the El Toro Loco was close by, at the bar.

Manning and Schwarz could hear muted conversations and the clacking of billiard balls, but their ears were alert to the sound of somebody coming back to find the missing proprietor.

Schwarz glanced at his watch again. "Ten," he whispered. "Nine."

"Jorge!" The speaker was irritated, and he shouted in Spanish at the kitchen door.

"Seven. Six." Schwarz mouthed the words.

There was a Spanish expletive and the sound of movement. The Latin Ranger was coming behind the bar.

Schwarz held up his free hand to continue the countdown on his fingers. Five. Four.

Maybe the angry Latin Ranger would just fix himself a drink and return to the public area of the tavern.

Three. Two.

The swing door to the kitchen opened.

Manning and Schwarz pushed their fingers in their ears hard. The Mexican gangbanger spent a foolish half second looking at them, trying to come to terms with a pair of heavily armed white men crouching in the kitchen with their eyes squeezed shut. Then he heard what sounded like a metal object bouncing and rolling across the floor of the bar, and one of his gang members shouted in a panic.

"Grenade!"

His lack of military experience showed in his reaction. The gang member half turned back to the bar to see what was going on. What followed was an eruption of light that slashed into his eyes with violent, destructive force at the same time as a wall of painful noise drove like nails into his brain.

Schwarz rode out the blast of sound that drilled into his head even through his fingers, then was on his feet in time to see the gangbanger stagger into the kitchen, falling into the screen door before flopping senseless to the ground.

Schwarz nudged him onto his stomach and quickly secured him with disposable handcuffs, then dragged him to his feet and walked him into the public area of the bar. Manning had gone ahead and met Lyons and Blancanales, who were coming through the front door. The floor was littered with moaning, writhing bodies, like the aftermath of some sort of strange nuclear blast.

"What's goin' down?" One of the gangbangers came out of the john, still dragging up the zipper on his jeans. "Hey, man, wait a minute. I'm cool!" He had never stared down so much hardware in his short criminal career.

With a quick flick of his Colt Government Model .45 pistol, Lyons signaled the gangbanger against the wall, where the teenager assumed the position.

"Been through this before, I gather," Lyons said, as he gave the kid a quick pat-down, removing a switch-blade and a cheap handgun from his jeans.

"Never like this, man! What did you do to them?"

"I'll kill you assholes! Nobody does this to me!" One of the gang members climbed unsteadily to his feet. If he saw the extent of the weaponry being wielded by his assailants, he was too stupid to care. He staggered wildly in the direction of Rosario Blancanales, flopping his fists through the white swarming flashes that would be clouding his vision for hours. Blancanales took a step to the left and hooked the man's ankle with his foot. The figure shouted wordlessly as he toppled, slamming into a chair before collapsing to the floor again. He was suddenly much more subdued. Blancanales cuffed his wrists quickly and efficiently.

The four-man version of Able Team made easy work of cuffing and organizing the fourteen members of the Latin Rangers, piling contraband on the top of the bar.

"Crack, coke, a little reefer and enough heroin to light up the entire population of San Diego for an afternoon," Schwarz said. "You guys are going down for a long time."

"No way, man!" shouted one of the older gang members. He was laying flat on his stomach with his wrists cuffed behind him, but was trying to see over his shoulder through his blinded eyes. "This is illegal search-and-seizure all the way! Our lawyer is gonna have us out of jail in five hours."

"We didn't say you were going to jail," Lyons

stated. "We said you were going down. You don't think we're cops, do you?"

"You can't do this, man!" protested the young man from the rest room. He was the only Latin who could actually see what was going on. "It's illegal all the way."

"Listen to me, you stupid punk," Blancanales stated flatly, leaning into the kid's face. "We've got something on every one of you guys. And we're not exactly concerned about bending the rules a little. Didn't you notice?"

"So what do you want with us, man?" demanded the older gangbanger on the floor.

"You Romeo Guitierez?" Lyons demanded.

"So what if I am?"

"We want to know what you guys had to do with the bombing of the Southern California Water Conservation Authority Dam yesterday."

It was as if Lyons had made a rude joke at a society party. All the gang members looked away. The older man on the floor seemed not to have even heard the question. The kid in the chair looked at the floor as if disinterested.

"This could take awhile," Blancanales said.

"We don't have awhile," Lyons retorted.

He announced loudly, "This is the deal. We are federal agents. We want answers."

"We ain't giving you no answers, man," Guitierez said. "You want to arrest us for possession, you do it."

"We're not going to arrest you for possession. Fifteen people died in California as a result of the collapse of the SCW Dam, including a national park ranger. Every man in this room is going down on federal murder charges."

"Hey, we didn't do it!" the kid protested.

"Shut up!" Guitierez shouted. "All right. I'll talk."

Stony Man Farm, Virginia

BARBARA PRICE SAT in a cushioned chair at the huge, horseshoe-shaped desk that served as Aaron Kurtzman's cybernetic command center.

"You believe them?" she said.

"Yeah, I believe them," Carl Lyons answered from the twin speakers on one of the computer monitors. "These guys are strictly street level. Guns and crack and heroin. They don't have the brains to pull off the sabotage at the SCW Dam. They don't even understand the implications."

Lyons was speaking into a specially configured cellular phone from the Ford Explorer in San Diego. The phone used an unusual encryption chip developed by Kurtzman and Hunt Wethers. The voice messages used by the phone could be decrypted only by a base unit positioned elsewhere in San Diego, like a safehouse, where the signals were further garbled and fed into the Internet and picked up via one of Stony Man Farm's dedicated T-3 connections. The mess of signals that merged into the Farm's systems required several levels of processing before coming out of the speakers as a recognizable voice. Price didn't understand how, but it all happened as seamlessly as a telephone call to a next-door neighbor.

"So what did you get from them?" Kurtzman asked.

"A few names. These are the people they were in contact with." He read off three names, all very indistinct, as Kurtzman tapped them into one of his computers.

"I'll do what I can with them," he said.

"I'm sure they're all fake dead ends," Lyons acknowledged. "But try this one, Aaron—Fawcett Frezchetti."

Kurtzman's fingers had the name entered into his system almost as soon as the word was out of Lyons's mouth, and he initiated a comprehensive search protocol that encompassed federal, state and international databases. The first-level search was performed in seconds.

"We've got something there. California and federal records on our man. You're right in his neighborhood."

Barbara Price walked around the desk and leaned over the table next to Kurtzman, scowling into the monitor. "He doesn't appear to have any clear-cut modus operandi. Looks like he worked for a few gangs on an off-and-on basis. Suspected of being a triggerman on a couple of hits for one of the L.A. Families in 1997, but that was never proved. His arrests have been for everything from distributing heroin to passing bad checks. This guy is a real mixed bag of tricks."

San Diego

"THESE DAYS Mr. Frezchetti is into recruitment," Carl Lyons said into the cellular phone. Out the window of the Explorer he and the other members of Able Team were keeping an eye on the front door of the El Toro Loco. Officers from the San Diego Police Department, called in by Price at their request, were just starting to arrive in droves. Inside they would find fourteen members of the Latin Rangers, each with drugs on his person, most with an illegal weapon as well.

"The Latins," Price asked.

"Yeah. Sounds like he has always kept his fingers

on the pulse of gang activity. Did some favors for the Latins in the recent past—kept them in product when one of their regular distributors came up short. Knows all the captains of street crime throughout the city, but manages to keep his affiliations at arm's length. He contacted the Latin leadership last week and promised them big bucks for an easy day's work. They met up with some badass guys late last night, drove out to the Water District in a panel truck and were put to work. They didn't even know what they were doing at the dam site. They got paid well. Like they could take a year off from the day-to-day gang business. But when they saw the dam blast on the news, they knew they were in deeper than they ever imagined. They were having a meeting at their favorite bar to try and figure out what they should do about their predicament.''

"How could they not know they were being set up by Frezchetti as stoolies?'' Kurtzman asked.

"They got greedy,'' Lyons answered. "You should've seen the wads of cash we lifted off these guys.''

"I've got an address for you, Carl.'' Just as Kurtzman rattled off a street address, Lyons hit the speaker button and his voice filled the Explorer's interior.

Blancanales was already putting the vehicle in Drive.

FOR ALMOST TWO DECADES Fawcett Frezchetti had managed to walk between the raindrops while collecting water in a tin cup. Suddenly, he was in a downpour and there was no way to keep from getting wet.

He had always been proud of his ability to operate on the fringes of the law without getting in the way of the police. Sure, he had been busted a few times here and there. But commensurate with the crimes he had committed, his jail time had been minimal. A drop in the bucket. The cops had nothing on him.

He had managed to keep out of the attention of law enforcement because he had kept himself a step removed from the crime organizations. Instead of getting in tight with one of the Families or one of the street-level organizations, he had stood on the sidelines. He'd done favors, small-time jobs here and there until the occasional big-time, high-paying jobs began falling into his lap. People started realizing he was well-networked. Bosses who needed eyes and ears and guns outside their own organizations began coming to him when things needed finding out or doing.

The situation had been achieved accidentally, but in retrospect it looked as if he had strategized to put himself in the position he was in. He claimed he had. He positioned himself as a very intelligent player of the various systems.

That had come back to bite him in the ass. Somebody had played him for a patsy, and he was about to take a major fall. He had to get out of this city while he still could.

He had heard the announcement of the dam collapse on the news that morning: fifteen dead, several missing, federal investigators on the scene. He had flipped on CNN and watched the coverage of the burst dam in the Southern California mountains and another in Peru. Fawcett Frezchetti knew he had been manipulated by some sort of an international terrorist group, whose scope was beyond his imagination. He was a pawn in a game of chess so huge he couldn't even begin to see the entire game board.

He turned on his police scanner with growing fear, and when he heard about the bust of the entire upper ranks of the Latin Rangers at the El Toro Loco, he knew he was in serious trouble. Somebody was going to be coming after him. The gang had no particular loyalty to him, especially when it dawned on them that they had been set up by him to take a fall. His name was mud.

So he and the gang were taking the fall for whatever organization had orchestrated the destruction of the dam. Now that he thought about it, this was the kind of manipulation and careful strategizing he had always claimed himself capable of. It was kind of ironic that someone had used such a strategy against him so effectively. It showed just how damned stupid he really was.

Stupid or not, he couldn't undo it now and he had to run, fast and far.

He didn't relish spending the rest of his life in a federal prison.

He began throwing things together. Just the small valuable stuff and enough clothes to get him through a few days. He had a wad of cash in his pocket, and that was all the money he had in the world. He had to be stupid, he thought—he was forty-two years old and had been playing the system for more than twenty years and didn't have anything more to show for it other than what he had accumulated in the past twenty-four hours.

Forget that. He would have to assess his priorities later.

Tossing an Accu-Tek BL-380 handgun into an old nylon Adidas satchel, he made for the door. Something caused him to detour to the front window of his apartment just long enough to glance out to the street. It had been ten minutes since he heard the call on the police radio for the El Toro Loco, but somebody was coming for him already.

He didn't know who it was and he didn't care. The

Ford Explorer was there to bring him down, he was sure of it. It slowed on the street and two men stepped out of the passenger-side doors before it stopped, moving with the professionalism of trained soldiers. The vehicle sped up again and disappeared from sight.

More men from the Explorer would be coming up the fire escape at the rear of the building in minutes. Frezchetti would be trapped in the middle.

"Shit!" His rage had nowhere to go. Just like he had nowhere to go. Impotent and trapped.

No way. There was always a way out. And he'd be damned if he was going to federal prison for the rest of his life. He would die first.

Think, dammit! He had to get out. He couldn't go down because the agents were coming up front and back. The stairs went to the roof, but the door was probably locked, as always. That left one escape route. The fire escape, going up.

He yanked open the window and scrambled onto the steel landing outside his window, dragging his satchel after him. He heard the squeak of tires as the Explorer's occupants spotted him. Doors suddenly opened and slammed shut.

Frezchetti started up the steps of the fire escape and almost immediately his legs began to scream. Lunch five days a week was an Italian sausage-beef combo sandwich with French fries at Mama's on Fourth Avenue. Had that crap been worth it? A voice inside him demanded insolently as he huffed for a better breath and strained up every step. He felt the vibration through the steel fire escape as the ladder was dragged down and someone started clambering the steps after him.

He looked up, mouth gaping open for extra breath. He was dismayed at how far he had yet to go—four more flights to the roof. The clatter of footsteps behind him was twice as fast as his own leaden steps.

"Frezchetti! Stop or I'll shoot!"

Frezchetti's terror grew in leaps and bounds. His aching legs fought past the pain and he increased his tempo, rounding the landings from one flight of stairs to the next faster and faster, ignoring the burning in his lungs. His hand reached into the Adidas bag for the Accu-Tek and he paused finally to point the handgun at the floor beneath his feet, firing one time. The .380ACP slug forced its way through the open grate below him but ricocheted wildly before reaching the pursuer, now just two flights beneath.

There was a chatter of automatic weapons' fire, and Frezchetti felt the stinging of tiny brick splinters flying off the wall into his face and neck. Only then did he realize one of his pursuers had remained in the alley and was targeting him from the ground with some sort of large firearm.

"Freeze, Frezchetti!"

The voice was distant, but commanding. Frezchetti considered obeying, then rebelled. He wouldn't be taken! His feet caught on one of the steel stairs and he collapsed on his stomach, managing to get the satchel underneath him to cushion the fall, but the stair edges slammed into his stomach and chest painfully and his right hand ached with pain. He pushed himself up again—no time to be in pain—and was relieved that he had at least held on to the gun somehow.

Furiously he climbed onto the roof of the building and turned on his pursuers, blasting blinding into the alley and the fire escape stairs, then pulling back before the answering torrent of automatic fire could reach him. Now he had the advantage. He'd be able to pick off the man on the stairs as soon as his head popped up over the roof, and he could stay far enough back from the edge to be out of sight of the guy in the alley.

He was safe. For now.

There was a sudden stream of muffled gunfire, and he turned to see the knob on the door to the interior stairway fall off in a mass of broken wood. The door swung open. Frezchetti started firing before he even had the pistol aimed, one shot after another, panicking. How had they gotten to the roof so damned fast? His advantage was blown! He had no way out!

The armed men in the stairwell pulled back, almost calmly. Of course they knew he was just about out of ammo and he'd need to change his clip.

"Give it up, Frezchetti," the man on the fire escape said, just below the lip of the building.

"No way."

"You're trapped, man."

"No way!"

Frezchetti turned toward the fire escape. He couldn't even see the guy but he fired anyway, then nothing happened. The gun was empty.

His time was up.

He turned to the east. The neighboring apartment building was just across the alleyway. It was two stories lower than the building he was standing on. At one point in his life he would have been able to make that jump. He started to run. His legs were wobbly, but he ignored that. Now he had to go beyond all pain and weakness. He pushed himself to greater speed, then vaulted onto the brick wall surrounding the roof and launched himself into open space, fisting the air for greater momentum, and knew at the very last moment that he wasn't going to make it. The gap was longer than he had judged. His body was weaker and slower. Voices on the roof behind him called out, but he didn't really hear them as he crashed into the roof edge of the next building at a fantastic speed, crushing his ribs into his lungs and shocking his body into near unconsciousness, so the grab he wanted to make never occurred. He flopped off the building and plummeted seventy feet to the pavement.

Santa Fe, New Mexico

COLLEEN DAVIS PARKED the Mercedes with two wheels in the grass, then strolled to the house, a soft-sided briefcase hanging at her side. The kid was on the front patio smoking a cigarette, evaluating her with hungry eyes. Her face wore a cold, amused smirk. She could feel his eyes moving over her like lewd fingers, and she enjoyed it. Enjoyed him wanting her, enjoyed knowing she had the power of her body to wield over him.

He would never make a move to take her. He was a fool but not that much of a fool. But the need was painful in him, driving him to distraction and ill temper. That was the power Colleen Davis loved.

The house was huge, even by American standards. Like half the houses in nearby Santa Fe, it was constructed in the Southwestern adobe style. But no adobe had ever been this huge. Clint Mahoney and his idiot son were wasting it. The rooms were mostly unused. Not that she cared, really.

The large, third-story library was where Davis and Mahoney had constructed a war room. This base of operations was outfitted like the strategic headquarters for a small army, with enough communications hardware and computer processing capability to run a medium-sized shipping company. There was plenty of incriminating evidence to put her, Mahoney and his idiot son away for life if they were ever tracked to the house.

If there was one thing Colleen Davis wasn't afraid of, it was the police. American police were pussycats. She'd taken a few, for strictly evaluation purposes. They weren't good lovers, and for the same reason—lack of drive—she was sure they weren't good fighters. Davis, on the other hand, had been trained by her father and brothers to be an excellent fighter. She was always armed, and her war room in the Santa Fe mansion had a small arsenal of staged firepower. She'd put up a good fight, if and when.

JARED MAHONEY CAME to the door of the large library that his father ridiculously called his war room. Colleen Davis had the wall-mounted television screen on as she booted up her bank of computers. Her eyes were shining, and her mouth was turned up slightly in the frigid smile that was the only genuine emotion the woman ever exhibited: cold satisfaction. CNN was replaying the footage of the California dam break for about the thousandth time that day.

"He shouldn't have let you handle it," Davis said.

Jared didn't respond.

"Now everything's a mess. If you'd managed to follow the plan, you could have at least kept a low profile."

That got his attention. "What do you mean by that?"

"The gangs your father hired. They got roughed up this morning. Somebody sure caught up to them in a hurry." She tapped on the printouts she'd made from an early Los Angeles Police Department report. "I was just going to call your father. Care to get on the line?"

Davis pressed a phone button without tearing her eyes from the words of the report. When Mahoney answered on the speaker she said, "It's me. There's a problem." She briefed him on the police report.

"It doesn't matter how much they know," she said. "What matters is the speed and the manner in which they were tracked down. This has the earmark of a high-level special forces team. The police are treating it like a gang attack. No attempts are being made to hush it up. Pretty bloody cocky."

"Relax," Clint Mahoney said, checking his watch. "That's what the gang was there for. To take the heat. They're a dead end. They're performing the function you intended."

"I know. But I'd estimated a full twenty-four hours before they were tracked down. Instead it took just six. Whatever agency is at work here moves fast, and they do it outside the boundaries of the law. They're exhibiting a pretty serious case of initiative." Her voice trailed off, distracted.

"You sound worried," Mahoney said. It was something of a joke. Davis wasn't the type to worry, under any circumstances.

Her response surprised him. "I'm going to keep a close eye on our operations. We might have attracted an unforeseen level of attention."

CHAPTER SEVEN

Northeast of Lima, Peru

The wide space in the mountain road that passed for a square in the town of Cinchona hadn't seen a tourist in fifty years. There were perhaps a couple of thousand people. A hundred homes at most had electricity and plumbing. Less than a dozen cars and trucks could be seen on the road.

"Wish we could have found a stealthier way into this burg," Carl Lyons muttered as Gadgets Schwarz steered the olive green Hummer around a crater in the road. The crater was full of water, a pond more than a pothole.

"Not likely unless you want to hike the trip," Blancanales said. "Or at the very least jump in and hike out."

"That would have been preferable to advertising our arrival," Lyons replied. "If we'd had a better handle on their location, I would have opted for it."

"Why don't you let me out here?" Blancanales suggested, leaning over the backseat and pointing out a ramshackle wooden public building of some kind.

"Tavern?" Schwarz asked.

"Yeah. Let's see how friendly the locals are."

Schwarz brought the Hummer to a halt next to a Jeep from the 1970s and Blancanales stepped out into the mud. A light drizzle had been falling since they went off the highway an hour earlier, and the old asphalt collected it in inch-deep puddles. Blancanales ignored the water, walking without hesitation to the doors of the tavern and pulling them open, just as a rugged-faced older mestizo was coming out. The man froze, his gaze boring into Blancanales with cold suspicion.

Blancanales didn't give him the satisfaction of a return look. He went to the small counter and stood by it until the man behind it approached him, his forehead wrinkled.

"A drink," Blancanales said in Spanish. "Whatever you've got."

The man's frown increased, and he put a can of beer on the counter. It didn't look cold. Blancanales pushed a few *nuevo sol* notes across the counter, knowing full well they were worth almost fifty U.S. dollars. In this village, it would be a fortune.

The man looked him squarely in the eyes. "Too much." He took the smallest bill in the small stack and gave Blancanales change.

The Able Team warrior leaned on the bar and pushed the tab on the beer. It hissed and foamed up slightly. Tipping it, he swirled a little beer in the grimy lip and poured off the resulting filth, then took a swallow. He was the center of attention, of course, but that didn't bother him. In fact, it might work in his favor if he played it correctly.

"Anyplace around here I can hire some men?" Blancanales asked the bartender.

"To mind your goats?" The bartender's face was straight, but his words were icy.

"I need something along the line of guards."

The bartender looked away and said nothing. Blancanales gave him a minute, swilled the beer and prodded again. "Think you can help me?"

"No. You've come to the wrong place."

Blancanales seriously doubted that. This man knew what he was after and was hiding it. Probably protecting himself. The village was likely held hostage by the mercenary group, if they were as numerous and ruthless as he believed them to be. One mistake would bring down a horrible punishment on the entire village.

Blancanales couldn't bring himself to be angry at the bartender if he was protecting himself and his neighbors from the petty retribution of thugs. On the other hand, this man might be in the pocket of the mercs to some extent. He was considering his options when a quick glance around the room gave him the distinct impression of a duality to the local population. There were Indians at the side table, heads hung low and talking quietly, giving wide berth to a mestizo group in the center of the room with a few Indian hangers-on. They were talking quietly to themselves, glaring at him furtively and laughing. The Indians outside the circle were mostly silent.

Blancanales strolled to the pair of large tables, wearing a thin smile and giving a wave of his beer and a *"buenos noches,"* that brought the men at the tables to a dead silence. "I'd like to buy you men a beer if you would let me," he added in Spanish.

After a moment one of them laughed harshly and boomed, "We'll let you buy us as many beers as you want."

"Good," Blancanales said, grinning and waving to the bartender as he pulled up his chair. "Maybe one of

you men could tell me how I could hire some body-
guards around here.''

"You can hire me!" the loudmouth said. "I work for
beer!"

More laughter around the table. Blancanales laughed
too, although he was pretty sure he was somehow the
butt of the joke. "I don't think you are up to my standards," he told the loudmouth.

"What do you mean by that?"

The laughter fell away like shards of glass from a
shattered window.

"I mean you don't have a gun. I need armed men,
maybe ten of them, for four days work in the mountains
about twenty miles south of here.''

"Why?"

"That's a secret."

The men exchanged glances.

"How do you know I don't have a gun?" Loudmouth
demanded.

"Maybe you do, but can you use it?"

"I can use it very well." Loudmouth spit the words
out.

"I need a lot more protection than one man can provide.''

"And how much are you willing to pay for ten men
for four days?''

Blancanales smiled and sipped his beer. "I'll talk
price when I see the men.''

"You will talk price now if you ever want to see the
men. I will not even get them for you unless I know
what you are offering.''

Blancanales shrugged slightly and put down the can.
"Thanks, anyway." As he walked to the door the loudmouth shouted, "Wait, wait." He hustled after Blan-

canales. "I will get you the men and the guns, and we will meet you here when you say. Then we will set our price."

Blancanales stared him down for a minute, then nodded. "Tomorrow morning. In front of this building."

The loudmouth grinned, revealing several missing teeth. "We will be here."

WHEN BLANCANALES SLID into the Hummer again, Schwarz started the engine and pulled the huge vehicle into the road in a sweeping U-turn.

"How did it go?" Lyons asked.

"I made lots of new friends. Slow up, Gadgets."

As they pulled away at a slow pace, Blancanales turned halfway in his seat and kept an eye on the tavern. The loudmouth mestizo emerged and jumped into the ancient Jeep, which started and jolted backward into the street, then spun on the pavement and took off in the other direction.

"That's our man," Blancanales said.

"I'm on him," Schwarz answered, pulling another U-turn that carried him into a ditch, onto the pavement and into another ditch on the other side of the road before they swerved back onto the asphalt.

"These people need to elect better Department of Public Works officials," Schwarz muttered.

"You guys need a better driver," Manning added.

They accelerated gradually, allowing the Jeep to put a substantial distance between itself and Able Team's Hummer. They watched it turn off the main road a full half mile ahead of them.

"I've got him," Schwarz stated, and accelerated to the turnoff, which took them in a sudden descent. They meandered through a neighborhood of simple wooden huts, devoid of electric light, and slowed to watch the Jeep barrel over the muddy dirt road, bouncing without concern through cavernous craters in the road. He followed the road's sharp left curve into the vegetation of the mountain.

"It's going to be dark in there," Schwarz muttered as he hit the gas.

"He'll spot us in a second if we use the headlights," Manning said.

Lyons regarded the overcast sky. "It'll be pitch black in an hour. Let's hope he gets where he's going before then."

Schwarz spun the Hummer along the sharp turn and left the town of Cinchona behind them. The trees and brush grew untamed on the sides of the narrow path, hiding even the dim illumination the cloudy mountain evening was giving them. They began a game of cat and mouse, speeding up to catch sight of their quarry in the straight portions of the road, then falling back quickly before he could spot them. Fortunately, the driver had the good sense to use his headlights, making him easier to spot in the deepening gloom. He was driving recklessly, spinning around curves over drop-offs that vanished into mountain crevices of untold depth. Schwarz's driving skills were put to the test.

Then they descended another hundred feet down a steep incline and spotted a turnoff ahead. There was no sign of the Jeep.

"Bring it to a stop before the turnoff, Gadgets," Lyons ordered. Schwarz hit the brakes hard, fighting the mud and inertia of the 3.5-ton Hummer. The vehicle's off-road tires scooped up the soggy earth by the bucketful and brought the Hummer to a halt a length short of the turnoff without skidding.

Lyons was out the door in an instant, scanning the forest on both sides of the road. To the left the road climbed the mountainside steeply. To the right, in the direction of the turnoff, it descended into what might be a valley, thick with trees and undergrowth as far as he could see.

He crouched on the ground and turned on the flashlight just long enough to examine the muddy road, then slid back into the passenger seat.

"We go to the right," he said. "Let's take it slow."

"We near something?" Manning asked.

"Not that I know of. I guess it just seems like we should be."

He explained his intuition no further, and Schwarz steered the wide-bodied vehicle into the turnoff. The road was a simple vehicle trail through the thick forest, clearly made by cars and trucks with less girth than the Hummer. It thrashed at the weeds and saplings, and left greenish paint on the bark of a few trees. Schwarz maneuvered it through the narrow pass, then braked again hard, staring out through the windshield.

"What've you got, Gadgets?"

"I thought I glimpsed light."

Lyons peered into the darkness of the road ahead. The clouds were thick, hiding the starlight. The way ahead was just about as black.

"This is as good a place as any," he stated. "Gadgets, get us off the road into the woods far enough to hide the Hummer. We'll proceed on foot."

Schwarz steered the Hummer thirty feet into the forest, maneuvering around trees and fallen logs, and turned the vehicle to facilitate a quick exit. The undergrowth closed behind it. There was no chance of it being spotted from the forest road, even in sunlight. They killed the engine and suited up for a march.

It turned out they had less than a mile of forest to traverse before they spotted open land ahead. Coming to the perimeter of a natural clearing, they observed a collection of well-maintained buildings lit with artificial light. In the deep dusk they made out a two-story, multiwindowed building they took to be a residence hall. A low-slung canopy on wooden supports covered two cars and three pickup trucks.

"There's my drinking buddy," Blancanales said. The man from the bar had parked his Jeep in front of a smaller building that hugged the far end of the residence hall. The smaller building was painted and had large, curtained windows and bright lighting.

"Residence for the head man in charge?" Manning suggested.

"That's a pretty good bet," Lyon said. "I think we'll find the man to answer our questions in that building."

"Shall we knock?" Manning asked.

Schwarz waved him to lead the way.

"I may have a more effective strategy," Lyons replied.

He began laying it out.

THE OLD INDIAN MAN was fetching twice as much water as usual. His back was creaking and groaning like an old tree branch about to snap in the wind. His fingers would barely close on the handle of the old zinc bucket.

He rested halfway up the hill, thinking that it was somehow ironic that the water was closer now, ever since the bursting of the great dam, so he could get it easier. But the bursting of the great dam had also been the cause for him to need extra water.

When he reached the old shack, he pushed the door in on its wooden hinges and set the pail on the packed earth floor, then scooped out the water with an old aluminium measuring cup.

He crossed to the low cot, which was piled with so many coarse woolen blankets they seemed to be shop inventory. But there was a man underneath the blankets, who might very well have died in the time it took the old Indian to go down to the river for the water.

Pulling several layers of the blankets aside, he examined the man's face. It was pale with a dark growth of beard, and the skin hung from the cheekbones like a thin cotton rag draped on sharp rocks.

The strange thing was that this was the face of a powerful man. Maybe an evil man—who could tell? But he had been brought low by fate.

He was breathing. That was a good sign. When the old Indian first discovered him on the bank he wasn't sure if the man was breathing or not. When he dragged him by his feet up the hill and rolled him on his stomach and pounded on his back, a small river had gurgled out of the man's throat. The old Indian had pushed on the man's back. The effort had nearly killed him. He wasn't strong himself anymore. The next time he checked, the man was breathing.

The sick man should be sweating, but he wasn't. The fever had already been coming to a full burn by the time the Indian managed to drag the man into the shack and leverage him into the cot. Then the man's face had been dripping with sweat. Now there was none. The man was severely dehydrated.

The old Indian knew he was dying.

He touched the cup to the lips of the man, letting a trickle fall into his mouth. The man didn't swallow or move. He just laid there, radiating heat, never opening his eyes or moving his lips.

The old Indian sighed.

He had seen many people die in his life—wife, children, friends and family uncounted. He knew what it was like to tend a man who was dying. He could feel the moment when the disease became too strong for the human body to battle any longer. This human body was long past that point. How it found the strength to sustain itself even now was a mystery.

Death was inexorable.

The old Indian wondered how he would possibly find the strength to bury the body.

SCHWARZ AND Blancanales emerged from the undergrowth at the edge of the forest on the north side of the compound. They crouched in the darkness and scanned for guards, finding two within their range of vision.

Those were their initial targets.

"He made a smart choice," Blancanales observed, nodding to the nearest guard, who had taken up a position in a dark spot against the wall of the residence hall, where the light from a pole-mounted flood lamp at the front of the building didn't shine. The guard didn't smoke, so there was no telltale glowing red ember, and he hardly moved, as if he were expecting a hostile probe.

"Maybe he's asleep," Schwarz suggested.

Even at that moment the guard walked a few paces, never leaving the shadow, and paced back to where he had been. They never saw more than a vague outline of the rifle he shouldered.

"I guess he's just good," Blancanales said. "He'll have to go first."

Schwarz evaluated the scenario. "I'm not sure how we'll accomplish that without giving him the chance to raise an alarm."

Blancanales checked his watch. "We'll just have to hope Gary and Ironman get the lights turned off."

MANNING CROUCHED in the weeds at the edge of the rocky clearing of the compound, peering into the darkness in both directions and waiting for movement while the seconds ticked off in his head. Then he lifted the NightTech 4.5-power Tasco NV250 monocular to his eye, adjusting the computerized brightness control until his vision was optimized. The night-viewing monocular utilized an internal light source that augmented the external light and provided a fourteen-degree field of view. If there was anybody walking the grounds, even in the faintly illuminated shadow, Manning would make him out.

"There," the big Canadian said softly, directing Lyons's vision into the shadows next to the building near the front door.

Lyons strained into the blackness. It took several seconds of concentration to make out the guard. "These guys are careful."

"You'd be paranoid too if you had just perpetrated what these guys did."

"Yeah. Or maybe they're just real pros. Let's be cautious. I don't want to underestimate them."

"Understood."

Manning observed the guard through the night sight for another few seconds, then nodded briefly. "His back is to us. This is the best opportunity we're going to get."

"Let's go. I'm ready for him."

Silently, Lyons rose from the brush and stepped into the open at the edge of the floodlights that illuminated most of the compound, and approached the residential hall swiftly. Every step brought him farther into the light, and every step made it more likely his approach would be heard.

Able Team had been sent into Peru equipped with automatic weaponry. Temporary team-member Manning carried an M-16 A-2. Carl Lyons had a Heckler & Koch MP-5 A-3, a submachine gun with a curved, 30-round clip. But for now Lyons was going in with a less substantial lead weapon. His Beretta 92-F was fitted with a sound suppressor forged by John "Cowboy" Kissinger, Stony Man's weaponsmith. He was also carrying a battle blade, which he intended to use if he got close enough.

He didn't. The guard sensed him. Maybe he caught the almost imperceptible whisper of Lyons's feet on the hard ground. Maybe he had a measure of the sixth sense some soldiers possessed. Somehow he knew he was no longer alone and he turned on Lyons quickly, swinging a Czech Vz58 assault rifle on its shoulder strap. He didn't have the chance to level it before Lyons triggered the Beretta handgun one time and sent a single 9 mm Parabellum round coring through his chest. He went down hard, the Vz58 clattering on the ground, even louder than the shot. Lyons cringed and grabbed for the guard, pulling him against the wall as deeply into the shadowy darkness as he could and stood at attention next to the corpse.

The night remained still.

MANNING WAITED just seconds after seeing the guard drop before he crept across the open ground to the generator shed set against a waist-high outcropping. A quick glance told him the door was secured with a hefty padlock, so he moved behind the building, finding a rubber hose from the massive, four-legged fuel tank. It parted under his knife, and gasoline started to fill a small depression in the rock. Next he ran in a crouch across seventy-five yards of empty space before coming to a stop with his back against the wall at Lyons's side.

The steady rumble of the generator took a full minute to sputter and die while the two men watched the windows above their heads and the flood lamps that lighted the compound exterior. The brightness of the windows began to yellow, and darkness crept out of the mountain forest to reclaim the clearing.

Shouts started almost immediately from inside.

"Party time," Lyons whispered.

"THERE'S OUR INVITATION," Schwarz said when the flood lamps turned yellow, then black. As the guards they had been watching started for the other side of the building to check on the generators, Schwarz and Blancanales moved into the open and crossed the compound at a run. A black section of the wall cracked open unexpectedly and a figure came down the stairs briskly, freezing on the bottom step when he saw the Able Team warriors barreling toward him. With a shout he made a reflexive grab at his armpit holster, but the butt of Blancanales's M-16 slammed across his skull and he flopped onto his face, unmoving.

Blancanales leveled the M-16 A-2/M-203 grenade launcher combo into the room as Schwarz yanked open the door, and spotted a dark figure bringing a weapon into target acquisition on the pair. Blancanales triggered the M-16 A-2, cutting into the gunner, whose hand locked on his trigger. A shotgun blast cut a hole in the floor.

Schwarz spotted one of the guards returning from the front of the building and triggered his assault rifle twice, putting the guard down cold, but the sound of more shots came from the left. Schwarz turned and saw the second guard in a firm shooter's stance, lining up his next shot for better accuracy. The Able Team electronics expert shoved Blancanales into the building. There was a blast and the doorframe splintered.

Blancanales gave his partner a quick nod of thanks. Schwarz stepped out again with the M-16 A-2 leading the way, snapped to full auto and chattering like a piece of metal-cutting machinery. It cut the second guard across the stomach, and the guy dropped to the floor in a heap.

The interior was black when the door swung closed, but a beam of light flashed beyond the next room. The man with the flashlight turned the corner and triggered his handgun, but Blancanales and Schwarz stepped away from the door and the bullets sailed through harmlessly. Schwarz moved into the doorway and fired a burst at the flashlight. It had been unwise of the man to hold on to it. It made a perfect target. The light fell to the floor, followed by the sound of a falling body.

They stepped through the next room into an empty, long hallway, Blancanales making a grab for the flashlight, flipping it off. Utter darkness swarmed around them, and they donned their thermal-imaging glasses, which turned the place green as they moved into the hall.

One of the doors ahead opened an inch, and they spotted the brightness of a human body peering out. In the blackness, the Able Team commandos were confident they remained unseen.

The face disappeared suddenly at the sound of gunfire outside the building, and in an instant they heard gunfire from the room. The gunner was firing on Lyons and Manning. Schwarz kicked open the door and rushed inside, leveling his M-16 A-2 as two men spun away from the window. Both had their automatic pistols gripped in two hands, and another fraction of a second would have found both acquiring a target on the Able Team commandos. Schwarz fired first, and Blancanales joined him an instant later. The gunners raised their hands and spasmed under the fire, dropping their weapons and falling to the floor.

CARL LYONS GESTURED to the rear as the generator gave up and lights across the compound dimmed and died. Gary Manning kept watch in that direction as Lyons kept an eye on the smaller building attached to the residence hall. Blancanales's friend from the tavern was still in there, and that was probably where they would find the man in charge.

The drizzle of the evening was now faded to a mist, which didn't fall so much as simply hang in the atmosphere. The clouds overhead veiled the brilliance of the stars and smothered the Peruvian complex in darkness. They could still see well enough to know when the door to the low building swung open and a man stomped out, shouting a name. His voice died when the night was pockmarked with rifle fire.

"Hands up!" Lyons said, cupping his hand over his mouth to redirect his voice. The figure spun his head, searching for the speaker in the darkness.

"I am pointing a gun at you. Put your hands up, or I will shoot."

Another man jumped through the door of the building and swung a gun into the night, triggering a short, blind blast that sent his comrade stumbling for cover. Lyons was better adjusted to the darkness, and he reached target acquisition on the gunner before the echoes of the blast had faded. The MP-5 A-3 stuttered in his hands, chopping into the gunner with a half-dozen 9 mm rounds. The other man froze, hands at shoulder level.

"Above!" Manning shouted.

Lyons recoiled against the wall with lightning speed, stepping away from the burst of gunfire raining from the second-floor windows. The gunfire stopped as soon as it had begun.

A head poked cautiously from the window almost directly above, then looked directly down on them. "All clear up here," Schwarz announced.

Lyons's prisoner was gone, and that probably meant he'd bolted inside the low building. The two men made for it, ducking under the windows and coming to a halt at either side of the door, which was almost completely closed. Manning nudged it open with his foot and fell back when the door splintered under a heavy-gauge shotgun blast.

Lyons left the Phoenix Force warrior guarding the door and hurried around the corner to the rear, where he found the nearest window closed and heavily shaded. The second window was open a bare inch to let in fresh air, and the shade had been pulled down.

Another blast erupted from the shotgun. Manning was making just enough of a nuisance of himself to keep the shotgunner occupied. Lyons drew his Tanto combat knife and tucked the seven-inch blade through the window opening, leveraging up the bottom of the shade. Inside, the blackness was thicker than the cloudy night, but the shotgunner was facing the other direction.

Lyons placed the barrel of the MP-5 A-3 on the windowsill and triggered a quick burst. The thump of the falling body and the clatter of the shotgun were accented with a moan of pain.

THE MAN KNEELING next to a pair of old cots had his hands gripped against the back of his skull. "I surrender! I surrender!" he shouted in Spanish.

Blancanales used his appropriated flashlight to blind the man, who blinked into the light, trying to see past it, with a look that was just a little too contrived. He leveled the M-16 A-2, in full view next to the flashlight. "On your face."

"What are you going to do to me?"

"Shoot you if you don't get down on your face."

"Please don't kill me! I swear I'll do whatever you want!"

He was putting on a convincing act of fealty without actually being cooperative. He might have been too panicky to think clearly, which is why he wasn't obeying his orders.

"I said get on your face. You've got one second."

The mercenary's bluff was called and he took the risk, making a quick grab at something behind his neck. His underestimation of his enemy was the death of him. The M-16 A-2 triggered a pair of rounds that pierced his skull. When he collapsed on the floor Blancanales saw that there was a small-caliber revolver clipped onto the collar of his shirt.

"Clear," Blancanales called.

The last doorway opened ahead of them. Slowly. A

shirtless man spoke in Spanish as he emerged into the hallway with his arms up. Schwarz covered him as Blancanales ordered him to turn in a circle. The man did so, his face calm and unconcerned, and he didn't hesitate when told to put his arms behind his back.

Blancanales secured the shirtless Peruvian in plastic handcuffs and satisfied himself that the room was now empty. They walked the prisoner to the end of the hall and out the door onto the steps that had served as their entrance.

The prisoner began to chuckle when a pair of headlights emerged from the forest and entered the compound, maneuvering quickly. The Jeep spun its wheel and fishtailed as it accelerated to the stairs. One of the windows rolled open and a head and shoulder appeared, the driver targeting the stairs with a handgun. Blancanales and Schwarz fell back through the door before the Peruvian shouted a loud, "No!"

The command had to have been heard because the shots were never fired, and as the Jeep careered away Schwarz was out the door again, shouldering the Peruvian down the flight of steps as he flipped the M-16 A-2 to his shoulder and sent a stream of 5.56 mm rounds chasing after the vehicle. The rear windshield spiderwebbed in three places before the driver took a hard turn to the left, turning to circle the building.

LYONS HEARD THE VEHICLE and peered around the corner as the Jeep tore past the steps and swerved under a heavy barrage of fire from the building. It traveled sideways over the ground for five yards before all four wheels caught and dragged it around the lower building, then turned sharply and barreled at increasing speed directly at the front door of the building. Lyons could only watch helplessly through the windows as he saw Manning's silhouette speed across the next window in the blazing high-beam headlights.

He listened to a further exchange of gunfire as he raced around the building, skidding in the mud himself as he rounded the corner and leveled the MP-5 A-3 at the vehicle. By then it was deserted.

Then he heard shots in the darkness, and he cursed silently. They were out there with Manning in the darkness, and he couldn't do a damn thing about it without perhaps killing the Phoenix Force commando.

MANNING FIRED the assault rifle at the Jeep as it swung into view, somehow missing the headlight. When it made a sharp turn directly at the front of the low building he knew he was the target, and he redirected the automatic fire into the windshield. The Jeep didn't alter course, heading at him at high speed, and Manning took off when it was just ten feet away and closing fast. The thin layer of mud on the rocky earth slipped from under his feet, and he had a quick vision of himself getting crushed between the front end of the vehicle and the wall of the building like a fly smashed on a tabletop by a fly swatter. He found the traction he needed, but the Jeep swerved to follow him, slamming into him with its front bumper and pummeling him into the wall. Manning felt lightning flash through his brain at the moment of impact and collapsed on his hands and knees, his vision swimming with light. He pushed against the ground, feeling the earth sway underneath him, disorienting him. One of the headlights was out, but the light that remained didn't clarify the situation. Manning had no choice but to flee. Once he had put some distance between himself and the Jeep he could get his bearings.

Legs of rubber were hard to run on, and the ground was suddenly as slick as wet ice. He careened to the left, unable to stop himself, until his feet flew out from beneath him.

There was a pair of gunshots, and he expected to feel the impact of bullets entering his flesh. His vision was clearing, though his head felt cracked open. He pushed himself to his feet and swerved deliberately to avoid more fire. Another pair of rounds drilled the earth to his left.

Something was very wrong. The impact with the vehicle had impaired his equilibrium. He couldn't seem to get his bearings. A mound of rock swam out of the chaos of the night. Manning slowed, but his unreliable legs collapsed him on top of it. He pushed against the rock and frowned at it, trying to determine what he thought he knew about it. Then he saw the nearby shack and smelled the fumes of gasoline.

When Manning realized he was at the generator shack, he knew exactly how to cut himself off from pursuit. Painfully, he crawled on all fours over the rock and found himself on a gentle incline. More shots rang out, forty, maybe fifty feet behind him. Although his vision was mostly clear, his ears were ringing like the aftereffect of a close-proximity explosion, so he wasn't sure if he heard the bullets impacting close by or not.

He found the strength to start trotting uphill. That lasted just a few yards before his feet refused to cooperate any longer and he collapsed. Weeds slashed at his face as he fell and knew he was outside the clearing. Since he couldn't see in the dark he tried to imagine the distance to the generator shed. He thought he was a safe distance away.

His clumsy fall had been loud enough to attract the

attention of his pursuers. Turning onto his back, he saw a brief flash from one of the guns. His best judgment told him that his pursuers were as close to the generator shack as they were likely to get.

It was now or never.

Manning crawled onto his knees and rose to his feet. Now where the hell was the damned generator shed? The night was swimming with demons. His chest was heaving with exertion.

Then, through the confusion in his damaged skull, he saw a strange glowing thing out in the blackness, distant and oddly spherical. For a fraction of a second he thought it was something unreal, another trick played by his brain. Then he realized he was seeing the light from one of the headlights on the Jeep silhouetting the gasoline tank perched next to the generator tank.

He grinned through the throbbing pain in his head. He had his target.

He squeezed the trigger on the M-16 A-2.

BLANCANALES AND SCHWARZ were creeping around the building when a distant rattle of gunfire reached them from 150 yards away. Suddenly, there was a burst of white light that rose off the ground. In that one microsecond they saw a figure on the hill—Manning, it had to be—collapsing where he stood, and three other gunmen within a few paces of the shed recoiling from the burst. But then the fire worked its way inside the tank.

It exploded with a blast of white light that slashed the generator shed to pieces, turning it to wooden shrapnel, cutting into the backs and legs of the fleeing gunmen. They were knocked down like paper dolls in a sudden gust of wind.

The conflagration waned until it was just a huge bon-fire that cast massive shadows across the compound.

Lyons raced into view and didn't even slow when he jogged past the fallen gunmen. They were out of the game. Blancanales and Schwarz were right behind him when he reached the edge of the mountain forest.

Gary Manning lay sprawled on his back, unconscious or dead.

Santa Fe, New Mexico

THOMAS MCDONOUGH TOOK the stairs to the third floor of the Mahoney mansion, entering what Mahoney called his war room. It was heavily equipped with communications electronics, including Iridium access to all Mahoney's contacts around the world.

At the head of a small meeting table sat a beautiful woman no more than five feet tall. With auburn hair and pale, freckled skin she looked like the Irish lass she was. Her boyish body had gently swelling breasts, and in her peasant blouse and trim-cut jeans, with just a green band holding in her long, flowing red hair, she looked like a high-school girl, not even old enough for marrying. In actuality she was in her midtwenties, with more than a decade of anti-British terrorist experience under her belt.

After the 1998 Irish peace accord referendum, Colleen Davis had seen the writing on the wall. An openly aggressive stance would no longer be tolerated. The fight for total and complete defeat of the British would continue, of course, but it would require more secretive and more persuasive methods. Disillusioned, she had left the land of her birth, the land where the people had surrendered to defeat like a million cowards, and moved to America.

Directed by other souls with similar sentiments, she found her way into the Mahoney fold. Mahoney's history proved him a patriot to the cause of a united Ireland and the punishment of the English. He quickly proved to her he was developing novel strategies for funding a new war against the British.

Mahoney already possessed a capable second in command in Thomas McDonough, but he required a brilliant strategist to organize his efforts. He also needed a beautiful, aggressive Irish woman to warm his bed at night. Davis gladly accepted both positions.

She sent for others she knew would be stifled under the yoke of the new Irish peace, Irishmen she knew would be choking in the thick atmosphere of betrayal to the cause by the people they had once considered patriots.

Martin O'Connell had come soon after, along with almost thirty disgruntled Irish fighters. O'Connell was sitting at the table at her elbow.

Only lately, and against the better judgment of his senior staff, had Clint Mahoney asked his young son to join the fold. Now Jared Mahoney was turning into a major risk.

"Well?" McDonough asked.

"Sit and listen," Davis said. She handed him a pair of headphones and reached to a nearby tape deck, where she started up a microcassette.

Mahoney's voice came through the headphones. He was speaking angrily to his son, telling him he had screwed up in San Diego. McDonough listened as the conversation turned to a heated confrontation. McDonough had been standing outside the office as it occurred and he had heard, distant and muffled, some of the original conversation.

Then the tide of the conversation turned as Mahoney presented his son with an offer of commission on his sales ventures with the American scientist, Joshua Icahn.

McDonough had been told about the plan by Mahoney. What he was interested in now was Jared's reaction.

When the tape was done, he took off the headphones and stared at Davis thoughtfully.

"Your reaction?" he asked.

"I think Mahoney's plan is sound as far as it goes," Colleen Davis said, tapping a pen on the tabletop. "Jared clearly doesn't have the belief in the cause that we have. What he needed was a real—for him—motivation, and Mahoney gave it to him."

"Motivation to do his best, sure, but not motivation enough to stop with the drugs," O'Connell stated flatly. "The boy's a screwup."

"Mahoney thinks he can get his act together," McDonough suggested.

"I don't," O'Connell declared.

"I don't either," Davis said.

"So you think we should take him out of our way?" McDonough asked emotionlessly.

"I don't think the situation is that desperate. Yet. We have got to remember that, screwup or no, Jared's death, even if accidental, would have a profoundly negative impact on Mahoney. Right now I think we want Mahoney as sharp as possible. We've got a lot of irons in the fire."

O'Connell nodded in doubtful agreement.

"But Jared remains a serious threat to the integrity

of our efforts,'' McDonough said. ''I'm especially leery of sending him into South America with Icahn. The doc is as much a screwup as Jared, just in different ways.''

''They'll have a couple of our people accompanying them,'' Davis reminded him.

''Not good enough,'' McDonough stated.

Davis nodded in agreement, then continued to nod as she came to a kind of decision. ''Then it is up to me.''

''It's up to you?'' O'Connell repeated in a question.

''To get Jared to take me into his confidence.'' She smiled, unbuttoned her peasant blouse low on her chest, and leaned over the table so that it fell open. ''Think he'll take this little Irish lass to his heart, boys?''

CHAPTER EIGHT

Stony Man Farm, Virginia

"How the hell could they let that opportunity slip through their damn fingers!" Hal Brognola bellowed, as he stared at two new reports. His big problems just kept getting bigger.

"It wasn't through any fault of theirs, Hal," Barbara Price assured him gently. She'd be the first to give the teams hell when they screwed up. This time they hadn't. "Able played it by the numbers. They didn't go in too aggressively. This guy Frezchetti had a few screws loose. The guys feel pretty bad about it, anyway, though."

"So we got nothing out of San Diego."

"Not a thing. Not a single lead."

"Dammit! What about Gary?"

"He's doing okay. He's got a pretty bad concussion and a rib cage covered with bruises. He'll live." Her casual tone told Brognola more than her words. She wasn't worried about Manning, so he wasn't going to. Not that he liked being cold-hearted, but there was too much going on to waste time on sympathy.

"Where is he?"

"Able got him airlifted offshore, to the *Roosevelt*, a Navy destroyer. He's being treated by the Navy doc."

"Airlifted him how?"

"Private helicopter. We chartered it out of Lima and had it pick up Gary at the probe site. It was the fastest way to get him to a doctor, and it avoided the need for U.S. aircraft flying into Peru, which could have opened up a can of worms."

"Good. And what intelligence did we gain for our trouble?"

Price frowned. "You're not going to like this."

Brognola groaned.

"There were two survivors of the probe. It got rough, and they weren't in good shape by the time everything was under control and Blancanales could start questioning them. But they had very little to say."

"Were they holding back?" Brognola asked.

"No. They just didn't know much. Pol was pretty confident they weren't protecting anybody. But whoever employed them went to great lengths to make sure his hired guns knew nothing about the operation.

"The operation went down like this," Price continued. "A month ago, a representative came to the merc compound in the mountains. He just showed up at their complex out of nowhere and hired them on the spot. He wouldn't say who he was or how he had heard of them, but gave them a hefty retainer and the promise of an impressive fee upon successful completion of the project. All in hard currency. U.S. dollars.

"The mercenaries were ordered to pick up an imported shipment of explosives, which was arranged for independently. Then they showed up at a meeting point a mile from the dam at the appointed time and place. Other mercenary teams were on hand. All were ordered to silence except when communication was absolutely required. There were four, maybe five men from the employer at the scene. They set the main explosive charges and supervised the setting of the auxiliary charges by other hired teams. Even though Striker managed to disable some of the explosives, the dam went down and the operation was considered a success. The mercenary team was paid in full, plus received a hefty bonus. They never learned any names."

"Peruvian mercenaries network like mercenaries in any part of the world," Brognola commented. "Did they recognize any of the others they saw at the site?"

Price nodded. "That's the one bit of good news I can give you. Rafael asked the same question. He knew the faces of two men at the site. They're Brazilian Indians, a tribe called Mitiya. The tribe was pretty much wiped out in their resistance movement during the late 1990s. When there was just a handful of them left, they gave up the fight and turned to mercenary work. They've helped out the Tupac Amaru once or twice. It's unclear if they were hired for those jobs or just did their fellow freedom fighters a favor. They've been implicated in some extortion scams against companies operating along the Amazon River, and one of their members was convicted in absentia in the 1997 murder of a timber company executive. In fact, that man was one of the two recognized by the Peruvian mercs at the dam site."

Brognola nodded. "We know anything about these Mitiya?"

"These aren't the peaceful Amazon Indians you see on Discovery Channel documentaries," Price said. "They're not terribly interested in retaining their tribal culture, although they are still based in a pretty remote location in the Amazon jungle. They've got a modern, well-equipped armory and a few floating tanks that take them in and out of the rain forest. Satellite telecommunications keep them in touch with the world. What we don't know about them is extensive—their numbers, their agenda, if they still have one, their customers.''

"But do we know where they are?" Brognola asked.

Price leaned over the conference table and buzzed the intercom. "Aaron, how's it going in there?"

"I was about to come in and show you," Kurtzman replied. "Give me two minutes."

He maneuvered his wheelchair expertly through the conference-room door a minute and thirty seconds later, spinning immediately to the computer set up beneath the screen monitor. He dialed it up in seconds.

"I've been trying to construct a database on the Mitiya," he said as he worked. "There isn't much to go on. I even culled my *National Geographic* electronic archives. You know you're dealing with a small tribe when you can't even find a *National Geographic* pictorial on them in the last one hundred years."

The screen came to life with a colorful, high-resolution map of the Amazon River. A tiny black icon appeared on the map at the Peruvian city of Iquitos and began following the river's course east through Peru, passing under the southern tip of Colombia into Brazil.

"This is the route I expect our friends the Mitiya are taking to get back to their Amazon home base," Kurtzman said.

Many miles inside Brazil the computer-generated cursor swung off the Amazon, following a tributary north until it came to a halt amid a collection of question marks scattered in the jungle.

"These question marks are my best estimates of former Mitiya villages. Any of these, or none of them, could be the base operations for the Mitiya mercenaries."

"How'd you come by this?" Price asked.

"I located a doctorate dissertation on the Mitiya done by an anthropologist from Brown University in Providence in 1967. It's in their electronic library," Kurtzman explained. "The dissertation wasn't too insightful, but the doctorate candidate describes his visits to seven Mitiya villages and their locations in reference to this tributary."

"What's their ETA?" Brognola asked, nodding at the display.

"That's a tough call, but I would guess nineteen more hours," Kurtzman answered. "This assumes a lot of factors. One is that they are returning directly from the dam explosion to their base. Two is that they make the trip using the watercraft we know they possess. If they have aircraft, all bets are off. I've accounted for the flow of the Amazon and this tributary, but a lot of other factors could affect their rate of travel, throwing my estimates off by hours."

"What we need to know is, can we have Able Team on the ground waiting for them when they get home?" Price asked.

Kurtzman grinned and said, "Absolutely. Maybe."

"Good. Get them there," the big Fed ordered briefly. "You've got authorization to make use of a U.S. Navy helicopter and personnel for the drop. Maybe the *Roosevelt* has equipment we can use."

"We don't need personnel, Hal. We've got Jack sitting on his thumbs in Lima," Price explained.

"Good. Let's get on it," Brognola stated. "Now, what's the deal in Turkmenistan?"

"Phoenix Force is still en route. The destruction of

the dam has been kept reasonably quiet for now, which is only possible because of its location," Kurtzman said. "The Red Cross is mobilizing, and a multinational humanitarian effort will be underway by dawn. There are several hundred thousand people affected in that part of the world, without the infrastructure to deal with it."

"It's the same story we've been hearing all day," the big Fed said. "The old water control systems have been taken out of commission for repairs, relying on the new water systems to take up the slack. When the new dams go down, there's no fallback option."

Price shook her head. "I just don't get it. Somebody is going to a lot of effort and expense to perpetrate indiscriminate genocide, but what's the point?"

The big Fed sighed, his shoulders slumping. "I wish I knew, Barbara."

Santa Fe, New Mexico

COLLEEN DAVIS LEFT her war room.

The truth was—and she would have admitted this to no one, not even to herself out loud—she was worried. The operation she and Mahoney had devised was intricate, dependent on the vagaries of international politics and the complexities of large-scale engineering she didn't understand. But most importantly it depended on the ability to effectively strategize the use of organizational units, which tended to operate the same regardless of their heritage. The gangs on the big-city streets of America were no mystery to her. Once you identified their motivation, they were the same as the street-level gangs of Belfast. Which were the same as the fighting units of the South American mercenaries.

They could all be expected to act and react to specific

patterns that she knew instinctively. She's been raised in one of those street-level Belfast gangs, after all, watching the behavior of the gutter warriors and learning to anticipate them. Honing her skills in the post-peace treaty splinter groups, she became one of the most respected terrorist strategists in Northern Ireland. The British wanted her badly. That made her smile. Even the Irish, those who knew her, those who'd caved in to the British demands, had learned to despise her. They'd swing back over to her way of thinking when the British were driven out of Ireland once and for good. When the punishment phase began.

She'd see to it.

But there were weak spots in the chain she was forging ever so carefully. One of them was right here, right now. Jared Mahoney.

Considering the Jared Mahoney problem had distracted her for days. Headstrong, rebellious as a teenager, he was the kind of man she would have purged from the operation months earlier. Except that his father was the reason the operation existed at all.

If only he was dedicated to the cause she wouldn't consider him to be such a loose cannon, but Jared Mahoney wasn't dedicated to anything except his drug habit and his hedonistic life-style. What he needed was inspiration, something to motivate him to succeed in his role.

Davis had no compunction about taking all the necessary steps to provide that motivation.

Tracking him down to his suite of rooms on the second floor of the expansive home, she walked in on him. The surprise was evident in his features.

"What do you want?"

"To see you before you leave."

At six inches closer than she had ever been to him before, she knew he could smell her skin, her perfume. She knew he would enjoy looking down on her face, with its pale, freckled skin. When she wanted to, when she relaxed the hard muscles of her face, she knew she could look as cute as an Irish teenager on her first date. She'd worn a loose top, cut in a deep *V*, showing him the pale swell of her breasts.

"See me about what?" he asked, distracted.

Davis didn't answer in words. Her physical acting skill was better than her dialogue. Reaching up to him, almost submissively, wrapping her arms around his neck, she drew his mouth to hers and kissed him deeply. She felt his body respond to hers with schoolboy eagerness.

It was almost too easy.

"You don't have to be at the plane for forty minutes," she said, putting an almost innocent hopefulness into her tone.

Jared Mahoney was about to speak. She knew what he would say. Why this, all of a sudden? Then he wisely shut his mouth and went along with the program.

"You have to go," she said thirty-three minutes later.

He looked at his watch. "Yeah."

She stretched out on top of the sheet, allowing his eyes to feast on her body as he redressed hastily. Now, finally, she knew he was going to want an explanation, so she beat him to it.

"I've been watching you for days," she said.

"I had no idea," he answered.

"I know. I suppose I come across as cold and heartless. I had to be, you know. Growing up the way I did. You understand."

Jared nodded, but he didn't understand. He'd been protected for most of his life by a mother who abhorred his father and what his father was.

"All the men I knew were cold and mean. Not like you, Jared," she said softly. She was reaching him in just the way she wanted to. She could see it in his softening eyes. "I knew you were different from all those men. Different from your father. I came to realize that you're the kind of man I've been needing my whole life. Do you understand?"

"Yes," he said, knotting his tie and sitting on the bed beside her, stroking her stomach and bare chest. "I just didn't realize how you felt."

She smiled sadly. "I know. I was trying to reach out to you—for days I've been trying. And I just couldn't. But then when I knew you were leaving on your trip and I realized I wouldn't see you for even more days maybe, I got afraid that this might be my last chance. So I somehow got up the courage to come to you."

He leaned down and kissed her. "I'm glad you did."

"I know you think this whole operation is a waste of time, Jared," she said. "But it is important to me, as well as your father."

"I know it is."

They parted like lovers. She watched him leave, then started to get dressed.

Jared had found his motivation.

By the time he learned it was a lie, he would have become nonvital.

Over Central South America

THE PERUVIAN AIR FORCE Hercules C-130B had been airborne since dawn. With the Andes Mountains far behind them, the landscape was a vast sea of green jungle cut by the blackish blue artery of the Amazon tributary that the map named Olora. Hermann Schwarz had been watching out the windows for the past fifteen minutes and saw no sign of life down there. Not a village, not a boat.

"We're coming up on it," Carl Lyons announced, emerging at the top of the stairs from the cockpit. "We're going to take a look around first, but let's be ready."

The ramp at the rear of the massive, four-prop aircraft swung down. Secured with safety lines, the three members of Able Team watched the passage of the endless green beneath them. When their Peruvian pilot brought the craft to four hundred feet, the tops of the tallest trees in the upper canopy of the Amazon jungle seemed close enough to grab, whipping by at high speed.

"Coming up underneath and a few hundred meters to the right," the copilot announced in flawless English over the intercom system.

The clearing was carried into view. Once it had been a village, but the people who tended it had departed years earlier, and the jungle was reclaiming it quickly. The wood and branch huts were just piles of rotting compost, and the few frame buildings that had once been there had collapsed. A single wreck of a riverboat, maybe thirty feet long, lay beached like a long-dead sea mammal in the shallows at the shore. Throughout the clearing the green, low weeds and shrubs of the jungle were flourishing, and a few saplings were already beginning to reach above the ground-hugging vegetation.

"That's not it," Lyons radioed the pilots. "Let's try target number two."

"Target two is coming up," the copilot announced a minute later. "Off to the right again."

The second village was almost completely obliterated. If the old wooden dock hadn't managed to somehow survive, sticking out into the Olora River like a finger, they might never have seen it. Under the encroaching growth in what might have once been a broad clearing were nothing but masses of collapsed wood and branches.

"That's a negative," Lyons told the pilots. "We'll try for three."

"Roger that."

"I hope this hasn't been a wasted trip," Schwarz said.

"You got something better to do, Gadgets?" Lyons asked gruffly.

"I could find something," Schwarz assured him, wiping the perspiration from his brow. The blanket of moist heat from the jungle had filled the Hercules until it was transformed into a flying steam bath.

"Number three, directly underneath," the pilot said.

The village materialized out of the jungle abruptly, a clearing about the size of a baseball field and bordered on all sides by dense vegetation—even the edge nearest to the Olora River had a wall of plant life cutting it off. But inside the border the ground was open, covered by low grass and bare earth. The buildings were small, framed, square houses, one of them topped with a handful of satellite dishes and antennae. In an instant the clearing had been swallowed up again by the jungle.

"That's it," Lyons said. "I saw no signs of life, but I don't want to chance getting targeted before we hit the ground. We'll bail out downstream, let the river carry us to them."

Schwarz and Blancanales prepped their supplies as Lyons returned to the cockpit for final instructions. The Hercules began an ascent again, providing the Able Team warriors with plenty of space to deploy their parachutes and, if their luck held, steer themselves away from anything that might hang them up.

When the copilot gave the word, the three men pushed the supply pack out the rear of the Hercules. The large, wrapped bundle tumbled end-over-end for just fifty feet before its chute deployed and slowed its descent. Blancanales, Schwarz and Lyons jumped after it.

A steady breeze, stronger than expected, carried their pack away from the river. Lyons wasn't worried about that, and he took the opportunity during his brief time airborne to scan the Amazon River Basin in all directions. Nothing could be seen that hinted at the presence of men, although looks could be deceiving. An army of several hundred men could have been hiding in plain sight. The surface of the Amazon River tributary was deserted as far as he could see. That meant little, as well.

He steered the chute in a broad circle to keep himself over the river, watching the pack disappear into the greenery and making a mental snapshot of the sky-scraping tree nearest to its position. Then he steered himself into a turn and came down in the river just a few steps from the shore, hitting bottom in three feet of water. In less than thirty seconds he had the chute gathered into a ball and stuffed into the rotting hollow of a log.

For a jungle landing, they had all come down with little trouble, and before the now-distant buzz of the departing Hercules had faded they started a march through the rain forest, finding their pack undamaged and making quick work of dismantling it. Within forty-five minutes of landing they were inflating the raft and stowing their equipment.

The dank heat of the afternoon was bringing out torrents of sweat, but they pushed off into the river and allowed it to carry them in the direction of the settlement of the Indians-turned-mercenaries.

A quarter mile from the compound they went to shore. As Lyons and Schwarz dragged the raft under cover, Blancanales retreated into the rain forest a few yards to set up the sat-link system.

The large briefcase opened to reveal the components of the sat-link unit nestled in foam cutouts. The twenty-four-inch dish unfolded like a fan and was mounted on a motorized base unit. The keyboard plugged into the base and with the flip of a switch the unit powered up. The dish needed no assistance to position itself. Like a chick waking up and immediately seeking its mother, the dish at once started searching the unseen heavens for a communications satellite somewhere in midorbit.

Blancanales tapped on the keyboard to initiate a protocol developed by the Stony Man Farm cybernetics team. It was designed for field use, which meant operability that was as automatic as possible. The last thing a commando in a dire situation needed to worry about was computer prompts and commands. With less than two hundred miles between them and the Colombian border, they were in a geographically ideal locale for making use of U.S. monitoring satellites.

The communications officer who took their call handed the mike over to Barbara Price.

"Stony here. Give me your GPS position."

The positioning unit fed the automatic positioning

satellite signal, triangulating the coordinates to the square meter. Blancanales relayed the information to Price as Lyons and Schwarz joined him, donning their combat headsets, which gave them access to the radio feed from the sat-link.

"We're sitting about a quarter mile upstream from target number three. Our flyover showed recent habitation, but we saw no indication that the village is inhabited now," Lyons explained. "They've got the entrance on the river camouflaged. I think we're going to find when we get there that it's invisible to passing watercraft. Which they don't get much of in this neck of the woods anyway."

"Carl," Price said, "everything we know and everything you've seen tells us this is a meticulous and ruthless group. They go to a lot of trouble to keep to themselves and only come into the outside world when they're paid well to do so. They're not going to be happy about company. I want Able frosty."

"We're on our toes," Lyons said. "Any further intel?"

"No. We tried to get Peruvian intelligence to find out anything it could about the Mitiya being in the city of Iquitos. They got nothing. If the Mitiya were in town, they kept a low profile. I was hoping to have narrowed the ETA, at least."

"We'll stay in touch, Stony Base."

The three serial-linked batteries in the sat-link's pack would keep it running twelve to fifteen hours, during which time they would have a satellite in place to transmit their audio signal to Stony Man on an irregular basis.

They retreated from the river, then turned to parallel

it, requiring a full hour to make a stealthy approach on the compound.

THE CLEARING had been carved out of the jungle long enough that the stumps had rotted out of the ground and the earth was compact from the passage of human beings. The large, almost perfect diamond was fenced in only by the jungle, with one of its corners almost touching the bank of the Olora River. After the enclosed acoustics of the jungle, walking in the small, abandoned village felt strangely vast and empty.

Able Team was in full jungle camouflage, including combat cosmetics, but against the whitewashed walls of the framed buildings they stood out, stark and surreal.

"This is Stony Base," Barbara Price said over their headphones. "Report if you can, Able Team."

Lyons didn't respond at first, giving his attention to the quiet compound and gesturing to the nearest building. Blancanales stepped onto a small wooden porch and pushed the front door open slowly as Schwarz maneuvered along the side of the building, checking out its rear. He scanned it and shook his head; nobody there.

"Quiet here, Stony Base," Lyons said. "Pol?"

Blancanales walked across the stark living area, with its unfinished wooden floors and walls, to a kitchen. A decades-old refrigerator hummed in the corner, a dusty boom box on top of it. That meant there was a generator somewhere. A swarm of ants crawled along the far wall. The table was nailed together out of roughly hewn wooden pieces.

"Pol?" Lyons repeated over the radio.

"Nothing yet. Nobody home."

He moved through the next doorway into a bedroom, where he found a drapery of dingy mosquito netting over the unmade, wide cot. Another tiny bedroom next to it contained three more low beds. The flimsy, ancient chest of drawers was crowded with plastic knickknacks and bottles of cheap perfume.

Of course there would be women among the Mitiya. Did they accompany the men when they traveled to Iquitos? A trip to the big city was probably a major event in the lives of this isolated mercenary community.

This meant they would use the opportunity to make purchases they couldn't normally make, especially after a major cash influx.

If he only got to go shopping a few times a year and spent the rest of his life in a jungle without exposure to the outside world, what would he buy?

Blancanales turned on his heel and strode back to the kitchen, pulling open the refrigerator and opening the interior door to the small freezer compartment. The compartment was stuffed full of frozen steaks, roasts and hamburger patties. He grabbed a plastic-wrapped T-bone and examined the label. No date. Freshness dating was a concept yet to be embraced by the supermarkets of Peru. He started going through the refrigerator, grabbing a cardboard carton of milk.

The date was there, imprinted in the cardboard.

The milk was going to be drinkable for another two weeks.

"I DON'T THINK we're alone," Blancanales reported simply.

Lyons slowly retreated to the side of the house along with Schwarz, out of sight of most of the compound.

"Explain."

"Fresh groceries."

"Maybe they got into hiding when they heard the

plane,'' Schwarz suggested, ''then they watched us come down. They know we're here.''

''So, where are they now?''

''This is a careful bunch,'' Lyons mused. ''They've had decades to become paranoid. They're probably still making use of the measures they developed during their rebel years. Like the camouflaged entrance to the village.''

''So they've got some sort of hiding place in the jungle, maybe in the village itself,'' Schwarz hypothesized. ''Whatever it is, it's close enough to run to in case of an assault.''

''Pol,'' Lyons said urgently into the radio, ''get out of there. We're sitting ducks.''

''I'll join you in thirty seconds.''

''You on the line, Stony Base?''

''We're following you, Able One,'' Price said. ''We've unearthed some intel that might be useful.''

''Able, listen up,'' Aaron Kurtzman said. ''I've managed to locate an old CIA report.''

''We're listening.''

''Suffice it to say Langley targeted a group of Mitiya briefly after an attack on some Americans in Brazil. They got their hands on this intel from the Brazilians. So this is very secondhand and very old. The Mitiya would send the women and children into the jungle and have watch platforms in trees surrounding their villages, usually in the tallest heavily leaf-laden trees. They'd put bowmen or gunmen in them with a clear shot at the entrance to the village.''

''Understood,'' Lyons said.

Blancanales stalked around the corner and hunched against the side of the building with his teammates.

"We need to move in toward the center of the village. Back here, their watch is probably not even visible."

Schwarz was thoughtful. "And we're invisible to them. So how do we use that to our advantage?"

"We drive them into the open. We burn them out."

THEY STUCK to the perimeter and charged from the rear of the house into the rain forest, then moved along the jungle floor watching the village through the undergrowth. Schwarz kept the M-16 A-2/M-203 combo aimed into the trees and watched the foliage above their heads. There was no telling for sure where the watch platform would be situated, which meant they couldn't be sure they wouldn't end up stumbling upon it.

Blancanales and Lyons kept an eye on the eerily quiet Mitiya village and the jungle that surrounded it, all bottom-tier trees that created a dark mass of green between twenty to fifty feet above the earth.

There was a section of the jungle that seemed to offer the broadest viewing area of the village, including the camouflaged entrance. Able Team halted and observed the trees through binoculars for a long minute.

"I've got them," Blancanales said, and pointed out one of the darkest of the trees, heavy with thick green leaves—an ideal spot. He had to train his field glasses on it for a full minute before he got movement. Then he focused on the face of an intent figure peering through the leaves.

"They don't have a make on us."

"Not yet," Lyon's agreed. "Can you light a fire on top of them, Pol?"

"Coming up."

Blancanales took advantage of the available time to set up his shot as precisely as possible. The trick was to place the incendiary grenade in the trees far enough above the mercenaries to drive them down without killing them in the process. This probe was about uncovering intelligence, not vengeance. The M-203 was being asked to send the grenade into a high-altitude arch and detonate it at about fifty feet off the rain-forest floor.

"Stony Base, we're about to engage," Lyons stated simply into his microphone.

"Affirmative," the Stony Man Farm mission controller answered.

Blancanales's shot was near perfect. The 40 mm incendiary grenade popped out of the launcher, arched across the open sky of the Mitiya compound and disappeared into the mass of green atop the tree where the mercenaries were staged. Yellow fire billowed out of the tree suddenly, revealing its branchy skeleton like an X-ray image.

The Able Team warriors launched themselves out of their cover at the moment of the burst, making quick time across the open ground in the few precious seconds available to them. As they homed in on the burning tree, the Indian mercenaries were falling and jumping to the ground. One of them had clearly been at a higher point in the tree and had been engulfed in the blast. He crashed through the branches, aflame, and hit the ground, unmoving.

One of the first mercenaries to come to ground spotted Able Team and realized he still had his weapon. He charged at Schwarz as he brought the Uzi into play. Before he could fire, Schwarz triggered his M-16 with a trio of rounds that sent the mercenary sprawling on his chest. Two other men reacted by running for the cover of the nearest shack. Lyons swept his MP-5 A-3 at the ground in front of them and triggered a stream of rounds. The mercs were unable to stop and ran directly into the stream of fire, collapsing as their legs were shattered.

The majority of mercenaries were hitting the ground and fleeing, if they were able. If enough of them could get to cover in the jungle, Blancanales knew they'd be able to drive Able Team away. He couldn't allow that to happen. Thumbing an HE round into the breech of the M-203, he aimed for the deep jungle and fired the round. The grenade flew above the heads of the mercenaries and struck a tree in front of them, exploding with a concussive blast that shattered the trunk and blasted the mercenaries in the face. Several were slapped to the ground senseless. The man in the rear collapsed heavily but rose again and veered into the jungle. Blancanales thumbed in another grenade and let it fly. It detonated with a decisive explosion that backlit the rain forest and ended in sudden stillness. The runner had taken a final tumble.

The last man aloft came crashing out of the tree with his shirt on fire, and his arms clawed wildly at the open air in the instant before he impacted the earth on an inturned foot. His ankle snapped with a heavy crack, then his shoulder hit the earth, smashing it beneath him. He was out cold, but the flames were extinguished.

CHAPTER NINE

*Mitiya Compound, Amazon Rain Forest,
Northwest Brazil*

"Able One here, Stony Base. We've got four captives.
Two aren't responsive, but alive."

"What about the two that are responsive?" Barbara
Price asked.

"They're less than cooperative," Lyons answered.
"They felt disinclined to answer our questions for quite
a while. Then we persuaded them to come clean with
what they knew."

"What persuaded them?" Kurtzman asked over the
line.

"They thought we had their families," Lyons said.
"They've got wives and children living with them here.
They're hidden in a cave in the jungle set up specifically
for that purpose. We haven't seen hide nor hair of them,
but the Mitiya fighters didn't know that. They thought
that from the intelligence we had of the compound we
had been spying on them and knew how they behaved.

"We're staying out of sight, holed up in one of their
central buildings, which appears to be some sort of a
community center."

"Good plan," Price said. "We don't know if you've

got all the mercenaries. Any of them or their wives or children could be hiding out in the jungle looking for a chance to peg you guys.''

''My thoughts exactly,'' Lyons said. ''Gadgets is keeping an eye out while Pol questions the captors.''

''Here I am,'' Blancanales said over the radio. He emerged from the smaller room at the back of the building, where the two conscious captives were tied up in chairs in different rooms. ''I've questioned them both. We got lucky in our strikes. Took out the two top men. They're demoralized. Add to that the perceived threat of killing off their wives and kids. These guys are in a sad state.''

''So what have they told you?'' Kurtzman probed.

''Not a damned thing,'' Blancanales said. ''They say they don't know anything, and I believe them. All the arrangements for the Bedoya Dam job were made anonymously, just like with our friends in Cinchona village. The Mitiya leadership was suspicious of working under such conditions, but all scum have their price. They were finally swayed by a large bonus. They were paid very well for the job, all in cash, and they never knew a thing.''

There was a morose silence over the sat-link as the Stony Man Farm staff digested this bit of bad news. Lyons waited patiently.

''All right,'' Price said finally. ''You did your best. At least we've shut them down. I suppose that counts for something.''

Lyons and Blancanales didn't respond to that. They were thinking that, with the stakes they were playing with, shutting down a bunch of know-nothing mercenaries counted for very little.

''Your extraction is on its way,'' Price continued,

sounding tired. "Jack's en route in a Navy chopper. ETA seventy-seven minutes."

"What about our friends?"

"The Brazilians are coming to get them. They're at least two hours out. You'll move the prisoners to a spot on the bank of the Amazon where your tributary intersects. The Brazilians will pick them up there. That way their families won't have the chance to come in and get them in the interim. But you'll have to move fast. The Brazilians don't know who it is that's taken the Mitiya down, and they might not be too happy if they knew U.S. paramilitaries were operating on their soil."

"Understood. Then what, Stony?"

"Working on that, Able One. Right now we just don't know."

Stony Man Farm, Virginia

PRICE AND Katzenelenbogen came through the door of the cybernetics lab with eager, but not hopeful looks on their tired faces.

"We've struck out, Aaron," Katz said. "Tell us you've got something."

"I wish I could." He leaned back in the wheelchair with his fingers laced behind his head. "There's nothing to tell you, yet. I've started going through the databases for more on our Mitiya friends. So far there's very little, and I don't think I'm going to get more."

"I think you're right," Price agreed. "I believe we're going to find out this is nothing but a marginally successful mercenary group without a solid link to the financial and organizational backing of the dam breaks."

"That leaves Phoenix," Katz said, glancing at the wall clock.

Price shook her head, her honey-blond hair brushing her shoulders. ''The lead Phoenix is following isn't substantial. My hopes there aren't high.''

Carmen Delahunt entered the room without a word, touching the control that caused the screen on the wall to switch from an FBI database display to a CNN broadcast. A reporter was standing on the Andes mountain perch that had become familiar to news watchers in the past day, set against the backdrop of the crumpled Bedoya Dam.

''...the investigation continues, as does the cleanup downstream. More than 230 bodies have been recovered up and down the stretch of Reyes River. Another two hundred people remain missing, but no bodies have been reported discovered since 5:00 a.m. this morning eastern time, making the likelihood of survivors slim indeed.''

The reporter signed off, and CNN switched to the San Diego dam-blast investigation.

No more survivors were likely to be found.

It was hard for Price to admit that she had still entertained hope of Mack Bolan's survival, but somehow she had. And every piece of information and every passing hour made that hope seem foolish. She tried to quash it and to convince herself once and for all that Mack Bolan was gone from this world. He had finally faced something monstrous and powerful enough to decimate his enormous vitality. It had taken a quarter million tons of collapsing concrete, but the Executioner was finally dead.

Maybe.

She couldn't help herself. The hope remained, even now, a full day and a half after the fact, despite her best wisdom.

Peru

THE OLD MAN'S HEART lurched and nearly came to a halt in his chest. He staggered away from the door and landed in a chair, breathing heavily.

He grabbed at his chest and leaned forward, over the floor, his eyes upturned in horror.

The corpse got to its feet and walked toward him.

"Stay back!" the old man begged.

"I'm not going to hurt you."

The corpse spoke English.

"You are dead?" the old man asked in his own version of imperfect English.

"No. I'm very much alive. I think I have you to thank for that."

The corpse had piercing blue eyes, the face strong and hard, perhaps cruel. But it was the face of a living man. The old man's heart stopped smashing into his throat quite so hard.

"I thought you were dead. I started to dig a grave."

"How did I get here?"

"I found you after the waters came down the canyon like a tidal wave. Now the river is deeper than before. You must have been swept away by the tidal wave, yes?"

Mack Bolan nodded and seemed to be peering into his own recent past. "Yeah. As clearly as I can remember it."

"You saved yourself. I found you above the waterline. You crawled out of the water. I found the trail of mud you made. Your body was covered in it. I washed it off as best I could. I tried to wake you, but you wouldn't wake up."

Bolan was thoughtful as he helped the old man to his feet. "I do have a headache."

The old man stared at him, amazed all over again. Then he opened his toothless gums wide and laughed. "You have a headache!" he said. "Young man, you have a knot on your skull like you started to grow another chin over your ear and you say, 'I have a headache.'" He laughed again.

The Executioner gave him a grim smile.

"Why didn't you take me to a town or to a doctor?"

The old man's amusement faded. "There is a town, but it is too far for me to go. I was born and I grew up there, but I will never go there again. It is too far and I am too old. People come to me once a month and bring me things I need. Sometimes they do not come." He shrugged. "There is no doctor. The last time I went there was to get a doctor. That was two years ago. I went to get a doctor for my wife. When I reached the town they said the doctor had left. Not enough people for him to take care of in the small town. It did not matter. My wife was dead when I got back from the town. So I had to bury her. That was hard, hard work. Too hard for an old man like me, and I knew I would never be strong enough to go into that town again. I am sorry about that. I am sorry if you feel I let you almost die."

"No need for that. You took me in. Got me out of the cold. That probably saved my life. I'm grateful."

The old man cocked his head like a curious dog. "I wonder if you would tell me what happened. Did the dam burst?"

"Yeah. I was there when it happened."

"That was the only thing that could have made such a tidal wave, I suppose."

"How far is the dam from here?"

"At least eight kilometers," the old man said. "I saw it once, a few years ago. When it was still being built. Men came and measured my house and said I would not be in danger of the rising water. What is your name, young man?"

"Mike Belasko," he said, and put out his hand to the old Indian, who took it in a claw crippled with arthritis. Even his mild grip made the old man wince.

"I am Tacna," the old man said, smiling again. "I'm very happy that you are not dead, Mike Belasko."

"I'm pleased myself. But I'm going to have to be a rude patient and leave you. I have something to take care of."

"Would that have to do with the bursting of the dam?"

"Yeah."

The old man moved to his single cabinet thoughtfully, removing a loaf of heavy, hard bread and a can of soup. He set the bread on the table and opened the can of soup with an ancient, rusty can opener. "You will need strength to get to the nearest town."

Mack Bolan was torn. He needed to get in contact with the outside world as soon as possible. It was imperative that he find out what was happening, and let Stony Man Farm know where he was.

But he was also weakened by lack of food. His body had been struggling for thirty-six long hours to fight off his injuries, without sustenance. When the salty, rich aroma of the soup reached him, his stomach growled expectantly.

He sat at the table to share a meal with the old Indian man who had saved his life.

Over the Caspian Sea

MIDMORNING in North America was early evening in the Central Asian states. The U.S. Air Force troop transport jet was now level at twelve thousand feet. It had flown north out of the Persian Gulf, straddling the Iraq-Iran border all the way into Turkish airspace, then making a broad, sweeping curve over Azerbaijan before heading in an easterly course over the Caspian.

"We're fifteen minutes from drop-off," the Air Force pilot announced over the aircraft intercom.

"You guys up for this?" asked the worried-looking Air Force crewman who had accompanied them, under strict orders to mind his own business.

"We've made high-altitude jumps before, mate," David McCarter said, with a casualness that the crewman couldn't tell was forced. Jumping out of an aircraft at twelve thousand feet was a proposition to take seriously. Even well-trained jumpers could experience any number of problems. The height made oxygen and thermal clothing imperative.

"Anything I can do to help?" the crewman added.

"Here you go." McCarter swallowed the dregs of his Coca-Cola soft drink and thrust the empty can at the crewman. He gave his team members the once-over, evaluating their state of preparedness. High-altitude face masks were in place. The equipment inventory they were going in with included lightweight enduro-style motorcycles for ground transportation.

"Stony Base here. How are your preparations going, Phoenix?" Barbara Price's voice was being relayed through the aircraft's radio.

"We're ready," McCarter said.

"I'm not going to be able to join you on the ground,

Phoenix,'' Price said. ''No satellite feed is available until 1900 hours your time. You'll have to go in without me.''

''We'll miss you, Stony, but we can handle it.''

As Price began feeding coordinates for the satellite uplink to Rafael Encizo, who would be charged with aligning the dish and getting them in contact with Stony Man Farm when the valuable satellite time became available, McCarter evaluated the team silently. There wasn't a more highly skilled or experienced paramilitary unit on the planet, but at the moment they were hampered by disillusionment. The loss of Mack Bolan, a man they had served with for more years and on more missions than some of them cared to remember, had shaken them. Now, the incomplete status of the team was a distraction. Phoenix Force was highly flexible and could operate in superlative fashion as a foursome, but the knowledge that Gary Manning was halfway across the globe, injured, status unclear, had a demoralizing impact.

''Stand by, Phoenix,'' Price said as she finished up with Encizo.

There was a crackle over the lines and a new voice came on. ''Greetings from the U.S.S. *Roosevelt*.''

''Gary! What the hell are you trying to pull down there?'' McCarter boomed.

''This is the life, boys. Lounging on deck, getting three squares on a tray, basking in the warm breezes of the South Pacific Ocean.''

''Enjoy it while you can,'' Encizo said with a grin. ''You're going to have some definite makeup work to do as soon as you get back in the fold.''

''Yeah. Talk about not pulling your weight,'' T. J. Hawkins, the youngest Phoenix Force member, piped in. His accent was all Texas, especially in casual conversation. "When's your vacation over?"

"Sad to say I'm flying back to the States tomorrow. Apparently there's paperwork I can lend a hand with at the Farm."

"Sorry to hear that," Hawkins said sympathetically.

"That'll teach you to duck when things go boom," Calvin James added.

Price broke in. "Gary's going to help us in the lab here at the Farm. We'll make use of his explosives expertise to help analyze the dam bombings. Any data you manage to scrounge up at the Turkmen sites could be useful."

"We'll keep that in mind," McCarter replied.

"Five minutes," the crewman announced.

"Good luck," Manning said. "Keep your butts out of the way of the bullets."

"See you soon," McCarter replied, happy to see the subtle but important change in the morale of his team. Hearing Manning's voice made all the difference. The emotional state was important even to the performance of the highly trained warrior. "Thanks, Stony."

Price's tone became very serious. "We've got damn little to go on at the moment, Phoenix. I'm hoping you'll dredge up something of value in this investigation."

"We'll do what we can, Stony Base."

Turkmenistan

THEY WERE in Turkmen airspace for less than three minutes when the crewman gave them the signal. The rear of the troop-transport aircraft swung down, filling the interior with the orange brilliance of the sun, low on the horizon and shining in directly at them. Below them, the world was covered with a blanket of gray haze that masked the landscape.

First the four Kawasaki motorcycles went in rapid succession, followed by the package containing the sat-link system. Next an armament package. Finally the four Phoenix Force warriors propelled themselves one after another from the rear door of the transport and into the bright, hazy sky over Central Asia.

They were going in heavy, which was nothing new for Phoenix. But they might be wasting their time on a wild-goose chase.

A U.S. surveillance satellite that dated from the Soviet era had been watching the Central Asian states at the time of the attack on the dams in the Turkmen foothills. It had been trained on Sheychenko, but had been refocused south after news of the attack reached the U.S. There was little to see, except a chance glimpse of what might have been a pair of large helicopters leaving the foothills. Before the satellite was out of range it had tracked the helicopters on a westward course that brought them down in the steppes near the western coast of Turkmenistan.

The steppes were vast and inhospitable, a stretch of desertlike wasteland forty miles wide and stretching 140 miles along the coast, bordering equally unpleasant marshlands. At a point sixty miles north of the city of Gasan-Kuli, the helicopters had disappeared at a point where no human beings were known to live.

The U.S. military was ready to hand the information over to the Turkmen military when Kurtzman latched on to it, less than five hours ago. It had been quickly decided to persuade the President for first crack at the target.

Descending, James spotted the gray Caspian Sea through the haze, far to the west. Beneath him the marshes were greenish, with patches of blue, clear water and brown, dry land. Using his field glasses he tried to peer through the polarizing haze, to find some evidence of human habitation in the wasteland, but he saw nothing. No road or building. No rising distortion of smoke.

James turned his attention to the gray-blue parachutes, which had blossomed well below him, and activated his own chute as he plummeted toward the equipment. As the mass of chute material erupted from the pack on his back, he heard it billow in the wind and he was yanked out of his free fall.

"They're on to us." It was Hawkins who broke the radio silence. "I've got a chopper powering up. North-northeast."

James quickly turned his field glasses north-northeast, picking up Hawkins in his line of sight, approximately one thousand feet below and one thousand feet north of his position. Beyond him there was a small distortion at ground level, and it took ten seconds of concentration for him to make out the shape of a large, black helicopter rising rapidly off a stretch of dry land in the marsh. He was impressed with Hawkins's perceptiveness. He might have missed the tiny movement of the still-distant chopper.

"They're going to reach us quickly. These blokes must have radar," McCarter stated. "Get down and get under cover."

"Getting down before they get to us might be a challenge, Phoenix One," James replied.

"I read you on that. Save your asses."

James dragged out the M-16 A-2/M-203 combo

tucked in with the gear on his back as the chopper ascended powerfully, presenting a broadside profile.

"It's a Helix," Hawkins announced, at the same instant James recognized the Soviet-era aircraft. "We're ducks on a pond."

"I'll distract him," James announced. "You guys get to the ground."

"You're on top. He'll target you last," McCarter said.

"I think I'll command his attention," James stated. He looked down at McCarter, floating nearly three hundred feet below, and gave him a brief wave.

"This I gotta see," Hawkins said.

The Russian KA-32 Helix helicopter swept up at the descending team of four with a thrum of power that was nearly left behind in the bright, crisp air, leveling off when it was still a quarter of a mile away and slowing to set its targets on the lowest jumper. Rafael Encizo was dangling like a worm, helpless on the hook with a hungry catfish homing in on him. The 7.62 mm machine guns buzzed to life.

McCarter and Hawkins could only watch.

James's assault rifle-grenade launcher combo dangled from his neck as he dragged on the chute to steer himself closer to the Helix while it slowed to a near stop. He knew he only had seconds to spare, but he also knew he was well out of range of the Soviet assault chopper. He released the chute drags and grabbed the assault rifle, aiming high and triggering a blast into the Turkmen sky. The distance and drop were well out of the ordinary, and he wasn't using tracers. All he could do was guess, adjusting the stream of 5.56 mm tumblers as he leaned on the trigger, trying to compensate simultaneously for the slow spiral of his now-uncontrolled descent. He knew the magazine was coming on empty when a shower of sparks started flying from the helicopter's twin rotors. The fire of the 7.62 mm machine guns halted in almost the same instant the ship veered away from the fire.

James didn't have time to evaluate the success of the enemy fire. Encizo might have just been cut in two. He'd worry about that later. He forced a hand inside his jump harness to get at another magazine for the M-16 A-2. The lanky black SEAL slapped it in place as the mile-distant chopper swept up in a circle like an angry hornet and leveled off a hundred feet above him, pointing at him. James had the distinct impression he was a whale about to be harpooned.

He triggered a useless barrage into the sky, up and out at the helicopter, which waited well out of range. The flash of rounds ended abruptly when the second magazine came to a lurching halt.

James grabbed at his harness quickly as the chopper accelerated at him with a burst of power to the twin rotors. The pilot was expressionless behind dark sunglasses. James allowed his face to register mounting panic as he spiraled away from the chopper, thumbed a high-explosive 40 mm grenade into the breech of the M-203 and grabbed at the parachute drags, bringing himself around again to face the Helix. It swept low, below the level of his descent, and came up again. As the assault chopper came face-to-face with the Phoenix Force warrior, the machine guns commenced a deadly barrage and James triggered the M-203, firm in the knowledge he was pushing the limits of the launcher's 375-yard range. In the instant the grenade was away, he grabbed the quick-release on the chute and actuated it. He heard the ripping of the machine-gun rounds as he plummeted suddenly through open space and heard the receding blast of the HE grenade.

He had avoided the flesh-shredding rounds of the machine gun only to open himself to a new form of death. The ground was huge and coming up fast as he grabbed at the emergency chute handle and deployed it, feeling himself forced suddenly out of a free fall into a controlled descent. But the earth was coming up fast, a giant hand about to smack him like a fly. He slammed into a flat section of ground, forcing his legs to descend into a controlled, shock-absorbing roll.

Somehow he managed to maintain consciousness, but he could feel the shock of impact rattling through his body. As he rolled onto all fours, he tried to push himself to his feet, but his right leg crumpled under him and he was on the ground again.

James watched the erratic course of the blasted helicopter above him. It didn't look fatally wounded, but it was going to need serious repairs before going into battle again. It had been worth it, James told himself, allowing the pain of the impact to wash over him.

"CAL!"

"Here."

Hawkins trotted at a ground-eating pace, coming upon his battered teammate behind a low wall of scrub brush.

"You injured?" Hawkins asked.

"I hurt. That's about all I know so far."

"I thought you'd be a sack of broken bones the way you came down. Man, you were moving fast."

"Tell me about it."

Hawkins took James's hand and hoisted him slowly to his feet. James was on his left foot, putting the right one down experimentally. It looked straight. Nothing broken. James winced a little when he put his weight on it, but the pain was receding with every passing second.

"I think I'll live. It just hurts like hell."

"This is going to slow you down."

"Negative. Just give me a few minutes to walk it off."

"We might not have a few minutes," Hawkins said, looking over the brush as the sounds of distance vehicles reached them.

James touched his microphone. "Phoenix One?"

"Good to hear your voice, Cal," McCarter said. "That move you pulled was bloody brilliant, but I thought we'd have to scoop you off the ground with a shovel."

"Not quite. Do you have a fix on the second wave?"

"Three jeeps coming in. We don't have time to get the bikes unloaded before they get here."

"We might want to make time," broke in Rafael Encizo. "I've spotted Helix number two coming at us hard and fast."

"These guys have the money for some serious transportation," Hawkins said.

"Phoenix One, you two take care of the jeeps while T.J. and I heat things up for the chopper."

"How do you plan on doing that?"

"More insidious trickery," James said.

"She'll be here in a few minutes—work fast," Encizo warned.

Hawkins grabbed the nearest of the fallen packs and hoisted it on his shoulders, bringing it to James's side. It took them all of thirty seconds to remove the remote-controlled .50-caliber machine gun from its case and set it up at the edge of a ground-hugging pillow of scrub brush. James was moving more easily now, and he was convinced the impact had only jarred him. He'd be bruised for a while, but there were no injuries he couldn't work off. He tucked the empty packing canvas underneath the brush hastily.

"How's our chopper?" Hawkins asked as he flipped on the radio receiver on the remote machine gun.

"I think they just spotted us," James said.

At that instant the air ripped apart with a torrent of 7.62 mm rounds that erupted from the belly of the assault chopper, slashing at the brush and long grass. The chopper was still a half mile away, but they could hear the tearing of the growth. They crept across bare ground, making their way 150 yards from the robotic machine gun and putting more space between themselves and the deadly Helix. The chopper hung poised in the air, slanted so the pilot could look directly at the ground not forty feet below his windshield.

"I hope David or Rafe didn't catch that fire," Hawkins groaned as he touched the radio on his headgear.

"No time to check. Here she comes."

The Helix was moving slowly over the rocky, empty ground, maintaining its angled posture, while Hawkins and James hunkered down in the brush. When the chopper was barely within range, James triggered a handful of rounds from the Browning machine gun. The fire sailed harmless under the belly of the Helix, but the chopper turned in the direction of the shots like a giant head turning its attention to some new area of interest. James depressed the small electronic button on the remote control and blasted the helicopter. A few of the rounds struck the chopper even as the aircraft retaliated with a blast of 7.62 mm rounds from the guns. James silenced the Browning abruptly.

The Helix was waiting for further response, hanging so still in the sky it was like a model hanging by string from a boy's bedroom ceiling. Then it slowly started to move in a wide circle, never moving its nose from the nest of brush where the Browning machine gun was placed.

"Ideal," James muttered as the Helix came directly between themselves and the Browning. The Phoenix Force commando had merely hoped to trick the pilot into coming into range. Instead, the cooperative mercenary had backed his aircraft to within spitting distance of the two men—and facing in the wrong direction.

"Target the rotors," James said above the roar as the chopper maneuvered to within one hundred feet of their stakeout position. He and Hawkins each stood and targeted carefully.

"Like shootin' goldfish in a kiddy pool," Hawkins commented.

The Helix reacted. The pilot or a gunner had been looking in the right place at the right time and spotted the two commandos. With a high-pitched squeal of overfueled turbines, the chopper veered up and away, but too late to save itself. The twin high-explosive 40 mm grenades left the M-203 launchers with virtually no recoil and detonated against the fuselage of the aircraft. Instantly the smooth thrum of the rotors turned to a sick chopping sound and the helicopter plummeted to the ground with a heavy crash of metal.

CHAPTER TEN

Rafael Encizo glanced back just long enough to see the evil-looking visage of the Russian helicopter nod forward in a distinctly uncharacteristic manner and plummet to the ground with a crack.

He offered up silent thanks to his comrades. With the chopper out of action, he concentrated on three military jeeps, probably Soviet as well. They rocked to a halt and their doors swung open, disgorging men who stared out beyond Encizo at the collapsing ruin of the Helix.

The effectiveness of the Phoenix Force attack had clearly taken them by surprise. Two expensive choppers had been taken out in just minutes.

The jeeps were too far off to be within range of Encizo's M-203, and McCarter was tucked in the brush to his left, another two hundred yards back. They were going to have to allow the mercenaries' vehicles to close in before engaging them.

The mercenaries overcame their surprise with a sudden flurry of action, jumping in their vehicles and spinning the wheels on the dusty earth.

Encizo knew the Turkmen mercs would go after the men who had just destroyed their valuable aircraft with a vengeance. That would be at least twelve men against James and Hawkins. Encizo knew his teammates could hold their own against tremendous odds, but he wanted to cut those odds a little. Call it a personal favor for a couple of buddies.

He duckwalked behind brush for ten yards, eyes locked on the progress of the jeeps, evaluating their path of travel and their speed like a lion looking for a likely wildebeest to bring down. Only there were no young or enfeebled in this small herd to choose from. He had to go simply with the one that came the closest.

It became apparent one of the jeeps was going to cut around a small rise that would bring it as close as could be hoped for. But Encizo was still going to be hard-pressed to get to it in time to take proactive measures without making himself an easy target. He scrambled across the hard-packed earth on all fours, paused before the last open stretch of ten yards to get his bearings, and decided to chance it. As two jeeps maneuvered around the rise to the south, all but their roofs and the tops of the windows were hidden, and the third jeep was veering north, trouncing over the uneven ground. Encizo sprinted across open land on an intercept path.

His rise was just five feet above the lower gap the jeep was taking, which meant he was directly in the line of sight of the vehicle's occupants. He saw their reactions when they spotted him, and there was a scramble inside to bring weapons to bear. Encizo reached the edge of the rise and threw himself into a long dive, bringing the M-16 up and out in a posture that brought him to a hard landing on his knees and elbows. The jeep skidded and fishtailed, coming to a halt in a dust cloud, and the door flew open. A mercenary in a battered Soviet army uniform, complete with threadbare hammer and sickle, jumped out and leveled a Kalashnikov rifle into the brush. Encizo triggered the M-16, sending a 3-round burst against the side of the jeep and dropping the gunner with a gut shot.

Encizo flattened against the top of the rise when a torrent of rounds drilled through the air inches above his head. The figure in the backseat had barely waited for his dead comrade to drop before firing over him at his ambushers. He had a bad, low angle, but Encizo could almost feel the bullets buzzing less than a foot above him. He listened for the inevitable pause, then rose and targeted the jeep's rear seat by memory, laying down a rapid burst of almost a dozen rounds that chased the gunner across the backseat bench and nailed him against the opposite door.

Encizo didn't wait for the body to collapse before flattening again to avoid the return fire from the pair of mercenaries who had leaped from the vehicle and taken cover on the far side of the jeep's hood.

The Phoenix Force warrior had secured a 40 mm grenade, but for a split second he reconsidered using it. The deadly bomb would doubtless end the current standoff, but it would take out the jeep, too. Encizo decided the vehicle might be useful, especially since he didn't know how well their motorcycles had survived the jump or when they'd have the chance to get to them.

This wouldn't be the first time he risked his neck for a piece of hardware.

As he changed the magazine on the M-16 and pocketed the grenade, Encizo rose on his hands and knees and threw himself into open space off the edge of the rise. For a half second he was airborne, watching the startled mercenaries hustle to bring their weapons to bear. The little Cuban landed on his feet on the sandy earth at the rear of the jeep, was driven forward by his flying momentum into a roll and ended up in a crouch on the opposite side of the jeep, facing the mercenaries from just six feet away. He triggered the M-16, sweeping a deadly figure eight of gunfire over them as one fled and one stood his ground. The fleeing mercenary dropped and rolled behind a nearby brush, somehow dodging the bullets. His companion absorbed a bloody collection of rounds and slammed to the earth, tossing his Kalashnikov at Encizo's feet.

A glance told the warrior that his backseat passenger wasn't going to protest as he jumped in the driver's seat and stomped on the foot pedals, slamming the jeep into gear and sending a spray of sand flying from the rear tires. He swerved forward and spun around the low mass of shrubs in search of the escaped mercenary. The merc was on the run, apparently uninjured, and he scrambled for cover in the waist-high clumps of vegetation when Encizo triggered the M-16 out the passenger-side window. The 5.56 mm tumblers were wasted into the barren Turkmen landscape.

Encizo dragged the steering wheel to the left, fishtailing briefly before whipping it back to the right. Now the mercenary was visible, and the man realized it at the same instant. He flopped back onto his face on the earth and pointed a 9 mm Bizon-2 machine pistol at the jeep.

Encizo ducked in the seat as he issued an obscenity in Spanish and spun the wheel hard to carry the vehicle away from the mercenary as a white-hot torrent of 9 mm rounds stitched the doors, side body panels and rear.

Encizo allowed the jeep to drift fifteen feet to an uncontrolled halt when the gunfire ceased. Crouching low, his hands flat in the sand that covered the floor, he could feel his patience running thin, the tension building in his gut.

Then he realized he was able to look out through a tattered opening that had been made in the rusty door by at least a pair of rounds from the machine pistol. He spotted the mercenary—a grizzled face and an ugly sneer. He was watching the jeep with intent awareness as he changed the magazine in his machine pistol.

Encizo scarcely breathed. He heard McCarter through the headphones asking him to report in. He ignored it.

The Turkmen mercenary slowly began to stalk the jeep, and Encizo recognized long years of battle experience in his behavior. He was sweeping the path before him with the machine pistol as if it were an extension of his hand.

Encizo set the M-16 on the seat at his shoulder, moving so slowly the movement was barely perceptible, and removed the Browning 9 mm handgun from its holster. Watching out his tiny portal, he reached up and over the top of the door and triggered a pair of rounds.

The merc had a look of amazement on his face. The machine pistol hit the earth at his feet, and seconds later he collapsed on top of it.

"Phoenix Two, talk to me," McCarter said urgently.

"You've got Phoenix Two," Encizo said finally. "Sorry. I was momentarily engaged."

"We've got a pair of vehicles buzzing around here taking potshots at us. Where are you?"

"I'll be there in twenty seconds, Phoenix One. I'll be in the third jeep. Do me a favor and don't shoot at me."

DAVID MCCARTER TRIGGERED a handful of rounds at the jeep as it spun past his position, then withdrew behind an earthen mound to avoid machine-gun fire from the Kalashnikov AK-102. The gunner in the passenger seat of the vehicle swiveled the weapon to make effective coverage without wasting rounds. Hemmed in, the Phoenix Force commander was trying to come up with a strategy for extricating himself from the clump of earth and brush when another jeep spun into view and braked to a halt. The vehicle was so covered with bullet holes it looked as if it had been given a leopard-print paint job.

"That you, Rafe?"

"I hear you, but I don't see you," Encizo answered in McCarter's headphones, and the figure behind the wheel of the jeep gave a brief wave. Then the vehicle that was harassing McCarter spun around the mound and braked to a halt. As the gunner in the passenger seat peppered McCarter's hiding place with 5.56 mm rounds, the driver shouted at Encizo's jeep. The little Cuban's M-16 appeared suddenly and swept the length of the merc vehicle with a full-auto blast of fire that tattered the tires and shattered the windows.

McCarter stepped out of cover and fired into the front seat, chopping through the spiderwebbed windshield and taking out the front passenger. There was still movement in the rear, and the Briton rushed close to the vehicle as the figure fell behind the front seats. He couldn't escape the Phoenix Force leader. There was no place for him to hide. McCarter emptied the rest of his magazine through the blurred side window until the glass was gone and the figures inside were lifeless.

Santa Fe, New Mexico

CLINT MAHONEY WAS STILL buttoning his shirt when he emerged from the stairway and grabbed the phone from

Colleen Davis. The woman's expression was quietly amused.

"Mr. Aya Endovik," she stated without emotion.

"Endovik? How did he contact us?"

"We haven't dismantled the secure number we used with Endovik," she stated evenly. "I haven't revealed to him that you're available. Shall I dismiss him?"

She was cold as a cuttlefish pulled out of the North Sea. Mahoney was constantly amazed that the warm and earnest people of Ireland could have produced a specimen of dispassion like Colleen Davis.

"He claims," she added, "that their Turkmen base is under attack."

Mahoney grabbed the phone out of her hand and nodded to the base unit. Davis punched the glowing membrane switch, and the LED display changed as he heard the connection go live in the receiver. Mahoney answered the line with the cover name he used with the CIS mercenaries. "Frank Merchant here."

"This is Endovik. What the hell kind of an operation are you running, Merchant? We've got a damn special forces group attacking us. You wouldn't believe the losses I'm taking here!"

"What kind of special forces?"

"A half-dozen guys maybe. They jumped in less than half an hour ago. They've disabled one of my choppers and completely destroyed the other. I've lost ground troops, too. The question is, how'd they find me? Answer me that!"

Mahoney felt cold anger. "Not because of leaks on my end."

"There were no mistakes at the Turkmen dam, Merchant. I assure you. This had to have come out of the U.S. Hold on!"

Turkmenistan

AYA ENDOVIK TURNED to the man at the radio who was gesturing to him urgently.

"Our men are not doing well out there," the radioman reported urgently. "At least one of the vehicles has been wiped out. I can't raise the other one. The third vehicle has a couple of the soldiers pinned down. They are awaiting orders."

Endovik shook his head and ground his teeth. "Tell them to get back now. We're pulling out. Do you hear me?" He stood and shouted to the others at the other side of the room, standing around nervously. "We're pulling out. Right now. Get it organized."

Endovik's lieutenants scrambled for the door as the mercenary leader shouted into the receiver. "Did you hear that, Merchant? I've lost more hardware and manpower in the last half an hour than in the eight years since I started this operation! Now I want to know what you are going to do about it?"

"I am not responsible for your losses, if that is what you're intimating," Mahoney said coolly, though his blood temperature was rising quickly. "What's the situation currently?"

"I've got four men in the field attempting to take them down," Endovik replied. "I'm going to pull them back in."

"Don't," Mahoney stated. "Instruct them to attempt to take their attackers into custody."

There was a moment of bewildered silence over the line. "Have you been listening to a word I've said, Merchant?" Endovik demanded. "These guys are deadly. Special forces. Well-equipped and highly motivated. My men can't combat a team like this."

"They can make the attempt," Mahoney said.

"Hold on!"

Endovik tossed the phone on the table and grabbed the mike set from his lieutenant, who was listening intently to the radio transmission coming from the jeep.

"Herik, what's your situation?"

"Taking fire as we retreat! We're trying to get out of range."

"Any chance you can double back on them and take them down?"

"We've hardly even spotted them. I can't even tell you how many there are. There's a hundred of these guys hiding in the bushes for all I know. They're scattered."

Endovik put the phone to his ear. "Merchant, they've got my men on the run."

"You, too?"

"I've survived in this business partly by knowing when not to take foolish risks."

Mahoney considered that, weighing his options and trying to restrain himself from giving in to his anger. He needed Aya Endovik to remain cooperative. Blowing up at him wouldn't achieve that aim. Playing on his greed would.

"I have a proposition for you, Endovik."

"I don't think I like the sound of it already."

"It would increase your fee by 150 percent."

There was silence on the line. Mahoney knew that would catch the Russian's attention. "Go ahead."

"I want to know who's behind this intrusion," Mahoney stated. "You take those men into custody and get me some answers, and you'll get that increased fee."

Endovik stood staring blankly at the radio unit, listening to the squeaks of voices still coming from the headset in his hand.

"I'm making no promises," he said by way of reply. "But I'll see what I can do."

HERIK YANKED the jeep into a wide, sweeping turn, putting distance between himself and the brushy rise that had erupted in a hail of fire, turning his windshield opaque and silencing the man in the seat directly behind him. There was a highly skilled special forces team on the ground. He was outgunned and he knew it. Suddenly he was on the run, intent on nothing except flight to safety.

He stomped on the accelerator and upshifted at dangerous speeds as he fishtailed through the brush. He'd left his attackers behind, but clearly there were others on the ground. They'd successfully taken out the other jeeps. He'd have to be ready for evasive maneuvers.

He never had the chance. When he spotted the soldier standing directly in his path, he knew he was dead. There was no way to turn off the path.

"Drive through him!" The mercenary at his side was also ex-Soviet army. A man good at his job. He aimed the Kalashnikov machine gun through the windshield, but he never had the chance to fire. The soldier's weapon triggered first.

Herik and his partner died instantly.

CALVIN JAMES FIRED the buckshot round from a distance of under twenty feet, then dived away from the careening jeep. The vehicle passed him with a roar, then tried to crawl up one of the embankments, fell onto its side and toppled onto its roof. James jumped out of the brush and pointed the business end of the M-16 into the passenger-side window as Hawkins came to his assistance, dropping to his knees and grabbing at the bodies. They hoisted them out of the vehicle roughly, before they could recover from the accident if they were still alive.

Only one of them was. The driver and front passenger had been obliterated by the savage buckshot round, the skin of their faces flayed. One of the men in the rear had caught a rifle shot in the neck. He'd been dead before the jeep flipped. The survivor was bleeding from three long slices along the left side of his face.

"Who's your boss?" James demanded, flipping the survivor onto his face in the sand and quickly handcuffing his wrists. The merc coughed and stuttered in Russian.

James grabbed him by the hair and lifted his head. "Who?"

"Aya Endovik," the man gasped.

"Who hired you to destroy the dams?"

The merc laughed, spitting blood. "I don't know that. You think they would tell me that?"

James hadn't thought they would, but there seemed no harm in trying.

McCarter's voice came through the headphones and Hawkins reported in. "We've just taken down the last vehicle, Phoenix One. We're questioning a prisoner."

"Rafe managed to apprehend one of those vehicles for himself. We'll be around to pick you up. See what you learn about the facility."

"Understood."

James nodded at the instructions, but noticed that his prisoner was now lying still, his forehead resting heavily against the earth. Playing possum, James assumed. But a pulse check told him the man wasn't acting.

"HE DIDN'T LAST LONG ENOUGH to offer up intelligence on the facility," James said apologetically when Encizo and McCarter arrived at the site of one of the chutes. It was the sat-link unit, and it had apparently survived the fall undamaged.

"How do you want to do this?" Encizo asked. "Tough to judge the reception we'll get based on the advance teams they sent out."

"Agreed. I don't want to open us up to surprises," McCarter said. "Rafe and I'll approach in the jeep. Cal, you and T.J. will come in on bikes. Rafe and I will allow you two enough time to circle their camp and come up from opposite directions. We'll see what we can see before charging in."

"We might have already wiped out the bulk of their manpower," Encizo suggested. "Otherwise I'd think they'd send out reinforcements."

McCarter nodded. "Dangerous to depend on that. Let's stay sharp."

CHAPTER ELEVEN

"Think we put the fear of God into them?" Encizo asked. Below them, two small convoys of ground-based vehicles were departing a ramshackle collection of buildings.

"I think they're trying to split us up so it's easier to take us down in small numbers," McCarter answered, checking his watch. Theoretically, their satellite uplink was going on-line.

The Phoenix Force warriors were outfitted in communications and cybernetics gear customized from the U.S. Army's Land Warrior program. Based on commercial communications, sensor and materials advances of the late 1990s, the Land Warrior system included an IHAS—Integrated Helmet Assembly Subsystem—using advanced materials for protection at lower weight, mounting a computer and sensor display for interface. That allowed Phoenix Force to view computer-generated graphics such as digital maps, intel and field personnel locations—all of which could be optimized and downloaded from Stony Man Farm via the sat-link.

Unlike Army soldiers, Phoenix Force packed in a single radio, allowing transmission among the entire team and with the Farm. When in Broadcast mode, transmissions could take place without hitting a transmit button.

Standard in the Land Warrior pack was a computer module and global positioning system—GPS—module. Most of the functions for the unit were enabled by a Remote Input Pointing Device, located on the pack's chest strap. Some operations were also enabled via switches near the hand, allowing for operation even while in a firing position. The frame of the equipment's backpack was configured of materials that allowed it to bend with the natural movement of the commando's body, for unparalleled field flexibility and maneuverability. Cables and antennae were constructed inside frame components, cutting down on snagging possibilities. Like the Land Warrior headgear, the body armor offered better ballistic protection without adding weight to the field package.

McCarter touched the transmit button on his hand control unit. "Stony Base."

"You have Stony Base," Kurtzman said.

McCarter quickly brought Kurtzman up to date on their situation. "You should be seeing six vehicles heading in opposite directions."

"Affirmative," Kurtzman said. "We're attempting to track their routes. You're going to have to give us some time on that."

"We're going in pursuit. Phoenix Four?"

"You've got Phoenix Four," James said.

"You're in position to take the northbound group," McCarter stated. "Remember, we need talkers."

"WE'RE ON IT." James spun the Kawasaki motorcycle in a standstill 180-degree turn and coasted down the hill above the compound, from which he had been monitoring the feverish activity below. It had been apparent upon their arrival that the mercenaries were beating a hasty retreat. It occurred to him that if they hadn't stopped to prep the two motorcycles they might have arrived in time to engage the mercenaries before they were in motion. But that line of thought was a waste of time, and he dismissed it.

Hawkins accelerated at his side, their pace leisurely as they evaluated the landscape ahead of them.

"They're going to be taking a dirt road that travels away from the hardsite and probably turn west or stay on a northward course," James said. "There's not much east of here. If the terrain cooperates, we can pace them and find a place to bring them to a halt."

Hawkins agreed and they accelerated in pursuit of the three military jeeps. All were so faded and rusted that their original camouflaged color could scarcely be ascertained, but the vehicles were roaring gutturally and making quick time along the twin trails of bare earth in the scratchy, dense growth of the Central Asian grasslands. The Phoenix Force commandos stood on the bikes when necessary to ease the travel over the irregular ground, and when they emerged out of the weeds onto the packed earth path a hundred yards behind the mercenaries, they found the travel little easier.

The commandos readied their M-16 combos, accelerating to bring the rear jeep into view as the road became unexpectedly straight over a half-mile distance.

The gunner in the rear jeep had been ready for the appearance of unfriendlies, and he yanked up a deck-mounted .50-caliber machine gun to target James and Hawkins.

Hawkins triggered his M-16 in a full-auto burst that cut up the rear of the jeep and slammed into the gunner, making him dance before the evasive swerve of the vehicle threw him into the road. Another backseat passen-

ger bounded behind the large machine gun without hesitation, ignoring the bursts that homed in on him from
James's and Hawkins's automatic weapons. The gunfire
failed to reach him before he triggered the big machine
gun.

"Let's git!" Hawkins shouted as a deadly torrent of
large-caliber rounds slammed into the dirt road, pushing
up divots. Hawkins twisted the wheel of his vehicle
savagely to the right and managed to catch an incline
that carried him onto a hillock that ended suddenly with
a four-foot cliff edge. Hawkins braced his body as he
sailed off it, rode out the impact with the earth, then
pulled away from the road, meandering the motorcycle
among the rises and grassy outcroppings, traveling
roughly parallel to the dirt track.

"Phoenix Four, this is really slowing me down," he
radioed to James, who had vanished.

"Me too," James replied. "But we can't risk getting
on the road again with that firepower pointed in our
direction."

Hawkins hit the gas when the way before him opened
up, sending his cycle rushing ahead with a burst of
speed. He spotted movement to the left, and saw the
last jeep appear between the irregular surface of the
land, then disappear again. Hawkins laid the M-16
A-2/M-203 across the handlebars and tried to maintain
his pace, watching the terrain as he waited for the jeep
to come into view again. When it did, he had less than
a second to make the shot. He triggered the assault rifle
in full-auto, scything across the gunner scrambling to
bring the machine gun into play. The enemy flopped
out of the jeep soundlessly and the vehicle bolted ahead.
There was at least one passenger still alive—one man
left to fire that machine gun.

If he could take out the passenger in the rear jeep, he and James would be able to get back onto the road again. The middle and front vehicles wouldn't be able to fire behind them without risk of hitting their own man. And the rear jeep would have no one left to fire that machine gun.

He twisted the bike to pull around a hump in the grassland, straightening fast when the rear tire skidded on the loose, dry soil. He released the gas and brought it into a sudden deceleration, contending with a series of moguls that rattled the lightweight bike. He accelerated again, feeling the hidden convoy slipping away from him and tightened his jaw as he sped up, doing his best to ignore the rattling in his bones and teeth. With a rush of satisfaction he heard the squeaking of brakes from the road to his left as the jeeps came to the end of their straightway and began meandering among the rises in the irregular grassland.

All but ignoring the possibility of sudden drop-offs or wall-like obstacles cropping up in his path, Hawkins sped alongside the convoy, a long, ten-foot-tall hillock separating him from the road. The rise ended abruptly and he found himself facing the rear jeep, its last surviving passenger making an alarmingly small adjustment to the .50-caliber machine gun to target the speeding bike. Hawkins had to make an instant decision. He braked the bike hard and triggered the M-16 A-2 simultaneously, without time to aim the weapon until he was firing, and he watched the jeep carry the machine gunner directly into the stream of his 5.56 mm rounds. The machine gunner saw his fate and dropped his weapon, raised his arms to protect himself from being carried into the stream, then tumbled backward out of the jeep as his torso was shattered by the automatic rifle fire, cracking his already lifeless skull on the packed earth.

Hawkins jerked the bike and accelerated, spinning through the gap onto the packed earth road. The driver of the last jeep was swerving as he tried to watch what was going on behind him and navigate the twists of the grasslands track at the same time. When he saw Hawkins emerge he froze, his head craned around almost a full 180 degrees. Suddenly he snapped forward again, and he yanked at the wheel to avoid running into a wall of earth. His jeep tried to crawl the barrier like a spider, failed to get a grip and somehow managed to power down the wall before flipping onto its roof. Bouncing violently, it swerved back onto the road.

Hawkins was already closing the gap, finding the open road a luxury. He tapped the transmit button on his chest.

"Phoenix Five calling Four."

"You have Four," James radioed back.

"I've depopulated the last vehicle. There's just a driver now. I'll use him as a shield while I try to pick off the others."

"I'm trying to overtake the leader, and it's not going well. This terrain is a bitch."

"I hear that."

"Don't go pushing them too hard, Phoenix Five. I need extra time to get in front."

JAMES PUSHED the engine on the motorcycle and shifted to a higher gear as he took advantage of his inertia to carry him to the top of a long, low hill and assess the situation below. He was a good hundred feet away from the road, with all kinds of outcroppings and dirt piles in the way, but he could see clouds of dust and glimpses of the racing vehicles. That glance had to be enough to determine their speed and position. Next he had to evaluate the terrain ahead of him—tricky business with all kinds of hidden places in the path where rocks, ruts and drop-offs might screw it up. He instantly determined the best pathway based on all available information and downshifted, revved the engine and pushed himself down the hill at increasingly velocity. The pathway was marked out in his head, and he followed it with blind precision, his active thought processes monitoring the landscape for nasty surprises.

A quick turn brought his front wheel down hard into a rut, and only his near-instant response saved the bike's front end from destruction. As soon as he saw the hole looming in front of him, he wrenched his body and the entire front end into the air, accelerating for extra push. His back and shoulder muscles screamed, but the front wheel missed crashing into the rut with disabling force, as the rear wheel thudded hard on the bottom of the hole and the front wheel crawled over the opposite lip. With another thrust of the accelerator, the motorcycle crawled out of it and sped for the road.

James knew he'd covered that distance at such reckless speed out of pure luck.

His luck didn't hold. The gunner in the front jeep had spotted him and was directing the .50-caliber machine gun across the road. When James's bike arced onto the packed earth path, the machine gun began to rattle ominously. James heard the powerful cracking of large rounds slamming into the dirt and the rocky walls. He steered back the way he had come and headed through a gap at top speed. Ahead of the jeep the road underwent a tight left turn. James knew there had to be a shortcut through the grassland and he found it, still moving fast and emerging onto an empty section of road a full ten seconds ahead of the jeep.

He braked hard, skidding the rear wheel on the sandy earth and coming to a stop facing the corner. The lead vehicle in the pack would appear very soon. James whipped the M-16 A-2/M-203 off his shoulder, thumbed an explosive round into the grenade launcher's breech, and fired it into the middle of the road as the jeep appeared. The round impacted where the vehicle would have been, but the driver had veered directly into the wall, saving the lives of his passengers.

While the jeep idled, its nose several feet up a steep hillock, James snatched a pair of CS grenades, pulled the pins and dropped the cans at his feet on the road, then spun the motorcycle in a circle and headed away from the convoy. Behind him the grenades exploded into billowing clouds of greasy smoke.

He had just purchased a few extra seconds of lead time.

Now what was he going to do with it?

Stony Man Farm, Virginia

THE WAR ROOM hummed with a life all its own. Every plasma and CRT display glowed with information coming in from around the world and above it.

"Satellite visual coming in on Phoenix Four," Akira Tokaido announced, evenly but urgently.

"Let's see it," Kurtzman commanded, although his eyes were locked on a monitor, evaluating field information from Phoenix Five's LW sensors and GPS.

"Here," Tokaido said. As Kurtzman's eyes wandered to a three-by-four-aspect-ratio screen it filled with the distorted satellite vision of the unbelievably uneven

Turkmen grasslands. They could see Calvin James, obviously on one of the motorcycles, speeding along the twin tire tracks of a dirt road.

"Pull back," Kurtzman said.

The image lifted away from James until the first of the three jeeps became visible on the screen, lurching after him and closing the quarter-mile distance between them.

"Bridge ahead," Tokaido declared, as the land a mile ahead of James suddenly opened up on the screen. Only a small, dark structure seemed to extend over it from the road.

Kurtzman stabbed the transmit button. "Phoenix Four this is Stony Base. There's a bridge ahead of you. Looks wooden to me. Maybe a good place to bring your pursuers to a halt."

"Don't know if I'll have the time to set up a roadblock, Stony Base," James said urgently. "They're coming up fast now. They're out for blood."

"Across the gully things get much flatter, Phoenix Four," Kurtzman cautioned. "This just might be your last opportunity to bring them to a halt."

"I'm going for it, Stony!" As he spoke the microphone picked up the distinctive rumble of machine-gun fire, and the feed from James went abruptly quiet.

"Phoenix Four, you there?"

"He's still up," Tokaido declared with a nod at the screen. James was putting the Kawasaki motorcycle to the test, taking it back and forth across the twin tire paths. But the satellite image didn't show him slowing or leaning the bike to the ground.

"Phoenix Four," Kurtzman asked urgently.

"He's going for the bridge," Tokaido said. A tiny

flash sparkled on the satellite image. "He's catching
autofire—"

"Cal!" Kurtzman demanded.

Turkmenistan

JAMES HEARD the sound of shattering stone just paces
behind the speeding motorcycle and danced to the left,
whipping right again to confuse the shooter. There was
nothing but line of sight between himself and his pursuers. But ahead of him was the structure of a wooden
bridge, thirty feet long over a chasm twenty or twenty-
five feet deep. He spotted the trestle on which it rested
in the middle of the expanse, made of old concrete. That
trestle wasn't going far no matter what he threw at it.

But the rest of the structure should disintegrate
nicely.

He whipped out another CS bomb, armed it and
tossed it over his shoulder when more machine-gun fire
homed in on him, listening with satisfaction to the braking of the jeep. But he heard it accelerate with grinding
gears almost instantly, directly into the oily smoke
cloud. The CS bought him less than five seconds.

Behind him the smoke yielded to the lead jeep, and
as soon as the cloud was left behind the machine gunner
trained the powerful weapon on his prey and fired another long, deadly blast.

James yanked out the M-16 A-2/M-203 while accelerating, thumbing a high-explosive round into the grenade launcher as the ground underneath the bike transformed to rough wooden planks that made a loud,
clanking noise. The wooden rail a foot to his left started
exploding into splinters, and James knew he'd be hit.
He swerved anyway, hard and fast, then felt the impact

of the .50-caliber round slam into his shoulder. The Land Warrior body armor stopped it, but the hit tossed him off balance and the quick movement he was attempting to compensate for proved too much for him. The motorcycle flipped sideways, and James hit the ground on the opposite side of the bridge, tucking the automatic rifle against his body and struggling to control the roll.

Stony Man Farm, Virginia

"PHOENIX FIVE, this is Stony Base!" Kurtzman shouted.

"You've got Five, Stony," Hawkins returned.

"Phoenix Four just went down hard," Kurtzman said, trying to peer deep into the grainy satellite digital-video feed.

"I'm coming into sight now, Stony. I'm about a half mile back, but I see the bridge. They're almost on him, Stony!"

"Can you get to him?" Kurtzman demanded.

"That's a negative, Stony—wait! Phoenix Four is up!"

"Say again?" Kurtzman glared at his display, praying it was true.

Turkmenistan

JAMES STAGGERED to his feet with the amazing realization that none of his limbs were dangling uselessly, and he tucked the M-16 A-2/M-203 hard against his battered torso, bruising his ribs. At this point, with his entire body feeling shattered, what was a little more pain? And he needed all the control he could muster to operate the thing. Through shock-blurred vision he saw the jeep coming at him, as big as a looming monster, just a couple of car lengths between it and the bridge. James triggered the M-203. As the standing figure in the rear of the jeep triggered the .50-caliber gun, the 40 mm high-explosive egg cracked open against the rear of the bridge.

James struggled to sharpen his cognitive ability. The jeep was screeching to a halt on the bridge, and it came to a stop within a few paces of the Phoenix Force commando, the off-balance gunner struggling to drag himself back into a standing position. From that proximity there was no way the terrorist would miss. The massive rounds would rip through James like a butcher's hacksaw through a side of beef.

He willed his feet to move, tracking sideways as he thumbed another HE into the breech, knowing he wouldn't have time to use it or get to cover before the machine gun commenced firing.

Then the bridge lurched and the machine gunner flung his hand in the air, flopping out of the rear of the jeep. The driver shouted maniacally and slammed the vehicle into gear. James saw what was happening. The bridge was now supported just on the one end. Where the explosive had hit, all structural integrity was gone, and the weight of the vehicle was tearing the supports on the good side away from the cliff. The surface descended a couple of feet with a crunch of breaking wood, then hung there.

The driver reversed, his passengers shouting at him, and as the front end of the bridge began to fall away from the cliff edge, he managed to reach the middle of the wooden structure, over the concrete trestle. The teetering of the wooden bridge stabilized.

The men sat in the jeep, afraid to move for fear of upsetting the balance.

James triggered the M-203 and watched the grenade impact on the bridge at the nose of the jeep. He heard the men shouting in terror as the blackened, smoking vehicle was pushed backward. As soon as the vehicle was off the trestle, the bridge tipped backward and the jeep plummeted into the chasm, slamming first against the cliff wall, then hitting the jagged, rocky surface below with a stupendous crash of metal and wood.

At the sound of a pair of shots from a handgun across the chasm, James ducked away from the edge and found a small rise in the land. He lay on his stomach, relishing the moment of rest to allow himself to come to terms with the physical battering he'd just received and looking for activity through the haze of smoke and dust.

The second jeep was stopped at the lip of the chasm, and the driver, fisting a 9 mm pistol, stood peering into the depths at the ruin, then back over the expanse to the other side, looking for James in vain. Behind him the third jeep was braking to a halt.

They exchanged quick shouts, then turned simultaneously as a rider on a motorcycle rumbled onto the road and laid on the trigger of an automatic rifle.

James snatched at his chest transmit button, ignoring the talk in his speakers. "Phoenix Five, this is Four. Get out of there, friend—they're cornered rats."

HAWKINS TOOK in the scene even as he received James's warning. The chasm was empty where the bridge should have been, and the first jeep was gone. The survivors had no way of escape except through him. Already the driver of the rear vehicle and the machine gunner in the second vehicle were scrambling to train weapons his way.

Hawkins shouldered the M-16 as he scanned for a way off the road, and saw none. Braking hard, he spun the motorcycle, vomiting dirt from the rear tire. The banging of a 9 mm handgun followed him as he pushed away and headed for the gap he had entered the road by. He felt the painful thump as one of the rounds slammed square into the middle of his back, stopped by his LW body armor. A fraction of a second later he heard the throaty roar of the machine gun start up and he spun wildly to the left, accelerated and spun back to the right, listening to the impact of the rounds as they nipped at the rear wheel of the bike. Then he reached his entry point and passed behind an earthen rise.

Hawkins slowed and circled, rustling in his pack for a plastique-and-detonator set while tapping at the transmit button on his helmet.

"Phoenix Four, what do you see going on from your vantage point?"

"They're still getting their act together. Wait—they're on the move, heading at you."

"I'll be ready for them."

"You're on your own. No way I can reach you, buddy."

"Understood. I can handle it. Are they sticking to the road?"

"So far."

Hawkins stomped on the kickstand and swung off the motorcycle, running for the rise and dropping on all fours as he reached the top and peered around the large boulder that rested on top of it. He evaluated the speed of the approaching jeeps, tucked the plastique behind the boulder and flipped on the detonator. He headed back for the bike on the run, jumping on it with enough force to push it off the stand. As the countdown in his head reached zero, he pulled away from the rise and thumbed the detonate button on the transmitter.

The boulder exploded like a volcanic mountaintop succumbing to the intense pressure of expanding magma, blasting the roadway with shards of rock traveling at asteroidlike speeds. Rocks slammed into the jeep at the front of the line, crashing into the body panels, destroying the glass and cracking open the driver's face, skull and flesh. His mangled body was tossed aside and the jeep spun sideways, lifting up on its side then tumbling upside down on the track.

Hawkins hunched over the handlebars of the motorcycle as the blast rocked the barren Turkmen landscape, wincing at the rattle of small stone and soil debris striking his body. Something hard thumped against his helmet.

Stony Man Farm, Virginia

AARON KURTZMAN DIRECTED the blurry digital image into the chasm that cut the track in two. The spy satellite was able to feed him low-resolution images at a frame rate of five per second, producing a jerky and sometimes confusing semblance of video motion. He was back in touch with James, and his relief was almost tangible.

"Can you get down into that chasm, Phoenix Four? We could use a photo of the occupants of that jeep."

"Affirmative," James answered.

With a clattering of fingers on the terminal, Kurtzman sped the satellite image cross-country, backtracking on the dirt road until he had a view of the jeeps from directly overhead.

"Phoenix Five—"

The image on the screen blurred, and when it cleared again one of the jeeps was sitting sideways in the road. It hung there for a couple of frames before flopping upside down on the road. The other jeep pulled to a halt within a few feet of the disabled vehicle, pausing as if indecisive. Without sound, the scene was eerily peaceful. Then the figures began jumping out of the jeeps in jerks and spurts of motion.

"Phoenix Five, this is Stony Base."

"Phoenix Five here. I just blew the hell out of something."

"You did yourself more harm than good," Kurtzman said. "You blocked the road on them. They're coming after you on foot. I count five of them."

"What's Cal's status?"

"He won't reach you for a while. David and Rafael are still chasing down the others. You'll have to consider yourself independent for the time being."

Akira Tokaido was watching a high-resolution digital image of a corpse's face scroll across his computer screen, nodding his head as if in time to some sort of music only he could hear—although the minidisk player hanging from his belt was, at the moment, turned off. He moved the mouse to grab the image.

"Coming your way, Carmen," he stated.

Across the room Carmen Delahunt nodded her head and intercepted the image as it flew onto her computer screen, like a shortstop snatching a lazy fly ball out of the air, and quickly initiated a series of search operations using software developed by herself and others on the Stony Man Farm cybernetics team.

Once a year the world's top hackers assembled for a convention in California, at which time they typically held a roundtable discussion to alert and advise world security experts about flaws in their safeguard electronic systems. Speaking under the cover of their on-line code names, the hackers were invariably two steps ahead of even the global security systems—a fact that never failed to make headlines.

One of the savants in the global hacker hierarchy was a secretive figure code-named Gregor, an acknowledged front-runner in security bypass strategy. His input had spurred high-level efforts to beef up Pentagon and other defense department electronic firewalls—and resulted in job offers from more government agencies than he could count.

He turned down all the offers. Those agencies didn't realize Gregor—alias Akira Tokaido—already had a government job of sorts.

Tokaido's software, manipulated by Carmen Delahunt, ripped mercilessly and automatically through safeguards, firewalls and security procedures of various international and American law enforcement and intelligence agencies, scanning for faces that matched those of her dead man. Due to the nature and geographic location of the operation, she was starting with Interpol, MI-6 and GSG-9 databases—those most likely to include Russians and Central Asians. As results began to feed into the terminal from the initial image, she assembled a report.

Across the room, Aaron Kurtzman could do little at the moment except watch. He seriously disliked having Phoenix Force in such a fragmented state. It unnerved him to realize Hawkins was maneuvering around the Turkmen landscape with five highly trained, highly motivated soldiers gunning for him. The bike would give him only so much of an advantage.

And now the motorcycle, according to the satellite image, had come once again to a stop.

"Talk to me, Phoenix Five."

"I've parked it, Stony Base. They're pissed off and acting rash, and I think I can take down one or two while they're in the open."

Turkmenistan

HAWKINS PULLED the motorcycle behind a mass of dense grassland brush and watched across the small open plain of ground-hugging grass for the arrival of what amounted to a small army. His last glimpse showed them in dogged pursuit.

The first mercenary jogged into the open with a companion close behind him, both realizing abruptly how precarious their position was. Too late for them. Hawkins triggered a pair of 5.56 mm rounds from the M-16 A-2, which punched the rear mercenary into a soundless heap on the scrubby grass. His companion reacted to the sound of the shots by retreating, without realizing his comrade was dead. He broke into a run after almost tripping over the corpse before Hawkins's second pair of shots cracked him in the small of the back and slammed him on his face.

When Hawkins's cover suddenly began to disintegrate, he cranked the gas and spun the motorcycle away from the gunfire. Three more mercenaries out there were tracking him, and he couldn't expect any assistance anytime soon.

How was he going to take them out?

CHAPTER TWELVE

"You want me to run away like a scared cowpoke?" Hawkins asked incredulously.

"I want you to save your ass to fight another day," Kurtzman stated over the airway in a voice that invited no argument.

Listening in, Calvin James couldn't help but grin. Even smiling, he discovered, was painful. He flung the hook over his head, producing a jolt of electricity in his shoulder where the machine-gun round had slammed into the bullet-resistant jacket. He was going to have a hell of a bruise flowering there. Above him the hook imbedded into the wood stump was all that remained of the bridge support, hitting at almost precisely the spot he'd been aiming for, and with a quick tug it was imbedded. He had taken the photos Stony wanted of the pair of dead men in the smashed jeep—although he seriously doubted they'd be able to ID what was left of the driver—and now was making his way back up to the track on the opposite side. Maybe he'd get there in time to actually do some good for the irate Hawkins.

He rode out the pain as he yanked himself hand-over-hand up the side of the twenty-five-foot wall and peered over the top, finding himself alone. The physical effort was actually doing him good, working out the unimportant, distracting aches. The shoulder throb wasn't receding, but he could live with it.

James clambered to the surface and started a quick trot after the three surviving hardmen.

HAWKINS BRAKED HARD at the end of the canyon. It was a dead end. As he cranked the motorcycle in a 180-degree turn, he stopped short, dropped the bike on its side with the engine still running and grabbed at a piece of vinyl support behind the seat where extra supplies could be tied down. He ripped off its screws with a heave, and Hawkins quickly jogged behind a small pile of fallen earth, laying the scrap of plastic where it was almost out of sight.

Speeding on foot to the mouth of the canyon, he circled around it until he was out of sight of the approaching gunmen. They were still on his trail, vivid on the small display screen of his Land Warrior headgear as three small blue triangles amid the chaos of the landscape. A single orange triangle indicated himself, and as he pumped up the incline that would carry him to a canyon overlook, he thumbed the chest control to expand the perspective of his LW display. The appearance of the second orange triangle at the edge of the screen was reassuring.

"Phoenix Four, this is Five. I've got your icon on screen."

"Phoenix Five, I'm seeing you too. What's going on?"

Hawkins was certain the gunmen on foot weren't tuning into their conversation. "The trap is set, Four. I planted a fake wreck in a confined space."

"Stony Base here," Kurtzman broke in. "Think

they'll fall for it?'' Kurtzman had the scenario on-screen and read Hawkins's intentions.

"No matter how they react it will probably involve splitting up to investigate," Hawkins said. "If I get very lucky, they'll be unfamiliar with the terrain and they'll all enter the canyon. I'll have three steers in a corral."

"If you are very unlucky they'll see through the ploy or they'll know the terrain," Kurtzman reminded him. "They'll all home in on your actual location."

"Roger that, Stony Base."

"Five, this is Four. I lost my horse but I might get there in time to lend a hand in the cattle drive."

"I'd be much obliged."

ENCIZO'S PALM SLAMMED into the steering wheel. "We should've taken the bikes!" he exclaimed, exasperated with himself.

They'd soon discovered the rearmost of three jeeps ahead of them was armed with a deck-mounted .50-caliber machine gun with a competent gunman behind it. It was very effectively keeping the Phoenix Force duo from closing in.

"Any advice, Stony Base?" McCarter asked.

"We're looking into it," Barbara Price answered. "There might be an opportunity coming up in about a mile."

"Explain, Stony Base."

"There's a hairpin in the road. We're trying to evaluate the details. Looks like there's a sharp decline, then a 180-degree hairpin, and finally more decline. If you can overcome some distance while the jeeps are on the curve, you'll be able to fire down on them a lot better than they'll be able to fire back."

"An effective way to use the terrain against them," McCarter stated.

"T.J.'s been making use of the local geology," Price added. "Maybe a small avalanche would be useful for you as well."

Encizo's foot slammed onto the accelerator.

"We'll see what we can do," he replied to Stony Base.

HAWKINS FOUND a spot overhanging the canyon floor that looked down on the turn. This was the point where the hardmen would see that the canyon came to a dead end. It would also be the spot where they would see the staged wreckage.

He alternated watching the mouth of the canyon and the images on the LW display. Extensive experience with the combat units and the earlier SIPE technology hadn't convinced him of their one-hundred-percent reliability. There was no electronic technology that could replace human observation. But the encroaching blue triangles turned into human beings at precisely the moment he'd judged they would. Hunkered down against the rock, he watched the three gunners slow in hesitation as they came to the canyon mouth. The rumble of the idling motorcycle reached their ears.

They decided on a leapfrog approach, and Hawkins couldn't have been happier as they went in, one after another, covering each other for brief spurts of movement through the canyon.

"I'm on the move, Stony Base. Keep me informed." Hawkins spoke in a low voice and crept away from the edge of the overlook silently, cringing against the crunch of dry earth under his feet. Catfooting to ground level, he started around to the mouth of the canyon.

"One of them has reached a sharp turn in the direction of the canyon," said Price's reassuring voice.

"The others?"

"Standing by. Standing by. Okay, the rear man is on the move, moving deeper into the canyon. He's with the front man now. Number three is holding back."

"His distance to the mouth of the canyon, Stony Base?"

"Eleven meters, Phoenix Four." Her presence in his head was strong, but soft, almost intimate.

"Keep me informed."

Choosing a buckshot round for the M-203, Hawkins also fisted a CS grenade as he moved stealthily toward the canyon opening.

"Movement," Price stated at the same time he spotted it with the peripheral vision of his display. "One of the front men is going in deeper. Number Two is staying put..." Her tone became suddenly urgent. "Three is retreating out of the canyon."

Hawkins saw it and reacted by stepping into the open at the mouth of the canyon with the M-16/M-203 leveled. He triggered the grenade launcher directly at the surprised hardman, who never had a chance to use the weapon at his side. The blast from the grenade launcher, transformed by the buckshot round into a high-power shotgun, was unbelievably destructive and instantly lethal. The nearest man disintegrated and from deeper in the canyon came a cry of pain as the second hardman took his share of flesh-shredding buckshot. Hawkins had pulled back from sight before the sound of the blast had dissipated, slamming the CS grenade into the grenade launcher. He stepped into the open again, already firing, depositing the smoke grenade on top of the ruin of blood and gore that had been his first victim. The brief glimpse he got before pulling himself into cover again showed him one man slumped in a bloody crouch and another figure peering around the bend into the canyon, agape at the horror.

Hawkins was wary but satisfied as the CS popped and the canyon filled with smoke. Two hardmen were alive and trapped, virtually helpless.

"Come out with your hands in the air!"

He heard the sounds of grunting and sobbing, and the wounded man staggered out of the canyon, weak from pain and blood loss, and coughing against the gas. His eyes were squeezed shut, and he went down hard when his foot hit a rock.

"Come toward me," Hawkins ordered.

"I'm dying!" The accent was Russian.

"Doesn't look like it to me. Unless I have to put a bullet in you myself."

The bloodied figure managed to creep in Hawkins's direction, trying to force his eyes open against the stinging effect of the gas.

"Stop. Hands behind your back."

Hawkins stooped and put plastic handcuffs on the man without taking his eyes off the canyon entrance, where wisps of smoke were now escaping.

"Come out!" he commanded loudly.

"Stony here," Price said. "He's retreated to the rear of the canyon."

"Can you use a hand?" The owner of the breathless voice was Calvin James, jogging into view at a distance and on the other side of the canyon mouth.

Hawkins knew James had just put in a hard couple of miles of full-gear running. "Stay put and I'll drive the last straggler right to you."

"Understood."

Hawkins was breathing hard himself by the time he'd climbed the incline to the canyon overlook. He wasn't trying to stay quiet now, and the gunner heard his approach, firing a barrage over the lip of the canyon before the Phoenix Force commando was in view. Hawkins popped in another CS grenade and stood only high enough to see the wall over the head of the last hardman.

When the second CS popped, the billowing gas sent the last hardman scurrying blindly through the canyon, falling heavily as he emerged from the heaviest smoke. Hawkins stitched the ground around him with M-16 fire.

The terrorist rose to his feet, coughing, unable to open his eyes, finally dropping his Kalashnikov rifle and pulling a handgun out of his belt, allowing it to clatter on the packed, hard earth. He staggered toward the mouth of the canyon with his hands in the air.

"Phoenix Four," Hawkins transmitted, "one mighty humble heifer coming your way, pardner."

"LET'S MOVE IN TIGHT. I'm going to hurry those bastards up," McCarter explained. "I don't want that arsehole in the rear to think about slowing down to cover his mates during the hairpin."

"Understood," Encizo said. As they came out of a short twist, he stomped on the gas. McCarter rode out the burst of speed as he was getting to his feet, leveling the M-16 A-2/M-203 on top of the windshield frame and aiming high, firing a wicked barrage. The driver of the closest jeep scrambled for cover and even the machine-gun operator dodged. The gunner quickly came to terms with the fact that the fire wasn't reaching them at their extended range and repositioned himself behind the weapon, but he had to hold on to ride out the swerv-

ing of the vehicle. The driver was running scared and
closing in fast on the next jeep.

The earth fell away to the right-hand side of the fleeing vehicles, and the road went into a decline. The pathway was narrow and steep, and had clearly been blasted
out of the side of a cliff. McCarter shouted wordlessly
as the obvious ploy materialized before them.

"It'll be like dropping water balloons out of an apart-
ment-building window," he shouted.

"Except the people on the sidewalk don't shoot
back," Encizo answered, bringing the jeep to a squeaking halt.

"Depends on your neighborhood."

The convoy of jeeps had entered the hairpin turn and
slowed to a crawl. McCarter could see why. The surface
was uneven and so narrow it barely accommodated the
wheelbase of the vehicles. The road was without a
shoulder, and a small twist of the wheel would send
them into oblivion.

"They've got a clue," Encizo said. He'd spotted a
sudden flurry of movement in the last jeep in line, which
suddenly backed up out of the curve, bringing the machine gun level with the Phoenix Force warriors.

"Get cover!" McCarter commanded.

"I'm going to bring it down on top of them." The
Cuban-born commando ran in the direction of the rear
jeep in what appeared to be a suicide charge. The gunner lined up the large-caliber weapon, unfazed by the
irrational behavior of his victim, and fired as Encizo
made a wild dive for cover. He reached his destination,
a man-sized thumb of rock protruding from the cliff
wall at the side of the road, as the .50-caliber rounds
pockmarked the ground and homed in on him. McCarter
was ducking low in the passenger seat and peered over
the dashboard. Encizo was in position but trapped while

the machine gunner was watching for him. Time to take the gunner's attention. McCarter stood, stepped out of the military vehicle and retreated to the rear, moving slowly and steadily until the machine gun was targeting him. Only then did he jump to cover behind the vehicle. A second later a deadly barrage of rounds clanked and whined off the bodywork and engine block.

Encizo had made a good approach, but he was still pushing the range of the M-16. He'd just have to make the best of it. His and McCarter's effectiveness was severely compromised until that machine gun was out of commission.

The little Cuban stepped around the thumb of rock and targeted the gunner, aiming high to account for a significant drop, and triggered a long full-auto burst. The machine gunner spotted him in an instant. Encizo tried to ignore him, instead straining to see the results of his gunfire. As the machine gunner twisted his deck-mounted weapon into target acquisition, Encizo spotted tiny clouds of flying dust and debris made by his M-16's rounds. He was still firing too low. He adjusted his aim and swept another six or eight rounds in a diagonal swathe across the rear of the jeep—he hoped. Then he withdrew to safety before he could see the results.

The expected machine gun fire never came, and when Encizo looked again the machine gunner had collapsed onto the road, wriggling like a half-squashed insect. Another man was scrambling for the machine gun, but it would take him precious seconds to get there. Encizo charged.

He raced down the middle of the rough trail as he loaded an HE round into the M-203 and targeted the rock wall over the jeep. The would-be machine gunner had a stroke of bad luck. He stood in the deck of the jeep as the deadly egg sailed within inches of his head and hit the stone at his shoulder. The explosion shredded his body viciously, obliterating the machine gun, cracking the jeep into pieces and generating a hail of rock that turned into a cascade of boulders and masses of packed earth. The jeep and its occupants were buried in seconds.

MCCARTER WATCHED the destruction of the jeep and jumped into the open, running to the edge of the road. The simple strategy became more complicated. They couldn't simply fire down on the rest of the jeep convoy due to an overhang. They couldn't see the road from where they were.

"No clear shots back there," he shouted to Encizo as he raced toward him.

Encizo was a few hundred feet closer to the hairpin, and when he stepped to the edge found he had a clear shot of the jeeps, which were now heading down the second incline. He thumbed another HE round into the breech of the M-203 and lined up a tricky shot. He had to place the explosive directly on top of or in front of the lead jeep to bring them all to a halt. He breathed and fired the round. Simultaneously there was a rattle of autofire and the lead jeep leapt forward with a burst of speed. The grenade missed the vehicle and impacted where it had previously been, blasting a fresh crater in the pockmarked path. The second jeep's front end lifted off the ground and skidded sideways, the driver leaning lifelessly onto the steering wheel. The passenger was screaming and clawing at his face as gravity took a firm hold on the vehicle and dragged it over the edge. Two figures in the back cried out as they were flung out of their seats into the open nothingness. The sounds of a crash rolled up the cliffside seconds later.

Two vehicles remained, and the middle one plowed through the new crater recklessly, grinding its underside against freshly exposed rock and bouncing out on the other side. Two men in the rear crouched on their knees, triggering blast after blast of defensive fire at their enemies above.

Encizo couldn't get near the edge in the face of the wild gunfire. He was as good as out of commission. McCarter couldn't see the fleeing vehicles and gambled on one last, desperate attempt to stop them.

"Fire in the hole!" he shouted to Encizo as he backed away from the overhang that blocked his view below and tossed an HE grenade onto the rock shelf. He jogged away and counted down mentally.

He fell on his face and covered his head as the countdown reached *one*.

He was probably just wasting explosives, and he knew it.

The blast felt like a thump in the rock underneath his body, and the air was filled with flying sand. When it settled McCarter was on his feet again, running to the newly trimmed overhang.

A great, one-ton chunk of rock had separated from the cliff at the Briton's feet and tumbled onto the road below, but it had been too late. The final pair of jeeps had passed beneath it with what had to have been seconds to spare. They had reached the bottom of the steep incline at the level ground and were pulling away onto a barely distinct trail that disappeared into the Turkmen steppes. They were already out of weapons range, and by the time Encizo had come wearily to McCarter's side they watched the jeep disappear from sight. Escaped.

"Stony Base, come in. This is Phoenix One."

"Stony Base here."

"We got zilch, Stony—"

"Hold on, Phoenix, hold on!"

Encizo looked at McCarter. Carmen Delahunt's voice had an odd ring to it.

They stood amid the chaos and death of their own making, on the side of a cliff in the middle of the Central Asian wasteland, and listened to nothingness on their radios.

"Phoenix One, this is Five."

"One here," McCarter answered brusquely. "Everything okay?"

"Phoenix One, this is Phoenix Four," broke in James. "Everything's good on our end. T.J. and I have a couple of locals in custody. But something's up at Stony Base."

"Like what?"

"We're clueless. I was hoping you'd know."

"Stony Base?" McCarter probed.

"Hold on, Phoenix!" Delahunt repeated urgently.

CHAPTER THIRTEEN

Stony Man Farm, Virginia

At the moment the call came through the line to Aaron Kurtzman, his eyes scanned the identification window at the bottom of his monitor and he froze.

It had been longer than he could remember that something shocked him so completely he was unable to move or act. But for five long seconds he did nothing but stare at the small display at the bottom of his screen, his mind churning.

Then he shook off the shock. He had men in the field. Phoenix was on the ground in Central Asia and in need of constant support. He simply couldn't afford to pay attention to the little window in the bottom corner of his computer screen.

Stony Man Farm mission controller Barbara Price had just disengaged communications with Phoenix Five, who had his situation under control. "Barb!"

Price looked at Aaron strangely, reading an unusual quality to his voice. A sort of suppressed amazement. "What's up, Aaron?"

"I'm transferring a call to you. I'm not free to take it."

Price assumed she was going to get Brognola on the

line—who else would the Communications Room have patched through to her during a mission? She heard the click in her headset as the call connected to her line. "This is Price."

"Striker, here."

Time abruptly halted. It was as if, for a fraction of a second, Barbara Price was in some other dimension.

"Mack?"

"Hope you didn't deal me out. I've still got cards to play."

"Thank god in heaven. We thought you were dead."

"I've felt better."

"You're hurt? Where are you?"

"Peru. Somewhere. A village by the name of Padilla. I'm on the only phone in the entire village."

"Answer my first question—are you injured?"

"I've got a hell of a headache. Probably a medium-sized concussion. More cuts and scrapes than I can count. Other than that I'm okay. All the limbs are working when I tell them to. I was dragged out of the river by a local and apparently I had a high fever for twenty-four hours." He paused. "I'm right in assuming it has been less than two days since the Bedoya Dam was blown?"

"Yes. Mack, this is incredible. I'm not kidding—we thought you were dead and gone."

"I'm not dead yet," Bolan said flatly. "I need a chopper in the Andes for my extraction. When we get a secure uplink you can tell me how we stand."

"I'll tell you we've got Phoenix and Able in the field now, trying to track down the parties behind Bedoya Dam—and the others."

"There's been other dams blown?"

"San Diego and southwestern Turkmenistan."

Silence.

"I'm not surprised. What's the situation in Lima?"

"Grim," Price said. "People have to have water so they're using what they have, clean or not. The cholera death toll is climbing by the hour and as it incubates it's going to get much worse before it gets any better."

"How close are you to fingering the perpetrator?"

"Phoenix is on the ground in Turkmenistan now, trying to round up the responsible parties. Able's tagged the doers in San Diego and Peru, but they were strictly hired help. If you've got intel that will take us to the brains behind these outfits, we'd sure like to know it."

"I do," Bolan declared succinctly. "Get me on a good line and I'll give you everything I've got. Where's Able now?"

"At least eight hundred miles away from your current position. They took out a merc base off an Amazon tributary in Brazil, and they're getting air transportation to a U.S. Navy destroyer currently cruising north of Chimbote. Gary's there under a doctor's care. You aren't the only one who's been knocked on the head in the past few days."

Bolan was going to question why Manning was on-site in South America, but that was an unimportant question that would be answered in time. "Get me on the same ship," Bolan said. "Gary can help bring me up to speed. We'll conference from there."

"Agreed. I've pinpointed your location," Price said as the screen in front of her located and displayed the Peruvian terrain. The village was a tiny dot hugging the foothills of the Andes. "I'll charter a helicopter out of Huánuco as soon as we hang up. Not terribly secure, but it's the quickest solution. I'll give the pilot coordinates for the U.S.S. *Roosevelt* and start working on landing clearances. I'll need to call in some favors with the Navy.''

"Fine."

"Mack," Barbara Price said, her voice suddenly soft, "it's good to hear your voice."

"Barbara, it's good to be heard."

Peru

MACK BOLAN PUSHED several U.S. twenty-dollar bills over the counter. The Padilla shopkeeper grinned widely.

"I could use some food."

The shopkeeper kept grinning. Bolan tried Spanish and got a better response. The shopkeeper ushered him to a table and brought out a half loaf of crusty bread and a beer, followed fifteen minutes later by steaming hunks of meat in gravy.

Bolan didn't like being in waiting mode, but there wasn't much he could do about it. Until he was briefed, until he had shared his information with the team at Stony Man Farm, until he had access to replacement hardware, ammunition and, most importantly, transportation, there was simply nothing more he could do.

He'd just have to sit and wait. The meat was gamy and tough, but tasty enough. The bottle of beer was cold and quenching.

The people of Padilla were lucky, the soldier considered. Their village was close to clean mountain streams. Not far away, in the sprawling metropolis of Lima, people as poor as these villagers wouldn't have easy access to clean water. So they drank whatever water they had.

Bolan had witnessed the quiet agony of poverty-stricken Third World children dying of cholera. In Southeast Asia he had seen it. In Africa.

Now in Peru. How many hundreds? Or was it already in the thousands?

Someone out there was directly responsible for those deaths and was guilty of mass murder. With every Liman child who died, the murderer's guilt compounded.

It wasn't a crime that could be allowed to go unavenged.

Stony Man Farm, Virginia

AT THE MOMENT Phoenix Force's combat situation came to an end, with the escape of the final two jeeps, Aaron Kurtzman turned to Barbara Price, still locked in conversation with whomever it was who had called on a line that had been assigned to Mack Bolan.

Carmen Delahunt had also been on-line with Phoenix Force when she saw his strange expression and saw him looking at Price.

"Aaron...?"

"Shh!"

The vivacious redhead turned to Price for a clue. The mission controller was the strongest, most in-control woman Delahunt knew, but at the moment she had moisture welling up in her eyes as she spoke into her headset.

Something had to have happened to one of the men in Able Team, although Delahunt hadn't even known them to be in combat at the moment.

McCarter, somewhere on the other side of the planet, was reporting on the poor results of their probe and his words were harsh in her ears.

"Hold on, Phoenix, hold on!" Delahunt said into her mike.

And what was up with Tokaido? The hacker had been watching Price himself; then Delahunt saw him start nodding and smiling, turning back to his keyboard with an uncharacteristic ear-to-ear grin. What had he figured out that she hadn't?

Then Price said something like, "Good to hear from you."

Good to hear from who?

"Stony Base?" asked the voice of Phoenix Force commander McCarter.

"Hold on, Phoenix!" Delahunt repeated.

Price disconnected her call, and an easy smile of intense relief welled up on her beautiful face.

"Mack," she announced simply, "is alive."

U.S.S. Roosevelt, *Atlantic Ocean,*
225 miles northwest of Lima, Peru

CAPTAIN LEON POLLIN STOMPED onto the bridge of the U.S.S. *Roosevelt*, still trying to suck bits of white bread from a tuna-fish sandwich out of his teeth. An uncomfortable sailor was following in his wake, totally unable to decide what he should do next. Asking the captain was out of the question.

Pollin halted inside his bridge so abruptly that the coffee in his white mug sloshed over the edge and dribbled on his shoes. He didn't notice. All he saw was a bridge devoid of a first mate.

"Wurtman!"

Wurtman stepped out of one of the communications cubicles at the rear of the bridge. "Here, sir."

"Let me see this damn fool communiqué!"

"Yes, sir."

Pollin was as hard-nosed and hard-assed as they came in the U.S. Navy, an attitude born of a sudden revelation that occurred on the streets of St. Louis when he was just seventeen years old and hiding in an alley. He'd just seen his best friend killed when one of their drug deals went bad. He'd missed death himself by inches. If the stranger they had just ran into had ever practiced with the revolver he'd pointed at them from just ten feet, he never would have missed either of them.

That moment of clarity revealed to Pollin that he was a worthless street hood. Unless he changed, he would get that bullet, sooner or later. It was inevitable.

But he had already dropped out of school and was unemployed. His options were few. He joined the Navy and, determined to make it work, got a formal education.

Make it work he did, with a lot of sweat and a lot of learning. Not too many years later, he was one of the youngest black U.S. Navy captains. He'd earned his position of respect and power. He didn't like people taking advantage of him.

At the moment, somebody was trying to do just that.

Be prepared to receive civilian helicopter and passenger in need of medical attention. Arriving approximately 1900 hours. Orders verifying this request coming via regular channels.

"Who sent this?" Pollin demanded.

"Unknown, sir," his second in command admitted, showing no fear. He'd worked with Pollin for months and knew the ropes.

"Unknown? Is this ship in the habit of taking orders from any fool who broadcasts on our frequency?"

"It came through a secure messaging system, although without identification, Captain."

"So how do you know it's legit?"

"I don't, sir. That's why I had it brought to your attention."

"We're not a hospital ship!" Pollin exploded. "Who the hell do these people think they are?"

"Captain, we've got a small aircraft approaching on radar," interrupted one of the bridge personnel. "Moving too slow for fixed-wing. Probably that chopper."

"They calling in?"

"Not yet, sir."

"When they do, tell them they aren't landing."

"The pilot says he's short on fuel, sir."

Pollin watched the hovering aircraft, sitting in the air a couple of hundred yards away over the swells of the Pacific, and shook his head incredulously. "They want to gas up, too? Do we look like a service station?"

Wurtman didn't bother to answer the question. "He says they've got about ten minutes more. Maybe fifteen. What if they go into the drink?"

"Then I'll have to go ahead and rescue them, I guess," Pollin said, challenge in his voice. "But until I get the order, that's the only way they're getting on this ship."

The call came through a moment later and a communications officer handed the phone to the captain. Wurtman was staring at the helicopter, a small, beetle-eyed Hughes dating from the 1960s. Wurtman didn't allow himself to smile as he heard the captain on the phone. "Yes, sir. Yes, sir. Of course, Admiral, I understand. Can you tell me though— Of course. Yes, Admiral.''

Pollin tossed the phone away and his voice was filled with exasperation. ''Well, let them land!''

WURTMAN WAS GIVEN the task of welcoming the new arrival for the busy captain. When the helicopter hit the deck, the pilot stayed aboard while the passenger shoved at the door and stepped out onto the pavement.

The man looked like he'd been through hell. His face was scratched and bruised. His clothing, black pants, shoes and shirt were ripped and tattered. Recently dried blood clung to his arms and hands, his scalp and his chin.

This had to be the passenger in need of medical attention the message mentioned.

But the dark-haired, bronzed-skinned man didn't look weakened. His blue eyes burned with a startling vividness, almost a tangible menace, and his powerful jawline gave him a hawkish appearance. The shredded garments revealed strong, muscular arms, and his hands looked as if they saw some kind of hard labor. All in all, he wasn't the kind of guy Wurtman would want as an enemy.

Wurtman wondered about this man. Clearly not military, or they would have been informed. On the other hand, not many civilians got VIP treatment on board U.S. Navy vessels. Some other government agency, maybe? CIA, perhaps?

The man was well over six feet, and when he stopped in front of Wurtman the young sailor had to look up to see him. Wurtman introduced himself in measured tones before he got too nervous.

''Mike Belasko,'' the man answered.

"Mr. Belasko, you look like you've been to Hades and back. Let me call you a stretcher."

"No, thanks. I'll walk. First I need to see one of my companions. The man with the head wound brought in yesterday."

"Right. Come this way."

He led the man belowdeck, down three levels, and along several long hallways. Belasko never fell behind, his powerful steps never lagging from weariness. Maybe his wounds weren't as bad as they looked. Wurtman halted in front of the door to the VIP guest rooms assigned to the other stranger. Belasko said a quick word of thanks and turned away from Wurtman, adding, "If you could send the doctor, I would appreciate it."

The sailor turned. As he made his way back down the hall to the sick bay, he found himself following a trail of blood drops that he was sure went all the way back to the helicopter landing pad.

MANNING STARED at the man in the doorway. Then he laughed out loud. "You look like death warmed over!"

"Speak for yourself."

Bolan's strong, bloody grip held Manning's hand for a long moment. "Jesus, Mack, it's good to see you! Everybody thought you were a goner."

"So I've been told," Bolan answered.

"Stony told me a dead man was going to come visiting me. That's all they were able to give me and I hoped to God it was you, but I couldn't let myself believe until you walked in the room."

"This room secure?"

"Who knows?"

"Then I'll be vague. How are you feeling?"

"Are you asking because you're so considerate?"

Bolan shook his head grimly. "I'm asking because I've got things to get done and I could use an assist."

Manning sat in stunned silence for a moment. "I think you'd better let Doc check you over before you start formulating new plans. I mean it—you don't look good."

Bolan shrugged. "Tacna did the best he could. His talents didn't extend to stitchery. Most of the abrasions were torn open during the hike out of the mountains to Padilla. The doctor's on his way."

Manning appraised the gaunt aspect of Bolan's powerful jawline. "You look starved, too."

"I had lunch in the village, but I could eat again."

After a quick knock the door opened, and the ship's doctor stepped in.

"The trail ends here," the young Navy MD muttered. "I'm taking you to the ship's hospital at once."

"Can't do it, Doctor," Bolan said. "I'm out of here in a couple of hours. Just stitch me up as best you can." He removed his shirt and pointed at a hideous, blackened gash that started at his right collarbone and extended down over his shoulder blade. His shirt was soaked with blood, which was running down his arm. "This is probably the best place to start."

"What happened to you, anyway?"

"I can't say."

The doctor opened a field medical kit he was carrying with him and began to clean the wound. "I know you guys are top secret and all that, but at least give me an idea of how you sustained your injuries so I know what to look for."

"I had a bad fall."

The doctor saw he'd gotten all he was going to get about the events precipitating the injuries, so he started to ask about Bolan's specific symptoms as he began sewing up the shoulder gash. Manning, meanwhile, called a nurse through his hospital intercom. By the time stitches had been placed in Bolan's shoulder, scalp and over his ribs, a huge lunch had arrived. Bolan started to eat as the doctor departed.

"Transportation is on its way?" he asked between bites.

"In fact, our favorite pilot brought us down here. He was hopping mad that he wasn't free to fetch you off that mountain personally. But he got the assignment of chauffeuring a very able-bodied group of men who were on a hunting expedition in the Amazon jungle."

Bolan nodded. Jack Grimaldi was a personal friend to the Executioner, and an ace pilot with a broader base of aircraft experience than most of the flyboys on the planet. He'd piloted everything from restored antique biplanes to prototype spy aircraft. He was also a warrior who had fought at Bolan's side time and again.

"ETA?" he asked.

"One hour, twenty minutes," Manning said. "More than enough time to get those X-rays the doc wanted."

"I can think of a more constructive and restorative way to spend the time," Bolan said. He finished the sandwich and stretched out in a cushioned guest chair, asleep within minutes.

CHAPTER FOURTEEN

U.S.S. Roosevelt,
Pacific Ocean near Chimbote, Peru

Captain Pollin received another call from the admiral. Wurtman decided it had to have been extremely persuasive, because when the third helicopter in two days was on a final approach to the Navy destroyer, Pollin himself was on hand to meet it, exhibiting his best behavior, with Wurtman at his side.

The three passengers and pilot crowded off the large transport chopper. They listened to Pollin's welcome distractedly. They weren't impressed by getting VIP treatment on a U.S. Navy vessel, and they were extremely eager to meet up with the other two arrivals. Within minutes they were being taken into the captain's briefing room, off the bridge, which was set up with access to a computer and telephone. The first two arrivals were already on the line with whomever it was they reported to. Pollin and his subordinate left them to it.

IT TOOK LESS THAN A MINUTE for Able Team and Jack Grimaldi to welcome Bolan on his return from the dead, then Manning punched up the secure channel that had already been established through the Navy communications link. What followed was a breakneck exchange of information between Able Team, Price and Kurtzman.

"There you are, Striker," Kurtzman said when Able Team's report was complete. "Now you know just about everything we do. And it isn't a hell of a lot. We have now found and neutralized teams of perpetrators in South America, San Diego and Turkmenistan. But they're all hired hands. None of them know why these dams are being targeted or who's behind it."

"That's where I can be of some assistance," Bolan answered. "Here's a name for you. Clint Mahoney."

"Just a minute," Kurtzman said, and they heard the lightning strikes of his fingers on a keyboard. In seconds the screen on the Navy-linked computer was coming to life with the face of a sandy-haired Irishman of about forty. It was a mug shot that dated back almost fifteen years.

"Is this the guy?" Kurtzman asked.

"I couldn't tell you. I've never seen him," Bolan admitted, staring at the screen, burning the images into his brain. "What's his background?"

"Hold on. I'm going to the Scotland Yard database for more," Kurtzman said, then he began summarizing over the small phone speaker.

"Clint Mahoney was born in Northern Ireland. His father was vehemently anti-British, and it looks like he was considered a violent offender even before the outset of the troubles. Father and son fled the island in the 1960s when they were identified as primary instigators of violence during what were supposed to have been peaceful demonstration against the British. These guys essentially helped initiate the violence. Clint was just a teenager at the time.

"The elder Mahoney died in 1974. Clint stayed in contact with his father's old comrades in arms," Kurtzman continued. "Early leaders of various Irish terrorist groups. Looks like Clint Mahoney returned to Ireland and tried to make a name for himself as a soldier. But even they considered him sadistic in his treatment of the English. Looks like the British blame him for the torture and murders of several young British soldiers. Eventually, the Irish groups considered him too dangerous to retain.

"So he was back in the U.S. by the late 1970s and started using his skills as an enforcer for various crime outfits. He's been implicated in twenty-three murders, according to FBI files. Known links with the most anarchic Irish independence organizations were retained, but he did no further work for them. Looks like he eventually became too dangerous for the Families to use—something to do with a hit on a Mob bookie who was found tortured to death, along with his wife and young daughter."

"This guy is a real piece of work," Price commented over the line.

"After that he played it low-key for most of the 1980s before turning to industrial extortion: he would buy specialized equipment, then drive up its price by sabotaging similar equipment from competing suppliers. He would then set off a bidding war for his equipment. He got rich and managed to avoid prosecution despite FBI and state organized-crime probes. CIA files say Langley became interested in him when it became apparent a large percentage of his profits were going to Ireland. But Mahoney managed to avoid serious charges and stayed out of jail." Kurtzman sighed. "That's about it. He's been steering approximately the same course for the past decade.''

Bolan said, "Now plug another name into the equation, Bear—Joshua Icahn.''

"Okay. Here he is.''

A new face showed up on their screen. This time it was a scrawny man whose bulbous eyes were circled by dark rings. His cheeks were shrunken, and his thin hair was naturally unkempt. If it hadn't been for the USC sweatshirt he was wearing, he would have looked like a starving street beggar from a Charles Dickens novel.

"Here he is in 1993,'' Kurtzman announced. "He's got a doctorate in environmental engineering and chemistry. Lots of job offers, but none of them worked out. A brilliant researcher, it looks like, but an abrasive personality.''

"A brainiac who doesn't play well with others,'' Jack Grimaldi summarized.

"That's about the size of it,'' Kurtzman agreed. "Not much on him for the past few years…'' His voice trailed off and the room on the bridge of the U.S.S. *Roosevelt* was silent as they waited for Kurtzman to come up with more for them to go on.

The sound of rattling keys came to a halt.

"Oh my,'' Kurtzman muttered. "Check this out.''

The sickly visage of Joshua Icahn vanished, to be replaced with a highly complicated exploded drawing of some sort of mechanical device. At the bottom of the screen was the legend, United States Patent Office Patent Application, September 29, 1998.

"Our friend has recently been awarded a patent for a method for desalination of seawater in large quantities,'' Kurtzman said. "Looks like he formed a corporation and attempted to obtain financing to build these devices. They must be big. They're talking about units for processing hundreds of thousands of gallons of water every year.''

Bolan nodded. ''Big enough that several units could supply a city the size of San Diego or Lima, or even the southern cities on the border of Turkmenistan. Anything about an Icahn-Mahoney alliance?''

''Still looking,'' Kurtzman said. ''I'm not finding it yet.''

''It's there. I'd stake my paycheck on it. Mahoney has teamed up with Icahn. Maybe bought him out or extorted controlling interest in the technology. Now he's creating a market for the technology.''

''I'll keep looking,'' Kurtzman said.

''Meanwhile?'' Lyons prompted.

''Meanwhile, I think it best that Able Team stay in South America,'' Bolan said. ''Since this was the first target, and since the less well-developed water distribution infrastructure in Lima will make the Lima situation desperate before that in San Diego, I'm betting this is where Mahoney and/or Icahn will make their sales pitch. I think we ought to have someone on hand when the pitch is made.''

''Agreed,'' Price said. ''What about you, Striker?''

''I'm going to call on Mr. Mahoney.''

''Then your destination is Santa Fe,'' Price stated.

''To hell with sitting on our thumbs in Lima. Send us with Striker,'' Lyons declared flatly. ''God only knows what he's going to be walking into in New Mexico.''

''I agree with your assessment but not your solution,'' Price replied. ''I want Able in Lima. I know it grinds your gears to be sitting around doing nothing,

Ironman, but that's just the way it is. Striker, I'll have a Stony blacksuit team waiting at the Santa Fe airport, with transportation. They'll be fully debriefed by the time you meet up with them.''

"ETA?" Bolan asked Grimaldi.

"Our jet is in Chimbote," he said with a grin and a shrug. "One hour from here to Chimbote, then seven more until we're on the ground in Santa Fe."

"Can you meet that schedule, Stony?"

"We'll do it," Price replied unhesitantly.

Bolan pushed back from the table. "Then let's move."

Lima, Peru

PASSENGERS GOING through customs at the international airport were heavily laden with boxes and bags filled with bottled water. Hastily erected signs warned foreign visitors that all water inside the city was considered unsafe to drink until it had been boiled. Jared Mahoney ignored it all. He didn't drink water anyway except to mix it with his whiskey. The alcohol killed the germs. He was anxiously looking forward to the coming days, and he was still slightly confused and taken aback by his farewell gift from Colleen Davis.

After months of barely speaking to him, ignoring him, why had she suddenly turned affectionate? She claimed she had been too shy, too hidden in her work, too protected by her tough facade. "Breaking out was difficult for me," she told him, when she was lying naked in his arms. "But when I found out you were leaving, I started to get sort of panicky. You understand? And that was the only way I could get over being too scared to make you know how I feel."

Maybe she was telling the truth. Maybe she wasn't. He'd worry about her later. Right now he wanted to get to the hotel, get out of the crowds. It was obvious these people weren't showering much these days. They'd fix that soon enough.

"There," he said to Icahn.

Joshua Icahn plodded along at Jared Mahoney's side as lifeless as a zombie. He looked morosely at the man Jared pointed to, a dapper figure in a three-piece suit carrying a sign with the Mahoney Corporation name printed on it. Two stiff soldiers waited at either shoulder.

"There's our ride," Jared said.

"I'm Jared Mahoney," he stated abruptly. "This is Dr. Joshua Icahn."

The diplomat introduced himself, but Jared wasn't listening. He handed the man his suitcase. He kept the carry-on for himself; he had a week's supply of crystal meth carefully hidden inside, and he wasn't about to let it out of his hands.

CHAPTER FIFTEEN

Santa Fe, New Mexico

The large adobe mansion stood on two hundred acres of New Mexico desert, five miles from the city of Santa Fe. The mountains to the west were sharply defined in the extraordinarily clean air. The sky was a brilliant blue, highlighted with streaks of white cloud. The desert scenery was almost too crisp and colorful, as if it were an artificially enhanced photograph, an effect of the dry, clean atmosphere, which was marred in the midafternoon by the cloud of dust that buffeted behind a hunter-green sports utility vehicle.

The grounds of the mansion were surrounded by no visible security fencing, but the mile-long, fresh-asphalt drive from the highway was blocked by an iron gate set into decorative brick pillars. The vehicle paused there. The black speaker panel set into the brickwork squawked with static. Then, "Yes?"

"Frank Hogen to see Ms. Davis."

"Repeat your name please?"

"Frank Hogen."

"You are not expected, Mr. Hogen. What is your affiliation?"

"Tragen Corporation. I am with my partner, Katrin

Tracy, and my vice president of engineering, Fred Spedeja. We're interested in negotiating a purchase of some
of the technology held by Ms. Davis."

"Please wait one minute."

It was more like five.

COLLEEN DAVIS FOUND the web page for Tragen Corporation and scanned it while her searches of other
global databases downloaded more information on the
company.

The picture that materialized was intriguing. This was
a high-technology entrepreneurship of the first order,
composed of just three main players and a tiny support
staff, yet generating millions in revenues—with minus-
cule overhead, nearly all of those revenues were profit.
Hogen, Tracy and Spedeja had started out in 1996 with
the purchase of a telecommunications technology that
specialized in converting low-bandwidth phone lines to
high bandwidth through a combination of software and
an electronic caching device. They contracted the manufacture of their components, sold tens of millions of
units in a few years and recently sold the technology at
a massive profit. Other technology acquisitions had occurred. Most of them, if not as wildly successful as the
data-transfer technology, were still pulling in consistent
substantial profits.

Hogen had a background in chemical engineering.
Tracy was a graduate of Reykjavik University, where
she earned a doctorate in thermal engineering. Spedeja
received his doctorate from MIT.

An interesting bunch. Almost idly it occurred to Davis that they might be fakes. She effortlessly broke
through the firewalls at Reykjavik University and soon
found herself pouring over Tracy's course-work grades

and her doctoral thesis on the dynamics of deep-well thermal energy harvest methodology.

That satisfied her that they were legitimate. So what did they want with her?

She saw no harm in trying to find out.

"PLEASE COME IN," said the voice from the black speaker grille, and the gate pulled open silently. The Land Rover rolled through and headed for the front of the sprawling low-profile adobe building.

"For a second there I thought they were going to tell us to go to hell," John Kissinger said from the backseat.

"Ye of little faith," Yakov Katzenelenbogen said, driving at a leisurely pace.

"We've got ourselves covered," Barbara Price assured him. "Aaron created so much electronic documentation on Tragen and its three principals we'll all probably get pegged for an IRS audit in the near future."

"Faith I've got," Kissinger said. "And I'm sure our paperwork is impeccably accurate. But these folks didn't have to let us in, whether they believe us or not."

"Now we just have to keep them believing us until we learn what we came to learn," Katzenelenbogen said.

The Land Rover pulled to a stop on the red cobblestone drive in front of the vast adobe house, where a front terrace was shaded under an awning lined with small potted trees. As they stepped from the sports utility vehicle, a young man opened the front door. Dressed in dark, casual slacks and shirt, and wearing a sport jacket to attempt to hide the handgun holstered under one arm, he smiled at them, a grimace that was completely without warmth. He clearly wasn't accustomed to receiving guests.

"Ms. Davis wasn't expecting you," he said with forced politeness.

"We weren't expecting to come ourselves until this morning," Price replied with an easy, relaxed smile. "Sorry if we're any trouble, but I think Ms. Davis will be interested in what we have to offer."

"I'm sure she will," he said acidly, holding the door for Price, then turning to lead them into a sweeping parlor. The room was decorated in a Western motif, with a cool, natural tile floor, a deerskin rug and a large stone fireplace. The furnishings were tanned leather, hand-made and very expensive.

"Have a seat," the young man said, and waved them vaguely toward the couch, leaving them as quickly as he could without breaking into a trot.

"Nice guy," Kissinger muttered as he sank into a chair so hugely overstuffed it was nearly as wide as a car. "You could measure this room in acres."

John "Cowboy" Kissinger was a tall man, broad across the shoulders and narrow at the hips, but the chair had the effect of making him look almost thin and frail. He appeared dapper and at ease in a slate-gray suit, but by his own standards he was overdressed. On the Farm he was normally to be found in much more casual attire.

Kissinger's eyes scanned the room's nearly hidden security components before he pulled off his dark glasses, folded them neatly and tucked them in his jacket pocket.

"Nice place," Katzenelenbogen added, examining some of the Anasazi pottery—genuine, he had no doubt—on a granite shelf. As he strolled to the sofa, he allowed his prosthetic right arm to hang naturally at his side, and with his left he overused the wooden cane. He was able to lean broadly to one side as he sat on the couch, and he managed to see out the front picture window far enough to make out a pair of casually dressed but disciplined-looking guards. Their automatic weapons were close at hand, and each had a holstered handgun on his hip. They were tucked in a shady corner of the house, tough to spot but with a broad view of the entire side expanse of the estate. He communicated this to the others with a quick glance. They had expected it.

The three of them had left Virginia at dawn, chartering a jet out of Dulles Airport in Washington, D.C., just in case they were tracked back that far.

There had been an obvious need to ascertain the validity of this target. Intelligence on the Mahoney organization had told them only that there was a base of operations outside Santa Fe. The threads that tied him to this house were thin at best. While Bolan was in transit, Price had deemed it best to make an evaluation of the site. If they came up with nothing, they might want to re-evaluate their intention to stage a hard probe.

As far as Katzenelenbogen was concerned, the presence of a pair of guards toting automatic weapons was enough to confirm the site. This had to be Mahoney's base.

Kissinger had come to a similar conclusion. There were no less than four hidden video pickups staged around the parlor. He couldn't begin to guess the number of microphones he would find if he really looked. Not that it mattered.

When Colleen Davis entered the room a few minutes later, they were all somewhat surprised to find themselves faced with what looked like a teenaged girl. She was petite, with narrow limbs and a curvaceous but svelte figure. Her features were Celtic and attractive, and, dressed in sandals, jeans and a white cotton riding blouse, she looked like nothing so much as a pretty Irish schoolgirl.

For her part, Colleen Davis was drawn to Barbara Price at once. The woman was beautiful. Her hair was strikingly blond, and the curves that her conservative, informally cut blazer and khaki slacks couldn't hide were blatantly feminine. Her features were a startling combination of natural beauty and innate strength, which her few strokes of makeup couldn't truly hide or improve upon.

"Good afternoon. I'm Colleen Davis," she said formally, but her green eyes were shining as they locked on Price's face, and she took her hand in a gentle grasp that lingered for a long intimate moment.

"Katrin Tracy," Price said, smiling with an easy, unaffected manner.

Davis found she had to almost physically shake herself free of the woman's presence to meet the others. She turned and greeted the suited engineer, Fred Spedeja, as he rose from his chair, then shook hands with Frank Hogen.

Hogen was an older man, but seemed ageless, which Davis found attractive in a fatherly way. Despite the cane, the prosthetic arm and the silver-gray hair, he sparkled with an incredible vitality in his deep-blue, crystal-clear eyes.

"Let me make you drinks," she said, the Irish brogue subtle yet potent in her enunciation, and headed for the marble-topped bar set into the wall. "Would you like to try some nice New Mexican white wine?"

"Certainly," Price said.

"None for me, thanks," Katzenelenbogen replied. "I'd take a mineral water, if you had some."

"That sounds good to me," Kissinger added.

"Of course. I don't have staff. I hate being waited on by servants," Davis explained as she efficiently uncorked an olive-colored bottle of wine with minimal fuss, allowing it to breathe as she plopped ice in a pair of tall glasses and filled each from a bottle of mineral water from the bar refrigerator. She reached down for a pair of wineglasses and brought everything to a coffee table on a tray.

"You flew in from D.C. this morning?" she asked pleasantly.

"Yes, as a matter of fact," Katzenelenbogen answered with a slight smile, taking the cold glass from her hands and raising it slightly. "Find this part of the country to be a little bit warmer than I'm used to."

Davis handed Kissinger his glass then. "Mr. Spedeja."

Kissinger smiled. "Call me Fred, ma'am."

Price was next to Katz on the large couch and Davis slid onto the cushion beside her as she poured the wine, as clear as water itself, into the glasses. Price's body language opened to Davis, turning to face her and putting an arm on the back of the couch. They sipped from their glasses, regarding each other over the rims, and smiled simultaneously.

"Delicious," Price said.

"Yes, it is very nice."

"I suppose you are wondering why we are here, Ms. Davis," Katzenelenbogen interrupted.

"Colleen, please," she said. "I think I have a pretty good idea, Frank, and I hope I'm not going to disappoint you. I've just done some quick research at tragencorp.com and got a feel for the business your firm specializes in.''

''Good,'' Katzenelenbogen said. ''And we know something of your own specialities, Colleen.''

Davis looked at him squarely, as if daring him to tell her.

''We know you've purchased the rights to some technologies patented by Dr. Joshua Icahn. As you've probably guessed, we're interested in purchasing those rights from you.''

''Specifically?''

Katzenelenbogen raised his eyebrows.

''I purchased a ninety-nine-year lease on the rights to *all* of Dr. Icahn's patented technologies,'' Davis explained.

Katzenelenbogen grinned smugly. ''I've studied that portfolio. We both know there's only one useful patent in the lot.''

Davis echoed the mirthless grin and waited for Katzenelenbogen to say it out loud. She was a cool customer, he was thinking. As young as she was, she refused to be intimidated by his age or by the numbers or bearing of the Stony Man team. As far as she was concerned, she had the upper hand. If these were true negotiations, he would have been at a distinct disadvantage.

''The water purification patent,'' he admitted finally. ''We want to buy it.''

''I'm not selling.''

Katzenelenbogen put his glass on the coffee table and leaned forward, launching into his sales pitch. ''I'm sure you know as well as I do the potential for the development of the technology, Ms. Davis, but the truth is you don't have the resources for developing it to that full potential…"

"Neither do you, Frank," Davis retorted. "Tragen Corporation doesn't have anything in the way of laboratories or manufacturing."

"But I've got the contacts," Katzenelenbogen answered. "As you've ascertained, I'm sure, I've been able to leverage and purchase all the expertise I need for the high-technology ventures I've embarked upon, regardless of their nature. True, large-scale desalination has little similarity to telecommunications, but I can guarantee you I have already lined up design laboratories for optimization of Dr. Icahn's technology, as well as electrical component and speciality, medical-grade plastic supply firms for the coils and separation membranes used in the process. I've got verbal commitments for the manufacturing and material supply for the cabinets and a transport infrastructure. Colleen, I even have an industrial design firm on retainer to make the units look good."

Kissinger added, "I've personally studied the capabilities of our contract manufacturers. They've got the staff to pull off large-scale production and very quickly. We can have a prototype built in a week and production under way in two."

"As I'm sure you're aware, Colleen," Katzenelenbogen continued with feigned eagerness, "there is no better time than the present for marketing these units."

Davis appeared anything but overwhelmed by their sales efforts, and she said nothing as they wrapped up, sipping her wine and meeting eyes with Price expectantly. "Aren't you going to put in your two cents' worth?"

"I think they've summed it up nicely," Price said

with a conspiratorial grin, making the most of the electricity sparkling between herself and Davis. "Anything I can say to convince you?"

"I'm afraid not," Davis said. "What you might not be aware of, Mr. Hogen, is that I purchased more than simply Dr. Icahn's patent rights. I purchased Dr. Icahn himself."

The look that passed between Price, Katzenelenbogen and Kissinger was of genuine surprise, and Davis didn't miss it. "He has been working with me for months on the optimization of his technology."

Katzenelenbogen shook his head, recovering quickly. "He might have invented the process, but he doesn't have the know-how to create an inexpensively producible unit out of it."

"You're right about that. We have also arranged for contract manufacture of the units. In fact, we've fielded prototypes in the past two months and are prepared to start production to order. I'm afraid you're too late, Dr. Hogen."

"Have you actually made sales of the equipment, though, Colleen?" Katzenelenbogen pressed.

Davis paused to consider that, then shrugged her shoulders very slightly, glancing at a diamond-studded watch on her thin, freckled wrist. "That I'll know in just a few hours. As I'm sure it will be public knowledge by the end of the day. Dr. Icahn and my salesman are meeting with Peruvian government representatives as we speak."

Another look passed from Price to Kissinger to Katzenelenbogen. Davis caught it all.

Davis put her arm on the back of the couch and rested her hand gently on Price's. "I'm sorry," she said with a genuine tinge of emotion, "to disappoint you."

"THE DEVIL IN A WHITE BLOUSE," Katzenelenbogen grumbled as they pulled out of the long drive onto the highway, leaving the adobe mansion behind them.

Beside him, Price nodded thoughtfully, her eyes focused on the distant mountains, then she gave a shiver. "She was creepy," she said. "Heartless and absolutely ice-cold. You could feel the frost in her fingers."

"She as good as told us she has no interest in saving lives," Kissinger mused. "All she wants is the profits from the technology."

Price grabbed the cellular phone from inside her blazer pocket and thumbed it quickly. In seconds a secure line opened to the communications center at the Farm, and she asked the officer in charge for Carmen Delahunt.

"What's up, Barb?"

Price quickly explained the situation described to them by Colleen Davis. "Find out what is going on in Lima, Carmen. Make your best use of contacts there. We've got one or two pairs of eyes in the Peruvian federal bureaucracy. Get me as much data as you can on this transaction. We'll be back at the Farm by 0800."

"I'll have a full report available for you by then," Delahunt assured her.

"Good. Give me Aaron, please."

Within seconds Kurtzman was on the line.

"How's the New Mexico desert?"

"A lot chillier than you would think," Price said. She was still experiencing the aftereffect of the curiously intimate interaction with Davis, but the sound of Kurtzman's voice was warming.

"Did you run into Mahoney?"

"Just his ice-princess, Davis," Price said. She related the details of their encounter. "I've already got Carmen combing for more on the sales meeting going on between the Peruvians and Icahn.''

"She said he was with a salesman?'' Kurtzman asked.

"That's the term she used,'' Price said.

"Any idea who?''

"None. I'm hoping Carmen will come up with that bit of information as well.''

"So, what's the plan? Are we still going along with Striker's intended probe of the place.''

"Yes,'' Price said. The question wasn't one of allowing or disallowing the probe. Bolan was intending to get inside the Santa Fe headquarters of Clint Mahoney, and there was very little the Farm could or would do to dissuade him from his set course of action. Bolan was, like few men in the world, his own boss. The question was whether the Farm would be lending a hand.

"The blacksuit team is fully prepped. The guys are sitting around waiting for the go or no-go.''

"Get them in the air,'' Price said. "Striker's scheduled to land in Santa Fe before midnight. They have plenty of time to get themselves set up before the 3:00 a.m. probe launch.''

"All right. Let's start going over the security system,'' Kurtzman said. "We'll map out everything you people encountered inside.''

Price switched the phone to speaker and cradled it in the dashboard unit. Kurtzman's voice came through the speaker for the others to hear.

"Along with the architectural drawings we've got on the house, we were able to finagle a satellite scan a few hours ago,'' he said. "Mahoney has apparently been doing some remodeling without getting the proper municipal building permits.''

"They've gone to great lengths to make the security system invisible," Kissinger stated. "I spotted several cameras covering just about every square inch of the interior, but I don't think most people would have even known they were there."

"Yeah. There were no obvious security surveillance optics in sight," Katzenelenbogen agreed. "But there were tiny little bug eyes everywhere."

"Somewhere there has to be staff to keep an eye on all those images," Price said.

"That's correct," Kissinger stated. "Even with motion detectors—which I'm sure are everywhere, too—they'd need humans to watch and react to intruders. I did see armed guards on the premises."

"Our thermal imaging shows a couple of hot spots inside," Kurtzman said. "One is a small room on the first floor, right off the courtyard. The heat signatures look like monitors to me. Six or eight of them, maybe more. The second hot spot is on the third floor. There's a variety of equipment there, from what I'm reading. Monitors, telecommunications, maybe a minicomputer or a heavy-duty PC."

"Mahoney's got his own little war room," Price said. "Actually, I'll bet Davis is the mastermind there. She's the one with the expertise, according to our profile."

"Any chance of Akira getting inside those systems?" Katzenelenbogen asked. "That might save Mack and our blacksuits the trouble."

They were closing in on the Santa Fe airport by this time. The chartered jet was waiting for them on the tarmac, refueled and prepped for takeoff.

"Unlikely," Kurtzman answered. "Although Akira's been at it for over an hour. He's got the IP pinned down, but Davis is too smart to allow him access."

"Akira's the best there is," Kissinger said. "Are you telling me he met his match?"

"Even Akira can't get through the security measures Davis is employing," Kurtzman said. "She's using the best firewall there is—she keeps the system turned off when she's not using it. Even a hacker extraordinaire like our guy can't get data off a drive that's not spinning."

"Then," Price said, "we'll ask Striker to flip the switch for us."

Las Vegas, Nevada

CLINT MAHONEY SAT at the desk in his suite at the Mirage Hotel, wearing lightweight headphones and staring at the tragencorp.com home page with his brow furled. He didn't like what he saw.

"What was their reaction to your refusal?" he asked. Davis's face, pale and impassive, was in a small window in the top-right corner of his screen.

"Very businesslike," she said with a shrug. "They were clearly disappointed. They could see the profit potential. But once they understood I had already taken the same marketing tack they planned, they knew they weren't dealing with a techno-geek open to manipulation."

Behind Mahoney, the prostitute on the bed murmured drowsily, annoyed in her sleep by the talking.

"Have company, Clint?" Davis asked, one eyebrow rising slightly.

Mahoney ignored the question. "Were they interested in the house?"

"You think they were checking the place out?" Davis said with a smirk.

"Why not?"

"You can't steal patented technology rights via burglary, Clint."

"Maybe they don't care about the rights to the technology," Mahoney answered. "Maybe they were searching for a link between the destruction of the dams and the company that will be benefiting from it."

"You still worried about that?"

"Damn worried," Mahoney spit. "Somebody has been on to us since the very start. That asshole on the dam in Peru—where in God's name did he come from? The raid on those stupid Indians. Not to mention the gang in San Diego."

"The man at the dam in Peru is buried under a thousand tons of concrete," Davis replied. "The South American mercenaries and the Californian gangs were set up to take the fall for us. You intended for those raids to occur. No surprises there."

"We never planned for a reaction as swift as the one we're seeing," Mahoney argued. "I get the feeling there's a highly organized group of some kind, trying to track us down."

"There's no way they could have that much on us," Davis said. "If there was such a group, it would have to be U.S.-based, which means you're talking about some sort of CIA-FBI task force. That kind of bureaucracy could never field a team fast enough to react with the speed we've witnessed in the South American mercenary probes and the San Diego gang takedown."

"So who did?" Mahoney posed.

"Locals," Davis said. "The Brazilians took out the Indians. The Peruvians took down the mercs in the Andes. The city police, maybe the FBI, took out the Latin

Rangers in San Diego. There was no single organization behind them. You're overreacting.''

"Maybe." He didn't sound convinced. "You never answered my question. Were the Tragen Corp. people interested in the house?''

Davis smiled and shook her head. "Only mildly. They have too much of their own money to be impressed by wealth and they didn't show the slightest interest in our security systems. I watched the tapes of their behavior prior to my appearance. Nothing suspicious.''

Mahoney considered this for a minute, then nodded. "We're two of a kind, Colleen. You're the daughter I never had.''

Davis cocked her head. She was about to comment on his take on their relationship, changed her mind and asked, "You still planning on returning tonight?''

"No." He pursed his lips thoughtfully, thinking fast, then said, "McDonough wants to spend another night on-site.''

"What for? We've put a dozen surveillance cameras in place.''

"He needs to get a feel for the site. He needs to go with his gut feelings on this.''

"Is he nervous?" Davis asked.

"No," Mahoney said. "Keep in mind this dwarfs our other undertakings. He's simply being extra careful.''

The prostitute had given up on sleeping. She came up behind Mahoney and kissed his neck, then stood rubbing his shoulders. Mahoney watched Davis assess the image of the naked young woman, a UNLV freshman. Even in Davis's low-resolution video feed, Mahoney knew, the woman would be exquisite. She was also very expensive.

"Nice," Davis said, smiling faintly, tiny in the laptop window. "Why not bring her home with you, Clint?"

"I just might."

Mahoney signed off and closed down the laptop. He quickly negotiated another twelve hours of service from the woman, then dialed the adjoining suite. McDonough picked up.

"Yeah?"

"We're staying an extra night," Mahoney said.

"What for?"

"Just a precaution. There could be trouble at the house, and I'd rather not be there if and when it goes down."

"Did you warn Colleen?"

"I was just talking to her."

"So what do we do until tomorrow?" McDonough asked.

"It's Las Vegas, my boy. We enjoy ourselves."

CHAPTER SIXTEEN

Santa Fe, New Mexico

By the time the four Hummers approached the estate, the moon had risen over the nearby mountain, illuminating a stretch of shadow-embraced open country that only the artificially illuminated grounds and pool broke.

"We're going to be spotted pretty quick in the open," mused the blacksuit commander.

"Maybe even sooner," Bolan agreed. "We have no idea what kind of electronic security system they have in place, only that it's extensive."

The blacksuit, a man named McDonald, nodded. "Let me send in one of my electronics guys. With his know-how and the intel we've got on this place, one man can sneak past their systems better than all of us. Once he's made his way through them, he'll have a good idea what kind of system is in place and how to go about taking it down without alerting enemy guns. Get us in nice and quiet."

Bolan considered that for a moment, then nodded. "Fine. But not alone. I'm going with him."

The blacksuit commander knew better than to argue with Bolan. "Okay. Let's get ready."

McDonald, during a military career heavy with combat experience, had never before found himself working for an outfit as strange as the Farm. He had been culled from the Navy SEALs for the job. Others in his outfit were from the Rangers and other U.S. military special operations groups. Down to a man they were specially requested by the Farm to serve on their blacksuit teams—although who actually did the requesting the commander had never known. He was also in the dark about the agency affiliation of the Farm. For all McDonald could tell, the Farm might even be some sort of independent agency, free of the constraints of the other military groups.

They sure acted like it.

There was also a distinct lack of military formality among the senior staff of the Farm. While they all appeared to have military training, no rank was designated. Some of the senior staff didn't even appear to be American. Even the names of the senior staff seemed subject to change on a rotating basis.

The man he was working with right now was no exception. The blacksuit leader knew him only as "Stony One" and "Striker." Who Striker was, what his capabilities were, why he was given virtually limitless authority by the Farm was beyond the blacksuit leader's understanding.

But this man, this Striker, had proved himself to the blacksuit commander on more than one occasion. Any doubts he might have had about working at this nameless stranger's side had vanished months ago.

Right now, Striker was clad in the same head-to-toe blacksuit and combat cosmetics as the rest of the team, and more than any man he had ever seen, this warrior looked at home in the darkness.

McDonald's electronics expert emerged from the

ranks, distinguished from the other blacksuits by a heavy black backpack and a small array of electronic sensing devices strapped to his wrists and combat webbing.

Bolan knew the man's capabilities and had, in fact, helped cull him from the ranks of the Rangers with special electronics training. He was one of the best on the planet at what he did. This night he was simply Blacksuit Four. Bolan said, "Tell me about our infiltration strategy."

"Sandy soil and low levels of precipitation make this location ideal for the use of buried sensors. We'll be searching for them," the electronics man explained.

"Motion detectors?"

"They'll be scanning for large mass signatures. They can't be sounding alerts every time a desert hare runs through the yard."

In minutes the pair set out across the sandy soil, hidden by the darkness of the mountain's shadow. Bolan's personal armory had been restocked by Stony Man Farm, and he was using a pair of suppressed firearms as his lead weapons during the clandestine part of the probe. The longer they kept themselves a secret, the better. The Beretta 93-R, holstered under his left arm, was silenced, courtesy of the Stony Man Farm armory. But even Cowboy Kissinger couldn't truly "silence" a firearm. The best he could do was stifle it somewhat, and either one of Bolan's suppressed weapons would make an audible noise when fired.

The blacksuit electronics expert was walking a few paces in front of Bolan, one eye on the ground and another on the small cone-shaped display on a handheld computer. At first glance it looked as if it were showing nothing but blue fog with a few pockmarks and pin-

holes. Bolan knew better. He recognized the display as
an ultrasound unit, broadcasting into the soil in front of
them and analyzing the bounced-back sound signatures.
He knew it wasn't looking for the security hardware—
a glass fiber cable might register as a plant root or as
nothing at all. What it was after was the telltale anom-
alous soil density where digging for the placement of
the security system cables and sensors took place. The
blacksuit came to a halt at the instant a small, thin line
appeared on the monitor. Bolan, looking over his shoulder, recognized it for what it was. The line stretched
across the ground in front of them, far too straight to
have been caused naturally. But it had been placed there
long enough that all surface evidence of its existence
was long gone. Looking at the spot with the naked eye
revealed no sign of whatever lay there.

"I make a conduit," the blacksuit whispered as he
fed new instructions into the palmtop computer. "I'm
looking for sensors and inputs. Here they are. Can't
make them out well enough for a precise ID, but the
fact that they're completely buried under the soil means
they're probably pressure-sensitive." A series of red
crosses appeared on the screen, set along the conduit
about every six inches, to judge by the gauge on the
screen. "They're positioned close together."

The problem was that they had no way of knowing
the level of sensitivity of the sensors. In all likelihood
they were sensitive enough to read a footstep within a
vicinity broad enough to result in 100 percent coverage
of the desert floor.

"Right here they're positioned close to one another,"
Bolan said. "Let's look for a gap." He gestured in the
direction of the looming mountain.

It took them ten minutes to find it, but then the blacksuit hissed victoriously as the display in his hands found a large change in the subsurface density, around which the conduit came to a complete stop. "Boulder, buried under the sand but too close to the surface to allow them to plant their monitors," he said.

Bolan nodded. "This is our entry point."

They slipped through the gap in the invisible protective field, then headed for the house, which they now approached from the southeast, finding no more security measures until they reached the building itself and crouched behind a decorative giant agave plant. The approach direction was advantageous, bringing them to within five paces of the house before they would emerge into the floodlights. Then they were vulnerable to digital video surveillance—if they were caught by one of the hidden cameras, and if the video feed was constantly being digitally analyzed for motion, the alarm would sound within seconds.

"Can you find the cameras?" Bolan asked.

"I'm not making any promises."

Bolan had full confidence in the man. Recruitment by the Farm meant the man was about the best in his field, anywhere. And the Farm equipment was state of the art. If this blacksuit electronics man couldn't find the cameras, then they probably couldn't be found.

"Got them," the blacksuit said. "Watch me make magic." He retreated three yards from the agave into the blackness and made quick work of erecting a small tripod on thin, hollow telescopic aluminium legs. The tiny laser snapped into a brace at the top, and a nearly invisible tracer laser dot appeared on the wall of the house. The blacksuit used a remote control the size of a silver dollar to adjust the laser's servomotors, which were themselves no bigger than pencil erasers. En-

sconced in blackness, they remained hidden from the
human or electronic monitors behind that camera during
the entire process.

When the tracer disappeared into the tiny black dot
in the adobe wall, Bolan knew the blacksuit had successfully found his mark. The magnitude of the laser
light was increased, and the camera became inoperative.
Inside, security personnel would be getting a strange
warning signal from the security electronics.

With any luck, one of them would be out to investigate within seconds.

The blacksuit crouched with Bolan behind the agave.
"Try to stay out of the path of the emitter. Depending
on the robustness of their equipment, the camera might
go functional again if the laser stopped scrambling it."

"Understood," Bolan replied. "Look sharp." He had
heard a small and distant click of a latch, and a moment
later a figure stepped out of a courtyard, through a black
archway in the east side of the building. The guard
glanced around perfunctorily, never seeing the hidden
wraiths behind the agave, and headed for the camera.
He peered into the hole where the camera hid and spoke
into his walkie-talkie. A revolver was tucked into a holster, strapped in place.

"Nothing blocking it," he said.

"You did something to it," the radio said.

"Naw, I didn't touch it."

"The interference changed. Now it's black."

"I'll open it up." The guard took a pen-sized screw-
driver from his shirt pocket, stabbed at a latch hidden
inside the wall and pulled open a panel no larger than
a paperback book.

Bolan struck, moving across the open space with the
delicate steps of a martial-arts master performing a rit-

ualistic rice-paper dance. The guard never heard the whisper of feet on the sandy soil, nor did he see a shift in the shadows. When the hand clamped like a solid metal claw around his face, he knew the instant terror that came with utter surprise. Then there registered in his nervous system the hideous sensation of biting metal, as cold as an ice shard where it passed through his flesh.

The blood burst out of his neck in a torrent, draining the life out of him in seconds. Bolan lowered the corpse to the ground and wiped the Ka-bar fighting knife on the dead man's clothing. Crouching, he pushed the camera panel closed again, then skirted the barely visible laser, allowing it to continue confusing the other watchmen. With a quick wave he summoned the blacksuit. Together they lifted the dead guard and carried him through the archway into the courtyard, depositing him in the gravel next to a quiet fountain.

The way was clear. A door to the interior was outlined in the blackness by light coming around its edges. Bolan, with a gesture of his hand, ordered the blacksuit to do the honors. The electronics Ranger grasped the handle and, on the nod from Bolan, pulled open the door. The Executioner's hand flew out in front of him and adjusted for the target in the moment that he spotted it. The stainless-steel Tru-Balance throwing knife sliced through the air in a deadly spin and impaled itself in the left eye of the shocked guard, the six-inch blade penetrating deep into the left hemisphere of the man's brain and turning him off like a light. Bolan stepped into the small guardroom, sweeping the 93-R over the area quickly before deciding there was no one else on duty. He grabbed the tumbling corpse under its arms and lowered it into the corner, out of the way.

The blacksuit was already taking his place at the controls, nodding to himself as he assessed the layout of the system. In fifteen seconds he began a controlled shutdown of the system. No one in the place would know their elaborate protection grid was suddenly inoperative.

"It's off," he announced quietly.

"Commander," Bolan said into his walkie-talkie, "all security systems have been taken off-line. I suggest you follow our route into the building. Move cross-country to the southeast side of the building. Look for an arched entrance to a courtyard and the entrance to a guardroom."

"Copy that, Stony One."

Bolan leaned over a monitor as the blacksuit pulled a map of the mansion and its electronic defenses onto the screen, comparing them to his mental image of the layout faxed to him from Stony Man Farm as he was flying up from South America. He quickly digested the new version of the layout and assessed the entry points he wanted. "These look like bedrooms," he commented, pointing out large third-floor rooms on the diagram. "I'm going up."

"Keep in touch," the blacksuit commented. "They've got every room in the house wired for movement, if not video. I can track you and alert you if anybody else is in your vicinity."

"Good," Bolan said. "I'll start with this room, then head down the hallway, in series."

"I'll be watching."

Bolan headed out the control room to a set of rear stairs, which he followed to the third floor, the heavily carpeted steps and the hush of an air-conditioner system masking his movement. Otherwise, the house was utterly silent. In the glimmering moonlight from a diamond-shaped, four-paned window, the Executioner emerged on the third floor in a peaceful hallway. The largest of the bedrooms was closest and he tried the door, without any hope of it being unlocked. The knob didn't turn in his hand. He extracted a key chain of anodized steel picks and inserted one carefully into the brass knob. The door opened with an unavoidable click.

He stepped against the wall as the door swung open with a tiny creak. The noise was too loud for his liking, but inside he heard no sudden rustle of bedclothes. After five seconds, he stepped to the door, passing into the room in a darting burst of movement that minimized his silhouette in the faintly illumined doorway.

Inside he hugged the floor and peered into the blackness, to which his eyes were adjusting rapidly, and saw movement from the bed's occupant. The figure sat up quickly and stared at the door, the whites of his eyes flashing as he tried to blink the sleep out of them. Then his gaze was drawn to the anomaly in the shadows and he grabbed at his bedside, snatching at something that lay on the table in the glimmering red glow of a clock radio. Bolan was across the room with the speed of lightning, slamming his forearm into the chest of the twisting figure and ramming it against the headboard. The body made a thump as it hit the wall and the figure retched on the bedclothes, gasping for breath. Bolan stood a few feet away, just out of the figure's reach.

"I have a gun leveled at your head," Bolan stated matter-of-factly. "You so much as sneeze and I'll shoot you dead."

"Don't shoot," the figure gasped, retching again. His distress, Bolan noted, was highly exaggerated. His Irish accent, on the other hand, sounded genuine.

"Are you Clint Mahoney?"

"Who?"

Bolan said nothing. He knew the lack of recognition was a pretense and he had the luxury of time to wait out the end of the game. He stood there, faceless in the blackness, until his silence unnerved the Irishman.

"I'm not Mahoney."

"Name."

"Marty O'Connell."

"Why is Mahoney committing mass murder?"

"He isn't committing mass murder, you moron. He's just blowing up some property."

"The cholera death toll in Lima might hit ten thousand within the month. Those murders are on your head."

"Listen, Yank, we just blew up some fucking dams!"

"Why?"

O'Connell's wet mouth curled into a sneer in the darkness. "For the money."

Suddenly he moved. He threw back the covers, trying to fling them up and over Bolan, as he rolled out the other side of the bed and made another grab for his handgun. Bolan easily sidestepped the blanket and tracked O'Connell's movement as much by sound as by sight. The suppressed Beretta coughed loudly, punching O'Connell in the shoulder. He shouted, wordlessly and full of rage, grabbing at the wound, then gulped as the second and third bullets slammed into his chest and stopped his heart.

CHAPTER SEVENTEEN

"Striker, this is Blacksuit Four." The Stony Man electronics expert sounded urgent over the headset.

"Striker here."

"There's movement all around you."

"I made some noise," he said simply. "What's going on in the hall outside bedroom one?"

"Two guards flanking the door, close proximity. Don't go out that way."

"That's the only way out," Bolan said with a mental shrug, picturing a pair of armed guards storming into the hallway and following the sound of the gunfire and the shouts to the door, then standing outside of it, unsure of their next step. Bolan took a similar position, hard up against the wall next to the door, so close to the guards he imagined he could almost feel their body heat through the wallboard that separated them. Seconds later the door pushed open a half inch, and Bolan fired through the narrow opening. The rounds tracked from floor to ceiling in a blast of sharp retorts.

There was a cry of shock from the first guard, and Bolan kicked open the door, reaching out to fire around the corner. Even for the Executioner, controlling the massive recoil of the 3-round burst was nearly impossible at such a wild angle, and there was no assurance he would score on guard number two. And there was no time to ask for a look-see from the blacksuit in the control room. Instead, he whipped around the doorjamb, counting on the wild fire to have slowed the guard's reaction time, and found he'd got lucky. The second guard was staggering away—from a wound or fear, Bolan couldn't tell. He didn't bother to find out. He pursued the figure with a single stride and emptied another three rounds into his torso, flinging him into the stairs.

"WHAT WAS THAT?" Bill O'Massey, one of Mahoney's old-time Irish friends, had recently arrived from Northern Ireland in need of sanctuary. He sat up in bed when O'Connell's dying shout reached them.

Colleen Davis wrinkled the pale skin of her forehead and tucked her sandy red hair behind her ears, as if it would allow her to hear better. There was a moment of silence. She strode to the closet for a stash of weapons stored there.

"Get up, dammit!"

O'Massey was about to protest when he heard a trio of machine-fired rounds, followed by another. By the time the sound of the third triburst reached him he was at Davis's side, where she was snatching up a pair of bullpup-design French FA MAS assault rifles. She slapped magazines into each of them, slipping both nylon straps over her shoulders, then grabbed at a Glock handgun. She retreated to the middle of the room, watching the door.

"At least put a fucking shirt on," O'Massey growled as he checked out his own armament.

Davis didn't even bother to acknowledge him. She turned to the window, which looked onto the well-lit grounds around the huge house. The night looked empty until she moved closer to the window and spotted dark, furtive movement close to the house.

"We're surrounded," she said without emotion. "SWAT team or special forces or something."

"How did they get through the security?"

"That doesn't matter now," she said. "What matters is getting out of here."

"Getting out? Why leave when we can stay and fight?"

"You can have it out with them if you want to, old man, but I choose my battles with a little more discretion. This isn't a fight for honor. This isn't a fight for the freedom of Ireland. This is a fight for a house. I don't care about the damn house."

Davis peered out the window again, seeing the way was now clear. She hoisted the window and clambered outside, grabbing at the aluminium rungs bolted into the roof, put there when the house was retrofitted for Mahoney for the singular purpose of facilitating an emergency escape. She hung from it for a moment, then swung her legs and curled her entire body up over the next rod, climbing onto the roof.

When O'Massey heard the blasts of large-caliber handgun fire in the adjoining room, he climbed out after her.

BLACKSUIT FOUR WAS squinting into the screen. Some sort of large shadow had moved over half of the camera just seconds after the last of the blacksuits completed a circle of that side of the building, then it was gone. It shouldn't have been there, thirty feet in the air. He quickly realized that someone might have moved in front of it while exiting one of the windows, although the aspect of the movement seemed too slow for that.

He turned his attention quickly to the camera in the other corner of the house, which covered only part of the same section of the grounds. Nothing.

"Commander, I've got unknowns on the ground on the north side of the main house."

"Negative, we just patrolled the north side."

"They emerged right after you guys passed, Commander."

"Armed?"

"Unknown. Their security camera coverage at that point leaves something to be desired."

BOLAN TUCKED the 93-R into the shoulder holster and pulled the Beretta M 3-P police shotgun from its straps. It opened the next door for him, shredding through the hand-rubbed pine. As it swung open, the man in the hidden corner unleashed a volley of autofire, sweeping it across the opening as if he expected Bolan to walk through it and get himself killed. The Executioner retreated a few paces as he made a quick assessment of the gunner's position on the other side of the wall, placed the barrel within inches of the wallboard and triggered.

The wall disintegrated with less resistance than the wooden door, and the gunner screamed in agony. Bolan heard the distinct rattle of the rifle falling, and at that signal he entered the room. The gunner was careening around the room like a rabid dog, half his face and chest flayed free of skin and his left arm cut to ribbons. Insane with fear and pain, he never saw Bolan jab the Beretta shotgun between his feet. He stumbled and sprawled to the floor. The impact knocked the breath out of him. Bolan grabbed at the fallen autorifle and ejected it through the window glass, then left the wounded man where he had fallen. If he survived, he might have answers to give. Right now he was in no shape to speak coherently.

"BLACKSUIT FOUR, this is Blacksuit Commander. Nobody on the north side of the building, although somebody just tossed out a rifle."

"Commander, Stony One here. I sent the gun. The top floor is cleaned out. Proceed inside and start cleaning up."

"Affirmative. We're moving in."

The blacksuit at the security controls was bothered by the unexplained something he had seen from the north-side camera, but he had no choice but to put it out of his mind as he assessed the ground-floor advance of the Stony Man blacksuit group.

"Commander, I make you at the east side entrance. Be aware of two or more armed guards who were stationed at that entrance. They're outside my range of vision at the moment—they're inside somewhere."

"How complete is your visual coverage?"

"Less than fifty percent. Nothing at all on the second floor."

"Understood. Team Three, move in."

THE BLACKSUIT COMMANDER left a pair of guards outside the east entrance and slipped in through a utility door on a raised wooden porch. An ex-SEAL blacksuit was guarding his back. They found themselves in a foyer with a stark white tile floor. Beyond them was a large kitchen, cold and sterile, illuminated by a single light over a huge stainless-steel stove.

"Blacksuit Four here. I've got you in the kitchen, Commander."

The commander, McDonald, glanced around momentarily for the camera and couldn't find it. Even inside, the security system was well hidden. He gave a brief wave. "Affirmative. How's it look?"

"To the south you'll find a dining room. I've got no visual there. To the west of the dining room is a living room or parlor. I've got full visual, and no one's home there."

McDonald faced the dining room apprehensively. He really hated going in without good intelligence, and right now they had none. The distinct advantage of possessing a partial set of eyes in the security man could quickly become a disadvantage if his teams used it as a crutch.

It wasn't the time to distract his men with an elementary lesson on maneuvers. He made a quick assessment of the blackened room next door, separated from him and his companion by a set of swing doors. He ordered the second blacksuit away from the doors with a gesture, grabbed at the wall switch and flipped on all the lights in the kitchen while nudging at the door. He pulled back as the startled figure in the dining room triggered his weapon. The rattle of eight rounds crunched into the swing door and into the kitchen walls.

"He's running scared, into the living room," Blacksuit Four stated quickly.

McDonald pushed his M-16 through the swing doors and aimed at the entrance to the living room, unleashing a deadly hail of fire. Three rounds chomped into the fleeing guard's back, flattening him on his face. The commander slipped into the parlor and kicked his gun away from the guard, then made a quick check for a pulse. The guard was stone dead.

"Others in the vicinity?" McDonald asked as his

companion came to his side and they instinctively took up watch on the other two entrances to the room.

"Nothing I can make out. I've got a hall and stairway to the north of your position, currently empty. There's another room to the east without cameras."

"Keep me posted."

BOLAN MONITORED the progress of McDonald and his blacksuit team, but his attention was centered on a quick power-up of the large, hardware-packed control room he discovered on the third floor of the building. In fifteen seconds the central computer was booted and various peripherals and terminals were coming on-line.

"Stony, this is Stony One. You should have access any second."

"Stand by. Yes, we just got in," Kurtzman said. "Good work, Stony One."

Bolan watched the main computer terminal, which displayed only a typical computer desktop. There was no indication on that end as the Stony Man Farm cybernetics team's specially configured search-and-download software pushed the CPU to the limit, electronically tapping in to its contents. Bolan removed a special cellular modem from his pack and found an auxiliary telecom outlet on the CPU, snapping it into place in a matter of seconds. Then he trailed the cable out for a couple of feet behind the unit and tucked the modem behind the desk. It should be found easily in a search, but only if somebody knew to look for it.

"Stony, how's it flowing?"

KURTZMAN'S EYES FAIRLY SPARKLED as he watched window after window fly across the screen, indicating the tremendous pace of data downloading from the Mahoney system.

"Fast and furious, Stony One."

"Anything more I can do here to speed things up?"

"Look for other computers or data storage peripherals that aren't hooked up to the system. Davis might have kept sensitive material in separate devices as an added security measure. Also, grab any and all disks you see lying around."

"Negative on that, Stony. No DVDs, no zips, no floppies. And all the drives appear to be tied into the system you've accessed."

"Good—" Kurtzman's voice locked suddenly in his throat as the windows blanked and a *data link severed* message appeared in bold red type. Across the room Tokaido cursed vividly. Within a half second, another message appeared: *auxiliary connection established.*

"Stony One, somebody just cut the T1 cable," Kurtzman said. "Your alternative measure is operable."

BOLAN PRESSED the transmit button on his headset. "Copy that, Blacksuit Commander?"

"We're on it, Stony One."

The download would have slowed tremendously. Kurtzman's cellular modem, as fast as it was, could never hope to equal the data transfer capabilities of a T1 line. But Davis or Mahoney, or whoever it was that had physically broken the T1 connection, would never know it was there and might never think to look for it. Even if disaster occurred to Bolan and the blacksuit team in the next few minutes, the data download would most likely continue uninterrupted.

"Blacksuit Four here. I've got them!" It was the electronics man, stationed in the control room.

"They're on the roof, over the northwest side of the building."

Bolan nodded to himself. They were directly above him. Made sense that was where the cable for the T1 fed into the building.

"Blacksuit Commander here. I'm on my way. The building appears clear. Keep the perimeter secure."

Good advice, Bolan realized, although unnecessary. The highly trained Stony Man blacksuits stationed around the estate knew better than to break their perimeter guard, even if it was for the purpose of hemming in the last known survivors in a hard probe.

Then he thought about Colleen Davis.

She had come across as highly intelligent, in control and mature beyond her years. That was the impression she gave Price, Katzenelenbogen and Kissinger. The fact that she hadn't panicked in the face of a violent raid by a well-trained antiterrorist team, and had, in fact, been cool enough to take time to sever the T1 line, bore out her disposition.

Now wasn't the time to underestimate a personality such as hers. She would have been careful enough to plan for a quick escape should it be necessary. She would make that escape—how?

Overland, avoiding the roads. She'd go into the desert. She'd have a capable vehicle staged for such an escape.

"Blacksuit Four, this is Stony One. There's a carport or garage somewhere."

"Roger that. A large one in front and a smaller garage on the southern end."

"Keep those garage doors closed if you can, Blacksuit Four," Bolan ordered as he bolted from the command center and raced to the stairs.

"Negative, Stony One. These home automation systems allow for local override of all systems. Anybody who wants to get out can do it with the flip of a switch."

"Can you monitor, Blacksuit Four?"

"Affirmative, Stony One. No movement—wait! Stony One, I have two figures in the small garage on the southern end of the house. Man, they just dropped out of nowhere. I think they came out of the ceiling."

That made perfect sense to Bolan.

Blacksuit Four quickly began feeding his news to the rest of the team. "They're moving fast," he added. "Looks like they've got a Hummer, and they're already out the door!"

Bolan hit the landing on the first floor with both feet and headed through a door that he knew would take him into the main carport. The lights were on. Blacksuit Four now had the entire estate blazing.

"Movement in the main garage! Is that you, Stony One?" Blacksuit Four demanded.

"Affirmative. Get those doors open!"

The garage doors began swinging open as Bolan jogged past the Lincoln TownCar and the Infiniti QX4 SUV. The Infiniti might be drivable in the desert, but it would never catch the Hummer on rough terrain. He found what he wanted in the last auto stall—a pair of Honda Valkyrie motorcycles. They weren't designed for the desert by any stretch of the imagination, but they were powerful. Handled correctly, such a vehicle might be able to catch up to the Hummer. He grabbed at one of the motorcycles, hoping the mechanics were as immaculately maintained as the well-waxed paint and polished chrome. The massive 1520cc engine thrummed to life smoothly and idled like a growling tyrannosaur roused from a nap.

"Blacksuit Nine here—they got past me. I nailed them with a dozen rounds. Their Hummer's fully armored."

"Stony One here. I'm in pursuit on two wheels."

Bolan fed gas to the 6-cylinder, 6-carburetor power plant and eased out of the garage.

"Blacksuit Nine here—I'm watching them head south-southeast into the desert. They're traveling with their lights on. You should be able to pick them up, Stony One."

"Affirmative." Bolan spotted Nine now, holding his position at the estate perimeter. Under the blanket of floodlights, the place was bright enough for a baseball game, but as Bolan raced off the pavement and into the desert he almost instantly needed his headlights. The rough terrain required constant vigilance. He veered to avoid a mound, then accelerated suddenly to clear a yawning ditch in the dirt that would have smashed his front end if he'd landed in it. He felt a surge of satisfaction at the snarling response he received from the Valkyrie. The machine had power to spare.

"Stony One here. Blacksuit Commander, there's another bike in the main garage. Get somebody on it."

"I'll send him after you within the next minute."

"Negative. Get him onto the highway, headed south-southeast. Keep him on the pavement. I'll stay in touch. We'll be able to pincer them. You on-line, Stony Base?"

"Stony Base here," Barbara Price answered. Kurtzman, Bolan knew, would be busy completing his data download, then launching all his resources into culling that data for useful information—an extensive project in itself.

"Have you got me GPS-positioned?"

"Affirmative, Stony One."

"I have visual on the fleeing Hummer. It's approximately one thousand yards ahead of me on an identical heading. Blacksuit Commander, who's joining us?"

"Blacksuit Eight here," a voice said through Bolan's speaker. "I'm heading out of the estate on the drive, and I can go just about as fast as you need me to on this baby."

"Stony Base here. I've got you pegged, Blacksuit Eight," Price stated. "Left on the highway and make use of some of that speed."

Bolan glanced toward the distant highway, but he couldn't make out the lights of Blacksuit Eight in the darkness. The man was simply there as backup, as far as Bolan was concerned. Hopefully he'd have the Hummer brought to a halt before Eight's path intersected theirs. He clicked on his high beams and accelerated suddenly, ripping over the irregular terrain at tremendous speed, which the Valkyrie handled effortlessly. Even the asphalt-trained suspension wasn't being tested by the rises and falls in the sandy, dry earth. It swept the occasional vegetation aside without notice. A shallow but large depression suddenly appeared ahead in the far-reaching high beams, and Bolan reacted with even greater speed, drenching the massive six-cylinder powerhouse with fuel and gripping tightly as the motorcycle roared forward with a throaty display of power, driving it momentarily airborne before its furiously spinning tires clawed into the soil again at the far side of the depression and dug through the soil, propelling Bolan back onto level ground.

The rear window of the Hummer flopped out of place, and Bolan twisted the handlebars of the bike as automatic gunfire sputtered from the vehicle's dark interior. The erratic motion of the vehicle and its pursuer made accurate fire highly improbable, but Bolan spotted the sudden plumes of dust rising just a few feet to the right of him.

He snatched at the Beretta shotgun, swung it onto the handlebars and transferred it to his left hand. The need to accelerate was more important than the need to brake, he reasoned. He'd just have to hope for no insurmountable details in the landscape. He jerked the accelerator as the gunfire paused and rode up hard and fast on the rear of the Hummer, swerving wildly, then leveled the Beretta. The automatic rifle fire recommenced, and the deadly hail of rounds chopped at the air in Bolan's path. He pulled out of the swerve, pulled back into it again, then fired the shotgun from a distance of twenty feet. Even over the voice of the Valkyrie Bolan heard the scream from the Hummer.

"Stony One here. The rear passenger is out of commission. I'm within ten yards."

"Stony Base here. I copy." Price began issuing new directions to Blacksuit Eight.

With nobody left to guard the rear end, Bolan could close in tight on the Hummer, and allow its behavior to tell him when the terrain altered. He moved in fast, raising himself in his seat to help ride out a series of small earthen trenches, then closed in on the right rear of the vehicle. The Hummer increased speed with a throaty roar, and Bolan matched it easily. He fired the Beretta police shotgun at the rear tires, but a large bounce lifted them off the ground as the blast filled the desert. Pieces of rubber shredded off the tires, but they refused to deflate.

The Hummer swerved at him as the driver realized the warrior's strategy, and Bolan's inability to brake nearly cost him his life. He released the gas and dropped the shotgun on its straps in the same instant, watching for one never-ending second as the rocketing motorcycle homed in relentlessly on the rear corner of the Hummer. By the time he closed on the brake, the seemingly inevitable impact was microseconds from becoming reality. Then he jerked hard, decelerating the motorcycle with inches to spare.

The Hummer swerved again, in the other direction, and swung into a 180. There was no time to search for the dangling shotgun. Bolan snatched at the .44 Magnum Desert Eagle as the careening Hummer swung broadside.

Colleen Davis was at the wheel. For a fraction of a second, for one of the few times in his years as a soldier, Mack Bolan paused in the midst of battle. The face of the driver was that of a young woman, with pretty pale skin and flowing reddish-blond hair, beautiful even in the garish blaze of the motorcycle's headlights. Bolan was reminded suddenly of another young woman he had known once, long ago.

Then a 9 mm Glock pistol appeared in the hands of the driver and the memory faded. She was Colleen Davis, murderer of children. The Glock fired at the same moment the blast of the .44 Magnum round filled the desert night. Bolan felt the sudden burst of pain as the 9 mm slug slammed into his rib cage, the force mitigated only partially by the body armor under his black nightsuit.

He pressed on the spot carefully. Nothing was broken, but he would have a large, ugly bruise on his ribs for weeks to come. A painful reminder of a moment of indecision.

Perching the massive motorcycle on its kickstand, ignoring Blacksuit Eight's approaching headlights, he walked to the stalled Hummer, the earth crunching under his feet. As he lifted her head, he saw that Colleen Davis bore a single black entry wound in her face, just above the left eye.

CHAPTER EIGHTEEN

Stony Man Farm, Virginia

"Check this out."

Kurtzman wheeled across the room, filled with curiosity. Still embroiled to his eyeballs in the suddenly under-control hard probe in Santa Fe, he hardly expected to be interrupted by Akira Tokaido unless it was absolutely vital—or highly unusual.

"What's up?"

"I tracked this as we were downloading all that data off the Mahoney system." The younger man tapped one of the dozen windows open on his screen. The download, in fact, was still underway. Now that the household in New Mexico belonged to Stony Man Farm, they could take their time about extracting every last byte of data.

"What is that?" Kurtzman asked. It was extremely seldom that he didn't recognize one of the application windows on his own system. This one showed nothing except a simple cartoon graphic of a pair of eyes looking around a corner.

"A voyeur," Tokaido said. "It's a little bit of software I built to look for lurkers on a server during an emergency download."

Kurtzman nodded suddenly. "I remember discussing this a year ago. You were going to implement this in our emergency download system."

"I was going to and I did," Tokaido said. "Then I more or less forgot about it until today. We've never raided a system with somebody watching us before. Then, when it came up as we started the download on the T1, I didn't want to bother you. So I went ahead and traced it back to its source. That was about the best we could do with it. Whoever he was, he was cut off when the T1 cable got sliced."

Kurtzman nodded. "And the source?"

"The Mirage. You know the big hotel in Vegas with the guys with the white tigers?"

"I've stayed there," Kurtzman said.

"Our lurker is there right now."

"Can you give me a room number?"

Tokaido shook his head. "You know what hotel phone systems are like. I got as far as the electronic switching system in their basement. After that, my trace got lost in the chaos."

"Too bad. Now tell me this guy didn't get into our systems."

"He didn't," Tokaido said. "Didn't even try, actually. Probably didn't have the expertise to trace us back to the source. Even if he did, you know he wouldn't stand a snowball's chance in hell of finagling his way through our security."

Kurtzman nodded. He knew how good Stony Man Farm computer security was. And he knew that there was no security measure in the world today that wouldn't be hacked tomorrow. "Good work anyway, Akira. I'm just not sure if this means anything."

"It means one of the key players wasn't at home in

Santa Fe when our teams let themselves in the front door. Whoever it was just happened to be accessing the system at the same time we were."

"Can't be," Kurtzman said with a frown. "Mack powered it up for us. The system wasn't on-line until that time."

A crease crossed Tokaido's face as he thought about that, slapping his blue-jeaned thigh with his thumb to an unheard beat. This was behavior Kurtzman saw often when the young hacker was headphoned and immersed in his heavy-metal music. When he wasn't wearing headphones, the behavior signaled sudden, furious thought.

"Then the only thing that makes sense is that somebody was sitting there waiting for the system to come on-line," Tokaido said, not liking this conclusion. "Somebody who knew the IP for this specific piece of hardware. Somebody's system was just sitting there waiting for activity to start. Or else they just happened to stumble onto us."

Kurtzman shook his head. "I'd say that's unlikely. I'm inclined to agree with your first idea. Somebody was keeping an eye on this system, just waiting for it to get up and running, then spy on whatever activity took place. Assuming they were able to watch what was happening."

"They were," Tokaido confirmed. "They had full system access, and I wasn't about to try to block them. I was afraid that if I did, I'd send our own download into toxic shock."

Kurtzman stretched backward in his chair, staring at the ceiling lights and pondering the implications. "So he had to be an insider. Why would an insider spy on his own computer?"

"Maybe as a security measure?" Tokaido posed.

"Why would they be expecting an intrusive system download?"

Tokaido shrugged, grinning and shaking his head. "I'm out of answers, boss. Maybe why it was will become more obvious when we know who it was."

Kurtzman nodded. "By determining who is not present at the Santa Fe mansion."

Santa Fe, New Mexico

KURTZMAN'S VOICE CAME OVER Bolan's headset. "Stony Base here. You on-line, Stony One?"

"I'm getting you, Stony Base." Bolan had parked the motorcycle on the front drive and was heading into the house, now securely in the hands of the Stony Man blacksuits. Lights were blazing inside and out, and beyond the flood lamps of the grounds, a half mile out and increasing their distance, the blacksuit Hummers were traveling rapidly in an ever-expanding search grid, just in case an unseen escapee was at large in the desert. They might have saved their fuel. Everybody who had been in residence when the probe commenced was inside the house still, with the exception of Colleen Davis and Bill O'Massey. And those two weren't going anywhere.

"It's urgent that I get photos ASAP," Kurtzman said.

Bolan looked questioningly at McDonald, the blacksuit commander, who had set up a small command center in the kitchen.

"McDonald here, Stony Base," the man said, touching his transmit button. "Photos will be downloading to you in ninety seconds or less. Incidentally, we've got a survivor."

"The man in the bedroom on the third floor," Bolan stated.

"Yes, sir. Blasted all to hell, but he'll live. My men are stabilizing him now."

Blacksuit Four entered the room with a small black plastic box no larger than a paperback novel. He waved it in the air briefly. "I got lots of good snaps of all of them. But none of them would smile for me."

"Give me that," McDonald said, his voice tinged with irritation. He didn't appreciate it when his men joked around in front of senior Stony Man staff. Especially this man, Striker.

But Striker's mouth was set in a firm line that was about as close to a grin as McDonald had ever seen.

The truth was that Bolan wasn't bothered in the least by a little bit of kidding around by the blacksuits. They'd just performed a superlative probe that, with its long list of unknown factors, had plenty of opportunity for crashes. If they were a little at ease now that the tension was lifted, he couldn't have cared less.

"Stony Base, you're going to be getting some bad news when you look at those pictures," Bolan said to Kurtzman

"What kind of bad news?"

"The missing-persons variety. Clint Mahoney's face won't be among the images you receive."

"Anybody else missing?"

"Yeah. Dr. Icahn."

"Davis?"

"She's here."

"Here she is. I'm getting her picture right now. She was looking better this afternoon."

"My fault."

"I have a feeling Mahoney and/or Icahn are on vacation.'' Kurtzman briefly explained the unusual eye-witness watching the Stony Man Farm download of data, and its trace back to the Las Vegas hotel.

''Strange time for a holiday. And not much of a lead. That's a large hotel,'' Bolan understated. ''But if it's Mahoney or Icahn, I'll find them.''

''You're heading to Vegas?''

''I'm out of other things to do, unless you've got a better lead for me to follow.''

''I'm sorry to say I don't,'' Kurtzman admitted. ''I'll arrange for you to take one of the blacksuit vehicles.''

''No need,'' Bolan said. ''I've got my own transportation.''

BOLAN MADE AN ATTEMPT to question the survivor. The man was barely conscious, and it soon became plain he had little in the way of useful knowledge about Mahoney's strategy. Whatever the man's plans were, they might be entirely out the window after the hard probe of his control center.

But Bolan didn't think so.

Leaving McDonald and his team to clean up the mess, he headed out. It was the middle of the night, and the road stretching between himself and Las Vegas, Nevada, was six hundred miles of the loneliest asphalt in America. Well before dawn he crossed into Arizona and found himself wishing it was light out. He appreciated the vast lonely beauty of the long stretches of Four Corners landscape. He felt for the people who lived there, their spirit all but destroyed, their endless suffering.

There was nothing he could do to help people such as the Navaho, Pueblo and Zuni.

Or was there?

When the early dawn came over the horizon, Bolan

was within sight of the startling green patchwork of land that was one of the Navaho agricultural cooperatives, where the People piped in the precious water from miles and miles away and carefully urged the soil to grow great, vivid fields of crops, forcing abundance out of the stingy soil of the desert.

Bolan's thoughts unwillingly pictured the results of the loss of that water. It wouldn't kill the Navaho. They'd survive. Subsistence would come, as it always did, from the federal government. But once again the ego of the People would have taken a blow, as they failed in their attempt to adapt to the world without committing cultural suicide. At the same time there appeared, all too vividly, an image of the turn of events that would bring about such devastation. He didn't want to think it was true. Maybe it wasn't. Maybe he was letting his imagination run away with him.

He was dog-tired, but the inertia of his soldier's will kept him awake and alert as the morning grew bright and hot, and soon he was wheeling the motorcycle across the great dam that watered the southwestern U.S.

The White House, Washington, D.C.

"THEY DID WHAT?" Brognola thundered.

"I'm sorry, Hal," the President of the United States of America said, opening his hands in a helpless gesture. He was somewhat taken aback. Not many men had the brass balls to raise their voices in the Oval Office. Even Hal Brognola—usually.

"They made a *deal?*"

"I thought it best you hear it from me," the President said.

"They signed away their souls to the devil," Brognola growled. "They paid the murderers of their own people for services rendered!"

"They aren't even convinced that Mahoney was behind the Bedoya Dam blast," the President said, his voice even and at its most reassuring.

"They know."

"There's no evidence to tie Mahoney to the crimes. Nothing convincing enough for the Peruvians. And they're desperate, Hal."

"I know they're in dire straits, Mr. President. I've been getting regular reports on the situation on the city streets in Lima."

"A city of millions of people," the President reminded him. "Red Cross and UN relief efforts are capable of just so much. They can't possibly hope to bring in the huge amounts of water a city of that size needs just to exist day to day. Lima needs a method for providing large amounts of clean water, and that's what they are buying."

"Just like Mahoney planned."

"Perhaps."

"They couldn't have cooperated with his terrorist efforts any more effectively," Brognola added bitterly.

"What would you have them do?" the President asked, shrugging, "allow their streets to become ever-expanding cesspools of disease? Or grab for any option that will help save their population? I know what I'd do."

Brognola looked up at him sharply.

"I would save my people. Worry about prosecuting the guilty parties later, after the damage control."

"The United States refuses to negotiate with terrorists," Brognola declared.

"This President of the United States refuses to let

vast numbers of his people die horribly when there is a way of saving them. No ethical leader would do so.''

With a flash of awareness, it occurred to the big Fed what the Man was saying to him, and he almost choked on the words. "Don't tell me you intend to purchase desalinization units from Mahoney?"

"I don't," the President stated flatly, sitting straight and businesslike in his leather upholstered chair, "but the mayor of San Diego does. And I sure as hell am not going to tell him he can't."

Brognola started to speak, but the President gave him an icy glare that silenced him.

"Two reasons, Hal. One—there's no evidence to tie Mahoney to the destruction of the Southern California dam, just as in Peru and Turkmenistan—evidence clearcut enough to convince the people who need that water. Two—Mahoney's technology is his only choice, literally. Without a huge supply of clean water, which no other government or agency in the hemisphere has any hope of providing, San Diego will literally wither and die. She'll be a bankrupt ghost town in months."

"She'll be bankrupt anyway," Brognola predicted, calmer but still breathing fire. "If Icahn has brokered his deal with the Peruvians, I can only assume his next stop is Turkmenistan. I have a feeling he'll walk out of that meeting with a bill of sale as well. When he gets to San Diego—the market with the most money—he'll conveniently claim his manufacturing resources are tapped out. He'll have to charge San Diego incredibly exorbitant rates. San Diego won't be able to afford it. They'll go to the state. California won't be able to afford it. Guess who'll foot the bill?"

The President regarded the big Fed for a long moment. "We'll see."

Stony Man Farm, Virginia

"WHO'S THAT?" Brognola asked less than two hours later, as he sat in the War Room with a sweet roll and a coffee. The roll was made with fruit out of the Farm's orchard and was delicious. The coffee was made by Aaron Kurtzman and was atrocious.

The screen showed a snarling young man's face.

"Mahoney's son, Jared," Barbara Price answered. "He's in his early twenties. They haven't exactly had a close father-and-son relationship, but they hooked up with each other recently. Mahoney found him rotting in jail on a small-time drug charge. He got him out and gave him a place to stay. Jared was living in Santa Fe until he and Icahn traveled to Lima together."

Brognola frowned. "This is Mahoney's salesman?"

"Not a good one, by all accounts," Kurtzman said. "All reports say he is arrogant, rude and almost always intoxicated. He goes through periods of extreme agitation that suggest he's using narcotics in addition to alcohol. But he managed to stay sober enough to strike a hard bargain with the Peruvian government."

"Only because the Peruvians had no choice," Price added. "They're paying a small fortune for each and every one of the two hundred desalination units they've promised to buy. The two-year deal will eventually gross Mahoney close to three-quarters of a billion dollars U.S. That's billion with a *B*."

"The Peruvians had to come up with fifty million dollars U.S. on the spot, just to close the deal. Jared Mahoney insisted the cash be deposited in a Mahoney account within an hour of signing the deal, or all agreements were null and void."

"He's behaving like an extortionist," Brognola muttered. "What's happening to that fifty million?"

"You're not going to like what we found. We started the trace as soon as we were alerted to it," Price explained. She had received the call within minutes of the conclusion of the big Fed's prebreakfast meeting with the President. "One disadvantage of Mahoney's little scheme is that he's trying to make it look perfectly legit. Which means the cash travels through legitimate channels and we can follow it."

"Follow it where?"

"Just about everywhere on the American continents," piped in Kurtzman. He touched a control that brought up the image of North and South America on a global grid on the wall-mounted screen. A thick red line began traveling across the screen, moving with sharp turns as Kurtzman explained. "It journeyed from Peru to Brazil, then to the Caymans, to Los Angeles, to Boston. Then it finally left the Americas." At this point the red line traveled into the grid of the Atlantic Ocean, heading on a vague northern-European course until it disappeared off the edge of the screen. "Each and every time it went from one Mahoney account to another, each one unknown by us and inactive until the transactions started. The trail was very well-planned."

"For what purpose?" Brognola asked.

"For creating red tape in case the Peruvians demand it back, if and when they decide Mahoney was actually guilty of causing their water-supply problems in the first place. Each of the accounts was owned by a distinct legal corporation of some kind, established by Mahoney for this one purpose. It might have taken him just a few hours to make the money transfers, but any legal action designed to drag it back along that trail would be subject to years of potential legal delays.''

"We thought Davis was the systems whiz," Price complained.

"She was. She set this all up months ago. Mahoney didn't have to know all the intricacies to make use of it this morning," Kurtzman explained.

"So where is it now?"

"Here's the kicker," Kurtzman said. "It was converted to currency."

"Where?"

Without a word, Kurtzman pressed a control and the screen scrolled to the right. The thick red line traveled at a steep angle into the North Atlantic and stopped at a tiny speckle of islands.

"The Faeroes?" Brognola asked incredulously. "Are you sure?"

"I'm sure."

"Mahoney could buy the entire island chain off Denmark for that much cash. Why there?"

To the left of the map appeared the face of a haggard, brutal-looking man in a yellow fisherman's raincoat.

"Clive White. An old friend of Clint Mahoney from the days of the Troubles," Price narrated. "He runs a pair of shipping vessels out of Eysturoy these days. But he's been to the U.S. to visit Mahoney annually for the past four years, and Mahoney stops by to visit him every once in a while as well. This intelligence is all courtesy of the British, by the way. They've been keeping a very close eye on him for the past decade."

"What did he do to warrant their attention?"

"Nothing that they have proof of, but they are sure he's the logistician behind a number of violent acts against English citizens. Murder, bombing, arson, rape, you name it. He was run out of Ireland after the peace accords in 1998, then changed his identity and managed to bury himself pretty deeply in his new life. The Danes probably don't even know who they've got living on their island.''

"Have you pegged him as the individual cashing in on the Peruvian down payment?'' Brognola asked.

"Yes.''

"Then what?''

"Within an hour of receiving the payment and taking the cash, White headed out to sea in his flagship vessel, the *Deep Seven*. For an ugly little fishing trawler, it's moving like a bat out of hell. We've been keeping an eye on him every minute we're able.''

Price hit a remote control that replaced the photo of Clive White with a low-orbit satellite black-and-white photo of the ocean. One of the Faeroe islands dominated the upper half of the shot. At the bottom of the screen the tiny dot of the *Deep Seven* was computer enhanced with red. In the next shot it had turned south, and in regular succession the next several shots, taken from various orbital angles and perspectives, showed it gradually heading southeast, deeper into the North Sea. All at once another ship appeared in one of the shots, and Price held the image on the screen.

"We don't know who that is,'' she said in answer to Brognola's unasked question. "The *Deep Seven* stopped at this point and waited for the other ship. Clearly it was a planned meeting. They sat in the middle of the ocean together until just twenty minutes ago.''

"Long enough to transfer the cash,'' Brognola mused, "and transfer something else aboard the fishing trawler in exchange.''

"That was our thought,'' Kurtzman said.

"What happened twenty minutes ago?" Brognola asked.

Price hit the control and the final satellite image was shown. The unknown ship was now sailing away, southeast, to the northern coast of Europe, perhaps the Scandinavian peninsula. The *Deep Seven* was continuing southwest, toward Great Britain.

"Mahoney works fast, you have to give him that," Brognola muttered. "He's had the money for less than a day, and already he's using the funds to renew terrorism back home."

"That was our assumption," Price said, nodding. "But it's only an assumption. We can't be sure until we see what, if anything, was transferred to the *Deep Seven.*"

Brognola nodded. "So let's take a look."

"I thought you'd see it my way," Price said. "Phoenix is en route to the North Sea from Central Asia. They were striking out in Turkmenistan, anyway."

"No more leads on our friend Aya Endovik?"

"He's fled Turkmenistan, and is probably holed up in far-eastern Russia by now. He has contacts there," Price explained. "His organization was essentially destroyed in the Phoenix raid when we decimated his ranks of officers. By spreading the word implicating him in the dam attack, we've made his name mud in his home country."

"Even the rabble are out to get him, now," Kurtzman added.

"Not worth pursuing, then?"

"We've got bigger fish to fry, in my opinion," Price said. "Endovik will still be lurking when this is all over. We can take care of him later. I'm confident he's no longer trustworthy in the eyes of Clint Mahoney. They won't be working together again soon.''

Brognola absorbed the facts, churned them in his mind during the time it took to swallow an antacid tablet and grind at the end of a fresh cigar. He agreed, as he usually did, with the rationale Price and Kurtzman had developed. "Fine. What's the strategy in the North Sea?"

"Depends on the behavior of the *Deep Seven* in the next eight hours," Price replied. "As Aaron said, this isn't your ordinary fishing trawler. She's cruising at forty knots at the moment and we think she can go much faster, judging by some of the distances she's covered today."

"Looks like she's heading directly toward England," Brognola stated. "That makes me a little uneasy."

"Yeah," Kurtzman said. "Can't be a social call."

"They can't make the British east coast before Phoenix pops in for a visit, no matter how fast their engines are," Price assured them. "Then we'll get some answers."

CHAPTER NINETEEN

Las Vegas, Nevada

At 10:00 a.m., Aaron Kurtzman provided Bolan with the room number for Clint Mahoney.

In the end the solution for locating Mahoney among the thousands of hotel guests was a simple task. Kurtzman simply searched for any room from which phone calls had been made to Lima, Peru.

There was just one. A suite, reserved under the name Frank Merchant. Bolan staked out the door for half an hour and struck pay dirt.

The man who emerged matched the photo the soldier had memorized of Clint Mahoney. The man who came to the door of the neighboring suite when Mahoney knocked was Mahoney's engineer, an Irishman named Thomas McDonough.

Bolan was just in time. They were checking out. As he stood in the small elevator lobby on the fourteenth floor, pretending to read a paper and occasionally glance at his watch, as if he were waiting for a tardy wife, he watched them heavily tip an arriving bellboy and pass off their luggage.

"We'll pick it up out front, son," Mahoney said to the bellboy, his accent perfectly American.

Bolan appeared to give up on his wife and touched the call button for the elevator. He rode to the lobby with the pair of terrorists, staring at the numbers of the LED display the whole way down. He slumped against the wall, looking as small as he could. But no change in posture could hide the strength in his physique, and he caught Mahoney giving him the once-over.

None of them said a word.

Bolan wondered briefly if he should just take out the pair of them right then and there.

At once he discarded the idea. The Mahoney organization, as wounded as it had been by the raid at the Santa Fe mansion the night before, was still alive and kicking. Cutting off the head of the beast wouldn't slow it at this stage. The trick was to get the entire body of it together and completely dismember it.

The list of names Stony Man Farm had extracted from the Santa Fe electronics system was extensive. Many of the major players in the organization had yet to be tracked down.

As Mahoney checked out at the front desk, McDonough put several dollar coins into a slot machine. Bolan left the hotel and made for the parking garage, then pulled to the front of the building. The front drive to the lobby entrance was so long he could straddle the Valkyrie at the curb fifty yards away from the entrance and still see every person who entered or left. He watched the Mahoney-McDonough baggage materialize on a bellboy's cart, and five minutes later a Suburban rolled past him and stopped at the curb. McDonough got out and tipped the bellboy again when he loaded the baggage in the rear of the big vehicle.

Bolan wished he'd had time to equip himself more thoroughly before this trip. He would easily have been able to get a small bug into that luggage during the period it was out of their sight. Then he would be hearing the entire conversation going on right now inside the Suburban.

He didn't dwell on it. He'd find some way of learning their plans.

"I'M ABOUT AN HOUR northeast of Vegas," Bolan reported on the cellular phone. "There's a small city around here called Overton, but we're a good twenty minutes outside it. Mahoney's just established himself a new base of operations if I'm seeing this correctly." He read the location to Barbara Price.

"We're on it. Anything happening there?"

"You could say that," Bolan replied, staring down from his hilltop perch into the fenced grounds of the house. "Looks like Mahoney's going to start a war with the state of Nevada. He's got vehicles arriving regularly. Three so far this afternoon. Mostly heavy-duty diesel pickups with caps and a few sports utility vehicles. They're unloading boxes of what appear to be explosives on the grounds of the home."

"Great."

"Yeah. They're going after the Hoover Dam. I don't think there's any way of denying it any longer."

"Do they have lake access?" Price asked.

"A private dock."

"Here we go," Price said. "I'm getting the details on the address now. He rented the house just twenty-four hours ago. Six thousand square feet of luxury estate on five acres of beautiful, unspoiled Lake Mead shoreline. Private dock and use of two small pleasure craft. Beauty and luxury in a rugged, secluded setting just one hour north of Las Vegas."

"Perfect vacation getaway for the overworked mass murderer," Bolan said. "Where's Able?"

"Still in Lima. I wanted them on the scene in case the opportunity arose to apprehend Dr. Icahn."

"That's not going to happen?"

"No." Price practically spit the word. "Instead, he's become the national hero." She explained how Icahn, along with the newly identified son of Clint Mahoney, had struck a deal with the government of Peru to sell them desalinization devices. "He'll take them for hundreds of millions at what he's charging," she said. "And with the strong economic trading ties Peru is developing, especially with Japan, Peru can't risk simply taking the technology and using it illegally. Peruvian patented technology trade would dry up overnight."

"I assume the doctor is trying to market his wares in Turkmenistan now?"

"Sure. With their recent oil deals starting to pay off, they've got money to pay for the technology."

"And the U.S.?" Bolan asked.

"Icahn and Jared Mahoney have an appointment to meet with the mayor of San Diego and his staff day after tomorrow. The assumption is that by that time Icahn will force Southern California to pay for start-up of the manufacturing. The U.S. taxpayer will end up paying twice or three times as much as the Peruvian taxpayer, who is already being ripped off."

"And it's all slated to fund a new terrorist war against the English," Bolan concluded.

"That's a good guess," Price said. "I've got Phoenix on that. They're scheduled to rendezvous with the *Deep Seven* in a few hours."

"If Able Team is just sitting on their thumbs in South America, get them up here pronto," Bolan said. "I want them prepped to take down Mahoney and his organization."

"What's the schedule?" Price asked.

"That's up to Mahoney," Bolan said, watching the slow pace of the activity below. "I have a feeling I'm only seeing the small tip of a very large iceberg."

"That would be correct," Price agreed. "The data we got out of the computer system in Santa Fe included a hierarchical organizational chart that includes at least forty U.S.-based men. All are identified strictly by code names, and so far we haven't found any way of getting the real names of these people. If and when we do, we can start going after them."

"I don't want to disparage your efforts, but I'm not counting on you finding that key," Bolan said. "Besides, we might not need it. If we wait, Mahoney is going to gather many of those men around him."

"The implication from what little useful data we're uncovering is that Mahoney's being especially careful about what he calls Phase Four," Price said. "And we can only assume Hoover Dam is Phase Four. This time he intends to use his own people for the operation."

"So the good news is Mahoney's organization will all be here in Nevada," Bolan mused. "If we can manage to take care of them all at once, this scheme can be stopped before it goes any further. The bad news is it'll be that much harder to shut down Phase Four."

"And if you don't want to scare them off, we can't call for outside assistance until the last minute," Price added. "It's just us Farmers."

Bolan considered the options, but his decision was already made. He would lay low for now. Let Mahoney gather his troops. Let him proceed with the preparations for the destruction of one of the most important civil engineering projects on the planet. Then, at the last minute, he and his companions, a collection of the finest warriors ever bred or trained, would strike. And strike hard.

"Get the blacksuit team here as fast as possible. When Phoenix finishes in the British Isles, plan on bringing them in. Then we'll all just sit here until the time is right."

"Hurry up and wait," Price stated.

"Yeah."

"Able will be on its way in an hour. McDonald's team, too. Both will join you by midnight," Price said. "Phoenix's schedule is a big fat unknown until they figure out what's going on. There's certainly *something* going on in the North Sea, but damned if we know what it is."

North Sea

"WHAT ARE OUR CHANCES of getting onto that boat?" David McCarter posed the question to the thoughtful figures in the aircraft's interior.

"Slim," T. J. Hawkins replied morosely.

"I can dive into it," Rafael Encizo said.

"That's a hell of a drop," McCarter pointed out.

"Difficult but not impossible," Encizo said. "They're moving fast but not faster than I can go during a controlled fall, and they're lit well enough. Finding the target won't be a problem."

"Then what?" Calvin James asked. "You get on board and take down the crew on your own?"

"You're not getting out of a little work that easily," Encizo replied. "I'm betting their attention will be fixed on the horizon. They'll be watching for patrol boats, not a single unarmed man. I believe I'll be able to sneak around long enough to cut some wires or throw some circuits. Stop them dead in the water. Then you guys can come alongside and join me for the cruise.''

Hawkins shrugged. ''Aren't we making this too hard on ourselves? Seems easier just to wait and see what'll happen when they dock. Surely somebody will search them.''

McCarter shook his head, a concerned frown creasing his forehead. ''I've got a bad feeling about this bleeding boat, mates,'' he said. ''She's not what she seems, that's obvious enough just by her speed. I'm not going to be happy until I've laid bare the rest of her secrets.''

FORTY MINUTES LATER, the *Deep Seven* appeared as a small batch of lights hugging the dark ocean. Phoenix Force's de Havilland aircraft was cruising high enough to avoid any suspicions the crew might have of the aircraft, as long as they didn't linger there unnecessarily.

''They sure as hell aren't going to expect some crazy son of a bitch jumping out of a plane in the middle of the night,'' Encizo said with a boyish grin.

''We'll be twenty minutes behind you,'' McCarter said. ''If you miss—''

''I won't miss,'' Encizo said. ''I've got zero desire to go floating around the North Sea in the middle of the night. See you on board.''

Encizo gave a brief wave as McCarter got the word from the cockpit and signaled the Cuban-born commando, who headed for the exit.

''PHOENIX TWO HERE. You with me Phoenix One?''

''I'm with you, Rafe.'' McCarter's voice came

clearly through the tiny headphones, while the whistle of the wind increased to a howl around him.

"Stony Base, you on the line?"

"Stony Base, here," Price said. Encizo's signal was being picked up by the radio in the de Havilland and added to the two-way communications system that was keeping the aircraft and the Farm in constant contact. "We read you loud and clear. How's your descent?"

Encizo heard the twinge of doubt in her voice. She wasn't one-hundred-percent confident in his ability to make this jump, either. Truth be told, Encizo was sweating in his blacksuit from the strain, both physical and mental, as he steered his body through the atmosphere to the perfect chute deployment point. "No problems out here," Encizo said, his voice brimming with self-confidence. "I'm deploying now."

He yanked the cord and tensed his body for the shock. When the chute bit the air, his descent slowed suddenly and yanked his torso out of its free fall. His limbs flopped like the arms and legs of a stuffed doll before he grabbed the risers and began steering himself and the chute after the fleeing *Deep Seven*.

The trawler's rate of travel made it about the fastest fishing vessel in Europe, but with the airfoil guided correctly Encizo caught up to it and hovered just above its aft end, watching for signs of activity. The only indication of life came from the forecastle, where the bridge windows afforded the pilot of the vessel a 360-degree view. A dim light glowed from within the forecastle, from a small, green-shaded banker's desk lamp and the luminescence from banks of controls. Encizo didn't know much about fishing-vessel control systems, but what he saw, even from that far out, didn't fit his image of a fishing trawler.

"Phoenix Two here. I'm seeing high-end electronics in the control room," Encizo reported over his channel to the de Havilland.

"To be expected," McCarter replied. "They'd have to upgrade the controls when they put in new power plants."

Which still doesn't explain why they had the high-end power plants in the first place, Encizo thought. He was trying to follow the movements of the figures on the bridge, which revealed just two men. The faint illumination didn't show him their features, and he had to make his best guess about the direction they were facing from their behavior. Not that he had much choice. He was dropping. His best techniques for stalling and gliding the airfoil gave him just a few extra seconds leeway. Finally the moment came when he had to glide onto the deck of the *Deep Seven* or ditch it in the North Sea.

He chose the vessel. With a sudden tilt forward he steered toward the deck, unable to tell whether he was being watched from the bridge or not. Guess he'd know if and when the bullets started flying, he said to himself. And if the bullets did start flying, he was just a few quick steps away from the ocean anyway.

His feet hit the deck running and he descended to his knees behind a fishing-net-crane control, twisting hard and dragging in the billowing material of the chute until it was wadded into a large ball. He hit the transmit button on his chest.

"Phoenix Two here. The Cuban has landed."

The crane's control was mounted on two-inch posts on the deck, presumably to allow water to flow under it instead of into it. He hastily stuffed the chute there. Encizo waited for no more than ten seconds—the time it took him to pull out a silenced 92-F and a two-edged fighting knife—then stepped into the open. The deck remained deserted. The perpetual hush of the ocean slashing against the quick-moving hull and the thrum of the unseen, improbable powerhouse engine were the only noises.

Encizo crossed the deck in a crouch, taking up a position behind a steel, deck-mounted container intended to house the nets when they weren't in use, and found he had a better view of the bridge from that position.

"Phoenix Two here."

"Stony Base here. Go ahead, Phoenix Two."

"I'm on deck, and I've got a pretty good view of the bridge. There are two crew members inside."

"What's your status, Phoenix Two?" Price asked.

"I've managed to stay undetected. There's no crew on the deck. This place sure is quiet."

"Stay sharp, Phoenix Two. There's got to be more than just the captain and his first mate."

"Roger that, Stony Base."

The darkness on the deck made the next stage of his search more difficult. He moved cautiously, quickly around the deck, moving from one hiding place to another. A drop in the breeze allowed the smell of fish to build up in Encizo's nostrils. He sniffed it, frowning. It was potent, but not nearly as strong as he would have expected from a working fishing vessel.

Maybe this wasn't a fishing vessel any longer. Maybe its use was relegated to other, less wholesome activities since it had been outfitted with its extrapowerful engines.

Finally he found himself crouching at the base of the wall of the forecastle. There was a small door set into the wall with a Danger: High Voltage sign emblazoned in letters that were almost unreadable in the darkness. Encizo opened the door and found the switch he was looking for.

"Phoenix Two here. I've found the emergency power cutoff."

"Roger that, Phoenix Two. Stand by."

Encizo listened as Price relayed a series of instructions to the remaining commandos in the de Havilland. Then she came back on the line.

"Phoenix One, Four and Five are on their way down. They'll hit the water in the next ninety seconds. I read them about one thousand yards behind you. They'll need about two minutes to have the raft inflated and running, another five to reach the *Deep Seven*."

"Standing by," Encizo said, melting into the deep shadows in a corner at the base of the forecastle wall. "Phoenix Five, you have any ideas how long we can expect the power outage to affect the control systems?"

T. J. Hawkins, the youngest member of Phoenix Force, was also the most up-to-date on electronics and microprocessor state of the art—which led to long, enthusiastic discussions with Aaron Kurtzman and Gadgets Schwarz that the other commandos found indecipherable and monotonous. But this time Hawkins's expertise was foiled by his ignorance of the system under discussion. "Unknown, Phoenix Two," he radioed back. "They could have anything going on in that bridge, including a battery backup that won't only save the system in case of a power outage, but allow it to continue to operate."

"Stony Base here. What are the consequences if that's the case, Phoenix Five?" Price asked.

"Then the *Deep Seven* might not even slow in her tracks when we cut her power."

That wasn't what Encizo wanted to hear. "Hey, I never bargained for pulling off this stunt all on my own," he transmitted.

"Relax. That's only a possibility, Rafe," Hawkins returned.

"We'll know in a hundred and twenty seconds, mates," McCarter cut in, with the beep of the on-target signal from the cockpit sounding behind his voice. "Stony Base, we're out of here."

"Roger that, Phoenix One."

Encizo listened to virtual silence. The rapid thrum of the engines below his feet notwithstanding, the dark emptiness of the night on the speeding fishing trawler was almost peaceful. He was experienced enough to know this was just the calm before the hurricane. He relaxed, allowing his body to melt into a yogalike state of highly lucid serenity. If there was one thing years of karate and kung fu training had taught him, it was that the most effective warriors were the dispassionate, relaxed, highly sensitized fighters. He wanted to be in such a state when the chaos commenced.

It wouldn't be long now.

At the 120-second mark he got to his feet, scanned the bare deck for movement, then crossed to the access panel for the power. First he reached into the deepest part of the cavity and placed a small, radio-activated explosive in place, out of sight.

The explosive was actually Plan B for stopping the trawler. Plan A was much simpler. With a small jerk, Encizo pulled the circuit breaker.

The thrum of the engine died to a murmur and then was gone, the trawler's speed dropping so quickly Encizo had to brace his feet to maintain his balance. He adjusted the circuit breaker so that it looked as if it had simply popped out of its slot, then descended into the shadows of the deck equipment.

Walking in a crouch, he made his way to the rear of the trawler, coming to a stop at a point where he had a 180-degree view of the sea to the northeast of the vessel. He dragged the thermal imaging glasses over his eyes, watching the empty water and listening to the suddenly quiet night.

The hush of the waves against the hull was nothing compared to the sound of the engine, and he easily made out the voices that approached from the front of the boat. They weren't happy voices.

McCarter's voice came over the radio. "Phoenix One here, Phoenix Two."

As the erratic sweep of flashlights crossed the night's darkness Encizo pushed the tone signal one time, generating a single beep at McCarter's end while enabling him to stay silent as the voices closed in. The Briton got the message and answered succinctly, "We're four minutes out."

"Where's the line run?" asked one of the voices.

"Right here."

There was sound of footsteps closing in, and a moment later Encizo clearly heard a man swearing under his breath on the other side of the container he was crouching against. Two men, he considered, unsuspecting and maybe not even armed. He could get to his feet and take them out with a single shot each from the silenced Beretta leathered against his rib cage. If the two of them were the total crew of the trawler, then the operation would be instantly controlled.

He discarded the idea when another voice, the third, called from the bridge window. "What's the problem?"

"Haven't found it yet. You sure it's not inside?"

"Yeah, I'm bloody sure."

Their voices were thick with an Irish brogue and the two were muttering bitterly under their breath as they hunted the deck.

"Here it is."

They had moved closer to the side of the deck and Encizo inched away, keeping himself out of their line of sight. Their flashlight's glow, even pointed down at the deck, was enough to make him visible.

"That's the hoist power feed," one of the men protested.

"Shamus says its the main feed."

"So what're we supposed to do about it?" Without waiting for an answer, the speaker turned to the bridge and shouted. "Hey, where's this feed line come from?"

"From the generator in the engine room," the man on the bridge shouted. "What's the problem?"

"Can't tell anything from here."

"Then look below!"

After more whispered griping, the figures on the deck stomped back to the forecastle and were gone. Encizo didn't allow himself to be relieved. They were nowhere near out of the woods yet. He wouldn't feel the smallest measure of safety until the rest of Phoenix Force was on board, and he scanned the steady swells of the sea with his thermal field glasses, finding it easy now to pick up the approaching warm spots on the cool ocean.

"Phoenix Two here," he said into his microphone. "I'm alone again."

"Everything under control, Phoenix Two?" McCarter asked.

"For the time being."

The small electric motor, specially noise-insulated for covert operations, was valiantly spinning against the rolling of the North Sea and didn't appear to Encizo to be getting anywhere. The small warm spot hadn't grown much in size as the door on the forecastle opened abruptly, slamming against the wall, and the two figures stomped out onto the deck again.

"How the hell are we supposed to know?" one of them shouted. "I ain't no electrician."

They headed directly to the panel in the wall of the forecastle underneath the bridge window and yanked it open.

"Yeah, it's tripped," he shouted.

"Well, reset it!"

There was a sound of metal actuation and the lights came on again. After the near-total darkness, even the warning lights and the bridge glow were bright, and Encizo stiffened as he lowered the glasses and realized he was able to make out the indistinct shape of the approaching raft, like a small mass of flotsam. Waiting impatiently, he heard the engines begin to come back on-line. He also heard the closing of the panel door. As the two men were walking away, Encizo grabbed the small radio control out of his pocket, opened the tiny window to the switch, and actuated it with a flick of his finger. There was a small burst from the panel, more of a sizzle than an explosion. But it did the trick. The power outage was sudden and complete, and the engine hum turned to a spinning deceleration, over which Encizo distinctly heard in the same instant the swell of profanity out of the two Irishmen and the distant hum of the electric motor on the approaching raft.

"Phoenix Two here," he hissed into the radio. "Kill your motor."

"Roger that," McCarter answered, and in the same instant the hum of the motor died in the night.

Encizo was relieved to hear no lull in the angry voices of the men on the deck as they marched back to the panel and ripped it open. They had failed to detect the sound of the small motor over their own voices.

"*Now* what?" It was the man on the bridge.

"Something burned up in there." The men were coughing now in the swell of acrid smoke issuing from the panel.

"How'd that happen?"

"It's your boat! You tell me!"

More footsteps and the door slammed again. Encizo risked a look, now finding three men on the deck, huddled around the open panel as the last wisps of smoke seeped out of it, into the night. The new arrival took the flashlight from one of the others and examined the cavity.

"The breaker's still in place."

"Something's gone and cooked the wiring," one of the others suggested.

"That shouldn't have happened. Should've just tossed the breaker again."

Encizo turned away just long enough to glance at the approaching raft through the thermal field glasses. By the time he turned back, the new arrival on the deck had his arm all the way inside the cavity and was feeling around the burned area. He withdrew it, holding something and glaring at it in the white illumination of the flashlight. Even from across the deck Encizo could make it out as part of his detonator. It took less than five more seconds for the man holding the blackened component to figure it out. He dropped it to the deck and strode purposefully to the entrance with a whispered command that the Phoenix Force commando couldn't make out.

"Phoenix Two here," he said into the radio. "They just figured out they're not alone. They've retreated to the interior."

"Phoenix One here—we'll join you in two minutes, Phoenix Two."

Encizo waited, feeling the charge in the night despite the utter silence from the ship and the sea. The bridge was dead. Not a peep came from the forecastle. The warm glow of the arriving raft had disappeared from his view against the side of the trawler and Encizo couldn't risk crawling out into the open to assist their boarding. For a fraction of a second he felt completely alone.

Then the engines began to thrum to life.

"Phoenix Two here—they've bypassed the breaker!"

McCarter DROPPED the tiny oar he'd been paddling with and snatched at the electric motor control as the message came through from Encizo. He'd figured out the situation himself when the heavy machinery sound reverberated with growing intensity from the hull of the trawler. The electric motor whined to life, coming to full power with far greater speed than the great throbbing mass of horsepower under the deck of the trawler. But the screws on the fishing vessel began spinning, and the sea at the rear began to turn white as the vessel pushed forward with amazing agility for such a large, ugly hulk of a boat.

"This is gonna be close," Hawkins said over the growing swell of noise. Crouched at the front of the inflatable raft, he could see the ladder on the side of the vessel, toward which they had been rowing. It was still growing closer, but the increasing speed of the trawler would soon start to outdistance the raft.

"She's pushed to her stops. This is all she's got," McCarter said.

"Give me the rope," Hawkins yelled to James, who was crouched in the center of the raft. James tossed the coil of thin nylon line to Hawkins, knotting it in seconds to the shorter piece of rope dangling from the front end of the raft.

"We've matched speed," McCarter shouted over the throaty rumble of the trawler engine. One glance told Hawkins it was the truth—at that moment the ladder on the side of the trawler stopped getting closer, paused where it was, then started moving away from them as the trawler reached the top speed of the tiny raft's motor and exceeded it easily.

"Phoenix Two this is Phoenix Five—can you be ready to catch a line?" Hawkins radioed.

"I'll try, Phoenix Five. Give me a count."

"Five. Four. Three." Hawkins stood on the front end of the raft. "Two." He crouched in a discus thrower's stance. "One."

The coil of rope sailed in a high arc, silhouetted in the brilliance that suddenly flooded the trawler as every light on board was turned on. Encizo materialized at the side of the boat just in time to snatch the coil as it floated into his hands, then disappeared again.

"I just roped me a boat," Hawkins shouted.

"Aren't you the cowboy," James said.

"Phoenix Two here. You're secure."

Over the engine's roar came the blast of a shotgun.

ENCIZO SPUN AWAY in a crouch, exposed for one long second as he sought cover. The figure standing at the corner of the forecastle was still facing the steel box that had been his hiding place, but he saw the movement out of the corner of his eye and spun in that direction. Encizo dropped below the lip in the opening into the cargo section, no more than two extra inches of wood protecting him from the blast of the 12-gauge as it thundered. The aim had been good—the wood shredded and splintered. He heard the man pump the weapon and wondered how many shots the magazine held.

He was in a bad place and he knew it. Flat, he was in the worst possible position for quick movement. He'd have to get to his feet, which would give the attacker ample time to fire another blast of buckshot.

He inched along the deck until he was looking around the cargo bay opening, but there was nothing he could see. As soon as the gunner came into view he'd be able to empty the shotgun at Encizo in the same instant the Cuban fired at him. The Phoenix Force commando was in no mood to exchange an eye for an eye. "Phoenix Two here. Give me a distraction—anything!"

Within seconds an eruption of automatic rifle fire slammed into the deck railing. There was no way it was going to reach the shotgunner, but Encizo had to trust it would take the man's attention for a fraction of a second. He sat up fast and found the man standing in the open just a few paces away, turning toward the rifle fire. At that instant he realized his mistake and turned back, but it was too late. Encizo fired three rounds into the gunner's chest.

Encizo jumped to his feet and ran to the forecastle, flattening against the wall with the Beretta close to his face. He made a quick evaluation of the scenario. If he had remained unobserved, the two men in the bridge—and he was still assuming there were only two other men on the trawler—would see their fallen comrade and believe he'd been shot from the gunfire coming from off the ship. The other Phoenix Force warriors were still sending the occasional round into the railing.

"Phoenix Two here. That's enough. Stay where you are for the time being. They'll have a clean shot at you if you try to get on board."

"Phoenix One here. We're standing by."

Encizo stepped quickly into the open, looking up at the bridge window, spotting one of the men glaring at the railing with a wrinkled brow. He spotted the movement far below and reacted quickly, raising a shotgun to target Encizo through the glass. The Cuban triggered the Beretta first, shattering the glass with the first round and following it up with three more 9 mm rounds, until he was sure the gunner was hit—he wasn't taking chances with all that glass getting in the way and potentially steering the rounds off target.

He listened to the thump of the body and the tinkling of glass as he moved against the wall again.

There was a long moment of silence.

Then he made out sounds of frantic movement on the bridge, lasting fifteen or twenty seconds. Then a blast of shotgun fire splattered the empty deck, followed a moment later by several rounds from a high-caliber rifle.

"Phoenix Two, this is Phoenix One. Talk to me," McCarter demanded on the radio.

"Phoenix Two here. That's cover fire. I'm out of sight, Phoenix One."

"Cover for what?"

"Unknown."

There was more activity, then a few more rifle bullets were emptied into the deck, followed by silence. Encizo inched along the wall, turned the corner and moved to the door. As he was about to open it, a small scuffle coming from the front end of the trawler caught his attention. He moved along the wall and peered around the front in time to see a figure on his knees in the lifeboat, dangling from its supports over the edge of the deck. He'd been watching for his attackers and spotted Encizo at once, firing the large-caliber hunting rifle he had tucked under his right arm. The Cuban retreated as the rounds crunched into the wall and deck where he'd been standing. Quickly, he hit the transmit button on his radio and explained the situation to the rest of the team. "I'm not sure he's the last of them, so watch yourselves."

"Roger that, Phoenix Two," McCarter said. "We'll join you momentarily."

Encizo chanced another look, just in time to see the lifeboat and its occupant descend below the level of the deck and disappear. He took up a careful shooter's stance with the Beretta supported in two hands, triggering twice at one of the pulleys. The end of the support disintegrated, and the sound of a scream reached him, then a splash, then nothing. He moved carefully to the rail and peered over the edge to find the lifeboat hanging by its nose by one rope, its rear end dangling over the water. The large, heavily shielded outboard motor was getting drenched by the North Sea swells. The occupant was long gone, lost and left behind in the cold, black ocean.

"I KNEW I'D END UP cleaning up this whole mess on my own," Encizo was saying minutes later as he was joined by the other three members of Phoenix Force on the bridge of the *Deep Seven*.

"T.J.," McCarter said, "think you can figure this

out?'' He waved at the bank of electronics that made up the controls of the fishing trawler.

Hawkins gave a low whistle as he regarded the computer system. ''Pretty spiffy setup for guys who just want to net a bunch of cod,'' he said. ''I'll get started.''

James started down the companionway into the living quarters of the trawler, carefully nosing his way ahead with a drawn handgun, just in case there was anyone lingering aboard, when he froze and swore viciously under his breath.

''Check this out,'' he called up to the bridge.

McCarter and Encizo stepped down the steep stairs and stopped beside him. The walls of the crew quarters had been ripped out to extend the cargo area. The stench of old fish catches lingered, but the vast space was packed floor to ceiling with canvas bags wired to a network of cables and power distribution boxes.

''Don't touch anything!'' Hawkins called from above. ''This boat is booby-trapped.''

''HERE'S THE SITUATION as I figure it,'' Hawkins told Kurtzman and Price minutes later over the satellite linkup he had established with Stony Man Farm. ''They're planning to destroy a major part of one of the English coastal towns. They've hollowed out the guts of the boat to put in as many explosives as they could fit. The computer system is using its global positioning input to drive itself directly to the target. They put in a high-grade power train to keep it going so fast no regular coast guard vessel would be able to get on board. They planned on escaping before they got too near the coast. We put a stop to that.''

''The system's got security programming, I assume?'' Kurtzman said.

"Yeah." Hawkins replied, sighing. "When I try to access the system, it tells me I have to enter a password correctly the first time or the system will blow the boat."

"Is there a modem? If we could get access to the system here, we could work on it from this end," Kurtzman suggested.

"We don't have time for that, Stony Base," McCarter broke in. "We've spotted lights already on the coast. We've got to get off this tub and blow her remotely."

"That's Lowestoft you're seeing, Phoenix One," Price stated. "Large city on the eastern British coast."

"I know it," McCarter replied. "Stony Base, if this trawler gets far enough into the dock before it blows, it could take out every building for blocks. We're talking thousands of lives lost."

"Understood, Phoenix One," Price said. "Plant your detonators and get out of there."

McCarter gestured below, and James and Encizo were down the companionway in minutes, staging their small explosives and detonators throughout the mountains of explosives packages. The process was completed in forty-five seconds.

"Let's get out of here."

The engine hum suddenly increased its pitch, reaching a high-intensity whine.

"What the bloody hell is going on?" McCarter demanded.

"She must be programmed to increase her speed as she closes in on the town," Hawkins said above the sound. "Safety measure against any shore-based coast guard vessels."

"Can't you slow it down?"

"Not without setting off the security system. She'll blow us all to smithereens."

"Then let's get off this bucket while we still can!" McCarter exclaimed as the vessel's high-speed vibration turned to a tooth-rattling shudder.

The four of them descended from the bridge in a hurry and crossed the tilted deck in an ungainly, spread-eagled gait to allow them to stay on their feet. The inflatable raft was bouncing and flopping on the speedboatlike wake of the big vessel, its thin nylon line stretched as tight as a guitar string. McCarter spotted the lights of the town approaching the trawler with nightmarish speed.

"Off!" he commanded. "Now!"

Without hesitation Encizo, Hawkins and James hurtled themselves into empty space off the rear rail of the *Deep Seven* as McCarter slashed at the nylon rope with his combat knife. The rope made a twang, and the inflatable raft disappeared into the blackness beyond the frothy light of the trawler's lights along with the Phoenix Force warriors. The lights of the town of Lowestoft were homing in on him, and McCarter knew his cushion of safety on either side was shrinking with every second. There was just one chance to detonate the mass of explosives a safe distance from the city without obliterating the Phoenix Force, and if he had to ride out the explosion himself then so be it.

Then his options disappeared in a flash. The engines of the *Deep Seven* were revving up, still faster. Their programming was designed to send them smashing into the docks at Lowestoft at their fastest possible speed, no matter if they were redlined and on the verge of bursting from their own exertion.

"Bloody hell!" McCarter shouted into the maelstrom

of spraying water and roaring mechanics. He ran to the rail, leapt into the open air and thumbed the detonator in his hand as his body descended into the blast of the trawler's slashing wake.

The water closed over him and for a fraction of a second McCarter held his breath. Then the ocean vanished in a spray of white fire.

CHAPTER TWENTY

"Oh, Jesus."

The Stony Man pilot was a major in the U.S. Air Force. He'd flown combat missions over Iraq during the Gulf War and had been a part of the long-term mission to control Saddam Hussein's ongoing belligerence against the world. He'd never seen anything like this.

The explosion erupted on the surface of the water and turned the night into day, illuminating the vast stretch of ocean with long shadows like a new dawn. The vessel had been moving so fast over the water that the raging fire continued to travel on the surface of the ocean as it grew into a monster, its tentacles reaching out toward the dock of the city of Lowestoft. The fire engulfed a whole line of darkened boats—a small pleasure craft, a restored windjammer and more ugly, squat fishing trawlers than could be counted in the short space of a half second when they were illuminated and then obliterated by the blast. The concrete docks endured the eruption as it rolled over them, but the wooden fittings and the rubber tires used to cushion the docked vessels melted in the fury.

The pilot had all but forgotten he was at the controls of the de Havilland, and he stared in helpless amazement as the billowing fire expanded in the direction of the wall of wooden structures on dry land. Some were warehouses, but some were seaside residences. The pilot could make out small windows and even wooden balconies hanging off the rear of the flats.

His teeth clenched hard, and he couldn't force his eyes to turn away as the blast yellowed in its core. The wall of flame slowed its expansion, then, miraculously, halted and died a sudden, implosive death. The monster collapsed upon itself and faded, leaving only a great ball of smoke and a hundred small fires. The buildings on the shore remained untouched by the conflagration.

"Thank God," the copilot stated. The pilot was startled. He'd forgotten he wasn't alone.

"Stony Base here," the radio crackled. "We've lost contact with Phoenix Force. Can you make visual contact?"

"Will attempt, Stony Base," the pilot radioed in return, banking the de Havilland to cross the explosion site.

He wasn't hopeful.

Stony Man Farm, Virginia

BROGNOLA HEARD the report of the explosion in his Farm office and hurried to the computer lab for more information, but he stood silent in the doorway as Kurtzman and Price coolly exchanged communication with the crew of the de Havilland over the British Isles. Nearby, Carmen Delahunt was monitoring British emergency channels for reports out of Lowestoft.

"We've got them," Price called over her shoulder.

"What's their status?"

"Unknown. We've arranged a helicopter pickup. Our

pilot reports seeing all four in the raft. Three are conscious."

Brognola didn't respond to that.

"We're having a radio dropped to the raft," Price added. "All their communications must have been knocked out by the blast or the water or both."

"We have an emergency medical team on that helicopter?"

"Of course." Price gave him a look.

"Stupid question," Brognola said apologetically. It *had* been a stupid question. Price and Kurtzman would move mountains to take care of their special operations groups. They were family.

Dammit! This operation was turning into a bad one. First Striker almost got blown to hell. Even now he was operating in the field with a probable concussion and bruised or broken ribs. Then Manning got laid up during the probe in the Andes. Now somebody else in Phoenix Force was out cold. Or worse.

He didn't want to think about worse.

"Let me know when you know anything," the big Fed said.

"Of course, Hal," Price replied with the slightest softness in her voice. She understood what he was going through, because she was going through it herself.

"When you get a chance," he added, seating himself at one of the empty communications centers, "connect me with Striker."

"STRIKER."

"It's Hal."

"What's up?"

Brognola paused, then launched into a description of the trials Phoenix Force was undergoing in the North

Sea off the eastern coast of England. He ended with a current status report. One man down, condition unknown, identity unknown. When he finished, Mack Bolan was silent on the line for a long moment.

"This one is turning out to be a real bastard."

"I was thinking along those lines myself," Brognola said.

"Most men would have been satisfied with making a lot of money," Bolan said. "Especially someone who started out poor and uneducated. Not Clint Mahoney. He's so fueled by hatred he's willing to go to all these lengths just to perpetrate violence against the enemies of his father."

"Exactly," Brognola agreed. "A cause he doesn't even have motivation to believe in himself."

"His upbringing at the hands of a fanatic was cause enough. Now he's passing it along to the next generation. When is his son scheduled to return to the U.S.?"

"Day after tomorrow. Word is he's already completed negotiations of a sale to the Turkmen government. He's extorting millions out of them."

"What's the destination of that down payment?"

"Unknown," Brognola said. "But I'd bet my government paycheck Mahoney has plans for it."

"As well as the funds he's going to get from San Diego," Bolan added. "But who will he negotiate with if he succeeds in knocking out the Hoover Dam?"

"Who won't he negotiate with?" Brognola said bitterly. "Half the cities in the Southwest get most or all of their water via the Hoover Dam water system. Those with the most money and the best proximity to a dirty or saline water source are the most likely customers. He can't possibly service them all. The cities without seawater access or the money to pay Mahoney will have to do without. Even the federal government couldn't come up with enough cash or resources to pay him off.''

"Rebuilding the Hoover Dam system?" Bolan asked.

"Would take years. By then we'll see billions in bankruptcies and dozens of deserted towns and cities."

"All for the sake of one man's misguided sense of justice," Bolan concluded. "We can't let it happen."

CHAPTER TWENTY-ONE

Thursday, 2:00 a.m., Hoover Dam,
Southeastern Nevada

Marine Captain Jackson Van Der Ling crossed the asphalt under the cold glare of the streetlight and marched up the steps, looking down on the surface of Lake Mead. The troop-transport vehicle was parked on the earth, looking out over the vast stretch of mirror-calm water. A Marine descended from the cab of the vehicle as he approached.

"What's the status?" Van Der Ling asked.

"Nothing to report, Captain."

"When's the last time you got reports from all the lookouts?"

"Five minutes, sir."

Van Der Ling nodded. That was about what he had expected.

He knew why he and his men were there. The sabotage of the dams in Peru, Turkmenistan and Southern California had received a lot of news coverage. The possibility of it happening again in the U.S. was highly improbable. But the politicians couldn't afford to be caught with their pants down. Not again. There had to be military protection on all the big dams just in case.

So Van Der Ling and his men were sitting on the Hoover Dam to cover some politician's ass.

He didn't like it, but it was part of the job. There were worse things than sitting out on the edge of a big lake in the middle of the night. The air was comfortable. The skies were clear. The worst thing that could happen was getting bored to death.

He never heard the approach of the blacksuited strangers. Never saw the flash of the shielded firearms. Never heard the cough of the suppressed weapons.

But he felt the sting of the impact like a sudden sharp bee sting against his neck. When he went to grab it, Van Der Ling realized his arms wouldn't function. In fact, his entire body was failing to respond to the signals his brain was sending them. He watched the earth approach and slam into his face, and he rolled, paralyzed, onto his back.

Van Der Ling stared up at the clear-as-glass sky. The stars were vivid and brighter than he had ever seen them.

Something was moving at the periphery of his vision—people, dressed in black and moving slowly. He heard the cough of suppressed weapons and the quiet, sudden cries of dying men. Van Der Ling felt removed from it all. Maybe he was already dead.

Then slow blackness crept over his vision, starting at the edge of the sky and speeding like smoke. He knew utter terror then. He was really dying. His consciousness was fading for good. When the blackness closed in entirely he would be over and done with.

There were worse last things to see than stars, he supposed.

The smoky blackness swarmed, covering up every point of light.

Then there was nothing.

"STONY ONE, COME IN."

"Striker here."

"We've lost contact with Hoover Dam."

Mack Bolan should have been surprised. There had been twenty-four Marines stationed at the dam. That was the best the U.S. government would do in response to Hal Brognola's pleading. It hadn't been enough. Bolan had known it wouldn't be.

"Give me a status report on the SOGs," he said.

"Able Team, including Manning and Grimaldi, is en route from Las Vegas in an Army CH-47 Chinook helicopter. ETA at the dam in thirty-three minutes," Barbara Price explained.

"Phoenix?"

"They'll be making a flyover in forty-one minutes," she said. "They're rested and prepped to chute in."

"McCarter?"

"Beat-up and probably suffering from a concussion, but he insists on leading the team down. He's a stubborn SOB, you know?"

Bolan refused to take the bait. "McDonald?"

"Standing by. The blacksuit team can be en route and on the scene about the same time as Able. Are we converging on the dam?"

"We are."

THE WARRIOR MOVED like a cat in the darkness, creeping across the bare landscape and descending the slope from the rocky perch that had served as his overlook for twenty-four long hours. Shrugging on the water-proofed backpack, he moved into the water slowly, without a ripple, and paddled with strong, easy strokes into the deeper water and around the outcropping that allowed him entrance to the shallow inlet of Clint Mahoney's rental house. Bolan ignored the twenty-six-foot Stratos SF, a watercraft that had been provided along with the rental of the house and which rested dark and silent on one side of the wide, new wooden dock. He headed for the sleek, forty-two-foot Carver, an Aft Cabin model outfitted with twin 350 Crusader engines, a lot of luxurious boat for a wide, peaceful lake like Mead. The engines were running at idle and the interior was well-illuminated, although Bolan had watched just one man board the craft. The sounds of activity from the house told him others were coming. Mahoney and his upper management weren't about to miss witnessing their most large-scale profit-making venture.

Bolan intended to join them for the show.

He eased through the water to the rear of the Carver and dragged himself up the ladder, standing on the swimming platform dripping for a long minute while waiting for signs of alarm from the interior. There was nothing. He crossed the sun lounge and peered into the top command bridge. A man stood there smoking a cigar and staring out into the night, a SIG-Sauer P-228, with a LaserMax targeting unit internally mounted, holstered under his left arm.

Bolan moved into the interior of the boat, allowing his Ka-bar fighting knife to serve as his lead weapon. He wasn't required to use it, as he found the dinette, enclosed lower bridge and two staterooms empty.

He had been standing by, waiting for a full day. But he was the consummate warrior, and he could wait a while longer if necessary. He moved into hiding in one of the staterooms, taking up a position out of sight of the door.

He listened as several men boarded the cabin cruiser, then the idling engine rose to a steady roar and the craft moved into deeper water. There were voices speaking urgently on the deck above him, and from the nearby sun lounge and dinette. He concentrated on distinguishing the men by their voices and position. In a few minutes he had picked out five individuals, one of whom had been addressed as Clint.

Bolan felt grim satisfaction. The boat by this time had moved far to into the middle of Lake Mead. There was nothing but blackness outside the small stateroom windows. It was just them and him.

They would be going down this night. Bolan made a silent oath to himself in the darkness. These murderers of innocent children would meet their fate. If they took Bolan down with them, then so be it. That was his fate, an inevitability he had long ago come to terms with. When the time came he would accept that fate with a warrior's grace.

If it came this night, he was ready for it.

WITH THE ENGINES spun down again, and the cabin cruiser moving along at a gentle couple of knots per hour, Clint Mahoney stood at the rear of the sun lounge and took the heavy glass from David Boyle. There was just a half inch of liquid in its wide bottom, which was fine. He wanted enough for a toast without slowing anyone's reflexes. There was still a good hour to an hour and a half before the final stage of the project was accomplished.

Recent news was distracting, but not dire enough to put a halt to this night's plans. When everyone was armed with a glass of whiskey, he raised his.

"We've had some bad news out of Britain, as you

all know by now," he announced. "Our friends have sprung a leak somewhere along their European pipeline. As a result, our first victorious strike against England was a great disaster."

He paused, as if offering up a moment of silence for a fallen friend, and to reinforce his disappointment.

"Our promotional campaign was scheduled for launch now. It has been delayed, of course. But I have been told by our friend the doctor that my son has successfully negotiated a contract with the Turkmen government that exceeded our expectations. In addition to financing construction of our new Central Asian manufacturing facility, the Turkmen government will pay us a guaranteed two million U.S. dollars per unit, with a guarantee of purchasing a minimum of one hundred units over the next year. Like our arrangement with Peru, a down payment was required immediately to hold that price. The down payment was made and is now on its way to our friends in Europe. Mr. Albright has assured me he'll be able to pull off stage two of our operation without the problems Mr. White experienced."

Bolan, listening intently, knew the man who was speaking was Clint Mahoney, and he mentally burned the name Albright into his memory. There was a man to be reckoned with, sometime in the future.

"Clint," one of his senior staff asked, "what if the leak wasn't out of the Faeroe operation. What if it came from our supply house?"

Mahoney waved his glass of whiskey, still held stiffly in position for a toast. But he was feeling less celebratory by the second. "Not likely. Our source has been an active global arms supplier for decades. They're highly reliable. They go to great lengths to keep themselves anonymous. That's one reason they're as expensive as they are.''

Mahoney spoke up suddenly, his posture stiffening. ''I will only work with professionals and experts. That is why I need to pay top dollar. That is the purpose of my extraordinary global capital-raising ventures. My long-term project isn't being executed out of some primitive thirst for power. I am intent on making a real difference. With my capital and with the extensive arms and explosives supply capabilities of our source, we can wreak high-grade havoc on the English. We will bring them to their knees, gentlemen. We will have them begging for mercy. Their politicians will have no choice but to pull themselves out of Ireland, along with all the English rabble they've planted on our island. We will—I promise you—accomplish what our compatriots failed to accomplish during the decades of the Troubles. And we most certainly will accomplish what the peace accords pretend to accomplish. We will restore the freedom and honor and church of our Ireland.''

Mahoney raised his glass solemnly, and then he drank.

''By this time tomorrow, we can start laying claim to the profits from our great destructive deeds in Peru, Turkmenistan and here in the U.S.,'' he added. ''We'll be done creating a market bigger than we can possibly serve. We'll have played both sides against the middle like no one else in history.''

''Do you still think that's the best course, Clint?'' Boyle asked. ''You're certain there's no chance the blowing of the dams will be linked to the sale of the water purifiers?''

''I'm certain,'' Mahoney said with a shrug that indicated he wasn't even worried about that outcome. He drained his glass. "Let's be on our way. I wouldn't want to miss our hour of greatest triumph. This time I'm giving myself the honor of performing the detonations." He patted his breast pocket.

The dual engines spun to high revs, and the screws bit the water, propelling the craft in a race across the massive, man-made lake.

"STONY BASE, are you reading me?" Bolan was still flat against the wall of the stateroom, whispering into his transmitter. He knew he couldn't depend on the satellite uplink he had erected on the hill near the Overton house much longer.

"Go ahead, Stony One," Kurtzman said.

"How are things proceeding at the dam?"

"Everybody's about to arrive and commence with the party. Are you going to be on time?"

"I'll be fashionably late, but I'm coming on the VIP boat," Bolan said. Quickly, he related his situation. He was also careful to give Kurtzman the details of Mahoney's speech. The unspoken reason for the debriefing was obvious. It was intel Stony Man Farm could use if Bolan didn't survive the night.

"My first order of business will be to find out more about the arms supplier," Bolan said. "He could be somebody we've never even heard of. I don't like the sound of that."

"Me neither," Kurtzman agreed. "Even if we stop Mahoney cold in his tracks, we'll have the European arm of the organization to track down. It might save a lot of lives if we can identify and castrate their hardware source."

"Absolutely."

"But that intelligence isn't worth losing your own life over."

"I'll give survival my best effort. Keep your ears open—I'm about to get company."

The door was opening. The man who entered wandered to the washroom door at the rear of the stateroom. Bolan had the Beretta 93-R leveled directly at the dome of his skull, ready to fire at any evidence that he had spotted the soldier. But the washroom door closed abruptly. The stateroom door swung shut and latched of its own accord. Bolan crossed to the washroom entrance, where he lay in wait, holstering the Beretta. When the man exited, Bolan grabbed him under the jaw with one powerful hand and slid the tip of the Ka-bar fighting knife into the man's gut. The fellow's eyes went wild with agony and breath hissed from his firmly clamped jaw.

"Don't move or I'll spill your guts."

The man lunged forward and tried to yank at Bolan's arm with his hands. The Executioner raked the blade across the captive's abdomen. "I said don't."

"I want the name of your European arms source."

The man's eyes wavered and crossed, and he tried to make some sort of plaintive plea. Bolan relaxed the tension in the hand that was almost entirely cutting off the man's breath, and the guy whispered like a miserable hound. "Kosim Bey."

"Spell it slowly."

The man did, concentrating deeply over the pain to get it correct.

"City."

"He's worldwide"

"City!"

"Alexandria, Egypt."

Bolan spoke into the headphones. "Catch that, Stony Base?"

"Yes, I heard it," Kurtzman said.

Bolan rapped the injured man on the jaw and perched him on the toilet. He closed the door, then inched open the stateroom door when the craft began to slow. With their eyes on the spectacle they were creating, the remaining four or more men would—he hoped—be less aware of the goings-on aboard their own vessel. Two of them were in sight up to their shoulders, standing on the sun lounge with their hands gripped on the supports. The third and fourth men could be almost anywhere—in the next stateroom, in the command bridge or on deck.

The soldier leveled the Beretta 93-R as he strode through the dining area to the companionway and cored both men with a pair of tribursts. They died on their feet, the first man losing his balance in death and toppling out the rear of the vessel, the second man collapsing on the sun lounge. There was a shout from above, and Bolan raced up the companionway, using speed as his advantage, aiming at the command deck and firing another triburst while he was still searching for a target. The trio of 9 mm rounds rocketed into the Nevada night sky, wasted: the command deck was empty.

He transferred the 93-R to his left hand while drawing the big Desert Eagle pistol with his right. The U.S.-made version of the big handgun was put together in the .44 Magnum configuration and fitted with a six-inch barrel. When he fired it at the fleeting shadow of a figure rising from the deck, the man flopped down lifelessly, and Bolan leapt up the companionway to the command bridge and through the wide window opening.

The Desert Eagle had drilled a hole in the man's chest and taken him down hard, his heart ripped apart by skeletal shrapnel. The deck was otherwise empty.

One man was missing.

Where was Clint Mahoney?

A faint click came through the hull. Bolan felt it beneath his feet. It was a belowdeck door latching, and he retreated to the front of the deck, far out onto the nose of the cruiser, where the lights from the command bridge and the interior windows barely reached. Mahoney, he realized, had to have been in the second stateroom or one of the heads.

Bolan was still dangerously exposed and he knew it, but anybody coming up from the inside would have to pass through the lower station and dining area. The soldier would see them far better than they would see him. For a long moment there was no further movement or sound from the interior of the pleasure boat, then Bolan saw a faint dark shape pass along the bottom of the window that showed him the lower helm station. He reacted quickly but didn't squeeze the trigger of the Desert Eagle. The shape was gone.

Then the thrum of the twin engines increased their pitch, and Bolan descended into a lower crouch as the vessel accelerated tremendously in a matter of seconds. Mahoney had to be hugging the ground under the lower helm, groping for the controls. The direction of the boat changed, too. It had been cutting a long, diagonal path across the wide open section of lake that ended at the base of the Hoover Dam. Now the nose of the craft aimed at the massive concrete wall as if intending to ram it.

The Executioner glanced back long enough to judge the distance. He had less than a minute prior to impact, but he wasn't at all sure Mahoney intended to end both their lives against the blank wall of the dam.

He aimed for the lower helm and triggered three rounds through the narrow window, smashing the glass and shattering the top of the steering wheel. Bolan advanced along the deck, firing another couple of rounds into the helm. He was ripping up the cabinetry but didn't appear to be doing vital damage to the controls, and he couldn't get so much as a glimpse of Mahoney.

Time was growing short as the massive wall towered over the forty-two-foot craft, and Bolan dropped spread-eagle on the deck. The sudden change in direction was going to come soon. The deck guardrail was thin tubular steel, just eighteen inches high, but it was all he had to work with. He tucked away his weapons and grabbed at the rail with all his strength.

Then the cabin cruiser turned so hard and fast Bolan was sure the craft would roll onto its roof, and his body slammed into the rail with tremendous force. The rail ripped out of the fiberglass deck, and the large section he was gripping separated from the rest and bent and flopped as if it were made of rubber. Bolan found himself airborne, the great concrete wall looming over him like a mountain. He released the useless steel. For a fleeting moment he expected to make impact with the dam itself. Every bone in his body would shatter, like a dropped porcelain bowl.

Then he splashed into the lake, water forced powerfully down his throat and nostrils, and white-lightning of pain slammed into his battered ribs and bruised skull. The whiteness threatened to cover him like a blanket.

Bolan pulled open his eyes and found himself struggling in blackness, blinded by the water. The sudsy foam of air flowed past him, but in different directions, as if gravity were being ignored and the foam no longer needed to find the surface. For a long moment in the chaos Bolan was unable to determine direction himself, and the screaming in his lungs and the burning in his head added to the confusion. Suddenly, for the first time, his amnesia about the final moments at Bedoya Dam vanished and he was bombarded with the memory of falling through the catastrophe of collapsing stone and exploding water. The past and the present mixed and blended until they were both happening now.

Then he recalled the crystallization of the survival instinct that had occurred during the cataclysm at Bedoya. He wouldn't stop fighting to survive. Not until his last cell was drained of energy. Not until his heart had grown entirely still. Not until the last synapse in his warrior's brain had ceased to fire with thought and will.

Bolan became still, ignoring the screaming of his deprived respiratory system, and allowed the inevitability of gravity to carry his body aright. Then he knew the way to the surface, and he stroked with strong, steady strokes out of the depths of the black lake and into the cool, life-giving air. As his face erupted into the night, he coughed out a lungful of water and sucked at the air, grateful to be alive. Grateful that he had another chance to complete the task at hand.

Above him, the Hoover Dam was a flurry of activity.

CHAPTER TWENTY-TWO

Stony Man Farm, Virginia

"Striker?"

"Contact lost," Carmen Delahunt stated flatly.

Barbara Price looked at the wide screen hanging blank on the War Room wall, feeling just as empty. She had a complicated battle to organize. There was simply no time to worry about one element.

"G-Force, are you with me?"

"Read you loud and clear, Stony Base," the voice of Stony Man pilot Jack Grimaldi said through the speaker system. The throbbing of the big CH-47 Chinook transport helicopter's rotors wasn't fully masked by the microphone.

"Status?" Price asked.

"Able Team is on the ground, off-loaded at the scheduled debarkation point. En route now to the Phoenix drop-off. ETA is forty-five seconds."

"Able One, you on-line?"

"Able One here," Carl Lyons replied. "I read you Stony Base. We're standing by."

"Phoenix One, this is Stony Base," Price said.

"Phoenix One here," McCarter said. "We check out and we're standing by for debarkation."

"Blacksuit Commander, this is Stony Base."

McDonald's voice answered immediately. "We're ready to move out."

Price nodded. The teams were nearly staged. "Akira?"

"I'm ready," Tokaido said.

"Aaron?"

"We'll have eyes in ten seconds," Kurtzman said.

"Carmen?"

"Marine backup is en route. I don't think they believe there's a problem."

"Five," Aaron Kurtzman announced. "Four. Three. Two. One. We have eyes."

The expansive wall screen flickered to life and filled with a broad thermal image. Cold and dark at the top of the screen, the massive dark wall of the Hoover Dam held the cool, deep lake precariously in its grasp.

"Give me a close-up of the activity, Aaron," Price said.

"Here it comes." Kurtzman played with the image, closing in on a section of the Hoover Dam almost directly above the ground-level generating station. A webbing of nylon ropes was strung over the side of the dam, and a frantic gray-suited work crew positioned the prepared explosive charges.

"Those look a lot like the charges Mack described at Bedoya," Price said.

Kurtzman nodded. "Yeah. But maybe three times as many." He sounded angry, and demanded rhetorically, "Where the hell did they get all that material without us knowing about it?"

A mental timer went off in Price's head. "Phoenix One?"

"We're on the ground, Stony Base," McCarter said.

Behind him Price heard the rush of rotors as Grimaldi's chopper took to the air.

"What's the status on Phoenix Three?"

"He's a little irritated about being left out of the action," McCarter said.

"Phoenix Three here," Manning said. "I'll live with it." Manning's battering had made the Navy doctors worried about his constitution. Price had given him orders to stay out of combat scenarios. Manning rebelled when the order came for the convergence of the Stony Man teams at Hoover, and they had compromised. Manning would stay with Grimaldi on the chopper, where he would serve as gunner and communications liaison. The chopper was equipped with a deck-mounted .50-caliber Browning machine gun.

Price transmitted a general message that went to Phoenix Force and Able Team as well as the blacksuit teams. "Stony Base here. Begin your approach as planned."

Hoover Dam, West Approach

ROSARIO BLANCANALES spotted the vehicles before they saw him. He signaled to the others, waited for his moment, then stepped into the road less than a dozen paces in front of the slow-moving Jeep. His M-16 spoke in the darkness, and the Jeep veered into the low shoulder. The backseat figure rose to his feet, but Blancanales never gave him the chance to fire the Galil assault rifle in his hands, stitching the gunner across the chest with 5.56 mm shockers. The driver caught one in the side of the head and slumped over the wheel.

Carl Lyons was out of the brush the moment the second and third vehicles swung into view, hurried along by the sound of gunfire. Lyons triggered a 40 mm high-explosive grenade from the M-203 launcher mounted under his assault rifle. The Jeep's driver didn't have time to evaluate the projectile. There was a thump, and a blast of fire cooked the vehicle's occupants in seconds. The third Jeep screeched to a halt several lengths behind the conflagration and spun into a rapid turn. Hermann Schwarz saw the last vehicle as his personal responsibility. He unleashed a full-auto barrage of rounds into the rear end of the vehicle, blowing both rear tires. The Jeep swerved on the disintegrating rubber and came to a stop long enough for Schwarz to draw a sideways figure eight with the chattering M-16, cutting down the three occupants.

"Able One here," Lyons transmitted over his radio. "We got a hot reception. I think they know we're here."

"Understood, Able One," Price said. "I'll pass that along."

Hoover Dam, East Approach

"STAY SHARP, mates," McCarter stated. "Able met up with a welcoming committee, and we might, too."

The road that crossed over the top of the dam and extended east into the desert was laid inside a canyon machine-cut into the living rock. Phoenix Force traveled atop it on foot. With a flick of his wrist, McCarter silently sent James ahead. The black commando sped over the rocky ground, watching simultaneously for traffic on the road and movement atop the rock. He dropped suddenly at a point thirty paces ahead of the others.

"Phoenix Four here. I've got three vehicles approaching on the highway. Give me a few seconds, and I'll give you a description." He raised his field glasses and watched the approaching vehicles, which were conveniently traveling without headlights, which would have messed up his night-vision optics. He got a good look. "Two open-top vehicles. Three in the first Jeep and two in the second. Automatic rifles all around. The third is a big SUV, number of occupants unknown. I suggest you stop them on your end, and I'll hem them in from behind."

"Phoenix One here. Sounds like a plan."

James hugged the earth as the three vehicles cruised past him, their attentive occupants unable to distinguish him in his night camouflage. He rose to his knees as they left him behind, moving into the road when a sudden barrage of automatic weapons' fire slammed into the lead Jeep, bringing it to an abrupt, lurching halt. The Phoenix Force commandos were invisible even to James in the darkness, and the second Jeep was trapped. It couldn't proceed forward, it couldn't retreat fast enough to avoid the withering fire and there was no visible enemy to defend itself against. The rear SUV's driver realized they were in a nearly impossible position for effective self-defense and decided on flight as the best option. James sent a single shot through the windshield as the driver finished his 360-degree turn. The hole that starred the windshield couldn't have been more accurate. The SUV wobbled into the carved-out wall, crawling up three feet before the incline became too steep, and it hung there, its engine groaning. When the door flung open James was ready for it. He deposited a single explosive grenade through the door. All glass ceased to exist when the great belch of fire burst from every window of the SUV. James hadn't counted exactly how many gunners were in the vehicle, and it didn't matter now.

"Stony Base here—Phoenix Four you've got another vehicle moving in fast."

"Copy that," James said as he scrambled for the burning SUV. In that moment he heard the whine of high revs as another Jeep screeched around the corner at high speed, and a torrent of autofire cut into the road at his heels. The Phoenix Force commando's quick footwork saved his life. He dived to the side, effectively placing the wrecked SUV between himself and the oncoming Jeep. He rolled as he hit the pavement, ignoring the blast of pain in his bruised elbows and knees, training his assault rifle on the place in the road where the Jeep might appear.

But it didn't.

"Phoenix One here. Four, you still with us?"

"Phoenix Four here," James said, giving a wave to the spot in the darkness where he thought his teammates might be waiting. "Alive and kicking."

He dropped low when a metal-chopping torrent of machine-gun fire began slamming into the burning SUV. Hugging the ground was the only defense. At any second one of those rounds might snake its way through the wreckage and find him.

"Phoenix Three, you guys in the vicinity?" James shouted into his radio.

"Way ahead of you, Cal," Gary Manning said.

"We're on them in three seconds," Grimaldi added over the radio. "Two. One."

The machine-gun fire coming out of the newly arrived Jeep sounded like the rattling of spare parts compared to the throaty roar of Manning's .50-caliber Browning machine gun. When James got to his feet, he spotted the chopper stuck in the air at a thirty-degree angle, with Manning strapped in behind the swivel-mounted weapon. The furious pounding was eating the Jeep alive. Within seconds the vehicle was nothing more than a pile of broken metal parts. When the machine-gun fire stopped, the Jeep was scarcely recognizable junk that started to burn in sputters and gasps.

"Phoenix Three here," Manning said over the radio. "I think I got them."

James waved at the big chopper. "I can confirm that you scored a few hits. Thanks, pal."

Stony Man Farm, Virginia

"THERE'S MAHONEY'S BOAT."

Price stared at the spot as Kurtzman panned the shot and closed in on the small shape in the lake many hundred yards from the dam.

"What's he up to?" Price asked.

"Watching, supervising," Kurtzman said.

"All the action is on the other side," Price argued. "And what is Striker up to?"

Kurtzman was silent for a moment. Then he said, "We can't chance sending Jack and Gary after him with Striker on board."

"Mahoney will be planning on going to shore before the dam is blown."

"Probably won't even bother with a dock," Kurtzman said. "He'll just drive it onto the shore. The boat's worthless to him without a lake anyway."

"You're right. Let's keep a close eye on his behavior. When Mahoney heads for land, we know we're running out of time."

Hoover Dam

THE PANEL TRUCK HAD BEEN brought to a halt directly in the middle of the dam. The roof was outfitted with reinforced sheet-steel guard plates to the front and rear. A pair of Spanish-made Amelia machine guns protruded from between the long slots in the steel guards—one fore, one aft.

"I'll try for it," Schwarz said, moving into the road long enough to aim the M-203 and send the high-explosive egg flying into the night. He was spotted at once, and the gunner unloaded the box-fed machine gun in a long, full-auto barrage that had to have consumed a full quarter of a 200-round ammunition box.

Schwarz sped for cover with the 5.56 mm rounds nipping at his heels. He heard the burst of the explosive but couldn't see where it had exploded. When he looked back at the dam, he found no evidence of damage to the panel truck.

"That's a negative," Lyons transmitted over the radio. "Flyboy, think you can get in close enough to take those guys out?"

"We're checking it out," Grimaldi replied. "They've got a steel shield for a roof."

Able Team listened as the helicopter moved in close and unleashed a .50-caliber barrage on the guard post, and heard the loud impact of rounds against the metal.

"We're wasting our fire," Manning said over the air. "We can't penetrate that roof. They're ignoring us. Wait—I see activity down there—"

Return fire erupted from the wall of the dam. A pair of snipers was situated on the opposite side of the wall, hanging in place from the nylon cords that suspended the workmen. Their Knight SR-25 semiauto sniper rifles popped the glass above Grimaldi's head, and he reacted with a quick twist of the rotor control, facing the big helicopter away from the dam and speeding out over the lake, avoiding a handful of rounds the snipers sent chasing after them.

"This is G-Force. We were chased off by snipers," he reported.

"There was somebody else wandering around down there, though," Manning protested. "Do we have anybody on the scene at the dam?"

"That's a negative," Price returned. "But Striker is no longer in contact with us. We assume he's still on the Mahoney watercraft in the middle of the lake. Is it possible you spotted him?"

"Can't confirm one way or the other, Stony Base," Manning said.

"Blacksuit Commander," Price ordered over the radio, "get your snipers to work on theirs."

"Affirmative, Stony Base," stated McDonald.

As HE FLOATED along the base of the concrete wall, feeling in the slimy green growth for a handhold, Bolan listened to the sounds of battle going on in both directions. He'd shed his waterlogged and useless radio and had no way of knowing how the battle went or where his skills were best placed. When he found the inspection ladder rungs set into the concrete wall, he started up without hesitation. He'd holstered his weapons. Soaked with water he couldn't trust either one of them to function properly. They were a last resort. He'd make use of the Marine-issue Ka-bar fighting knife and see what kind of pickup weapon he could acquire.

A blast of machine-gun fire came from the top of the dam almost directly over his head. He flattened against the concrete wall, at first thinking he'd been spotted, ready to let go and make the long drop back into the water. Then he realized the fire wasn't aimed at him at all, and no enemy was visible over the top of the wall. He was spurred on to greater speed, reaching the top of the dam and scrambling over the wall, where he curled against the traffic barrier as a helicopter swung over the road and unleashed large-caliber machine-gun fire at a parked, black panel truck. There was some sort of battle-shielded structure on top. It was pretty well placed to defend land-based encroachment from either direction.

As the helicopter swerved away to avoid rifle fire from the other side of the panel truck, Bolan crept to the vehicle, climbed the mounting rungs and peered into the protected compartment at the top of the truck.

A pair of gunners squatted on their hands and knees, carefully watching the road in both directions. Each was embracing a swivel-mounted Amelia machine gun. Two-hundred-round ammunition boxes filled the interior of the compartment as if the gunners had settled in for a long war. Each also had a handgun holstered on his hip.

Bolan wasted just fifteen seconds waiting for a distraction that never came. Then he acted, slithering over the low barrier rail and attacking silently, swiftly and mercilessly. He stepped to the man on his right, grabbing him by the forehead and dragging the fighting blade across his throat, then spun and slammed his bare heel into the second gunner. The man was in the midst of turning, suddenly aware of an intruder, and received the impact in the soft flesh just above his left hip. He bent double, the air expelling from his lungs with a grunt. Bolan moved over him, dropping the knife and grabbing his head in both hands.

The gunner seemed to know what the Executioner intended, and he let out a great short yelp of fear. Then his head was twisted with a powerful, violent wrench that tore his vertebrae apart at the shoulders. The body collapsed limp and lifeless.

Bolan quickly examined the construction of the shelter. For quick assembly, the massive steel plates were connected with thick bolts and heavy wing nuts. It took him just seconds to unscrew the eight connectors holding on the roof and shove off the massive steel plate. It clattered to the road, and the soldier grabbed the nearest Amelia, resting it on top of the steel side shield, and aimed it down at the small building.

"Hey, we've got a problem up here," Bolan shouted.

The first face that emerged from the enclosure was that of Thomas McDonough, the brain behind Mahoney's dam-blasting projects. Bolan recognized him easily from the photos supplied by Stony Man. At first he stared at the Executioner with a kind of irritated confusion.

Then realization came all at once, and McDonough turned for a hasty retreat into the shielded enclosure. Bolan triggered the Amelia, which stopped McDonough in his tracks and held him there for seconds, dancing him like a doll on the strings of a spasmodic puppeteer.

He collapsed in pieces.

Bolan armed himself with pistols belonging to the dead gunners and grabbed spare boxes of ammo for the Amelia. He draped the machine gun from his shoulder by its strap and stepped onto the ladder to clamber down the side of the panel truck when the throb of whirling rotors reached him and the big CH-47 Chinook troop-transport helicopter descended toward him from almost directly above, hanging just a stone's throw off the lake side of the dam.

"Hey, Sarge!" the pilot shouted through a huge grin. Bolan threw Grimaldi a wave, then clambered to the surface of the road and jogged across it, feeling the warmth of the long-since-set desert sun still radiating from the blacktop.

Normally, the building was used for a box office and starting point for the tour of the dam, and it housed the elevator that descended down the middle of the structure. Now the building was empty, but the wall of the dam was filled with workmen, some of whom apparently knew that Mahoney's defenses had failed spectacularly. They were descending the long nylon lines as fast as possible. Bolan couldn't, wouldn't, allow these murderers of innocents to escape. There had to be no chance for them to ever gain freedom to perpetrate their evil. He stepped onto the narrow wall at the top of the magnificent dam and stared down as if into oblivion, squeezing the trigger on the Amelia machine gun and launching a spray of fire.

The workmen hung like insects on the massive wall and gazed up in horror at the Executioner. Balancing on the rim of death, entirely unprotected, he risked his own life to end theirs. Like ants hosed off a window, the relentless spray of the machine-gun fire brushed them off the concrete wall and sent them skidding and flopping down the incline to the deadly impact hundreds of feet below.

The Amelia's box of two hundred rounds emptied and the machine gun chugged dry. The night became eerily still.

Then the explosions began.

CHAPTER TWENTY-THREE

"They're in combat black. Heavily armed and taking no prisoners!"

"How did you even let them get on the ground?" Mahoney demanded.

"How should I know? They're coming out of nowhere. I can't even begin to guess how many. These guys are fucking invisible. Special Forces or some damned thing."

"What's your status?"

"We're about to be overwhelmed," the dam base commander said.

"What? How can that be?"

"We're retreating to the interior."

"Don't!" Mahoney ordered.

"It's our only hope for survival."

The base commander shouted wordlessly, and the radio transmitted a heavy impact, like a body slamming into the earth.

"I'm hit! I'm down!"

"How bad?" Mahoney demanded.

"Bad." The base commander's voice became lethargic and strangely contemplative. "Very bad."

"Listen to me! How many explosive units are in place?"

There was a moment of radio silence.

"Answer me!"

"Six. Just six. That's all." There was a long, heavy sigh, and Mahoney knew he wasn't getting anything more out of his unit at the base of the dam.

Mahoney felt strangely alone in the dark silence, more alone than he had felt in decades, since the death of his father. He had found brotherhood in his companions, bound together in mutual love for their homeland and for the dark determination to go to any length to save it. A few of those comrades had been wiped out at the house in Santa Fe. Many more died in one bloody, horrific moment aboard this very craft just minutes earlier, when the madman had ripped through the pleasure craft like a berserker. Mahoney had barely been able to shake him off the craft, leaving him alone with the corpses of his comrades.

In the brief glimpse he had obtained of the stranger's face it had looked bizarrely familiar, and only now did it occur to Clint Mahoney where he had seen that face before.

Bedoya.

"Holy Christ," he said under his breath.

It simply couldn't be. It was impossible that any man could have survived the crash of Bedoya. Yet it was true. He knew it suddenly and irrevocably. And if the man had survived Bedoya, then he had to have been the mastermind behind the destruction at the house in Santa Fe.

The thought of that man walking inside his house was the sort of intimate transgression that curdled Mahoney's blood.

Then it occurred to him suddenly that if that warrior

had survived Bedoya, he would most certainly have survived Mahoney dunking him in the lake.

He was still alive. Maybe he was swimming to shore. Maybe he was swimming through the darkness after Clint Mahoney on the Carver pleasure craft.

The thought filled the man with more fear than he had known in most of his adult life. He gazed into the blackness of the lake as if he expected to see a monster lunge out of it and engulf him. He engaged the screws and pushed the accelerator, forcing the vessel into a hard 180-degree turn before straightening and flying away from the dam at full speed. When he was another quarter of a mile away, he allowed it to drift to a stop— and then he heard the sound of the machine guns at the top of the dam. He grabbed the radio.

"McDonough, come in."

"McDonough's down! He's dead!" It was McDonough's second in command.

"What!"

"The fire's coming from our own guard station! It must have been taken!"

"How did that happen?" Mahoney demanded.

"Shit! Get out of here! Go dow—" The transmission became a screech of terror underscored with the rattle of machine-gun fire. Eerily, Mahoney could hear the delayed echo of the fire as it floated over the still water toward the boat.

Then he knew where his nameless adversary had gone upon being thrown into the water. Mahoney had deposited him within easy striking distance of the machine-gun bank.

"I've undone myself," Mahoney said to the empty boat. His comrades agreed with that assessment—it appeared that the bloody, strewed corpses responded by nodding their lifeless heads in the rocking of the boat.

Six explosive packages were in place. He tried to remember the engineering schematics McDonough had devised. He had recommended a minimum of eighteen shaped charges to effectively puncture and open the Hoover Dam. Twenty-four charges had been planned, just in case, as a safety margin.

Six charges wouldn't even come close. But they just might damage the dam enough to have long-term negative effects.

Most importantly, it might be enough to bring down his adversary and wash away the Special Forces team at the base of the dam.

The charges wouldn't have been linked, but that wasn't a problem. Each was designed with a secondary detonation system, tied in to Mahoney's cellular pocket-sized controls. The Southern Nevada cellular phone system would transmit the signals.

He thumbed the controls, his eyes alternating between the small, illuminated plastic keys of the portable-phone-sized controller and the distant, illuminated battle ground of the dam. The Amelia was firing again, a steady pounding that went on and on.

Idly, it occurred to him that the six explosive charges just might do enough damage to adversely affect the level of Lake Mead. He might be committing suicide. He contemplated making a run for the shore, to the landing site where the two Lincoln Towncars were staged as escape vehicles. But that would take precious minutes. He couldn't give his adversary that much time to get to safety.

Mahoney hoped his son would continue the enterprise

he had started. It seemed unlikely that Jared would possess the initiative to do so.

It didn't matter. Not now.

Mahoney hit Enter on the phone and blissfully listened to the explosions commence.

BOLAN DROPPED the weapon and dived for the nearest nylon rope, ripping the skin of his fingers against the concrete. As the tremor hit, he wrapped the rope around his wrists and grabbed in vain with his free left hand. He felt his body swing away from the wall as the structure, against all odds, moved. Then he fell back against it, hard and fast, his shoulders and back absorbing the impact. The white lightning flashed through his consciousness again. If he surrendered to it now, he thought vaguely, it was going to be a long way down.

He slapped the concrete wall and felt another nylon rope fall into his hand. In an instant he twisted it around his wrist, then managed to twirl his body, braiding the two ropes for added stability. He'd slid a good eight to ten feet down the ropes, and now he could feel and smell the friction-burned flesh of his palms.

The second explosion rocked the warrior's world.

"REPEAT, THE DAM IS blowing!" Manning shouted over the speaker.

For Barbara Price, time slowed as the satellite image of the Hoover Dam, electronically gathered from low geosynchronous orbit, shuddered on the big wall display screen.

"Blacksuit Commander this is Stony Base—get your team to high ground now!"

"Copy that, Stony Base, we're on our way," McDonald radioed. "But our options are limited."

"Understood. Good luck. Phoenix and Able, back off."

"We're way ahead of you there," McCarter replied.

"Roger that—" Lyons began, but his words were cut off as the second explosive shock pounded through the Nevada night.

The tiny gray streak on the screen that was the Hoover Dam belched part of itself into all directions. The small gray splotch that was the CH-47 Chinook helicopter swung low over it.

"G-Force, what are you trying to do?" Price ordered. "Pull up now."

"Negative, Stony Base," Grimaldi replied.

"G-Force, one good size chunk of concrete is going to send you and Phoenix Three to the ground in a big hurry."

"I'm aware of that, Stony Base," Grimaldi replied. It sounded as if he were talking through clenched teeth. "I've got Striker in sight at the top of the dam. I'm going in for him."

Price knew it was foolhardy and that she should be ordering Grimaldi and Manning to pull out to a safe distance.

She said nothing.

BOLAN IGNORED the fresh flow of blood gushing from his knees and feet where they had dragged against the surface and raised his head to the sound of heaving chopper rotors. The big Chinook was hovering over the top of the dam, tilted nearly on its side. As Jack Grimaldi battled with the controls for stability, Gary Manning dangled from his safety harness and played out the lifeline.

The third concussive explosion crashed through the night, vibrating the very atmosphere that supported the aircraft as well as the dam itself. Bolan deliberately went limp when the impact hit, flinging him up and out, and managed to execute a judolike fall as he cracked into the wall again. More flesh ripped.

The soldier's first thought was for the chopper. It was re-establishing itself above him. His second thought was for the dam.

The explosions had started at a point only a hundred feet below the apex of the huge structure. Mahoney was blowing everything he had. The lower devices hadn't been staged. Each explosion came twenty feet nearer to the dangling Bolan.

The Executioner walked along the face of the dam and found the topmost explosive package. He freed one hand from his support ropes long enough to slice the webbing that held in the explosives and draw out the cellular receiver that would detonate it. The package was actually made up of several one-hundred-pound explosive packs. He shrugged the hundred-pound mass of webbed explosives onto his shoulders and made a quick grab at the lifeline harness from the chopper.

"To the boat!" Bolan shouted at Manning.

Manning gave an okay signal with his finger and thumb and radioed Grimaldi. The harness began reeling them in as the chopper began an almost directly vertical ascent.

The fourth explosion came so close that a shower of concrete debris slammed into Bolan from below, imbedding a thousand tiny pebbles deep into his flesh like the pricking of a lava shower. He clung hard to the lifeline with one arm and refused to release the explosive mass with the other.

The chopper rose and cleared Bolan over the top of the dam, then raced out over the agitated lake. The stop-watch in the warrior's head had counted fifteen-second intervals between the detonation of the packages, and right on cue, now far behind him, he heard the fifth package blow. Below him he spotted the Carver pleasure craft, sitting in the water, facing the dam as if waiting for the real show to begin.

The red light on the cellular receiver in his hands was warm and steady, and there was ten seconds to go when Bolan saw Clint Mahoney look up at him from the command bridge. His jaw dropped.

In that moment, Mahoney knew the identity of the man hanging precariously from the belly of the huge, buglike aircraft. He knew what it was the Executioner had draped like a spider's egg sac on one shoulder.

Mahoney knew he had lost the battle. His adversary, his nameless executioner, was victorious.

Bolan's count was at four when Grimaldi brought him to the perfect dropping point high above the bobbing watercraft. He released it and watched it sail in a long, low arc through three, then two. At the one count, as Grimaldi took them out of there, Mahoney made a last-chance effort to stop the irreversible chain of events. He tossed the cellular controller into the cold, dark lake.

He was seconds too late.

The package blew when it was just eight feet above the deck of the cabin cruiser. The explosive force slammed into the pleasure boat, smashing it deep into the water like a child stepping on a floating toy in a bathtub. There was a short-lived crater in the face of the lake. When the water flowed in and refilled the void, the plastic debris began rising to the surface. The metal pieces sank. The human scrap scattered and was gone.

CHAPTER TWENTY-FOUR

California

When the private long-range passenger jet came to a stop at the end of the runway, Jared Mahoney expected it to turn and head for the private hangars at San Diego International Airport. But the aircraft just sat there.

"What's the problem?" he asked over the radio to the cockpit.

"We've been told to sit tight. There's heavy commercial traffic in our way. It'll be clear in three minutes."

"Whatever. Hurry it up."

Jared Mahoney needed a fix and he was getting jumpy. The flight had been three hours longer than he had planned, and his supply of meth was depleted.

Icahn stiffened in the seat across the wide, carpeted isle. "What's going on?" he demanded as he stared out the window.

The front hatchway opened in that instant. Jared jumped to his feet, dragging at the Para-Ordnance P-12 tucked in the overnight bag on the seat beside him. He held it behind his back, his adrenaline slamming through his body and his head reeling with his need for a fix. This wasn't good. This couldn't be good.

When he saw the man walking in through the hatchway, he knew there was trouble.

The man had dark skin and black hair, and piercing blue eyes from which no secrets could be concealed. He was dressed in casual khaki pants and a white cotton shirt, both of which were cut loose to accommodate a network of bandages that covered his limbs, head and torso.

This was a man who had ridden through hell and somehow lived to tell about it.

"Jared Mahoney?" he asked in a voice that was quiet, yet tinged with authority.

"Who the fuck are you?"

The dark-haired man suddenly had a big, black handgun pointed directly at the youth. "Jared Mahoney, I presume."

Jared's skull trembled and his hands shook. He didn't know what was happening, but he couldn't let it happen. He pulled the P-12 from behind his back and leveled it at the stranger. The gunshot that filled the narrow confines of the luxury jet didn't seem to come from the P-12.

It wasn't until he felt the rivulets of blood dripping inside his clothes did Jared Mahoney realize he'd been shot in the stomach. He tried to level the P-12 another time. The stranger once again beat him to the punch. This time, Jared was knocked onto his knees on the thick carpet. He fell on his face between the seats and felt nothing more.

More armed gunmen entered the jet's cabin. There had to have been eight or ten of them on the tarmac surrounding the aircraft. As the stranger extracted the Para-Ordnance handgun from the fingers of the dead man, Dr. Joshua Icahn looked as if he were about to vomit. When he could no longer make his legs work, he sank shakily into his seat.

"You struck a hard bargain with the people of Peru and Turkmenistan," the stranger said. "I wonder if you would consider renegotiating those contracts?"

"Yes," Icahn said in a whisper. "Of course."

The stranger nodded. He didn't smile. Icahn somehow knew, with absolute certainty, that this man would have killed him, too, if he had given the wrong answer.

AFTER ICAHN WAS HANDED OFF to the Federal Bureau of Investigation at San Diego International, Bolan found Grimaldi lovingly prepping the Cessna Citation aircraft leased for him by Stony Man Farm. Bolan sat in the copilot's seat as they taxied and lifted off the runway, the craft's nose pointed into the rising sun.

When they reached eighteen thousand feet, Jack Grimaldi clapped him lightly on his left shoulder—one of the few unbandaged parts of Bolan's body. "We've got this entire jet to ourselves. Go take advantage of it. Have a drink. Eat a steak. Take a nap."

Bolan nodded. "Maybe I will."

He took Grimaldi's suggestions to heart. He was battered and empty, in need of refilling and rejuvenation. He warmed up two of the meals the catering service had provided and devoured them, washing them down with a couple of beers.

The people of Peru, Turkmenistan and San Diego would get their desalination technology at cost. The Red Cross was hopeful that it could help stem the tide of infectious diseases in Lima and that fresh water would eventually help break the hold cholera had on the city. Still, hundreds would die as a result of weeks of bad water. In the Turkmen cities the damage in terms of human lives was still being assessed.

Brognola had been right. This had been a hard battle. McCarter and Manning would be recovering for some time. Several blacksuits had been wounded by falling rock in Nevada, and one blacksuit warrior, a young Ranger, was being sent home to his family in a wooden box.

Some battles in the War Everlasting were harder than others.

Mack Bolan laid across two seats and willed himself to sleep.

It didn't come easy.

Gold Eagle brings you high-tech action and mystic adventure!

THE Destroyer™

#118 Killer Watts

Created by

MURPHY
and SAPIR

A military experiment gone wrong creates a supercharged fiend who deals shocking death from his very fingertips, and Remo and Chiun are charged with shorting out this walking psycho power plant.

Available in February 2000 at your favorite retail outlet.

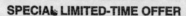

James Axler

OUTLANDERS™

ARMAGEDDON AXIS

What was supposed to be the seat of power after the nuclear holocaust, a vast installation inside Mount Rushmore—is a new powerbase of destruction. Kane and his fellow exiles venture to the hot spot, where they face an old enemy conspiring to start the second wave of Armageddon.

GOUT11